Picking

UP THE

Pieces

Picking

UP THE

Pieces

LOVE LESSONS BOOK TWO

ELIZABETH HAYLEY

WATERHOUSE PRESS

Copyright © 2019 Waterhouse Press, LLC
Cover Design by Waterhouse Press
Cover Images: Shutterstock

ISBN: 978-1-64263-239-2

Dedicated to all of our fans who waited
[not so patiently] for this book to be released.
Remember, happy endings are always more
satisfying if you're teased a little bit first.

chapter one

m a x

I swirled the amber liquid around in the tumbler, my eyes mesmerized by the movement of the fluid. Ignoring the techno music behind me as I gazed into the glass, I willed myself not to think of how the ice had diluted the Jack Daniels just enough so that the color perfectly matched the gold flecks in her hazel eyes. It'd been nearly five months since I'd seen her. And they had been the longest five months of my life.

The light brush of a delicate shoulder made contact with my bicep, pulling me from my trance. I inhaled deeply, gearing myself up to don the mask of a happy playboy. This didn't use to be a mask for me. It used to *be* me. Not anymore.

Sliding my eyes to the left, I smirked. I appraised my visitor's body, her ample, firm breasts that were accentuated by a black, low-cut halter top, her flat stomach, and a firm ass that was hidden by tight jeans as she leaned forward on the bar. *Mmm, she'll definitely do.*

Noticing that she had my attention, she turned her body

toward me, lifting one hand to her hip while the other remained resting on the bar. "Oh my God. It *is* you." Her smile grew as her eyes drank me in, much like I had done to her. She clearly liked what she saw as she bit her lower lip and pushed her chest out a little farther. "I'm Jenna, and I'm a huge fan."

Aren't they all? My mind flashed back to that day in the airport nine months ago. *She* hadn't had a damn clue who I was, nor had she cared. Though she couldn't hide how I affected her. The way her breathing had hitched when she first saw me. How her eyes had followed me through security. How her body had reacted to my dirty words. And even after she had given in to me, she was still able to shock the shit out of me by wanting nothing to do with me afterward. It had been hot as hell. "Nice to meet you, Jenna. I'm Max." I kept my eyes trained on hers, my face serious, as I extended my hand toward her.

"The pleasure's all mine," Jenna purred as she slid her palm against mine.

I released her fingers quickly and turned back toward the bar. "Can I buy you a drink?" I asked as I sought out the bartender. *I need to get drunker. Now.*

"Sure," she replied, clearly perplexed by my sudden shift in behavior. Jenna sat down on the stool beside me, keeping her body turned slightly in my direction.

I made eye contact with the bartender and put up my index finger, beckoning him over.

"Mr. Samson, another round?" he asked.

"Yeah. And"—I gestured toward Jenna—"whatever she's having."

"Coming right up."

I took another deep breath, wishing I had been a little closer to alcohol oblivion before Jenna had made her move.

Meaningless conversation while sober was not my idea of a good time. She clearly knew what I was after, and she was also clearly after the same thing. Her body language and flirtatious response made that obvious. But I wasn't in this to enjoy her company. I was in it to forget. And I couldn't do that sober.

💚

Two hours later, I was drunkenly fumbling with my keys, trying to unlock my door while keeping my lips on Jenna's. I finally turned the lock, pushing the door open as I backed her through the doorway. I threw my keys in the general direction of my hall table and lowered my hands to cup her ass and pull her into my pulsing hard-on.

My dogs ran to greet me, but I ignored them as I worked my lips down Jenna's neck and we clumsily moved toward the stairs. And as I began pulling her top over her head, I silently thanked God I was as wasted as I was. Otherwise, I would have remembered how I had done this before: ripping another girl's clothes from her body as my mouth owned every inch of her skin on our way up the stairs to my bedroom.

I might have even remembered how I had lowered that girl onto the steps, unable to keep my hands off her long enough to complete the journey. And I definitely would have remembered the feeling of her finally becoming mine, only to realize that she didn't want me after all. *Yeah, it was definitely better to not remember any of that shit.*

I was almost tempted to lift Jenna and carry her up the stairs, but as I swayed slightly, I thought better of it. Instead, I pulled my mouth away, grabbed her hand, and led her toward my room. Once there, I pulled Jenna back to me, her hands flying up to my chest to regain her balance. My lips owned hers as I worked the button on her jeans with my fingers. I pushed them to the floor and then reached up to pull my blue polo shirt over my head. Kicking off my shoes, I undid my jeans quickly, yanking them down to reveal my pulsing erection.

Jenna immediately fell to her knees and took my long, hard length in her hand. I struggled to resist thrusting against her warm palm as I felt myself get harder at her touch. She began to stroke me slowly, teasingly, lifting her eyes to mine slightly and licking her lips. The action made me conscious of my desire to have her tongue swirling around my dick instead.

I nestled my hand in her honey-colored hair as she brought her face closer to my cock. At last, she flicked her tongue over my tip before she allowed my hardness to push past her lips and plunge into her warm mouth. *God, this feels good.* She moaned as she continued to suck, which caused a vibration to radiate through me.

"Jesus, fuck. Just like that," I said as I guided her back and forth. Watching those tight lips around my erection was enough to make me come. My head lolled back as I allowed myself to be overwhelmed by sensation.

Jenna's hand worked the base of my shaft as her mouth took me as deeply as she could. I grunted in pleasure. This girl knew how to give one hell of a blow job.

She worked me over with her mouth for a bit longer before I reluctantly pulled her back and urged her to her feet. If I waited any longer, I wouldn't be able to stop myself from coming in her mouth. And I wanted to be buried deep inside of her when that happened. As she rose, she reached behind her, unhooked her bra, and let it drop to the floor.

I palmed her huge tits in my hands and teased her nipples.

I knew they were fake. Then she hooked her thumbs in her panties and lowered them until they joined her bra on the floor. I guided her backward until her legs hit the mattress. She reclined on my bed and pushed herself toward the headboard, her eyes never leaving mine. Lying back, she spread her legs like an open invitation.

My eyes took her in, from her shapely legs to her long, soft neck. But I didn't look at her face. Because as much as I told myself I wanted to forget, what I really wanted was to pretend. Pretend that Jenna wasn't a stranger. Pretend that *she* was the one I wanted in my bed.

And as I rolled a condom onto my cock and covered Jenna's body with mine, thrusting into her fully, it was all I could do to refrain from calling her Lily.

❤

I was roused the next morning by a cacophony of doorbells, knocking, and my friggin' dogs barking at whoever waited at my front door. But worst of all was the rise and fall of breathing beside me. I turned my head to the left to take in my visitor. *Shit.* Burying my head in the pillow, I desperately tried to remember her name. *Gina, Jamie, Jenna?*

The banging downstairs was relentless, so I pushed myself up from the bed and reached down for the pair of jeans I had dropped to the floor the night before. The woman in my bed stirred at my movement and smiled as she opened her eyes to gaze at me.

She started to say something, but I spoke before she had a chance. "Stay here." I turned to leave, but not before noticing how her smile faded at my gruff order. I stalked out of the room, through the hall, and down the stairs. "I'm coming, I'm coming," I yelled as I descended. Yanking the door open fiercely, I was ready to give the person on the other side a piece of my fucking mind. But just as I was about to release an onslaught of obscenities, my eyes registered who was standing before me: my mom.

"Good morning, Max," my mom said sternly as I stood there speechless.

Finally, my words came back to me. "Good morning. Uh, I'm sorry. Did I know you were coming?" My question sounded more like an accusation than I'd meant for it to.

"Do I need an invitation to come see my son?"

Shit, she's pissed. "No, of course not. I just...wasn't expecting you. What time is it?" I asked as I stepped back from the door so my mom could enter.

"Eight thirty."

Okay, good. It's still morning. At least I didn't look like a total loser, sleeping through a Wednesday. "It's good to see you, Mom." Maybe the flattery approach would make her stop looking at me like she wanted to beat me with a wooden spoon.

"I bet," she huffed, directing her eyes at the floor.

When I followed her glare, I inwardly cringed. Tossed haphazardly on my hardwood floor was a pair of stilettos. *Fuck.* There were only two options in a situation like this: either claim they were mine or ignore them completely. And as I stood there, actually considering which was the lesser of the two evils, my mom chose for me.

"Sorry to interrupt your"—her eyes lifted to meet mine so that I could witness the disapproval that came with her words—"slumber party, but Jack called me this morning. He's incredibly concerned, to say the least, as are your father and I."

Tightly closing my eyes, I envisioned all the ways I could murder my agent. It would need to be slow and painful, much like this conversation. *How dare that fucking asshole call my mom? I'm not a goddamn child.* "There's no need to be concerned, Mom. I have it all under control." As soon as the words slipped out, I knew things were about to get worse. My mom hated when I lied to her, and I had just uttered as big of a lie as I had ever told her. I was far from having anything in my life under control.

"Oh, really," she scoffed, "because it doesn't seem like you have it all under control. Jack said he's been trying to get in touch with you for weeks and you haven't returned a single one of his calls. Supposedly a local sports network wants you to do some guest pregame coverage for the upcoming hockey season. He said it could turn permanent. Were you aware of this?" Her anger faded as she spoke, and sadness took its place. Tears wet her eyes.

It ripped me apart. I hated seeing my mom hurting, especially when I was the cause of it all. This woman was the only female on the planet who gave a fuck about me, and all I did was hurt her. I wished I could be a better person for her. But I couldn't. We all needed to face the facts: I was a Grade A asshole who would be a constant source of disappointment to my family. *I need a drink.* "Mom, I'll handle it. Please, don't worry about this stuff. I mean, it's not like I *need* to work. I'm just waiting for the right opportunity to present itself."

She began wringing her hands as she listened to my bullshit. "Things don't just present themselves, Max. You need to work for them. And don't you dare tell me not to worry. You know damn well that I have *every* reason to worry."

I had no response to this. The truth was, she did have

every right to worry. If I cared more about my well-being, I'd be worried too. I was a mess. "I'm sorry that I'm such a pain in the ass." I dropped my eyes to the floor, unable to look at her as I spoke.

She sighed heavily and brought her hand to my cheek. "Max, look at me."

I lifted my eyes hesitantly.

"I love you. I will always love you, and you've made us incredibly proud in many, many ways. But there is a great life waiting out there for you, and I'd be lying if I said it didn't pain me to see you content to just let it all pass you by. I know you're hurting and I know you're bitter. But no one can make any of that better except you. It's time to deal with your problems and start working to fix them. It's time to grow up, darling."

Her words didn't surprise me. I had said variations of them to myself over the past few months. But saying them and doing them were two different things. I just wasn't up for fixing my life right now. "I'll call Jack today," was all I could offer her, and it sounded as halfhearted as it felt.

She simply nodded, knowing damn well that I wasn't going to call. "Okay then, I guess I'll head home. Your father said he'd have breakfast waiting when I got there. If you hear about a death due to food poisoning, just remember that my will is in the safe in my bedroom closet." She shifted even closer to me, the weight of our conversation slowing her down, making her seem weary.

I leaned down so she could kiss my cheek, but she withdrew right before her lips were about to make contact. I looked down at her to see her staring behind me, and I turned to see what had caught her attention. *Fuck!* Standing on the stairs, wearing my T-shirt but no pants, was Gina/Jamie/Jenna.

"Sorry to interrupt. I just wasn't sure if you wanted me to make you some breakfast before I left for work."

Breakfast? Is this bitch insane? "No, I'm fine," I said through gritted teeth. "But help yourself. The kitchen is that way."

The . . . girl seemed to take the hint, because she scampered off in the direction I pointed. By the time I turned back to my mom, she had already opened the door and was beginning to pull it closed behind her. But she stopped before it closed all the way and, without turning back toward me, began talking. "You know, you can sleep your way through this entire state, Max. It'll never fill the void she left. It'll only make it deeper." And with that, she closed the door the rest of the way and left.

I stood there for a minute, just staring at the door. Nothing I could say would justify my recent behavior. I knew that she was right, but there was something about having it actually said out loud that affected me on a much deeper level than it had before. I finally ran my hand through my hair and turned toward the kitchen, wondering if I could get another blowjob before I got this chick the hell out of my house.

chapter two

l i l y

Standing in line at the coffee shop, I deliberated about my order. Today was my first day back to work since the summer ended, and if previous years had been any indication, I had a day of long, boring meetings ahead of me.

But I needed to tread a delicate balance with my order. Too much caffeine and I'd be itching to get up and move around. I made it a habit of sitting on the aisle during in-service days so I could take frequent breaks. If I took any more, people would start to think I had irritable bowel syndrome or something. But the alternative didn't seem feasible either. Too little caffeine and I'd fall asleep in the auditorium seat. Of course, Glen McCallum, one of our history teachers, dozed off routinely at thirty-minute faculty meetings and no one said shit to *him*.

Finally deciding on a medium mocha latte, I dropped my eyes from the menu above the baristas' heads and leaned to the right to count the number of people ahead of me. As usual, I was running late. *One… two… three…* I felt my muscles tense involuntarily. *Shit. No, that can't be him.*

I hadn't seen him in nearly five months, and I had been to this coffee shop dozens of times since then. Of course, my summer schedule had been much different from Adam's. I rarely rose before ten thirty in the morning, and he'd already be at work by that time. The chances of us running into one another here would have been slim to none.

As he ran a hand through the back of his thick blond hair and waited patiently for his order, my heart pounded so loudly in my chest I was certain he'd turn around to see what the noise was. I could leave without being noticed. Just remove myself from the line and slip out the door.

But I couldn't. Well, I *could*. I just didn't want to. There was no denying that I had thought about him often since our breakup, despite the fact that I had become more independent and self-assured. If Adam met the new me, he'd surely realize I had changed. The selfish Lily who needed a man to love her and accept her had vanished. I loved and accepted myself, and that was enough. Sure, I *wanted* someone to share my life with. But I didn't *need* someone.

In order to get his attention, I thought briefly about pushing in front of him and making some asinine comment like I had on the day we'd met. But I thought better of it. Instead, I let my eyes appraise his strong shoulders beneath his baby blue dress shirt.

I no longer felt rushed to get to work. I would happily stare at him for as long as I could.

The line moved up as the barista slid the large coffee Adam's way. He picked it up quickly and moved confidently toward the cream and sugar station against the far wall, where he poured a generous amount of milk into his cup and swirled it around.

I didn't even have to look at his face as he turned to leave to know I'd been wrong. Adam drank his coffee black with just sugar. The man wasn't him. I'd just wanted it to be.

❤

After our compulsory "welcome back" breakfast in the cafeteria, our principal, Mr. Murdock, told us we had a ten-minute break before the first meeting would commence in the auditorium. The herd shuffled through the halls, some eager to start the new year, but most just wondering where the summer had gone.

Tina and I found seats on the aisle as the superintendent rose to speak. "Good morning, everyone," Dr. Edwards began once the noise from the crowd had died down. "I hope that all of you have had an enjoyable and relaxing summer. I know I did." She rambled on for a bit about her vacation to California, and then directed us to the big screen that had lowered behind her on stage. "As many of you know, I like to open with a slideshow each year. Usually, we show pictures of school events: the plays, field days, concerts. But this year, I thought I'd show the people behind all of that. I thought I'd show all of you because *you* are the ones who make those things happen. A few weeks ago, I sent out an email asking for pictures of your summer vacations, and I received an overwhelming response. Thanks to all of you who contributed." Dr. Edwards stepped to the side as the lights dimmed and the slideshow began to play. The song "You're the Best" began to play as pictures of the teachers flashed on the screen. I couldn't help but think that the song didn't apply to every face I saw.

My eyes stared blankly at the screen ahead of me as I took

in the pictures of Erin Sutton's honeymoon in Barbados, Ryan Lonoff and his two sons huddled around a campfire, and Kim Flynn and her husband, Matt, with their family at the beach.

Some more slides flickered on the screen as I got lost in my own daydream. The last time I had been in this auditorium with music playing and the lights off, I had been on the other side of the curtain, lost in Max's dirty words and the rough touch of his powerful hands. I had been in my own world, oblivious to what was happening around me. And I don't just mean at that moment. Things were happening around me... to me, and I hadn't been aware of them until it was too late.

Tina interrupted my trance with an elbow to my side and a goofy laugh. "It figures you'd send one of you eating," she joked as she pointed to the screen where there was a close-up of me in Italy devouring a slice of pizza.

I had sent several pictures when Dr. Edwards requested them, and of course she had chosen a close-up of me eating. *Why did I even send that one to begin with?* The waiter had taken my picture from a few feet away. I was sitting outside a trendy bistro at a black wrought-iron table for two, but the other chair was conspicuously empty. I couldn't help but wonder if the rest of the faculty noticed that as easily as I had. I hoped they didn't.

"Wow, you *did* manage to stay away from guys while you were traveling through Europe by yourself. I didn't think you could do it," Tina said incredulously. *So much for my hope that people wouldn't notice.* "I sure as shit wouldn't have been able to."

"Well, almost," I said with a forced laugh. "I didn't have it in me to avoid France like I'd hoped. I met a hottie named Nikolas. We did go out a few times. Just to late dinners and a soccer game, but that's as far as I would take it. You weren't kidding about the vibrator thing, though. I wish I would have listened to you and gotten one before I left. It would have come in handy on more than one occasion."

"You know I've never steered you wrong," Tina replied. "I'm full of all kinds of good advice. Now my next suggestion is for us to take a break. Murdock's getting ready to speak, and I need to mentally prepare myself before listening to him for any length of time."

I felt my smile spread to my eyes as it became more genuine. "Let's go," I said as I nodded toward the auditorium exit.

❤

Five minutes later, we were back in our seats. Mr. Murdock had already begun speaking, and since I felt more refreshed after my break, I paid attention.

"I know you're probably all wondering what this year's theme will be," he said excitedly. I didn't share his enthusiasm. "This year our focus will be 'hands-on teachers.' Or, as you'll often hear us refer to it, 'HOT.'"

He laughed loudly at his lame pun.

"Ha, they've gotta be kidding us with this. I don't even wanna know what they mean by 'hands-on teachers.' Is this for real?" I asked Tina, who was already jotting down the acronym in her notebook and laughing about it.

"Well, you already had the 'hands-on' part mastered *last* year, so it should come easily to you." She snickered at her own joke, and I rolled my eyes, though I couldn't help but be somewhat amused.

Just when I thought our new theme couldn't get more embarrassing, the assistant principal began passing out green T-shirts with the slogan "We are HOT." *Nope, they're definitely not kidding.*

I spent the rest of the morning going back and forth between planning out the first month of school and playing on my phone. Before I knew it, our lunch break had arrived. As I made my way up the aisle, I heard Mr. Murdock's deep voice beckoning me. "Miss Hamilton, I need to see you quickly before you go."

I had no idea what he could want, so I told Tina to meet me in the lobby and I'd hopefully be out in a few minutes. As I approached Mr. Murdock at the front of the auditorium, I noticed a thin young girl with short black hair standing quietly beside him. "Lily, this is Trish. Trish, this is Lily Hamilton. She'll be your mentor for the year."

Did I hear him right? Mentor? Unless Trish needed someone to show her the most discreet places to get off on school property, I didn't think I was the right person for the job. *Do I even have a say in this?* I opened my mouth to speak, but Mr. Murdock beat me to it.

"Lily is one of the best teachers we have," he said. "The kids love her, and she has some pretty innovative ideas in the classroom. I thought she'd be a great person for you to learn from during your first year." My mouth closed as I felt a look of confusion sweep across my face. "As we say here at Swift now, she's HOT. And Lily, I do apologize for not asking you in advance to be Trish's mentor, but she was a last-minute hire, and knowing you're a team player, I knew you'd be on board."

Trish grasped her weak hand around mine and shook it tentatively. "I'm so excited to meet you, Miss Hamilton," she said in that eager "first-year teacher" kind of way. "I wanna be a HOT teacher too."

"No, it's not a HOT teacher. The *T* stands for teacher, so you're saying teacher twice," Mr. Murdock corrected her. I could see how confused she was by his explanation. "Never mind," he said. "Forget it."

Fuck me, this is gonna be a long year.

♥

I returned from lunch eager to set up my classroom, but after glancing at the afternoon agenda, I realized that we only had about an hour of time to ourselves that wasn't taken up by meetings. Putting up bulletin boards and arranging desks would have to wait until after I met with Trish. She was clearly in need of a little guidance if she was going to survive her first year.

As I popped my head into Trish's classroom, which was just down the hall from mine, I saw she already had her room set up. Her desks were arranged in groups of four, and brightly colored paper decorated her bulletin boards.

"Wow," I said, gesturing around the room, "looks like you're all ready for the year. Do you have a few minutes to talk? I thought I'd just go over a couple of important things with you. You know . . . like where the vending machine is and the quickest exits to the parking lot," I said with a smirk. "And to see if you have any questions."

"Thanks, I think I'm almost all set. I'm just finalizing my syllabus now. Do you wanna look it over?" She moved from her seat so I could sit down at her computer.

My eyes scanned the document, and for the most part,

it looked professional and covered all the necessary basics of the class. It wasn't until I got to the end that a clear problem jumped out at me. "Wait, is this your *home* number?" I asked, pointing to her contact information.

"My cell. I wanted to make myself as available as I could to the parents and the students." Her voice beamed with excitement. It was sweet. Naïve, but sweet.

I shook my head. "You don't wanna do that."

"But if a student has a problem with homework, or a parent is concerned about their child, I'd like to be able to help."

"Okay, I get that. But that's not gonna be why they call. A kid's not gonna call about homework. They're middle schoolers. They'll call to prank you. And the parents who call will call at all hours. You don't wanna open up that door because once it's opened, it can't be shut. You can't give students and parents access to your personal life." I didn't realize just how ironic that last statement was until I heard myself speak it. "Trust me on this one."

Eventually Trish acquiesced, though I could tell she thought I was hurting her chances of forming instant connections with her students. I explained the basic school procedures: attendance, referrals, policies, and what to expect on the first day. This was her first teaching job since she'd only graduated in May, and I could tell she was eager to learn the lay of the land. So when she launched off into a monologue about how she was going to change the lives of all the troubled youths at Swift, I had to step in and bring her back down to reality.

"Look, this may seem harsh," I began, "but you aren't going to make the difference you think you'll make. Kids like Jake Robinson," I said, pointing to her roster, "he won't have a pencil most days. If you give him one and he actually uses it to write his name on his paper, consider that an accomplishment."

Trish looked at me like I had just told her I'd mowed her puppy down with my car. On purpose.

"I know you probably think that's harsh. But I'm just being honest. It's the biggest mistake teachers make. The ones who think they can change every child's life are the ones who get burned out and feel like failures when it doesn't happen. I don't want you to feel like that. You're not Hilary Swank in *Freedom Writers*. No teacher is. And by the way, hanging out with students is never an excuse for ruining your marriage to Patrick Dempsey." I wagged my finger at her sternly before allowing a smile to spread across my face. My last comment served to lighten the mood for both of us. "No matter how good of a teacher you are, you can't change *every*one. And you have to be okay with that." I could see Trish's face begin to relax a bit, but the sadness in her eyes remained. "You have to be okay with the fact that you may only change *one*. And you have to be okay with maybe not even knowing you did. My point is that you just have to do the best you can and be happy with it... because your best will never feel good enough." *Jesus, I can be a real downer.*

Trish hesitated for a moment, clearly trying to process my words. "Thanks," she said sincerely. "I guess it's better to know that going in. Kinda takes some of the pressure off."

"Yeah, no pressure. And don't worry about all those initiatives. They'll come and go. Just try to go with the flow around here. Don't take anything too seriously, and don't— and I can't stress this enough—don't go to any meetings that aren't mandatory. You accidentally show up to one voluntary meeting, and it's all over. Next thing you know, you'll be the head of some new committee and your notebook will have so many acronyms scrawled across it, it'll look like a bowl of Alphabet soup after a night of heavy drinking."

"Okay, so no giving my phone number to students, no taking things too seriously, and no showing up to extra meetings. I think I got it. Anything else?" she asked with a shy smile.

I shrugged. "Just try to have fun. I mean, that's why we became teachers to begin with, right? So we could be perpetual kids?" I turned to leave but stopped short of the door. "Oh, one more thing: no waiting 'til the last minute to make copies. We always run out of paper."

❤

The first week back was interminable. But as I strolled through the parking lot toward my car at the end of the day Friday, I became acutely aware of the fact that I needed exercise more than usual. Sitting around all day didn't agree with me. Well, I mean, the sitting around was fine. I had done that willingly for most of the summer. It was more that I was forced to sit through stuff I didn't feel like being bothered with that had me so restless.

Either way, I knew that a trip to CrossFit was in order. My roommate, Amanda, and I had been going for a few months now, and both of us had gotten noticeably toner. I was glad I left my traditional gym for CrossFit when Amanda had suggested it. The motivation that the CrossFit coaches provided was something that other gyms lacked unless you paid for a personal trainer. And I sure as hell couldn't pay for that on a teacher's salary.

Sixty-three kettlebell swings, forty-five push-ups, sixty

box jumps, and six hundred meters later, I was finally back at my apartment ready to wind down for the day. It was only six thirty, and I was friggin' exhausted. I grabbed a bottle of water from the fridge and headed toward the bathroom to take a much-needed shower. As I passed the cordless phone in the living room, I noticed the light on the phone blinking to notify us that we had an unheard message. *Probably just a courtesy call.* Our families and friends knew to call our cells.

I pressed the phone to my ear and entered the code for our voicemail as I turned on the shower to let it warm up. I expected to be deleting whatever the message was immediately. But as I heard, "Lily, honey, this is Marjory Samson . . . Max's mom," I bolted out of the bathroom so I could hear better.

My heart skipped a beat or two at the mention of Max's name. *Did something happen to him?* I hadn't spoken to Max since he left for his new job back in the spring. "Sorry to call you at home," she continued. "I hope you don't mind me looking up your number. Anyway, I'm calling because Max has a job opportunity, but he's not returning his agent's calls. He's really just . . . I don't know." I could tell Marjorie wanted to say more but was restraining herself because she probably knew Max wouldn't want me to know all the details. "He's just not himself. I tried to talk some sense into him, but I couldn't get through. I know how close the two of you were. You're the only one I thought he might listen to." She ended her message by thanking me and requesting that I call her back to talk when I had a few minutes.

Before hanging up, I'd jotted down her number, though I wasn't sure whether I'd planned to call back. She'd said that she thought *I'd* be able to talk some sense into him? *Me?* There was no fixing Max Samson. But as much as I told myself that he was way beyond repair and much too broken, I couldn't help but feel guilt over the fact that I had been the one to break him.

Well, shit.

chapter three

l i l y

Marjorie's call had ground my senses to a halt. I was utterly lost as to what I should do. On the one hand, I didn't owe Max anything. He had fucked up one of the best things I'd ever experienced because he was stupid, selfish, and vindictive. I needed all that bullshit back in my life like I needed a scorching case of herpes. *Okay, that settles it, then. I simply won't return Marjorie's call. Except . . .*

Max wasn't all bullshit. He was funny and capable of such profound thoughtfulness that I had actually started to think of him as more like Adam than I had originally given Max credit for. If the past five months of relentless soul-searching had resulted in nothing else, I had finally allowed myself to accept that I had felt very real things for Max—things that went beyond friendship.

At the time, when all my X-rated high school drama had gone down, I had tried to convince myself incessantly that we shared only a physical connection. Even when I hadn't been able to deny that there was *something* there, I convinced myself that it paled in comparison to what I had with Adam. But now, I wasn't so sure of that.

And though my romantic feelings for Max had been extinguished by the supreme pain I felt after losing Adam, I couldn't deny how my skin prickled whenever I watched a hockey game or heard the word "doll." So where did that leave me?

Totally fucked, that's where.

This game of moral ping-pong continued throughout the weekend. I was thankful my parents had come into town to spend Labor Day weekend with me. Traipsing around Philly to visit all the tourist sites was a welcome distraction. Though I was a little bummed that I had to miss a birthday party for Kate, one of my CrossFit coaches. Amanda had gone, but I still felt bad that I'd missed the celebration. It also would've been an excellent excuse to get wasted and forget all this nonsense.

Plus, I missed out on the drama of Amanda's ex-boyfriend showing up and our CrossFit coach Shane pretending to be her new slam piece. I was shocked to hear he came to her rescue, especially after she called his dog his girlfriend and made oral sex jokes at his expense last week. That girl was truly one of a kind.

Even with all the running around I did with my parents, the weekend still dragged. But I had to give them credit. They had been surprisingly supportive since my breakup with Adam. I think they knew the toll it had taken on me and decided not to be their usual overbearing selves. Instead, they had just been there for me. And their effort had brought us closer.

After dropping them at the airport Monday morning, another horrible thought crept into my head: I had to go back to work the next day. It's not that I minded working. I just liked *not* working so much more. I wrote lesson plans for the week and created some assignments to get the year rolling. As I looked at the papers spread all over my bed, I glanced down at my phone to check the time. Three twenty p.m. My shoulders slumped as I realized a devastating fact: I was a total loser.

And as the word loser flitted around my brain, my focus returned to Max. Not because he was a loser, but because I had lost him. And his friendship. My brain was suddenly rapid-firing emotions and thoughts that made everything simultaneously lucid and confusing. I had hurt Max long before he had hurt me, therefore deserving his day of reckoning in more ways than one. I had broken him. All this I already knew. But what I hadn't fully contemplated until now was that cutting off Max had broken a piece of me too. I was never more myself than when I was with him. So maybe, just maybe, this was my chance to not only help heal Max, but to heal myself as well.

💔

I woke up Tuesday morning so alert and clearheaded, I didn't even need my daily jolt of caffeine. Monday's epiphany had already convinced me of the right thing to do, but I had forced myself to sleep on it anyway. I was almost surprised that the night's restful sleep hadn't wavered my resolve at all.

But as I drove to work, doubts started creeping in. It would be a tricky path to navigate, getting close to Max again without getting *too* close. Could we have a regular friendship? Would he be able to keep his womanizing hands to himself? And, most agonizing, would he even want to see me again? I had worked so hard to distance myself from the selfish, immature girl I had been five months ago, but would he even let me get close enough to him to prove it?

More questions like this plagued my thoughts all morning. I tried to make a good first impression and be the attentive teacher my students deserved, but it was a struggle. When third period rolled around, I took a deep breath. *One more class and then my free period. I just have to get through forty-five more minutes, and then I can call Marjorie.*

I had just told my students to open their textbooks to page twenty-five when I heard a knock at my door. I looked over and saw Trish, eyes wide, face flushed. "One second, guys," I said to the class as I hurried to the door.

Trish stepped back so I could open the door and walk out into the hall. I pushed the door closed behind me, leaving it open just enough that I would hear if the kids starting pummeling each other. "Trish, what's wrong? You look like you just got caught having sex in the supply room." *Damn, the supply room! Why had I never thought of that? Wait . . . shit . . . focus, Lily.* Maybe I hadn't changed as much as I thought I had.

"I . . . I . . . Oh God, Lily, I'm going to be fired."

My mind quickly made a list of the things that one would have to do to get fired from here. Trish didn't look the type to find sixth graders attractive, so that was out. I looked intently at her pupils. No, she definitely wasn't high, so we were all clear there. There was no blood on her clothes, so she hadn't murdered anyone. I was stumped. "Trish, slow down. What do you mean you're going to be fired?"

Trish took a deep breath in an attempt to force down her rising emotions. *This chick needs to get it together.*

"One of my students told me that I was the worst teacher he'd ever had and that he was going to tell his dad to call the principal and get me fired." Her eyes began to glisten as she fought back tears.

Jesus Christ, what am I gonna do with this girl? "Why did he say you were the worst teacher?" Maybe this insanely dramatic display was warranted. Maybe she had offered to sell him some meth, or karate chopped him in the throat, or slept with his father. *Wow, I probably should've left out that last thought.*

"I assigned them homework, and he said he wasn't going to do homework on the first day of school. I said that was fine, but then he'd earn a zero for the assignment." Her lips formed into a pout as she willed back the tears.

I stared at her intently, waiting for her to continue and tell me about the part where she had flipped out on him and called him a little prick or something. But she didn't say anything else. I closed my eyes and shook my head slightly. "Wait. That's it?"

"Well . . . yeah."

"Trish, you're not getting fired. If teachers were fired every time a student said we were bad at our jobs, human resources would have to put a revolving door in. He was angry. He'll go to gym, blow off some steam, and forget all about it by lunch. Don't worry about it."

Horror swept across Trish's face. "But, he has gym *after* lunch."

Man, this girl was really missing the point. "Listen, it's understandable that you're nervous, and you want all the kids to like you, and you want to be perfect at your job. But it's not going to happen. They're kids. They say things they don't mean all the time. You're the adult, and you need to act like it. Don't let them rile you with idle threats or they'll walk all over you all year long. Keep a cool head and everything will be fine."

"Okay, you're right." She released a deep breath. "God, you must think I'm a total lunatic." Her eyes stayed on the floor as she spoke, as if she were bracing herself for my response.

"I think you're a passionate teacher who has a lot to learn. Just like every other first-year teacher in the world. It'll get better. I promise."

She looked up at me and smiled broadly. "Thanks, Lily. I really appreciate your help. And sorry for interrupting your class."

My comforting words had clearly put her at ease. Restraint was starting to suit me. Who would have guessed? "Don't worry about it. I prefer to spend as little time working as possible, so I welcome the disruption," I said with a wink.

She smiled at me again as she said goodbye and headed down the hallway.

I giggled to myself as I reentered my classroom, thinking about how much fun it would be to get Trish drunk.

❤

The bell rang, signaling the end of third period, and my stomach lurched. *Okay, Lily, time to man up and get this over with.* I yanked open my bottom right desk drawer and reached into my purse, pulling out my phone and the scrap of paper I had written Marjorie's number on. I dialed and then took a shaky breath as I listened to the rings. My breath hitched when I heard the voice that was somehow so familiar to me, despite my only having ever heard it twice before.

"Hello?"

I cleared my throat before speaking, my nerves frazzling. "Hi, Marjorie. It's Lily."

❤

After my conversation with Max's mom, I'd been on edge the rest of the day. I'd gone to CrossFit after work to relieve a little stress, but once I got home and had nothing to think about except my phone call with Marjorie, my nerves got the best of me. I couldn't wait for Amanda to get home. I needed to sort this shit out, and I obviously couldn't do that on my own. So when she finally walked through the door at nearly ten thirty, I basically attacked her.

"Were you at work this whole time? What the fuck have you been doing? I've been waiting to talk to you."

"What is so important that you can't wait to tell me?" Amanda asked.

"Well, I actually need your advice on something."

"You? Need *my* advice? You must have *really* gotten yourself in a jam. What is it *this* time? Three men? A professional athlete, a hot dad, *and* a billionaire?" she asked with a laugh.

I rolled my eyes at her sarcastic accusation.

"*Four* guys? You horny devil. When are you gonna learn your lesson?"

"Shut up, asshole," I muttered, my mouth unable to resist lifting up into a smile.

"Just trying to make you laugh." She shrugged. "And it worked. What is it really?"

"Well..." I trailed off, embarrassed that Amanda hadn't been as far off as she'd predicted. "Max's mom called me today."

"Max's mom? Why?" Amanda's face grew more and more confused as she thought about what that could mean. "He's not back in town, is he? Lil, you can't do this to yourself again.

You're just beginning to get back to normal. Don't."

I quickly decided that I couldn't tell her he was back in town. Not after the way she'd just reacted. And if I couldn't tell her *that,* I certainly couldn't tell her Max's mom had revealed he'd never left to begin with. "No, he's not back. But his agent's been trying to get a hold of him. There's a possible job opportunity, but Max won't return his calls. He won't listen to his mom either. She just thought maybe I could get through to him. That's all."

Amanda breathed deeply and allowed the awkward silence to linger as she waited for me to continue. When I didn't, she finally spoke. "You're not gonna call him, are you? After everything that happened?"

"It wasn't all his fault. I just thought maybe I could help him."

"You can't be serious? Last week I came home to find you crying about what happened last spring, and now you wanna start this shit again? He's not a fucking charity case, Lily." I could see the pain and anger in her expression.

"You're right," I conceded. "I won't call him." But as I rose to get ready for bed, one thing became clear. Amanda *was* right; Max wasn't my responsibility. Still, I couldn't help but feel a pang of guilt knowing that part of what I had told Amanda had been a complete fucking lie.

💔

Tuesday night, what little sleep I managed to find was plagued with strange dreams. I woke up in a cold sweat after a nightmare where I found myself trapped in a cave with a caged tiger. Slowly and steadily, he clawed at the lock, and I knew eventually he'd break out and attack me. I could see light at one end of the cave, but I would have had to pass the tiger to escape. I didn't think I could make it past him without at least his paw scratching me through the cage, so I stayed in place, screaming in the hopes that someone might hear me. No one ever did.

In another nightmare, I woke up in my childhood room to find that it had been painted red, not the lavender that I'd grown up with. I had risen from my bed and run my hand along the freshly painted wall, wondering who'd chosen the color and how they'd painted it while I remained asleep.

There was only one explanation for my odd subconscious visions: I was fucking nuts.

When I wasn't having nightmares, I found myself wide awake, playing out my future conversation with Max in my weary mind. Would he even pick up when he saw my number? Would he be excited to talk to me? Would *I* be excited to talk to *him*? Would our conversation begin with idle small talk as if we were two friends from childhood catching up after years of unintentional separation?

In my mind, I pictured our conversation going easily. It would be obvious that he was happy I'd called, but he'd hide it with a cautious voice. He'd ask me why I contacted him. I'd explain what led to my call: his mom's and my overall concern for his well-being and success. Then, after we'd each caught the other up on what we'd been up to for the past five months, we'd say our goodbyes amicably.

There was something to be said for wishful thinking. Unfortunately, the only thing I could say for it in this situation was that it didn't work. At all.

I called Max on my prep period from the school phone. I

had convinced myself that he wouldn't answer otherwise.

When he did pick up, his slow voice revealed that my call had woken him. At eleven fifteen in the morning. On a weekday. "Max?" I'd said it as a question, though I'm not really sure why.

"Yeah, who's this?" His voice held curiosity with a clear hint of annoyance.

"It's Lily."

"Lily? Is everything okay? Where are you calling from?" I could sense the worry in his voice, as if I'd only call him if something serious were wrong. And I guessed he was kind of right.

"I'm calling from school. Everything's okay." I paused, realizing what I'd said hadn't been entirely true. "Well, kinda. I...talked to your mom. She's concerned. Jack called her because he couldn't get a hold of you. There's an opportunity—"

He cut me off before I had a chance to explain further. "That's why you called? Because of my mom?" What little curiosity that had been present in his voice earlier had vanished. It now held pure frustration.

"I just wanted to make sure you knew about the opportunity. It's at a local sports station for a guest—"

"I know what it is." His voice grew louder, and I heard a female in the background ask if everything was all right. "It's fine," Max assured her quietly, pulling the phone away from his mouth. "Go back to sleep. I can't do this now," he added gruffly. I knew that last sentence had been meant for me.

The dead air on the other end of the line only served to confirm it. *Shit.*

chapter four

a d a m

"Come on, Eva. We gotta go. It's only the second week of school and you already missed the bus." My voice sounded angrier than I'd intended. I should have cut Eva a little slack because she was used to getting a ride from me, and I knew taking the bus this year would be an adjustment. But I couldn't hide my annoyance. My morning drive to the new housing development I had been overseeing took me over an hour each way. Now, since I'd be leaving over twenty minutes later than usual, I'd be sitting in rush hour traffic. I probably had more than an hour and a half drive ahead of me.

Eva pulled the straightener thing through her hair for what seemed like the hundredth time. "I'm almost ready. I just need to put on mascara."

"You don't need mascara. You look fine. And when did you start wearing makeup anyway?"

"Ugh," she grunted in disgust as she put the straightener on the bathroom countertop and threw her makeup in a bag.

"'Fine' isn't good enough. And I've been wearing makeup for months. You don't notice *anything*. I'll just do it in the car," she huffed. "Let's go."

The drive to school took even longer than expected as Eva told me repeatedly to slow down and be careful going over any speed bumps for fear of ruining her makeup. "Where'd you learn how to do that anyway?" I asked, nodding toward some powder thing she had in her hand.

"Brittany's mom. She taught a bunch of us at a sleepover." Her voice seemed more chipper than it had before we'd left the house. Only ten minutes earlier she'd been ready to give me a third-degree burn with that hair contraption, and now she acted like it had never happened. *Teenagers.*

"*Brittany's* mom?" I raised an eyebrow and looked over at her, hoping that she'd pick up on the reason for my question without my having to spell it out for her. Brittany's mom was not the female influence I wanted for Eva. Her skin stayed perpetually bronzed, even during the winter thanks to baby oil and tanning salons. And to my knowledge, she didn't own one article of clothing that didn't cling to her body like plastic wrap. I wasn't sure what she did for a living, but some of the other fathers and I had speculated on more than one occasion.

Eva flipped the mirrored visor up roughly, letting it slap against the roof. "Yeah, Brittany's mom. Gosh, what's your problem today?"

There's the Eva I remember so vividly from earlier. "Sorry," I replied with a slight shrug of my shoulders and a smirk.

"Just drop me off over there," she said, pointing to a side entrance of the building that was about thirty yards away from the main doors. "I don't want people to see me getting out of your car."

As ridiculous as I thought that was, she was still a thirteen-year-old girl, and I didn't want to embarrass her. I rolled my eyes, but began to veer down the driveway toward the entrance Eva had requested.

Until I saw her. Lily. Walking up the sidewalk toward the school. My mind scolded itself for even thinking her name. And as if by reflex, I slammed on my brakes and threw the car into reverse.

"What are you doing, Dad? I said up there." Eva directed me to the doors she'd requested.

"Uh, I'm gonna drop you at the edge of the parking lot." I searched for an excuse that would seem believable. Somehow, telling Eva that I didn't want to run into her teacher from last year—you know, the one I'd been screwing—didn't seem like an appropriate response. "The buses are pulling up. It'll be easier to turn around. And it's not cool to be seen with me, remember?" I quickly added, hoping that would strengthen my argument.

Eva seemed to accept the excuse without question, and I sighed internally with relief. But she had always been observant, able to read people better than most. "What are you looking at?" she asked as she shifted her eyes toward the school.

Shit, shit, shit. Was I that obvious? I was surprised at how easily I recognized Lily from twenty-five yards away. Her wavy brown hair had grown longer, almost reaching the middle of her back. And her skin was still golden from the summer. But as much as I didn't want to think about her, didn't want to see her, I couldn't stop moving my eyes up her bare legs, imaggining the soft curve of her ass under that tight skirt. And as I ogled her, my mind reminded me how difficult these last five months had been.

I'd had nothing but time to think about what had happened between us. And the simple truth was that, as painful as the summer had been, my life was easier without her. She had been disloyal. And selfish. And these were transgressions I didn't think I could forgive. So I had made an attempt at moving on. I'd even gone out with a few women, though nothing too serious.

But even though I didn't want to think about her, my dick had other plans. It twitched at the sight of her confident stride as she made her way toward the building. With no luck, I willed myself to look away, to shut my eyes. I tried to think of anything but grabbing her by the waist and pulling her against me. Anything to rid myself of my sex-filled visions. But to no avail.

For once, I was thankful for Eva's short attention span. She had already gathered her things and exited the car, seemingly forgetting about her question. *Thank God.*

But as she shut the door, I realized that dropping the subject completely would have been too good to be true. "Oh, that's Miss Hamilton," Eva said excitedly as she popped her head in the window one last time. "I loved her."

As Eva made her way toward the building, my eyes remained on Lily, penetrating her with my gaze. "Me too," I whispered.

I waited until she entered the building before I reached down to adjust myself through my pants. *This is gonna be a long fucking day.*

💔

Normally, my drive down the Pennsylvania Turnpike gave me

time to relax, sip my coffee, and listen to sports radio in peace. Despite the length of my commute, it was the one point in my day when no one bothered me. No one asked me about last-minute design changes or how to use our drafting program—something most of the guys had received adequate training on and should know how to use by now. The drive gave me time to *not* think.

But today's ride didn't provide that same respite I had grown to appreciate over the course of the past several weeks. My mind was plagued with thoughts of Lily. I hadn't expected to see her, though I didn't know why. She worked at the school, for God's sake. It shouldn't have been that much of a surprise. But I still hadn't been prepared, especially for the physical reaction I'd felt. I'd spent the past few months fluctuating between being disgusted by her and missing her. Finally, my emotions had melded into a kind of melancholic ambivalence.

But I wasn't feeling ambivalent today. I couldn't deny that I'd felt something. I just wasn't sure what that *something* was. Part of it was physical, and I could easily chalk that up to being a guy. There was no denying that she was still hot as hell. But what else had I felt?

For once, I was thankful when my phone rang. It was John, the new intern, asking about the build materials for the Ashcroft Development. "Did you look in the Ashcroft folder?" *Jesus, it's like fucking* Romper Room *there. Can't they do anything without my help?* "All of it should be on the computer where I showed you last week. I'm driving. I can't look it up now." I heard John whistling as he searched the computer for the file that held the material specs. *I wish I could be that carefree when I work.*

"Okay, got it, Mr. Carter."

I hung up the phone quickly before John had a chance to fire off his next stupid question.

❤

My babysitting duties continued when I arrived on the jobsite, and I had to spend the first fifteen minutes re-explaining the difference between the Berkshire and Evanston floor plans. I started up my computer in the trailer that served as my office and opened the CAD program. "The Berkshire has a connecting bathroom between two of the spare bedrooms, as well as a sitting room off the master. Other than that, they're nearly identical. You should know this shit, Joe. You're in charge when I'm not here. I can't hold your hand every goddamn minute."

"Sorry, Adam. Got it. Won't happen again," Joe said apologetically before exiting the trailer.

"Rough morning, Adam?" Cecilia asked, handing me a fresh cup of coffee. Her warm smile greeted me as she swept her graying hair away from her face.

"Just a little," I said with a shrug.

"Eva?"

Sure, let's go with that. "Yeah, teenage girls." I raised my eyebrows and let out a long sigh. "I don't know what I'm gonna do with her some days." I took a swig of the piping hot coffee and burned the roof of my mouth. "Guess I was a little short with Joe there, huh?"

She chuckled softly, and the fine lines around her mouth and eyes became more pronounced. "Nah, he deserved it. Even *I* know the difference between the Berkshire and the Evanston, and I'm just the site receptionist."

"You're not *just* anything. Don't sell yourself short. What would I do without you, Cecilia?"

"Probably be as gray as me," she replied, smiling. "But that reminds me ... Jeff's coming home from college for the weekend, and he's bringing his girlfriend. I was wondering if I could leave at noon on Friday so I could pick them up from the train station. I haven't met her yet."

"How am I gonna survive a half a day without you?" I asked, only half kidding.

Cecilia already knew the answer to her question before I could give it and thanked me with a kiss on the cheek. "You're a sweetheart, Adam."

And as I watched her return to her desk, I was suddenly overcome with the desire to hear another voice saying those same words.

chapter five

m a x

As I pressed the two hundred and sixty pounds above my chest for the thirtieth time, I was thankful for a little relief. Carefully, I eased the bar in place on its rack and sat up to take a breather. One more set of ten, and I'd move on to incline dumbbell presses.

In the last few months, I'd really focused on my workout routine. It's not like I'd ever been lazy. I'd always been athletic and kept in shape. I guess I'd just found myself with extra time to kill lately. No job. No girl. Well, maybe too many girls was my *real* problem. I needed something to focus my energy on.

The last time I'd been this serious about a workout regimen had been a few years ago when I'd still played for the Avalanche. Somehow, despite my recent weakness for wings and whiskey, getting back to my old routine helped me pack on an extra fifteen pounds of solid muscle. And my chest and arms showed it.

I kept to a strict schedule: a serving of MUSCLE MILK

with skim milk for breakfast and a performance drink before my workouts to supply me with strength and energy. This last part was vital since my late nights often left me tired and run-down.

While the rest of my life spiraled into chaos, the one aspect I seemed to be able to control was keeping in shape. Five to six days a week, I went to the gym, rotating my workouts between my upper and lower body. And I could still knock out three miles in a little less than twenty-five minutes. Not bad for a guy about to turn thirty.

I wiped the sweat from my face and neck with my towel and made my way over to the chest fly machine. "That's a ton of weight, isn't it?" an airy voice asked from behind me as I leaned over to move the pin lower on the weights. "Two hundred pounds? Are you gonna lift all that?"

I turned around to see a cute blonde standing behind me. "That's the plan," I said. As she reached back to adjust her long hair she had tied up in a ponytail, her tits rose higher on her chest. Images of how my hands would fit perfectly around them flitted through my brain. Of course, I couldn't be sure without checking. I felt my lips spread into a slight smirk at the thought.

As I sat on the bench, I made no effort to conceal my wandering eyes as they traveled up the length of her legs to her tight black shorts. *Fuck, she's hot.* The thought of taking her back to my place for a post-workout shower crossed my mind. And judging by the way she was biting her lower lip as she watched me exercise, my proposition wouldn't even be a hard sell. *I can't wait to have my teeth on that lip later.*

"I'm finishing up here," she said. "Just gotta stretch." And as she leaned forward to loosen up her hamstrings, I imagined licking the sweat that glistened between her breasts.

This is too goddamn easy. "Yeah, me too. Two more sets here, and I'm done." I rushed through the rest of my reps and extended a hand as I finished my second set. "I'm Max, by the way."

"Max," she said with a playful smile as she took my hand in hers, "it's a pleasure to meet you." But I wasn't prepared for the next words out of her mouth, and as she said them, her warm hand felt like ice against my skin. "I'm Lily."

Oh, you've gotta be fuckin' kidding me.

Needless to say, I got the hell out of there as quickly as possible. I wasted no time wiping off my machine, grabbing my water bottle, and bolting to my car without so much as a goodbye. As I sped home, I wondered what the fuck had happened to me. A name shouldn't matter. Half the time I didn't remember their names anyway.

But she shared a name I couldn't forget. And there was no way I was taking Lily back to my house and into my bed. Well, let me rephrase that. There was no way I was taking *that* Lily back to my house and into my bed.

But the other Lily—the *real* Lily—she was another story. She could come in my bed anytime she wanted to. Literally. And I'd pictured that plenty of times: her under me, on top of me, in front of me screaming my fucking name as I made her shake with pleasure. But that was all I had of her: old memories and stale visions that I feared would begin to disintegrate with time.

I had gone months without speaking to her, and then

when I'd finally heard from her last week, I'd been a complete asshole. *Fuck, why had I been so rude?* I'd blown her off, and I was sure she'd heard Stephanie or Sophie or whatever the fuck her name was in the background. To make matters worse, Lily had texted me over the weekend to say she'd only been trying to help and she was sorry if she'd upset me. There was no denying I'd been a complete dick. But I didn't need her help or her fucking sympathy, and I'd gotten defensive.

Finally home, I turned on the shower and stepped out of my boxers, allowing the cool air from the vent to brush against my body for a moment. When I slid open the shower door and stepped under the steaming water, I knew I needed to wash more than just the sweat from myself. I needed to wash away the guilt I felt for how I'd treated her.

❤

I was surprised when Lily picked up on the second ring because I half expected her to let it go to voicemail. "Hello," she said quietly. *Maybe she didn't look to see who it was before picking up.*

"Uh . . . hey, Lily. It's Max."

"I know. Your name came up on my phone."

Fucking idiot. "Oh, right. Listen, about the other day . . ." I let my voice trail off in the hopes that she'd pick up where I left off and relieve me of my embarrassment. She didn't. When silence lingered between us, I forced myself to speak again. "I shouldn't have hung up. I mean, I should've let you talk. You can talk now." I knew as soon as I said that last sentence, it had come out wrong.

"Really, can I? Thanks."

Damn. I knew I deserved every bit of sarcasm that she delivered, but that didn't stop the sting. Not knowing what the hell to say to change the direction of the conversation, I stayed quiet and hoped *she'd* fill the silence this time.

"Look, we don't need to make this conversation any longer than it has to be. I just wanted to tell you there's an opportunity for you to be a guest analyst on TV. Did your agent tell you that? It could turn into something big. Something permanent. Don't be stupid, Max."

"Too late," was all I managed to force out. *God, I really have a way with words today.* "Listen, I'll think about it. Things have been ... uh, crazy lately."

"Crazy? How crazy can things be? You're not working. What have you been doing?" Her voice was accusatory.

I had to rein in my defensiveness. Her tone pissed me off, but I knew that if I snapped at her again, I'd regret it forever. "Um, listen, Lily. I know that I was rude last week, and I'd like to get together. Maybe explain some things. Clear the air. Can I buy you a drink?" The way I saw it, this was the best of both worlds. We could say what we each needed to say, and I could avoid doing it sober. "How 'bout Dino's? They have a beer garden there. We'll grab some pizza, a few beers, and talk."

"Okay, when?"

The quickness of her response surprised me. I needed a little time to collect my thoughts. Plus, I didn't wanna seem too eager to see her. A week and a half seemed like a good amount of time to let things cool down a bit. "Uh, how 'bout Saturday the twenty-first? Late afternoon?"

"Um, let me see." She got quiet for a few moments, probably to look at the calendar on her phone—which made me think about how I had absolutely nothing going on. Ever.

"That should be fine. I'll see you then, I guess."

"Yeah, okay. See you then. Oh, I'll text you about the time when it gets closer." *Does it seem like I have a life now? Probably not.*

"Okay. Oh, and Max," she added just before hanging up. "Try not to be such an asshole this time."

I dropped my hands and stared down at my cell phone screen as I heard the line go dead. I couldn't help the soft, rumbling chuckle that escaped my throat as I replayed the conversation in my head. *Well, that went well.*

chapter six

a d a m

"Eva! Where's my hair gel?" I lifted my head up toward the ceiling of my bathroom. *You just had to give me a girl, didn't you?* As I continued to ponder all the reasons God could have for punishing me, I heard Eva's voice yell from downstairs.

"What?"

"You heard me. Where is my hair gel?" Getting ready for a date was already nerve-racking enough without my thirteen-year-old running inadvertent interference.

The next time Eva spoke, she was behind me. I watched her reflection in the bathroom mirror as she leaned against the doorjamb munching on a brownie. "What makes you think I have your hair gel?" She examined her brownie closely, her refusal to meet my eyes giving her away.

"Eva," I warned.

"Okay, okay, it's in my room. I'll get it."

Watching her walk away, I came to a disturbing realization. Eva had just entered her teenage years. I still had at least five years of this kleptomaniacal liar. I wasn't sure both of us were going to survive.

She returned to the bathroom and thrust the bottle of hair gel at me with a gruff, "Here."

Deciding my sanity had a better chance of staying intact if I ignored her rudeness, I took it from her. "Why did you take this anyway? It's *men's* hair gel."

"I was experimenting." She shrugged, before turning on her heels and heading back downstairs.

I thought for a second. "Experimenting with what?" I finally called after her, unable to quell my curiosity.

She stopped abruptly on the landing and looked at me with annoyance before spitting out, "With sex, Dad." Registering the look of horror that swept across my face as I nearly vomited *Exorcist*-style all over the bathroom, Eva rolled her eyes before adding, "Seriously. What do you *think* I was doing with it?"

I stared at the bottle in my hand, no longer wanting it anywhere near me. From this day forward, I would always associate it with a father's worst nightmare. My head spun as I looked from Eva to the bottle, from the bottle to Eva. "I ... I ... Jesus Christ, Eva, please tell me you were using it on your hair."

"Obviously, Dad. God." She stomped down the rest of the steps and left me alone to wonder if there were any convents that accepted children.

I stared at the offending bottle of hair gel, knowing that I needed to use it, but not sure I could handle squirting liquid from it. "Fuck it," I muttered before throwing it in the trash can. Messy hair, I could deal with. The thoughts that were now plaguing my frontal lobe, I couldn't.

I ran my hands through my hair before walking back to my room to grab my wallet and spray myself with cologne. Quickly checking my watch, I realized that I was running late but stopped to take one last look in my bedroom mirror. Having decided to put in a little extra effort, I'd ironed my light blue polo and khakis neatly. I flexed my bicep and was pleased with how the sleeve of my shirt fit snugly around my muscles. Satisfied with my appearance, I jogged down the steps and started toward the front door just as my mom entered.

"Hey, Mom." I placed a quick kiss on her cheek. "Thanks again for staying with Eva tonight."

"No problem, Adam. I love having girl time with my granddaughter. You look nice tonight. Who's the lucky lady?" My mom slid past me to hug Eva.

"I'm not sure, actually. I mean, I know her name, but not much beyond that. My friend Frank's wife hooked us up." The entire situation was pretty awkward. Claire had been telling me about her friend Marnie for weeks. But it wasn't until Frank showed me a picture of her that I relented. It was a little grainy because he had taken a picture *of* a picture with his phone, but I could still make out her light blond hair, slim figure, and pretty features. I just hoped not much had changed since the picture had been taken. But in the end, what did I really have to lose?

"Well, have a good time," my mom called to me as she guided Eva into the living room.

"Thanks. You too." I watched my two favorite women in the world snuggle next to each other on the couch and start talking a mile a minute about who-knows-what. A smile tugged at my lips as I walked out the door and closed it behind me.

Marnie lived in Gladwyne, an affluent town about twenty minutes from my house. From what I gathered from Frank,

Marnie had married well and divorced even better. But she had seemed sweet and genuine on the phone, so I suppressed my nagging suspicions about her and asked her out to dinner.

My GPS guided me to a high-rise that screamed overpriced condominiums. I pulled up to the front of the building where I saw a familiar woman speaking to the doorman. I quickly put on my hazard lights, put my car in park, and jumped out. "Marnie?"

"Adam?"

"Yes." I walked confidently up to her and shook her outstretched hand. *Score one for me.* She was even hotter than her picture. Her low-cut green dress clung tightly to her body in all the right places, allowing me a glimpse of her cleavage without even having to try. *Nice.* And as my gaze lowered down to her flat stomach, I tried to resist stealing a look at her toned legs. Thankfully, her deep blue eyes caught mine right before I could take my visual molestation any further. "Nice to meet you," I said quickly.

"You, too. Really nice." She bit her lower lip as her eyes traveled the length of me.

I shifted my shoulders uncomfortably and cleared my throat. "You ready to go?" Her predatory gaze discomfited me. While it was always nice to be appraised appreciatively by the opposite sex, Marnie looked like she wanted to chain me up in her basement and make me her love servant.

"Definitely."

Marnie slipped her arm through mine and I guided her to the car. Once she was shut safely inside, I released the breath I'd been holding and looked back at the doorman. Maybe it was just a figment of my frazzled imagination, but I was pretty sure he winked at me. I took a few deep gulps of air before climbing into the driver's seat next to Marnie and starting toward the restaurant.

❤

Dinner was initially uneventful. Conversation flowed easily, Marnie stowed her roving eyes, and I started to loosen up. She told me about her ten-year-old son, Tyler, who was diagnosed with autism when he was three. Her husband had withdrawn from the family after the diagnosis, feeling short-changed that he didn't get the "perfect" son who would be a junior version of him. After four more years of enduring a cold and distant man, Marnie finally filed for divorce and her now ex-husband completely disappeared from their lives, other than the child support check she received from him every month.

I shared my past about Eva's mother, how she'd been unable to cope with the prospect of being a mother and left me to raise Eva alone. Then, with the heavy stuff out of the way, the conversation shifted to lighter topics like hobbies, favorite vacation spots, and where we'd gone to college. I was feeling really good about this date.

Until Marnie ordered a third martini. And then a fourth. And then a dessert wine. I watched her guzzle alcohol like she had been deprived of liquid for two days. Shock raged through me as she began to sway in her chair, giggle like a lunatic, and slur her words. By the time the waiter brought the bill, Marnie was obliterated. She had inched closer to me, nearly tipping off her chair in the process, and began running her fingernails up my thigh. My brain and body fought to get on the same page, but both were starting to short-circuit.

My cock stiffened slightly at her touch, and arousal coursed through my body. I'd have to be blind not to be attracted to her. She had the best tits money could buy, and they accentuated her narrow waist. She was strikingly beautiful. The entire package would make any man horny as hell.

But my brain was firing off warning shots left and right. Something about Marnie screamed shark, and I didn't want to be caught in the water when she decided to strike. I had heard stories about women who seduced men, lured them home, treated them to a good time, only to threaten them with police action if they didn't pay up the next morning. And Marnie fit the stereotype I had built in my head. I wasn't about to risk my future for one night of pleasure.

As I drove back toward Marnie's house, the internal battle waged on. She continued to pet me as I drove, never reaching my dick, but getting damn close. My brain suddenly flooded with memories of another time when I had been in this situation. Only that time, I had been in a movie theater and had actually respected the woman touching me.

The overt sexual behavior Marnie delivered was cheap and fleeting. So unlike what I had felt in the theater that night. But, of course, I had also been a different person back then. It still amazed me how much I had changed in five months. The core of me was still the same, but I was more guarded, less trusting, and a little . . . colder toward women.

I had been on numerous dates since Lily, and while I still hoped to meet my perfect match, I was also enjoying the search. Sex no longer had to mean something to me. It clearly hadn't meant much to *her*, and from what I saw at Eva's school the other morning, she was doing just fine. I could be just fine too.

But did this feel fine? *Fuck.*

My mood took a downturn as Marnie instructed me to pull into a parking space off to the right side of her building. I now had absolutely no intention of having sex with her. But, since she was drunk as shit, I needed to at least make sure she got inside okay.

Marnie surprised me when she led me around the back of the building, nearly falling on the uneven ground three separate times. I held her arm as she stumbled onto a back patio and began fumbling with her keys. I released her so that she could unlock the sliding glass door.

"Once I get this open, I'll get rid of the babysitter. Then we can enjoy the rest of our evening," she slurred.

It was on the tip of my tongue to tell her not to bother. There was no way I was getting it up for this chick now. She was a fucking mess.

As Marnie continued to struggle with the door, I thought it was odd that the babysitter hadn't come to investigate the noise or called the cops to report the pair of psychopaths trying to break in. It was then that I noticed how dark it seemed to be inside. Was her son afraid of light or something? Shit was getting weird. Fast.

I was just about to ask Marnie if she needed help with the door when I heard glass breaking, followed by a slew of hissed obscenities. *Great, now we are definitely getting arrested.* "Shit, are you okay?"

"Yeah, yeah, I'm fine," Marnie uttered. She finally slid the door open and stepped inside. "Come on in. I'll be right back."

I stepped into her home and quickly began to wonder if I had entered *The Twilight Zone*. Since it was pitch black inside, I brushed my hand over the wall until I hit a light switch. Flipping it on, her dining room lit up.

From what I could see of her house, it looked tidy and well-decorated. Well, except for the blood splattered all over the floor. *Wait... what? Jesus Christ!* The hardwood floor that stretched from her dining room and down an adjacent hallway looked like a scene from *CSI*. Fine, my ass; Marnie would have needed to have cut off her entire goddamn hand to produce that much blood.

I turned the corner and glanced down the hallway, half expecting to see Marnie's corpse slumped against a wall. I noticed that all the doors were shut, and light peeked out from beneath only one of them. Since the blood trail led to that door, my suspicion skyrocketed. Were the babysitter and Tyler in one of those other rooms? Were they vampires? No, they couldn't be. Otherwise they'd have flocked to the plasma all over the floor. *What the hell is wrong with me? When did this night take such a bizarre turn that I started believing in vampires?*

I was just about to wash my hands of this entire situation and get the hell out of there when one of the doors opened. Marnie stepped out into the hall with a towel wrapped around her hand. And absolutely nothing else. She was stark naked as she leaned against the wall in an attempt to look sexy. It didn't work.

"Uh, Marnie, are you... okay?" I had no idea what to say in this situation. I briefly looked around to make sure there weren't hidden cameras somewhere. Being on a show like *Punk'd* or *What Would You Do?* seemed highly plausible.

She used her shoulder to push off the wall, but only made it two shuffled steps toward me before slinking back against it for support. "I'm fine. Though I'm about to be better."

The fuck you are. "Is Tyler here?" I had to know what was

going on with this kid. There were pictures scattered around the apartment of a boy. Some of the pictures even had Marnie in them. So she definitely had a son. But where the hell was he?

"Of course. He's in there." She gestured toward one of the closed doors with her head, nearly throwing herself off balance.

"With the babysitter?"

"No, I sent her home." Marnie began to stumble toward me, her shoulder still resting against the wall. She reminded me of the scary little girl in *The Ring*.

"When? I didn't see her leave."

Marnie stopped suddenly, her face taking on a glint of anger. Well, as angry as it could look considering how plastered she was. "I told you I was getting rid of her. As soon as I walked in, she went out the front door."

"Marnie, listen to me. I know that didn't happen. I would've seen her. Is Tyler really here?" I became hyperaware of my surroundings, my paternal instincts kicking in. Something was very wrong here.

"Why are you so worried about him? He's fine. He's always fine. I'm sure he's sleeping soundly in his room."

Always fine? Jesus Christ. I suddenly realized that this probably wasn't the first time this crazy bitch left her autistic kid alone in his room while she went out, got hammered, and propositioned a virtual stranger. As she reached up toward her breast to fondle her nipples, I realized I'd had enough. "Um, I need to make a phone call. I just want to check on Eva. I'll, uh, I'll be right back."

"I'll be right here, wet and ready," she cooed.

I dry heaved at the image her words conjured. Practically running onto her back patio, I slid the door closed behind me and fished my cell phone out of my pocket.

"9-1-1. What's your emergency?"

"Yes, hi, I... There's a woman... I'm at her house, and I think... Listen, she's totally fucked up, and you need to get someone out here." I had no idea how to describe what had occurred over the past ten minutes.

"Sir, is this an emergency? We don't have time for prank calls tonight." The operator sounded annoyed and seemed unsure if she believed what I was saying.

That makes two of us, sweetheart. "Trust me, it's an emergency. She's bleeding profusely, heavily intoxicated, and I'm pretty sure she locked her special needs son in his bedroom. Oh, and she's completely naked."

"What's the address?"

I was momentarily stunned at how the operator doubted my initial request for help but completely believed the incredulous tale I had just told. *Probably because you can't make up shit like this.*

I gave the operator the information and waited outside for the police to arrive. I had told her that I was around the back of the building, so I wasn't surprised when, about five minutes later, I saw the movements of flashlight beams.

The cops sauntered up to me, and the larger of the two began speaking. "You the one who called 9-1-1?"

I nodded.

"Okay, so what's your story?"

"I don't have a *story*, officers. Everything I told the operator is the complete truth."

"Well, then why don't you tell us what you told the operator?"

I recounted the events of the night, and I could tell from

their expressions that they didn't believe me. I didn't blame them. I wish I didn't have to believe me either.

"All right, stay here. We'll go check it out."

They disappeared into the house, and I let out a deep breath. Thank God this was about to become someone else's problem. I was going to kill Frank and Claire for setting me up with this piece of work.

The shorter officer came back outside about two minutes later, looking frazzled. "Okay, sir. You can head home now."

That was it? They didn't need me to make a statement? Nothing? "You don't need me to do anything else? You sure?"

"Sir," the cop interrupted sternly, "trust me. Do yourself a favor and get out of here as quickly as possible." He then turned around and went back inside.

No need to tell me twice. And as I sprinted to my car and peeled out of the parking lot, I gave serious thought to taking a vow of celibacy.

❤

The phone only rang twice before I heard the familiar gruff, "Hello."

"I'm going to fucking murder you. Like a real murder. One that involves waterboarding and pliers."

"Adam? How ya doin', buddy? I guess your date didn't go so well last night. What? She didn't put out?"

"Are you kidding me? Have you ever even met that head case? She should be locked up in an asylum for the criminally insane."

"You serious? I met her once. She's smoking hot. And she looks like she knows her way around a dick."

"I bet she does. Lots and lots of dicks would be my guess." I recounted the story for Frank, who listened with rapt attention. When I finally finished, he remained silent for a few seconds.

"That's it?" he asked.

"That's it? What do you mean, 'That's it'? Haven't you been listening? You set me up with a fucking sociopath."

"I think that's a little dramatic, don't you?"

"Um, fuck no, I don't think it's dramatic. What the hell is the matter with you?" I was beginning to wonder if I were the crazy one.

"So, you didn't fuck her at all? You didn't even get a blowjob out of her or anything?"

"You are frightening me on so many levels right now, I don't even know what to say."

"How about you say that the next time a naked chick throws herself at your cock, you'll fucking act like a man and screw her brains out?"

"I ... Have you been evaluated? Because you may really benefit from some professional help."

Frank let out a guffaw. "Maybe I can visit the same person Marnie's going to be court-ordered to see after you got her busted by the fuzz."

"You're making it sound like I did something wrong here. I possibly saved a child's life last night. I'm a fucking hero." Okay, I may have gotten a little ahead of myself with the hero comment.

"Hero, my ass, pal. You call me up, and instead of giving me the vital information, like if her pussy's shaved, you go on about how you walked away from a hot naked woman because *she's* the crazy one."

"I need to hang up."

"I swear, you could fuck up a wet dream."

And on that note, I clicked the End button on my phone and slunk back into my desk chair. As my head spun from everything that had happened in the past twenty-four hours, I knew only one thing for sure: I needed new friends.

chapter seven

m a x

I glanced over at my alarm clock for what felt like the five hundredth time. Five thirty. God, why couldn't I sleep? I rarely ever had issues nodding off, but the previous night I'd been restless. *Fuck it.* I rolled out of bed and started to put my running gear on. *May as well be productive.*

I had hoped that the run would tire me out a little, but it only energized me more. Well, maybe it wasn't exactly the running that had my adrenaline spiking. Maybe it was a certain person who I would be seeing in a little more than twelve hours. I muttered a curse under my breath as I thought about how much she was still able to affect me.

I hadn't even seen her yet, but the prospect of being physically close to her, being able to smell her scent and look into those beautiful hazel eyes was making me feel shaky and manic. Memories of her ran through my mind like an X-rated slideshow—her big, perky, and perfectly round tits that fit in my hands as though they were made to be there, her sculpted legs wrapped hungrily around my waist, and her beautiful face brightened with light freckles that lit up with every smile she threw in my direction. *Shit.*

My legs shook and my chest burned when I returned home an hour later. I stripped from my sweaty clothes as I climbed the stairs and headed for the shower, turning the nozzle all the way to the right. Frigid water was exactly what I needed to quell the burning heat that was blazing within me. I had to push this shit out of my mind. I couldn't meet her tonight with all this running through my brain. As I placed my palm on the wall beneath the showerhead and exhaled a deep breath, I started to force myself to relax.

I hope she wears something tight.

Damn it.

When I arrived, I chose a seat at the bar. A table felt too intimate, and I didn't want to make her uncomfortable. Even with my back to the door, I still couldn't resist the urge to turn around and look at it every thirty seconds. I pushed my beer bottle back and forth between my hands on the bar impatiently, stopping to glance down at my large Bulova watch. It was still a few minutes before six o'clock; she wasn't late yet. But I was annoyed anyway.

Why was I the only one who had cared enough to be early? Why did I care at all? Lily had ripped my heart out and stomped all over it. I didn't owe her this meeting. And I especially didn't owe her an apology. What had I been thinking?

Suddenly, my body tensed and my skin prickled. I knew that when I turned around, she'd be there. I cocked my head to the side, looking at her out of the corner of my eye. She scanned the bar and stopped on me, her lips lifting to a small smile. Shiny and perfect, her hair looked as though she had just stepped out of a shampoo commercial. A fitted purple CrossFit T-shirt formed snugly to her body, and her jeans settled casually on her hips.

Suddenly my annoyance turned to anger. How dare she look so fantastic? I had been a mess for the past five months, and she looked like a fucking model. If there had been any question whether or not I had meant a damn thing to her, that question had been answered. If anything, she looked better. I guess kicking me out of her life had done wonders for her. *Fuck this.*

I quickly turned back toward the bar, not acknowledging her approach. Thank God I had the wherewithal to meet her in a bar. I held up my beer bottle to the bartender, signaling for another.

"Hey, Max. Have you been here long?"

"No, not long," I said simply. She had been there five seconds, and I was already being a dick. But I didn't care. The bartender set the bottle in front of me, and I brought it directly to my lips and took a swig.

"Anything for you, miss?" the bartender asked.

Lily looked over at me for a split second. When I didn't make any move to look back at her, she replied, "Just water for right now."

"Comin' right up."

"So, what's been going on?" Lily asked, discomfort evident in her voice.

"Nothin' much. Just figuring some things out. What about you? I didn't know you did CrossFit," I said with a snort.

She looked confused for a minute before looking down at her shirt. "Oh, yeah, I started it over the summer. One of our coaches was in a competition in the city today. I came right from there."

"Huh. I didn't peg you for a trendy exerciser."

"What does that mean exactly?" She narrowed her eyes at me, probably trying to figure out what the hell my problem was.

Truth be told, *I* wasn't sure what my problem was. I had been excited, and somewhat nervous, to see her all day. But now that she was there, I was pissed off and edgy. "It's such a fad. I didn't think you'd be someone who would buy into the hype."

"I'm not sure how something that has been around since two thousand and has millions of participants can be considered a fad."

"I just hate all those people who act like CrossFit is the best thing that's ever been invented. Like anyone really cares how many burpees you can do or how much weight you can jerk."

"Speaking of jerks, I thought I told you not to be an asshole."

"You told me to *try* not to be one."

"What's your problem? You tell me you want to meet up so you can apologize, and I agree, only to show up and have you be a complete dick for no reason?" Her face flushed as anger started to flood into her. *Now* we were on a level playing field.

"I'm being a dick for voicing my opinions? Aren't you a teacher? Shouldn't you be encouraging people to speak their minds?"

"Oh, you want us to speak our minds? No problem,

playboy. Just let me order a drink, and maybe dinner and dessert, since I'll probably be here awhile. I have *plenty* to say to you." She motioned to the bartender and ordered a gin and tonic.

What a bitch! She'd ordered that drink on purpose; I knew she had.

When the bartender set it down in front of her, she brought it up to her lips, but turned toward me before taking a sip. "What's the matter, Max? Bring back memories?"

I was immediately transported back to the plane. Back to how good it had felt to touch her, hear her breathing quicken, watch her chest rise and fall. I had even been turned on when she'd told the flight attendant to ignore the drink I'd ordered for her and to bring a gin and tonic instead. She'd been so pigheaded. I knew right away that I had to have her. It was this memory that reminded me of how much I had loved her once. But the way she threw this memory in my face made me hate her in that moment.

"No good ones," I retorted bitterly.

Lily's face showed no sign that my comment had stung her, but I knew it had. Because I knew *her*. Better than anyone.

"So, what did you tell loverboy you were doing tonight? Since I'm sure you haven't suddenly developed a penchant for truth-telling in the past five months, I bet you came up with something interesting." I hadn't even thought about Adam until this moment. I was sure they had worked things out, but I hadn't dwelled on it.

I'd been so consumed with thoughts of her for the past couple of weeks that he hadn't sparked a single moment of brain activity. Until now. Because now, I was bordering on rage, and the thought of him with Lily amplified it. I was starting to feel like Carrie at the prom, capable of wiping out every living being in this bar if it would make me feel better.

She drew back a little at my comment and stared at me as though she were trying to figure something out. "Why would I tell him anything?" I could hear the caution in her voice.

She's probably worried I'm having us filmed so that I can send him the footage. Damn. That actually would've been a good idea. "I guess you wouldn't. Lying by omission is probably preferable to lying outright."

"He doesn't care where I am, Max. I have no reason to lie. I haven't even spoken to him since April."

Wait… What did she just say? "You're not with Adam?" My question had sounded more eager than I'd meant for it to.

She shook her head slowly as her eyes bored into me.

"Oh," I said flippantly. "I guess I just assumed you were still together." I didn't want her to know how thrown I was by this information. I wasn't exactly sure how I felt about it, but I definitely felt something. Relief maybe?

"Why the hell would you assume that? After the shit you pulled, what would ever make you think that he'd want to see me again?" She leaned slightly toward me, making it clear that she had no intention of backing down.

"The shit that *I* pulled?" My voice was louder and strained as I tried to resist the urge to scream at her. "You're fucking delusional, you know that? Everything that happened was shit *you* set in motion. He doesn't want to talk to you because he isn't interested in associating with deceitful liars who fuck people over for the fun of it." I knew that calling her a liar again would piss her off even more, but I didn't care.

I waited for her to run away sobbing like a typical girl would have. But as she looked me up and down in disgust, I remembered why I had always been so drawn to Lily. She wasn't like typical girls.

"I'm not the only one who fucks people over for fun, you selfish prick. You knew where we stood from day one. I lied to Adam; you're right about that. So I deserve every hateful word he would ever hurl at me. Not that he ever would, because unlike you, he's not a spoiled child. But, you? You were complicit every second. I *never* lied to you. And you were a willing accomplice in Operation Fuck Over Adam. So don't you dare sit there and act like you're better than me, because you aren't."

I'm not sure how the tension in our postures, the clear agitation on our faces, or the venom in our voices could be in any way inviting to a stranger, but evidently it was, because I suddenly felt a soft tap on my shoulder. I whirled around and saw a cute redhead standing behind me.

"Excuse me," the interloper purred. "Could you get the bartender's attention for me?"

"Sure thing, doll." I let one corner of my lip lift in a half smile. The girl no doubt thought that the smile was my way of flirting, and in a way, she was right. But it was mostly because I knew how badly it would hurt Lily to hear me call someone else "doll." It might even kill her. And right then, that was what I needed. I needed her to hurt like I did. If I had been in my right mind, I might have noticed how acidic my tongue tasted as the word left my mouth. Even my body knew that term would only ever apply to one person. But I had left my right mind behind three insults ago, and it wasn't coming back anytime soon.

The bartender took the woman's order and then walked away. I kept my eyes on her seductively, luring her in for the kill.

"You look really familiar. Have we met before?" she asked as she held the straw to her mouth.

I loved these coy games women played. "I don't think so. But I'm glad we're meeting now, doll. I'm Max." As I held out my hand to her, I heard the stool on the other side of me push back. *I knew the second "doll" would get her.*

"I'm certainly glad to see you haven't changed, Max. Now I don't have to feel guilty for wishing that your sorry ass gets hit by a fucking train on the way home. And hopefully that bitch is with you when it happens." Lily grabbed her purse and started toward the exit.

But the redhead wasn't willing to let Lily's comment slide. "Guess some girls can't handle it when something better comes along and takes a man's attention."

The anger immediately left me and was replaced by amusement as I watched Lily stop dead in her tracks and turn back toward us with menacing slowness. My eyes darted between the two women. *Oh, this is going to be good.*

I sat back a little so that I wasn't in the direct line of fire.

"Better? Really? Because desperate women who approach men instead of being approached are always the better option." Lily was trying to remain cool, but I could see the tightness in her shoulders. She was ready to pounce on this chick.

"I'm clearly not so desperate that I'd waste time flirting with a guy who obviously isn't interested." Apparently, the sexy stranger was ready to do some pouncing of her own.

"You have two seconds to get the hell out of here before I deflate those monstrosities on your chest and you're out five grand."

I hadn't had many opportunities to see sober Lily

threatening physical harm to another female. It was fucking *hot*.

"Please, you ugly bitch. Stop embarrassing yourself. It's painfully obvious that *you're* the one everyone wishes would leave." The woman was obviously impressed with herself as a cruel smile lit up her face.

Even I was almost offended by her remark. She was extremely attractive, but had nothing on my Lily.

"Max," Lily growled at me. "I am two seconds away from using a very unsavory term. So, if you don't want a repeat of our nightclub experience last year, I suggest you get rid of this trash. Right. Now."

And just like that, the memory sprang to mind. Some girl had insulted me, and a drunken Lily had called her a sloppy cunt. It was priceless. And as I mentally replayed the vision of Lily, eyes wild, swinging her body around toward the offender, I couldn't contain my laughter. It started as a smile, that quickly transformed into a chuckle, that then grew to a full-on belly laugh. And as I erupted, Lily's lips began to twitch until she was laughing right along with me.

I'm not sure when our visitor left. It was too difficult to see with the tears clouding my vision. The only thing I could focus on was the sound of Lily's laughter as she sat back down beside me.

chapter eight

l i l y

Surprisingly, I awoke refreshed and upbeat on Monday, and that almost *never* happened. In the morning, I took the time to brew some fresh coffee before I left for work, and I even managed to pack my lunch: tuna with a salad, apple, and a small bag of organic popcorn. I'd been making a conscious effort to eat healthier when I could because I didn't want all my hours at CrossFit to go to waste.

The day moved quickly as I immersed myself in work, and the next two days were much the same. The students I had this year seemed genuinely nice. They asked intelligent questions, offered to help put the laptops away properly, and seemed to thoroughly enjoy the class. They made it a pleasure to come to work each day. But I hoped I hadn't jumped the gun on my assessment of them. It was still only September. In years past, the beginning of the year had only been a honeymoon phase. Then October came. And with it, spawns of Satan. But I had high hopes for this year's kids.

Unfortunately, Trish wasn't faring so well in her classes. As her mentor, I had the responsibility of speaking informally with her on a regular basis to answer any questions she might have and to give her advice.

But Wednesday afternoon was the first *formal* meeting of the year, when the mentors and mentees from all the district's schools got together to meet with the administration about any issues they were experiencing. The topic of the lesson was classroom management. Thankfully, though the meetings were monthly for the new teachers, mentors only had to attend once in September and once in May.

And two times was plenty. Though new teachers—who were just getting acclimated to facilitating a classroom of students on their own—could benefit from such instruction, classroom management was not a topic that I felt I needed to work on. I never had a problem in that area, and after years of teaching, I didn't think I would start now.

Trish, on the other hand, was a complete disaster. Instead of telling me privately about the behavior issues she'd been having in class, she apparently thought that a group setting would be the most appropriate place to share her struggles.

After Mr. Coulson, the Director of Curriculum and Instruction, played a video of a well-run classroom in California, Trish's hand shot up. As she spoke, tears threatened to fall from her eyes. "My class doesn't look like that," she said.

"Well, what *does* it look like, Trish? Please, share with the group."

No, Trish. Please don't *share with the group.* I felt my eyes grow wide with embarrassment as I anticipated what she might say.

"I found out this morning that the kids who sit against the

wall in my fifth-period class have slowly been chipping away at the drywall behind my poster of Edgar Allan Poe," she blurted out. "They were all laughing today, and I saw them crowding around one spot, so I knew something was going on. When I managed to get them out of the way, I saw that they'd dug a hole through the wall. You can see through the other side into the stairwell."

Even Mr. Coulson didn't know how to respond to that. And *he* had a comment for *everything*. Before she had spoken, there'd been no doubt in my mind that whatever Trish was about to say would be awful, but I had no idea that her kids had been reenacting *The* fucking *Shawshank Redemption*. I briefly wondered why I hadn't seen Tim Robbins emerge from her classroom with pieces of drywall in the cuffs of his pants.

Over the course of the next few hours, we managed to talk Trish down from her proverbial ledge. Though at least now if she got the urge to "jump," she could just climb through the hole in her wall and throw herself down the stairs. I had to admit, the image made me laugh.

Somehow, even after the meeting, I still felt energetic enough to go to CrossFit before heading home. By the time I walked in the door, it was already after eight fifteen. I jumped when I heard Amanda scream. Not so much because of all the yelling. I was used to her crazy behavior. I jumped because I hadn't expected her to be home. She almost always got home after me.

I heard running water, mixed with Amanda's cursing, coming from the bathroom. "Fuck, fuck, fuck! Ouch! Jesus Christ!"

"Amanda, are you okay?" I knocked on the door, unsure of what could elicit such urgent screams.

"Uh, yeah. I just . . ." She sighed deeply before continuing. "I sprayed myself in the eye with sex toy cleaner." She opened the door and thrust the bottle my way. "Can you read this? Should I call poison control or something?"

"You're ridiculous. Just keep splashing water on your eyes. It'll come out. The stuff is made to go on things you put in your body. It's not poisonous." I couldn't help but laugh at her. This kind of stuff always happened to Amanda. "How did you do that anyway?"

As she flicked on the light and held up the vibrator she'd been clenching in her hand, I instantly became sorry I'd asked. "I was cleaning this in the dark. I couldn't see which way the bottle was gonna spray. I just started pumping, and it sprayed in my eyes." She pulled a hand towel off the rack and dabbed her face dry. "I didn't even get to clean this yet," she said as she ran the vibrator under the water and sprayed the cleaner cautiously toward it.

"Why does every conversation I have with you revolve around sex?"

She shrugged. "'Cause I love sex. And when I can't have it with someone else, I like to have it with myself. Speaking of . . . there seems to be a little more pep in your step the last few days," she nearly sang. "Tell me about him."

"Who?"

"What do you mean 'who'? Whoever has you so happy. You've been walking around with a goofy smile since the weekend."

"I have?" My question was genuine.

"Yeah, you have. Don't tell me you didn't notice."

"Um, no, not really." I hadn't noticed I'd been *happier*. More energetic? Definitely. More upbeat? Maybe. But happier? That was an emotion I thought had left me months ago. I'd seen Max over the weekend, and it had gone well—once we'd gotten past our little spat in the beginning, that is. The rest of the night had gone better than I'd expected, full of easy conversation and light laughter. We had *fun* together. I kept waiting for the bomb to drop, but it never did. He even divulged his interest in the job prospect his agent had scored for him. Max Samson opened up to me, and the shock had nearly killed me on the spot. He'd texted Monday to thank me for meeting with him and told me he'd text me later this week. But we were still so far from what we were when we were at our best. And our "best" was never all that good to begin with. We had a long way to go. Maybe I was just happy we'd begun the journey.

"Oh, before I forget, do you wanna go play pool Saturday? Steph and Danielle wanna go. We can drink and make stupid bets."

Thank God for Amanda's ADHD. If there was one thing she was good for, it was a random change in subject. "Sure, but I know better than to bet against *you*."

❤

Friday afternoon I got a text from Max.

Wanna meet up tomorrow night? A buddy of mine's in a band and he's playing at a bar in the city tomorrow. Could use a little company.

Remembering my plans for the pool hall with Amanda, I wrote back.

I might be able to go later. What time?

He doesn't go on until 10:30 I think.

That could work. I can probably get there a little after that. Text me the address and the name of the place.

As I put my phone back into my desk, I wondered if it was really wise to begin an ongoing relationship with Max, even if it was just a friendship. It was one thing to discuss his career prospects. It was another to hang out with him for the fun of it. Was I just rationalizing it by telling myself that he needed a good friend? Someone who could get him through the mess he'd made of things? But, more importantly, was I really the person to help him do that?

Saturday morning I occupied myself with CrossFit and a pedicure. I tried not to think about seeing Max, but my effort had the opposite effect. We had felt so comfortable last time we'd seen each other. Well, we had *eventually.* Things weren't comfy initially. But I could only imagine that things between us would only get easier, especially since the complication of sex had been removed from the equation. Because I sure as hell wasn't going down *that* road again.

I got ready for the night early, quickly deciding on snug

white pants that stopped just above my ankles, small heels, and a light green top. As always, Amanda was running late, still straightening her hair when I walked out of my room. She pulled herself away from the mirror to appraise my choice in attire.

"Who are you all dressed up for, Lil? We're just goin' to the pool hall."

Shit. Had it been that obvious that I'd given more than my usual thought to my appearance? "Nobody," I replied, hoping my quick response would cause her to drop it. "Can't a girl just look nice?"

As she ran her eyes up and down the length of my body, I was sure she didn't believe me. "Nobody, my ass. You look *hot.*"

"Do I?" I asked with a quick spin. Despite the fact that my appearance caused Amanda to question my intentions, it felt good to know that she thought I looked nice. She wasn't one to dish out serious compliments often.

"Yeah, you totally do. If I were a guy, I'd fuck you."

Yup, that seems more on par for Amanda. "Aww," I replied in my best southern accent, "you really know how to make a girl feel special."

But there was no evading Amanda when she wanted information. Especially when it came to sex. "So is the new mystery man comin' tonight or what? I'm dying to meet the guy who can put a smile like that on Lily Hamilton's face. He must be *damn* good in bed."

Shit. Now *she thinks I'm happy because I'm sleeping with someone.* "No, I might go out with him afterward, though. And who said I was sleeping with him?"

"Who said you *weren't?*"

I needed to dodge her questions. And fast. "Let's talk about who *you* may or may not be sleeping with, shall we? A certain Shane Reed will be there tonight, right?" Amanda definitely had a thing for our CrossFit coach, even if she wouldn't admit it. And who could really blame her? He was blond, built like a fucking gladiator, and funny as hell. She'd been hanging out with him recently and had invited him out that night so she could embarrass him in pool since he'd done the same to her when they'd gone rock-climbing last weekend. Shane was in for a real surprise. He had no idea Amanda could kick anyone's ass in pool thanks to her grandfather's tutelage when she was young.

As I'd hoped, my plan worked like a charm. Amanda averted her eyes back to the mirror as she denied my accusation with a laugh.

God, that was almost too easy.

❤

Once at the pool hall, my suspicions were confirmed. It didn't take long for Shane and Amanda to make a bet—one that resulted in them kissing, regardless of who won. I gave Amanda an I-told-you-so glance as she pretended to be grossed out by the thought of kissing Shane.

"Not a word," she warned me.

The first game went as I'd anticipated. Amanda played the dumb blonde role perfectly, asking about how to hold the cue and missing easy shots. But I knew she'd take him in the second game since it was best out of three.

Under normal circumstances, I would've been entertained by her performance. But I was distracted knowing that in a few hours I'd see Max. When I pulled my phone out of my purse to check the time, I was surprised to see a text from him. What did he have to say that couldn't wait until later?

Any chance you can get here earlier?

> *Why? I thought your friend doesn't play until later. I'm at the pool hall with Amanda. I'm her ride home.*

Is there someone else who can take her home? I need you to get here. It's kind of an emergency.

This was going to make me look like a horrible friend to Amanda, but Max sounded desperate. Well, as desperate as you could sound through text, and it worried me. When we'd first talked, I'd promised myself that I would make every effort to help him get his life back on track. If that meant leaving Amanda to flirt with Shane on her own for a bit, well, that was a casualty of war. "I'm gonna get going," I said reluctantly.

Amanda gave me a confused glance as she eyed up her next shot. "But you're my ride home."

For a moment, I felt bad. That is, until Shane chimed in. "I'll drive you. It's no big deal."

Thank you, Coach Shane. "Perfect." And it was. I could leave early without feeling bad that I'd ditched a friend, and Amanda could get some more alone time with Shane. I sent Max a quick text.

> *On my way. Be there soon.*

And as I settled into the driver's seat and threw my car into drive, I laughed. One of us needed to be saved at a bar again. And it felt good to be the one doing the saving this time.

chapter nine

m a x

I was fidgeting helplessly, my eyes darting pensively toward the door every few seconds. *Where the hell is she?* She had said she was on her way over an hour ago. Silently cursing my decision to come down to the city early, I picked up my whiskey on the rocks and damn near drained the glass. She must've hit traffic. And as the nasally voice across from me continued to garble out sounds that my brain refused to process as words, I cursed every motorist between here and wherever the hell Lily was coming from.

My leg started jerking violently, making the chair I was sitting on creak loudly. I didn't care. The creaking was preferable to the high-pitched nightmare that was *still* prattling on about God-knows-what. I rubbed my hand over my face, wondering if this was my purgatory. Was this how I was meant to atone for being such a prick all these years?

I lifted my glass to my mouth and glanced toward the door again. "Oh, thank you, Jesus."

"Huh?" the voice puzzled.

"Oh, uh, nothing," I said sheepishly. Then, bellowing across the bar and waving my hands like a lunatic, I yelled, "Lily! Hey, Lily, over here!"

Lily returned my wave with a smile and walked toward me. Why was she walking so slowly? *Come on, doll.*

"Hey. Sorry it took me so long to get here. Traffic was—"

I interrupted her by throwing my arm around her shoulder and pressing a kiss to her temple. "No big deal, hon. I'm just *so* glad you're finally here." I threw my gaze at the hyena across from me, hoping that Lily would understand the role I needed her to play. But all I saw on her face was shock. *Shit, I shouldn't have kissed her. I caused her to short-circuit.* "Lily, this is..." I hesitated. My mind drew a complete blank. *What the fuck is her name?*

"Stacey," the hyena answered for me. "Men. Their attention is only ever on one thing."

Wait, was she intimating that I didn't remember her name because I was too absorbed in thinking about fucking her? *Gross.*

"Sorry. Yes, this is Stacey, and she's been talking to me for the past *two hours* about, well, everything you could ever possibly think of." I spoke with a smile, but it was tight and I hoped that Lily would see right through it. I studied her intensely, and it clicked. She narrowed her eyes at me, and I felt an instant of fear. She wouldn't screw me over on purpose, would she?

Finally, Lily stretched out her hand. "Hi Stacey, so nice to meet you. And thank you for keeping Max here company for me." As she spoke, Lily poked her fingers into my ribs unnecessarily hard, which caused me to buck forward and wince.

Message received.

"Oh, so you two are…?" Stacey inquired, surprise and disappointment showing on her face.

Worrying that Lily was beginning to feel bad for this harbinger of boredom, I quickly interjected. "Yes, this is my girlfriend, Lily. Remember, I told you I was waiting for her."

I shot a quick look to Lily and widened my eyes in an attempt to convey the level of crazy we were dealing with here. This bitch was a stage-five clinger if I ever met one. I had told her on at least five occasions that I was meeting my girlfriend, and she had pretended not to hear me every time—a complete dismissal of reality. It would have been impressive had it not terrifyingly reminded me of the plot of *Misery*.

Anger sparked in Stacey's features as she snapped at me. "No, I absolutely do not remember you mentioning anything like that."

Here we go.

"Oh, I'm so sorry, Stacey," Lily apologized. "Max here is so forgetful sometimes. It's the syphilis."

Yeah, it's the… Did she just say syphilis?

Stacey looked horrified as Lily continued, leaning in closer to the hyena as though she were imparting highly classified information. "Yeah, I'm actually not his girlfriend. I'm his nurse. His mind is deteriorating so rapidly, I don't even bother to correct him anymore."

"Oh, that's terrible," Stacey drawled as she put a hand to her chest.

Dramatist.

I tightened my grip on Lily's shoulder as a warning. One more comment like that, and I would rip off her arm and beat her with it.

"I know. And the herpes is only making it worse."

"Okay, well, I think that's enough of that. I have a table waiting for us, Nurse Lily. Shall we?" I glared at her as I spoke, wishing horrible things on her: male pattern baldness, impetigo, leprosy.

"Yes, let's," she replied with equal agitation. Then she turned toward Stacey and hugged her. "Thank you so much again. The last time he was left alone in the city, we found him in an abandoned building with no pants. Or underwear." She hissed out the last sentence, leaving the implication of her words hanging heavily in the air.

Stacey's mouth fell open as we marched off. I was as appalled as Stacey, though obviously for different reasons. Lily, however, wore a smug smile on her face.

"Jesus Christ, Lil. Was all that really necessary? What if she blabs that shit to the papers?" We turned around a corner to where the band was setting up. As soon as we were out of Stacey's line of sight, Lily rounded on me swiftly and punched me in the gut. Hard. I let out a sputtering cough, wheezing from the force of the blow. "Holy fuck!" I yelled when air returned to my lungs. "What the hell was that for?"

Lily stepped directly into my personal space, a place I was none too keen on having her since she'd assaulted me seconds before. But she was staring at me like she was debating what to do with my body, so I quickly decided that the best defense was a good offense. "Did I tell you that your shirt really brings out the green in your eyes? Because it does. Really." She was still staring me down, clearly trying to get herself under control before she spoke to me. *Shit. Compliments almost always worked.*

"You motherfucker."

So much for control.

"Tell me you did not drag me away from my friends so that I could save your ass from a woman." She stopped and awaited my reply. When she didn't receive one, she continued. "You're not saying anything. Why aren't you saying anything?"

"I also take back the CrossFit comment. It's clearly doing wonders. You look beautiful. I didn't think you could get any more gorgeous, but let me tell you—"

"Max, stop complimenting me for Christ's sake. It's cheap and meaningless when you do it to try to fix a situation *you* fucked up."

"But you hit me. Can't we be even?"

"Even? Did you smoke crack earlier today? You told me you had an emergency—"

"I think I said it was *sort of* an emergency." She reeled back to hit me again, so I threw my hands out to block her. She had really grown violent over the past few months. "Okay, okay, you're right. It was a dick move. But, in my defense, did you *see* that woman?" I shuddered at the memory.

"Yeah, I saw her. What was wrong with her?"

"What was wrong with her? She looked like a Furby."

Lily's mouth drew up into a smile, but she quickly repressed it. "Oh, stop. She did not."

"Now who's smoking crack? And you *hugged* her. I'm surprised you didn't get a rash from her five o'clock shadow."

Then Lily turned serious. "Max, listen to me. Don't ever do that again. I was panicking the whole way here. And you took advantage of the fact that I'd hurry down here to help you. I want to be here for you. I want to be your friend. Because despite my better judgment, I missed you over these last months. But if you pull some dumb shit like this again, I will be burying you in an unmarked grave in a pet cemetery. Got it?"

"Yes, Miss Hamilton," I replied in a monotone. But when she started off toward the exit, I quickly followed her, grabbing her arm. "Wait, wait, I'm sorry. I was just kidding." Pulling her back in front of me, I released her arm and blew out a breath. "I promise. I won't do anything like that again. I apologize for making you worry."

She thought for a moment, probably trying to figure out whether or not she believed me. In the end, she must have decided that she did. "Okay, apology accepted."

"Thank God," I sighed. "Now, you ready to hear some music?"

"As ready as I'll ever be," she replied with a wry smile.

We walked closer to the stage. The band was still setting up, so the crowd hadn't followed us into this section of the bar yet. Standing there in a comfortable silence, I took in the sight of her. I hadn't been lying. That green shirt highlighted the subtle sparkle in her eyes I'd noticed the first time they met mine in that airport. And those tight white pants fit her lean legs perfectly. I suddenly wondered if Lily knew how beautiful she was, if she'd appreciate hearing it. But I shook off the thought, figuring that she'd love to hear it. Just not from me.

"So, she talked your ear off for two hours, huh?" she said slyly as she cocked her head in my direction.

"Two horrendous hours. I was nice at first. That was my undoing. Once I realized that she was never going to leave me alone, I had to call in the cavalry."

"Why didn't you just excuse yourself and then find a new seat?"

"I did. Twice! She followed me both times. I made a valiant attempt at listening to her for about three minutes. But then she started talking about her porcelain doll collection, and I panicked. That's when I moved the first time. I lasted almost four minutes the second time. And then came the story about having her grandmother's ashes sitting on her nightstand beside her bed. That's when I knew it was time for escape number two. But she sniffed me out like a bloodhound and started jabbering again. That time I didn't even try to listen. I just tried to keep calm and wait for you to get here and save me."

Lily was no longer trying to hide her amusement. She smiled widely as she visualized the scene in her head. "It couldn't have been *that* bad."

"Listen, I'm not sure if you saw the white string of spit on the side of her mouth, but I saw it. I also had to keep dodging it as it flew out of her mouth randomly like a slingshot. So don't tell me it wasn't that bad. I lived it, and I'm telling you that my life was in mortal danger back there."

"Whatever you say," she said, smiling, flipping her chestnut hair over her shoulder as she turned her attention back to the band.

I gazed at her a moment, appreciating the simple beauty that encapsulated Lily Hamilton. I wasn't sure how many more times she'd forgive me after I screwed up, but I was glad that she hadn't given up on me yet. And as the smile spread across my face, I realized that her inner beauty might be even more alluring than the outer beauty.

As the rest of the night passed, I found myself wishing that I could freeze time. Being friends with Lily was easy. Natural. And for the first time in six months, I started to feel a little hope that my life wouldn't be shitty forever.

chapter ten

a d a m

As October passed, my schedule began to calm down a bit. I only had to check in periodically at the new home site because the guys seemed like they were finally able to function without my constant supervision. And Eva managed to get into the groove of the school year. She decided to play volleyball and seemed to have a handle on her grades. We'd gone to a few Sixers games together, but I had to admit I was thankful when she went to a dance and a few sleepovers. It gave me some time to do my own thing.

When Halloween arrived, I was glad Eva had decided against the Miley Cyrus costume she'd originally planned. When her friend Christina suggested that she and a few of her friends dress as the *Pretty Little Liars*, I couldn't have been happier. I knew it would be a significant improvement on her first choice. Well, maybe *significant* wasn't the correct term. *Slight* might be more accurate. It certainly beat the image that had haunted my nightmares for the past few weeks: one that involved my scantily clad thirteen-year-old daughter prancing around the neighborhood with a shaved head and a sledgehammer.

I'd let her stay out later than usual because the girls had planned to go back to Christina's with their candy and watch a movie. I knew she was growing up, and this would be one of her last years trick-or-treating, so I wanted her to enjoy the time with her friends. But like any concerned father, I waited by the door until Christina's mom dropped Eva off a little before eleven thirty. As she skipped through the door wide awake, I'd pretended to be asleep on the couch so she wouldn't know I'd been waiting up for her.

A while later, I heard her settle in for the night, and as I crept to the top of the stairs, I couldn't resist peeking in her room to see her sleeping peacefully. Now I could do the same.

The next morning, as usual, I packed Eva's lunch and said goodbye as she left for the bus. I planned to head into the office for a bit to do some drawings and wanted to go to Eva's volleyball game after school. With my laptop bag and a bottle of water in hand, I headed out the door.

For weeks, I hadn't managed to get to the coffee shop before work, but since I had a light day ahead of me, I decided a relaxing morning was in order as well. I would enjoy a cup of coffee and read the paper quietly—something I hadn't done in a while. As I entered, I realized just how much I'd missed the smell of freshly ground coffee beans. Since I wasn't in a rush, I figured I'd wait until the line died down a bit before I ordered. So I swiped a newspaper off the rack by the door and settled myself into a high-top table by the window.

As customers made their way through the door, the crisp autumn air mingled with the warmth of the coffeehouse. I paid little attention to what was happening around me, happily engrossing myself in the paper for a few minutes until I glanced up to see that the line had gotten considerably shorter.

I wasn't much of a coffee snob, but for some reason, I had the urge to try something new. My eyes stayed fixed on the menu above the baristas' heads—a menu I wasn't at all familiar with because I never deviated from my usual order. As the line dwindled, I inched my way closer to the counter and studied the choices before me: lattes, macchiatos, cappuccinos, espressos. I had no idea what to get. But when my turn came and the barista stared at me for a moment, I knew exactly what I wanted: the usual.

"Large hot coffee, two sugars, right?" the barista asked, sliding the tall cup my way.

I was immediately confused. I didn't even recognize the small blond girl working today. There was no way she would have recognized *me*, let alone know what I wanted to drink. "Right, how did you...?" My voice trailed off.

"I didn't," she replied with a shrug. "But *she* did."

I spun around in the direction of the doors and stretched my head around the line behind me to look out the glass. I barely heard her when the girl at the counter told me my coffee had been paid for too. I'd been too captivated by who I'd seen outside.

Just as she'd gotten into her car, my eyes locked with Lily's for a split second. A second that seemed both too long and not long enough. And as I watched her drive away, I was surprised by my first thought. *How did she know how I took my coffee?*

I put the cup to my lips and let the smooth familiar taste slide down my throat, thinking that despite my fleeting craving for change, I ultimately always came back to what I already loved.

chapter eleven

l i l y

What was that look? Was he confused? Was he happy to see me? He didn't *look* happy. I couldn't describe what I saw on Adam's face when his gaze caught mine as I'd entered my car.

Though I'm not sure why, I hadn't expected Adam to realize I'd even been there. As I stood in line, I'd glanced behind me to see him reading the paper alone. I'd been overcome with the urge to sit down across from him. To be staring into his bright green eyes like it was seven months ago and our lives together were in our future instead of in our past.

But I couldn't do that. He'd never allow it. Not after what I'd done to him. So I did the only thing I could do for him in that moment: I'd bought him a cup of coffee.

And now that he knew it'd been me who'd bought it for him, I didn't exactly know how I felt about it. *Wait ... that's not true. I know exactly how I feel about it. Like an asshole, that's how.* As I pulled into my space at work, I shook my head and silently scolded myself for thinking I could become some stealthy coffee Robin Hood, doling out java to all those I'd wronged.

Note to self: avoid the coffeehouse for a few weeks.

❤

Work passed rather quickly, and I knew that later that day I'd have the luxury of focusing on someone else's problems instead of my own, namely Amanda's problem with coming to terms with her feelings for Shane.

Scratch that. Maybe Amanda's problem was *my* problem too. She burst through the door at five thirty, clearly irritated I was dragging her to CrossFit that night. She tried to recover by putting on a brave face and remaining stoic as she changed for the gym. "Ready to go," she nearly sang, plastering a fake smile across her face as she headed for the door.

I followed her out, donning a grin that I hoped mirrored hers to show her how ridiculous she looked. For someone with such a hard exterior, Amanda could be so damn transparent sometimes. After she'd called me last Sunday morning to "rescue" her from her night at Shane's, she'd spent the remainder of the week freaking out. She couldn't handle her feelings for him, so she'd run. And as far as I could tell, she was content to keep running.

But last night, I'd finally called her out on avoiding him, which she denied. In an effort to prove that she didn't have real feelings for Shane, she'd agreed to go to CrossFit, a place she'd been trying to avoid like some sort of airborne STD for the past four days.

Though, the thing I should have remembered about Amanda was that, when she felt backed into a corner, she came at you like a pit bull. So when Shane pulled her into his office for an airing out of their bullshit, she fought back in the most effective way possible: she said whatever she thought would hurt him the most with complete indifference.

From my protective perch a few feet away from the office door, I'd been too busy sending threatening glares to the nosy CrossFitters to thoroughly eavesdrop. But what I did hear made me cringe. She denied all feelings for him. Denied all connection. He put himself out there for her, and she trounced all over every ounce of his ego. It was ... terrible.

And as I watched her storm out of his office, I knew I was looking at a facade—a protective mask that she'd adorned to aid in her escape from Shane. But the thing about a mask is, it doesn't cover the eyes. And that's where I saw it: regret. Her eyes swam with it. So I followed her silently back out to my car, knowing that I was in for one hell of a ride home.

It wasn't until we pulled away from CrossFit that Amanda finally let go of all the tears she'd been holding back for the last week. As much as I wanted to talk to her, I couldn't bring myself to try. What could I say that would make her feel better? That she was an idiot for running? That she should accept her feelings for what they were instead of pretending she felt nothing?

Over the past few months, she'd been hanging out with Shane more frequently. I could see their relationship slowly progressing from a friendship to something more intimate, especially over the past few weeks. I knew they had kissed after the pool hall, but I didn't know anything more had happened until she had called me from his house the morning after the wedding they'd gone to together. Though she would never admit it, Shane was perfect for her. He was witty, playful, kind, and smoking hot. Ultimately, he was a male version of Amanda, minus the intense fear of commitment.

Why did she have to be so dense, so blind to what the rest of us could see? She could claim they were just friends all she wanted—that theirs was nothing more than a platonic relationship that had gone a step too far. I knew all about taking a friendship where it should never go. And while I would never make that mistake again, Amanda's situation wasn't the same.

Because I realized what Amanda didn't. She loved him. She had to. Because your heart didn't break like that for someone you didn't love. I knew what it was like to lose someone you loved when it could have been prevented. It was the kind of pain that could even reduce a ballbuster like Amanda to tears. And my heart hurt with a familiar ache just watching her experience it.

💔

I tried to leave Amanda alone most of the weekend in the hopes that by getting a little space, she would come to her senses and talk to Shane. But by Tuesday afternoon, she'd already joined a new gym. *So much for coming to her senses.*

I'd been so preoccupied with making sure she didn't hang herself with the cord of her hair straightener that I hadn't even thought about my "encounter" with Adam.

Until Wednesday morning, that is.

chapter twelve

a d a m

"Eva, you ready?" I walked toward the front door, not waiting for her to reply. I stood there, trying to force patience into my countenance. It was nearly friggin' impossible.

Finally, she bounded down the stairs and eyed me suspiciously. "Why are you standing there like that?"

"Like what? I'm just waiting for you." My eyes narrowed in confusion. *Why am I answering to my thirteen-year-old daughter?*

"Waiting for me, why?"

"So I can have you help me drag a body from my trunk," I said with an eye roll. "So I can take you to school. Why else?"

Eva checked her phone and then looked back at me as if trying to fit pieces of a puzzle together, but no matter how she spun them, they just didn't fit. "I haven't missed the bus. Why are you driving me?"

"I thought I'd be nice and drop you off. Am I not allowed to do something nice for you?" The look on her face let me know she wasn't buying it. The truth was, I didn't offer her the ride to be nice. I did it in the off chance that I'd get to see Lily. I wasn't entirely sure what I was going to do when I did see her, but I'd figure all that out when the time came. "Fine," I sighed. "I read a story in the newspaper about a bus driver who kidnapped one of the students on his route and held her hostage for three weeks before they found her. She's so traumatized that she hasn't spoken in four months. I guess the story makes me a little nervous about you riding the bus."

Her eyes narrowed. "Are you going to pick me up in the afternoon too?"

Shit. "No."

"Why not?" She put a hand to her hip and awaited my response. *When did she become so skeptical?*

"Because I don't view sixty-year-old Doris Callahan as much of a threat to your safety. Can we go now, please?" Thank the Lord her afternoon driver was a female. Otherwise I would've been totally fucked.

Eva's face softened, and she dropped her hand from her hip. She started toward the door, but stopped in front of me, suddenly wrapping her arms around my torso.

"Thanks, Daddy."

I hugged her back firmly and dropped my cheek to the top of her head. "Anytime, baby. It's my job to keep you safe." *I am really going to burn in hell for this one.*

Eva pulled away, bounced out the door, and got in the car. As I locked the house, I hoped that, however things played out with Lily, it was worth lying my ass off to my daughter.

♥

Eva had actually kissed me on the cheek before exiting the car and making her way into the school building. I should've felt disappointed in myself for getting her affection in such a devious manner, but I was eating it up. The way I saw it, this was retroactive payment for all the things I had done for her over the past thirteen years that I hadn't gotten a shred of appreciation for. Like talking to her about her period. I was *definitely* owed for that one.

But Eva had left the car five minutes ago, and I was still at the end of the driveway leading up to Swift Middle School. I had scanned the teacher parking lot and didn't see Lily's car. *She's probably running late, as usual.* Why I was still sitting there though, I didn't know. I just couldn't bring myself to pull away. So, instead, I sat there like a third-rate stalker, hoping to catch a glimpse of a woman I wasn't even sure I liked.

Then I saw her. I had somehow missed her pull in, but I hadn't missed her walking toward the school. And as soon as I caught sight of her soft brown hair blowing gently in the wind, the confidence of her gait, and the cool collectedness on her face, I knew why I was still sitting there. I damn well did like her. Maybe even loved her. And I had about fifteen seconds to determine what to do about it before she stepped into the building and I lost my chance to do anything.

"Fuck it," I muttered as I threw my car in gear and drove toward the school entrance. She was approaching the front doors, and I felt my opportunity slipping away. I racked my brain for something to say, but nothing came. Finally, I just said anything. "Thanks!" I yelled as I leapt from my car, not even bothering to close my door. I watched her jerk to a stop, but she didn't turn around. *Does she not recognize my voice?* I immediately realized what a stupid question that was. It was *because* she knew it was me that her body was so tense. Maybe this had been a mistake.

"Uh . . . Lily, I just wanted to say thanks for the coffee." I stood there, waiting for her to turn around and acknowledge me in any way. Christ, this had *definitely* been a mistake.

Finally, after what felt like hours, she turned around to face me. I watched as her eyes looked me over, and I prayed that she liked what she saw. "Hi," she ground out, clearly at a loss for anything else to say.

I felt my eyes widen, waiting for her to continue. This shouldn't feel so awkward. At least not for me. *She* was the one who had betrayed *me*. Yet I couldn't shake the feeling that both of us owed something to the other. Though I couldn't, for the life of me, figure out what I could possibly owe *her*.

When she didn't speak, I felt the urge to clarify, if for no other reason than to end this debacle as soon as possible. "The coffee the other day . . . I just wanted to say thank you." I was clearly on the verge of setting some sort of record for repeating myself. *Come on, Carter; get your head out of your ass.*

I noticed her lips lift slightly before spreading into a small laugh. "Yeah, you said that already. And you're welcome, by the way."

I thought that her silence had been weird, but hearing her speak to me was even more disconcerting. Not to mention that she had just called me out on my redundancy, thereby highlighting my awkwardness. "It surprised me, that's all." At some point today, my brain would catch up to my mouth and prevent this stupid shit from leaving it. But evidently my mind had not yet reached that point.

Confusion lit up her face. "That I'd buy you a cup of coffee?"

"No... well, yes, that too. But I was more surprised that you knew how I *took* my coffee." I felt like a teenage girl who harped on the fact that a boy knew her favorite color. But I couldn't help it. The fact that she knew this small detail meant that she had *wanted* to know it. That she cared enough to pay attention to the subtle idiosyncrasies that only someone who loved you would think to notice.

"Black. Two sugars," she said simply, as though it were information that was obvious to everyone who knew me. It wasn't. "I've always known that, Adam."

It shook me a little to realize how much I loved hearing her say my name—how much I wanted to hear her say it again, preferably in a more intimate setting. She licked her lips, and my need to hear her say my name again morphed into a need to hear her scream it as I slid inside her, as I branded her so everyone knew that she was mine.

"Well, I should probably get going. I don't want to be late."

I was tempted to point out that she probably already was, but thankfully my brain caught that comment before my mouth spewed it. So this was it? This was how things ended? Did I want that? Did she? "Right, sorry," I quickly grumbled, sounding much harsher than I had intended. I softened my voice before I spoke again. "I don't want you to be late either. I guess I'll talk to ya later."

The last part slipped out. It was a standard farewell. An easy substitute for goodbye. But with Lily, it held countless possibilities. I could talk to her later. If I wanted to. And as I watched her walk toward the school, my heart ached with how badly I wanted to.

♥

Two days. Two torturous days of thinking about her and how fucked up our entire conversation had been. Couldn't I have played it cool? Just one time? I glanced over at the clock next to my bed. Two fifteen a.m. I had barely slept the previous night and was having a repeat performance this evening as well.

It wouldn't have been so bad if I could just figure out what the hell I wanted. I shouldn't want Lily. She had destroyed me. The entire time she was dating me, she was also seeing that cocksucker, Max. How could she do that and have genuine feelings for me?

It wasn't like we had been dating for years and the relationship had gone stale. Not that that would have provided a valid excuse for her behavior, but at least then I could've understood on some level. But we had only been together a short time. We were still in the honeymoon stage of our relationship, and she had fucked around on me. I couldn't reconcile *that* Lily with the one I thought I knew. The one I had loved.

My Lily was kind and caring and considerate. She was gentle and sincere. Suddenly, my mind was plagued by the Lily I had known. How her hand fit perfectly in mine. How my arms felt at home when they wrapped around her. How her lips melded to mine in a blissful frenzy whenever we were together.

I thought back to the last time I had been with her—how perfect she'd felt when I pushed inside of her. How her soft moans had made me harder than I had ever been in my life. And when her orgasm ripped through her, her pussy had clenched down on my pulsating cock, milking the come from it in long, bursting squirts. But as great as that had been, it hadn't been enough. I'd needed to have her again, but that time, I took her mouth. The thought of that warmth enveloping my hard cock caused my entire body to tingle.

And as I remembered the feel of her tongue swirling over my tip and drinking me dry, I couldn't stop my dick from hardening at the thought. Involuntarily, I lowered my hand under the covers, grabbed tightly, and tugged with long, hard strokes. As I continued to work myself, I let my mind wander. To think about how, after she had sated me with that delicious mouth, I had wanted to return the favor. To show her that our relationship was about give-and-take.

I gripped my shaft harder, pulling faster as my mind replayed the images of my fingers having their way with her body, thrusting inside of her until she came all over them. I remembered telling her we needed to go on a vacation so that I could touch her for an entire weekend without interruption.

It was that memory that caused my orgasm to come barreling down my spine. That image—of touching her like she belonged to me—that caused me to finally explode, catching the hot bursts of semen in my hand.

It was in that moment that I knew the truth. She couldn't have faked that passion. She couldn't have feigned the physical reaction she had to me. *Holy fuck. She had loved me.*

♥

I woke up the next morning feeling lighter than I had in months. My relationship with Lily hadn't *all* been bullshit. We had felt very real things during our time together—things that had stuck with me throughout the last however many months, no matter how much I tried to deny their existence. The only question I was left with was just how much of our relationship *had* been bullshit. And as I swung my legs over the edge of my bed and ran a hand through my rumpled hair, I decided it was time to find out.

❤

I sat at my computer screen, my email open, and the cursor blinking. This had seemed like such a great idea three hours ago. But now that I was faced with the task of following through with my plan, it seemed less appealing.

Already having drafted and deleted five emails to Lily, I was beginning to get frustrated. I was supposed to be reviewing our budget for our current project, but I couldn't focus on numbers right now. Well, there was one number I was able to focus on, but I had sworn to myself that I wasn't going to use it.

I had barely been able to hold a conversation with her when I had a clear purpose for doing so. There was no way I'd be able to sustain idle chitchat. So I had opted for an email instead. But there was so much to consider. Did I try to be funny? Did I immediately get to the heart of the matter? Did I ask some random, mundane question about the school? I grew more and more frantic as the minutes ticked by.

Finally, with my new motto of "Fuck it" ringing in my head, I began typing again. This time, I just let my fingers do the talking and hoped for the best. Once finished, I previewed what I had written.

Hi Lily,

It's Adam. I just wanted to say that it was good seeing you yesterday. And, in the spirit of paying it forward (or in this case, paying it back), I wanted to get you a cup of coffee as well. So here ya go. One caramel macchiato. Enjoy.

I inwardly groaned at the hokiness of putting a virtual macchiato in an email, but I clearly couldn't get past this loser behavior. I quickly hit Send before I had a chance to contemplate it any longer. And as soon as my email went cruising through cyberspace, on its way to the one person who could possibly hold the key to my sustained happiness, I regretted including the picture. I probably didn't need to start off with "It's Adam" either since the sender would be automatically listed. *Fucking asshole.*

But whatever. What was done was done, and now the ball was in her court. She'd either write back or she wouldn't. No need to obsess over it. Nothing more I could do now. Might as well get to work. Staring at my monitor wasn't going to help the situation. I was just going to clear my mind of all things Lily and... *Holy shit, was that a ping?* I catapulted myself closer to my monitor as I vise-gripped my mouse. There it was. An email from *Hamilton, Lily.* I couldn't help but feel relieved at the swiftness of her response. I allowed my eyes to drift down to the body of her email and took a deep breath.

Hey Adam,

It was great to see you too.

"*Great!*" She'd written "*great.*" That had to be a good sign.

Though I'm thinking it's less great since you sent me a picture of the thing that I need most in the world right now. I'm jonesing in the worst way. So, I'm sorry to say that I will not be enjoying your poor excuse for "paying it back." Better luck next time.

P.S. Shouldn't you be working? :)

By the time I realized just how broadly I was grinning, it was too late. I was too far gone and already typing my reply. It was frightening how insanely happy I was that she had joked with me like she would have done seven months ago. Filled with certainty that this wasn't all a huge mistake and that I owed us both a second chance, I again gazed over my reply before hitting Send.

Let me make it up to you. If you're around tomorrow morning, stop by the coffeehouse and I'll buy you the real thing. Around 9?

P.S. Shouldn't you? ;)

I sent the message off and bit at my thumbnail as I awaited her response. I felt like I had when I'd asked Melissa Price to the junior prom. Though, when Lily's reply came through, it blew Melissa's response out of the water.

See you then.

I exhaled the first deep breath I'd been able to release since this whole email nonsense had started. Sinking back into my chair, I thought about how this felt so . . . right. It was a do-over. And I was sure as fuck going to make sure it went right this time.

chapter thirteen

l i l y

Coffee. With Adam. Tomorrow morning. Had he just asked me out? Maybe not asked me out in the traditional sense. He'd only said that he would make it up to me by buying me a cup of coffee. *That would make us even, right?* I'd bought *him* one. Now he'd buy *me* one. Just friends having coffee together.

But the thing was, we weren't friends. I'd never been just friends with Adam.

So what would this be?

A wave of anxiety ran through me that nearly rattled my core. Was Adam giving me a second chance? Did I even deserve one? I'd spent these last seven months rehashing, analyzing, and critiquing what had happened between us. And the only conclusion I could come to was that it had been entirely my fault. I'd been wrong to think that I could resist Max, even though I really *had* loved Adam.

Because it's not that simple.

It didn't matter that you only loved one person. Everyone

had urges, sexual desires that when presented with the opportunity were difficult to ignore. The key to being faithful was to avoid putting yourself in a situation where you'd be tempted to act on those desires.

It meant avoiding drunken nights in clubs where you and your friends danced with hot guys. Because you might just be tempted to kiss one of them.

It meant leaving happy hour early before you and that coworker you've had a crush on for the past few months were the only ones left and he offered you a ride home. Because you might just take it.

Being faithful wasn't something people just were. It was an action. It was a choice. It said so in a *Cosmo* article I read recently. *God, that's a great fucking magazine.*

❤

By Friday afternoon, I felt spent. The students had been writing persuasive essays about whether or not they should get paid to go to school. Not surprisingly, most of them said they should. On the Smartboard, I projected an example of how their paper's heading should look. And though they gave it a genuine effort, when Sam Christianson put the words "Your Name" at the top of his paper instead of his actual name, I briefly lost all faith in America's future generations.

"No, Sam," I said, chuckling, "I just wrote 'Your Name' up there so you'd know that your own name goes on the top left. Type 'Sam Christianson.'"

"Oh, okay," he said as he changed the font to some large illegible script that I'd already told them they weren't allowed to use. And when he typed his name all in lowercase letters,

I couldn't help thinking that a future career as a smut writer looked better and better.

❤

As I made my way out of CrossFit a little after eight, I crossed my arms at the bitter chill that stung my cheeks. We'd had some unseasonably warm weather for the past few weeks, but suddenly, in early November, it seemed winter had come early. I cranked up the heat in my car and turned on my headlights as I pulled out of the parking lot.

I'd told Tina and Trish that I'd meet them for a few drinks at a nearby bar that had a psychic on Friday nights. I wasn't too interested in seeing what my own future held, though. To be honest, I was a little frightened of psychics. Something about the way their eyes always looked glazed over. But the thought of getting Trish drunk was just too good to pass up.

Unfortunately, when I opened the door to my apartment and saw Amanda gorging herself on a gallon of ice cream, I thought maybe I'd have to take a rain check on my girls' night. She'd been avoiding Shane for weeks. But instead of getting better, she seemed to be getting worse. I couldn't stand by and watch her self-destruct while I did nothing. "Why are you already in your pajamas eating an entire carton of ice cream?" I asked, accusation plaguing my tone.

I was sure she thought I'd already gone out for the night when she jumped at my question. She gave some sarcastic answer, asked me why I was there, and then went back to her DVR'd episode of *Sons of Anarchy*.

"Don't be a smartass. I'm going out in a bit," I answered, studying her closely. She seemed to have lost a little of what made Amanda *Amanda*. When she'd walked away from Shane, she'd walked away from a part of herself too. "But by the looks of you, I actually don't think I'm going anywhere. I've let this go on long enough...you, avoiding Shane...avoiding me... avoiding your own feelings. Let me take a shower. I'll be out in ten minutes. You better be ready to talk then."

Damn. Charlie Hunnam would have made one hell of a Christian Grey, I thought as I glanced at the TV before making my way down the hallway to shower. Just when I'd been hoping the size of his dick would have made up for his strange accent, he'd backed out of the role. *Fantasizing about fictional characters? Christ, I'm becoming* extra *sexually frustrated lately.* Maybe it was finally time to invest in that vibrator Tina had suggested last year.

❤

Saturday morning I was up before the sun. I'd slept surprisingly well, despite the nervous energy I'd been feeling most of the day Friday. Even if my conversation with Amanda hadn't opened *her* eyes, it had opened *mine*. As I'd spoken about Amanda, I'd spoken, too, about myself and the mistakes I'd made. I'd told her that everyone deserves a second chance, even a dumbass like her. I'd given my friendship with Max that chance. And now Adam was giving me mine. And if *he* thought I deserved it...well, then I guess so did I.

I put on one of my Under Armour ColdGear shirts and some sweats, and threw my hair up before heading out the door for a run. The brisk morning air woke me up, and I'd gotten in three miles before heading home to shower.

I'd somehow managed to keep my mind clear from

thinking about Adam for much of last night and this morning, but as the hot water sprayed against my skin, the smell of my vanilla body wash brought me back to the last time I'd been with him. We'd made love by the couch in a way that made a silky slickness run down my thighs at the thought. Afterward, we'd been in this same shower together. And my mind filled with images of rubbing soap along his solid chest and down the length of his cock until he hardened again. My heart raced at the memory, and I bit my lip to replace the emptiness my mouth felt without him thrusting inside it.

I rubbed the loofah across my chest and around my neck as I let the water hit my face and make its way down between my legs. I needed this man. Physically, emotionally, I wanted all of him. But I would take the pieces as he'd offer them. At his pace. If he even offered them at all. For now, just the thought of him was enough. Dropping my loofah, I let my hands sweep across my slippery breasts until one hand drifted down to calm the ache between my thighs.

Instantly, my own hand became Adam's fingers skirting my clit... teasing me with subtle pressure until I craved him inside me... He sucked hungrily at my opening and slipped his tongue in and out in soft, deliberate strokes. This was what I imagined as I closed my eyes and rested my head against my forearm on the tile wall, working my way to a much-needed release.

My breathing quickened as I tapped gently against myself to thoughts of Adam's lips on my throat, his long fingers urging me over the edge. I felt my legs get weaker, shaking with every roll of my hips. I needed this. But as much as I tried, I just couldn't get myself there. *Fuck!* I banged my head toward the shower wall in frustration, thankful that my arm was there to take the impact. *Yup, definitely going to need to invest in a vibrator. And preferably a waterproof one.*

By eight thirty, I had settled myself into a high-top table by the window of the coffeehouse. I wanted to make sure I was there early because, for some reason, I didn't want Adam to be waiting for *me*. Even though he'd offered to buy my coffee, I'd ordered my own when I'd arrived, figuring I'd drink it while I waited and collected my thoughts. Then, when Adam arrived, I would have another.

I sipped on my beverage while I tried to wait patiently. But I was on edge, unsure of what the two of us would have to talk about. It was one thing to say a quick hello in a parking lot or exchange cute emails when each person had time to carefully compose their response. It was another thing entirely to sit there across from one another like everything that had happened between us hadn't happened at all.

And it was probably even worse to sit there across from one another knowing it *had*.

"Morning." I was awakened from my internal monologue by the sound of Adam's voice. Good thing I was early. It was only eight forty-five. "You already bought yourself a cup," he said, gesturing toward my coffee. "I thought it was my treat?"

"Uh . . . yeah, sorry. I thought I'd be ready for another one when you got here. I'll have another in a bit, though. Thanks."

"Okay, well, let me grab a drink and I'll be right back."

Once Adam got in line, I spent the next two minutes staring at how his perfectly round ass looked in his fitted dark jeans. It didn't take me long to remember how sexually frustrated I'd felt since that morning, and by the time he arrived back at the table, I was wiggling in my seat, trying desperately to find a position that would dull the ache between my legs.

"You okay?" Adam asked, a curious grin on his face.

Could be better. "Yeah, just trying to get comfortable."

"So," he said, placing his coat on the back of his chair and taking a seat, "what's new?"

God, this already feels so awkward. Neither one of us would be able to make more than idle small talk. *Maybe it was a mistake to come here.* "Um, nothing really." I searched my brain, trying desperately to find something to talk about. Anything. *Let's see, what's new, what's new? I made a mess of my life and yours... Wait, that's not new. Shit. I joined CrossFit... Who the hell wants to hear stories about CrossFit? Nobody, that's who. I tried to get myself off in the shower this morning to thoughts of you... it didn't work. Yeah, like I'd ever fuckin' say that. Think, damn it. Got it:* "I went to Europe over the summer."

"Really? Where? Who'd you go with?"

I gave him a brief overview of my trip—famous museums I'd visited, beautiful cathedrals I'd enjoyed, the delicious food I'd tasted. And he seemed genuinely interested as I shared some of the details. But after I revealed the fact that I'd gone alone, he'd gotten quiet.

Did he think I'd gone alone because of *him*? I'd gone alone because of *myself.* Maybe it had been a mistake to talk about Europe. *Maybe I* should *tell him about CrossFit or my masturbation attempt. Shit.* I needed to get the attention off me before I said something stupid. "Did *you* go anywhere fun this summer?" I asked, hoping to alleviate some of the tension that seemed to have settled over the table since Adam's arrival.

"The beach."

Oookay. Guess we're sticking with short answers. I sat for a moment, listening to the sound of both of us sipping on our drinks, the cappuccino machines steaming behind the counter, the meaningless chatter of the employees. "Are we gonna talk about what happened between us?" I asked suddenly.

My question not only seemed to surprise Adam, but it also surprised me. But I was immediately glad I'd said it.

Adam's face softened as he seemed to be deciding how to respond. "I don't know. Should we?"

"I'm not sure. Maybe. We're not doing so well attempting to talk about anything else."

Adam moved his coffee cup between his hands nervously. "Nothing either one of us can say will change what happened last spring. I'm not sure if we should even be doing this right now." Finally, Adam looked up, and his eyes met mine. "I just... When I saw you the other day... I couldn't *not* see you again."

I wasn't sure what I saw on his face as he said those words: *I couldn't* not *see you again.* Behind his composed exterior, I was sure I'd seen pain. Pain that *I'd* caused. But I also thought I saw a spark of hope glistening in his eyes as he looked at me. Hope that maybe, despite everything we'd been through, everything I'd done, *this* time might be different. "I couldn't not see you either," I said quietly.

Adam swept his tongue across his lips before he spoke. "We... we were never really friends. We had feelings for each other so quickly after we met. I just can't do that again." His eyes bored into mine, as if he saw some secret answer written there.

I tried hard to maintain my upright posture. But inside, I was slumped over so far my head hit the table. I'm not sure when I had allowed myself to get my hopes up, but I had. And his words were like a knife to the chest.

When he resumed speaking, his voice was low, and I mentally braced myself for his imminent rejection. "I have to protect myself this time."

Wait . . . what? Did he say "this time"?

"So can we try that first?" he continued. "Try to be friends? See where things go?"

It took me a moment to register that he hadn't told me to go to hell and burn there for all eternity. It took every fiber of willpower I possessed to prevent myself from leaping over the table and dry-humping his leg. "Friends," I replied with a genuine smile, which he returned. "Well, now that the elephant's out of the room, let's have a normal conversation. Oh, and another cup of coffee," I said, shaking my cup to show it was now empty.

Adam chuckled softly as he rose to throw my cup away and get me another. The look on my face must have let him know I didn't know what was funny.

"At the coffeehouse . . ." he explained, "talking about elephants. Did you ever read that book by the way?" he smirked.

Water for Elephants. How could I forget? "Yeah," I laughed. "Actually I did."

"See, now we have something to talk about. Caramel macchiato, right?" he asked as he turned toward the counter casually, not even really waiting for me to reply.

"Actually," I said, "make it a mocha latte."

"Mocha latte?" he asked, his voice raising in disbelief. "When did you change?"

I shrugged, a shy smile gracing my lips. "I'm not really sure."

chapter fourteen

m a x

"So how many people are coming?"

"Should be about twenty. I didn't want anything too huge."

Trevor turned his head in the direction I had been absently staring at while we talked. "Are we waiting for someone in particular?"

Sharply snapping my head back to him, I let loose with an uneasy grin. I hadn't realized I'd been staring until he called my attention to it. "Uh, no. Just my parents," I offered quickly.

"Right," he said with a smirk, clearly knowing that I was lying.

In that moment, I hated how well he knew me. I guess that's what happened when you kept friends around that you met in elementary school. They got really good at reading you. Though it probably wasn't all that difficult to see through my excuse. Lily and I had fallen into a comfortable friendship, talking a few times a week and even hanging out every once in a while.

I couldn't resist immediately looking back at the entrance to the private room my parents had rented for my birthday. It was a Monday—a shitty night for a party—but I liked celebrating my birthday on the actual day. Who wouldn't want to honor the day I came into the world? That was a great fucking day. Not that I remember it, but I'm sure it was.

My parents had wanted to throw me a party, and I relented because, well, who wouldn't want a party? But my mom had also insisted because, as she said, "You only turn thirty once." I wanted to counter that I remember her turning forty-nine quite a few times, but decided to keep that comment to myself. I had kept the guest list small because I wanted everyone to be comfortable and have a good time. Once you started inviting agents, former teammates, and business associates, shit would get out of hand. And I would also have had to spend more time glad-handing and kissing ass than I was up for on *my* birthday. So my mom had contacted a local restaurant and rented one of their back rooms. My only stipulation was that the room had a bar, and she hadn't let me down.

Trevor started speaking again, but I zoned him out as I saw her. *She came.* When I'd mentioned the party to her, I hadn't been sure Lily would actually make it, thinking it might be too weird for her to hang out with my family and friends. She had told me she'd come, but part of me didn't want to get my hopes up. I couldn't quite figure out why I instantly felt relieved when I saw her.

My shoulders dropped and my tension abated. *She looks fucking fantastic!* In the five seconds it took for her to see me sitting at the bar, I had already completely taken her in: her black tights, cream silk shirt, black ankle boots, just enough makeup to accentuate her natural beauty. *No wonder I'd wanted to fuck her as soon as I'd laid eyes on her in that airport.* When her eyes finally landed on me, her face lit up with a broad smile, and she started making her way toward me.

"Oh, so *that's* who we've been waiting for," Trevor mumbled beside me.

I cut him a quick sideways glance, which only made him chuckle. Then, I turned my attention back to Lily just in time for her to put her arms around my neck and squeeze.

"Happy birthday, old man."

"Thanks. And old, my ass," I retorted with mock indignation.

She giggled and thrust a small wrapped box at me. "Here, this is for you. Obviously."

"Awesome. I'd say you didn't have to get me anything, but I'd be lying."

She shook her head before putting that bright smile back on her face.

"Should I open it now?" I asked, unsure of what the protocol was for opening gifts once you hit thirty. I normally just tore everything open immediately, but maybe I was supposed to be more mature now that I'd entered a new decade.

"Whatever you want. It's your birthday."

"I love your attitude." I ripped the paper off the gift and stared at it. I looked to Lily and saw the smirk she was trying to suppress. "You got me a whistle?"

She couldn't hold back anymore and allowed the laugh she had been choking back to escape her lips. "It's a rape whistle. So that the next time you get stalked in a bar by a cougar, you can summon help."

I laughed with her. "You asshole. This is a horrible gift."

She wiped tears from her eyes and then reached toward

me with a card in her hand. "Here's your real gift."

I snatched the envelope from her hand and tore it open, pulling out a card—something silly about getting so old my body was starting to fall apart. *Yeah, right.* Inside the card were small colorful slips of paper with writing and drawings on them. I examined them more closely, reading each one. Realization dawned on me slowly as I looked over them: coupons.

About ten coupons that Lily had made, each promising me something different. One was redeemable for a late-night pickup, no questions asked. Another was to be used in place of an apology. *Shit, she probably should've given me more of that one.* There were coupons for a free hug, for an accomplice in crime, for a corny joke when I needed a laugh.

As I sifted through them, it dawned on me what the real gift was. Her friendship. Lily was offering me another chance to be close to her. Not romantically, but still intimately. I suddenly realized why I felt such relief when she'd walked into the party. It was because she was my friend—probably my best friend—and things just weren't as good when she wasn't around. I decided in that moment that this would be enough. I wouldn't screw up with her again by trying to force things to go in a direction that we didn't both want. If friendship was what she was offering, then that's what I would take. And that was *all* I would take.

I sifted through my pile of coupons and handed her one.

She looked down at it before smiling sweetly at me. "Since it's your birthday, I guess I can let you slide with a free one." Then she slid her arms back around my neck, and I inhaled her as I wrapped my arms around her, speechless at the gift she had given me and confident that it would be the best one I would receive this year. Especially since I was pretty sure no one else's tits would feel *this* good against my chest. Friends be damned, I was still human. The fact that I restrained myself from running my tongue down her neck should've spoken volumes to my dedication to our new relationship.

We broke apart before the embrace became awkward, as if there was a set amount of time a hug between friends should last. Trevor cleared his throat beside me, and I wished that he had gone the hell away. "Lily, this is my good buddy, Trevor. Trevor, Lily."

Trevor extended his hand toward her, and Lily shook it, but her face was cool and impassive. *Huh.*

"Nice to meet you, Lily. I would've spoken up sooner, but I didn't want to ruin the Hallmark moment."

"You too." Her response was clipped, and she looked away from him quickly, dismissively. I stared at her strangely for a moment, but before I had time to dissect her behavior, I heard another familiar voice over my shoulder.

"There's the person I've been waiting all day to see."

I watched my father approach, wide-eyed and beaming with his arms outstretched, ready to give me a big hug. Even knowing that it wouldn't be as fulfilling as the one I got from Lily, it did always feel good to get a hug from my dad. He somehow always managed to convey so much with it: his love, his pride, his devotion. When he got closer, I moved slightly toward him to receive the embrace, but he simply pushed my arms out of his way.

"Out of my way, Max. I need to hug this pretty girl."

This man did not *just diss me on my birthday.* But when I looked over at Lily, I couldn't say I blamed him. I'd have gone straight for her too.

"How are you, my dear?" my dad asked as he wrapped his arms around her.

I turned toward my mom, who had been following right behind him. She simply shrugged and let a soft giggle escape from her lips.

I reached my hand up to my dad's shoulder and gently ripped him away from Lily. "Listen, old man. Don't forget who chooses what home you go into when Mom gets tired of your cranky ass."

He laughed that hearty laugh that I loved and smiled. "Stop threatening me and get over here."

He pulled me into a strong, chest-constricting embrace that made me feel so loved I could barely stand it. I stored this memory into the recesses of my brain so that I could one day pull it out and remind myself to hug my own child exactly like this.

"Sorry we're late," my mom said as she edged my dad away from me so that she could move closer. "I give your father one thing to do, and does he do it? Of course not."

"Aww, come on, doll. Max would've understood if we hadn't brought him a card."

"You forgot to get me a birthday card? What kind of father are you?" I asked, acting insulted.

"Listen, if I had to remember to get all my children birthday cards, I'd have little time for anything else."

"Dad, I'm your only child."

"Semantics," he declared as he waved a hand at me.

"Did you forget to take your pill or something?" I asked, trying, but failing, to keep the amusement from my voice.

"You mean my Viagra? No, I made sure to take that," he replied as he wagged his eyebrows at my mother.

"Bill, stop that! How embarrassing," my mom huffed as she walked over to Lily and gave her a hug and quick kiss on the cheek.

"Thank you for making my thirtieth birthday traumatic, Dad. Nothing like a good ole Dad-violating-Mom story to make shit memorable," I grumbled as I watched my mom give Lily an extra squeeze before releasing her.

"Today is the perfect day for such talk. How do you think you got here?"

"Dad, I swear, if you don't stop talking, I'm gonna puke."

"Anyway," my mom interrupted, "here is your card. We'll put your gift over on the table with the others. Bill, can you go check on Aunt Gladys?"

"Hell no!" my dad yelled at the same time I said, "You brought Aunt Gladys?" I felt an accusing glare creep onto my face. *What the hell were they thinking?*

"Who's Aunt Gladys?" Lily asked.

I heard Trevor laughing behind me. *Asshole.*

"Oh, Trevor, I didn't see you. How are you?" my mom asked as she moved toward him to greet him.

"Forget him," I whined, blocking her path. "Why did you bring Aunt Gladys?"

My mom's features grew stern as she reprimanded me. "Because she's your great-aunt, that's why. She has as much right to be here as anyone else, and you will be nice to her or I swear to you, Max, I will kill you."

This wasn't the first time my mom had threatened me with bodily harm, but it always made me laugh. My mother had never touched me with anything other than love and affection. Maybe if she had, I wouldn't have turned out to be such a prick. "Okay, Okay, I'll be nice. But where is she?"

My dad replied quickly, "Bathroom."

"Oh, no," I groaned.

Lily looked at us, completely perplexed. "If you need

someone to go check on her, I'd be happy to . . ."

"No," my dad and I both yelped in unison, resulting in an icy glare from my mother.

My dad gripped Lily's shoulders like he was warning her about her imminent death. "Lily, whatever you do, stay away from the bathroom when Aunt Gladys is in there. Please, dear, promise me. Promise!" he hollered at her when she didn't immediately reply.

"You two stop this right now," my mom scolded as she elbowed my father in the ribs. "Aunt Gladys just has some bowel problems is all. It's not *that* bad."

"Not that bad if you're comparing it to gutting a human," my father muttered under his breath.

Lily looked horrified at the three of us and then burst out laughing. She was nearly hysterical when we all joined in, tears streaming down our faces.

"What did I miss?"

We all laughed harder as we whipped around to look upon Aunt Gladys hobbling toward us. My stomach cramped as I walked over to give her a swift hug and thank her for coming.

"So, Aunt Gladys, everything, umm . . . go okay?" my father asked, trying like hell to maintain a straight face. *Goddamn him for asking this question.* We all shook as we tried to restrain ourselves.

"Yeah, all good. Left something fierce in that toilet, though. Where's the food?" And with that pearl of information, she walked away from us in search of hors d'oeuvres.

We all looked at each other before rolling with a new wave of laughter. I gripped my hand on the bar to keep myself from doubling over onto the floor.

"Jesus Christ, why would she tell us that?" I said as I tried to catch my breath.

"I don't know, but I'm so glad she did," Trevor sputtered.

"All right, all right, enough." My mom sniffed as she wiped her cheeks dry. "Come on, Bill, let's go say hi to everyone."

"Right behind ya, doll."

I couldn't help glancing over at Lily at my dad's term of endearment. This hadn't been the first time he'd said it, and she had to have noticed it by now. Her smile slipped a little, and she shuffled her feet slightly before darting a quick look my way. Running my hand through my hair, I attempted to rein myself back in.

"Okay, people, time to go trolling for cougars. I'll see ya around." Trevor plopped his drink down onto the bar and made his way out to mingle.

"Is he serious?" Lily asked when he had gotten out of earshot.

"Sadly, yes."

"Gross," Lily whispered.

"Yes, yes, it is. He's actually quite popular with the over-forty crowd."

"Sounds like quite a guy," Lily said dryly.

She clearly didn't like Trevor, but I couldn't figure out why. I was about to ask her, when I realized I didn't give a shit. I didn't want to get into any serious conversations tonight. It was my birthday and I planned to enjoy it.

Lily and I chatted for a while as various family members and friends came over to wish me happy birthday. After about a half an hour, the servers announced that they were ready to bring out the first course. We all made our way to the lone long table in the middle of the room. My mom directed everyone where to sit like a dictator as my dad made hand signals behind her back, mocking her in the most loving way possible. When she rounded on him, he threw his hand to his hair and smiled at her sheepishly. Even she couldn't hide the smile that lifted her lips as she slapped him softly in the stomach.

I ended up between my dad and Lily and was just about to pick up my fork and dive into my salad when I heard the clink of a glass.

"Excuse me," my mom interrupted.

Oh no. She wouldn't.

"I just wanted to take this opportunity, since we're surrounded by family and friends, to say a few words about Max."

Yup, she's gonna do it. I plopped my elbow on the table and sank my head into it. I felt a sharp poke in my ribs and turned to Lily, who mouthed, "Behave" at me.

"Thirty years ago on this day, November twenty-fifth, nineteen eighty-three . . ."

I groaned as my mother slipped into her teacher voice and improved her posture as though she were giving the Gettysburg Address. My father kicked me harshly under the table to stifle me. I pitched forward slightly so that I could grab the abused area on my shin and accidentally caused the table to shake. Hearing a throat clear, I directed my eyes to my mother, who raised her eyebrows as if to ask, "Are you done?" I straightened in my chair and mentally prepared myself for the embarrassment that awaited me.

"As I was saying, on that day, at ten fifty a.m., the most beautiful thing happened to me—"

"Beautiful may be an exaggeration," my father interjected before he seemed to remember that he was not part of this monologue and fidgeted in his chair uncomfortably under my mom's intense stare.

I happily returned his kick from a few moments prior and watched as he winced in discomfort. *How's it feel, old man?*

"Like father like son, I guess," my mom quipped, causing everyone to let loose a short murmur of laughter. "At ten fifty a.m., the doctor told me that I had a son. I remember my eyes filling with tears as he placed this tiny, beautiful baby into my arms. I couldn't even believe that he was mine. And as Bill hovered over me, trying to get a peek at his son, I turned my head toward the window. It was beginning to snow. It lasted for only a few minutes, but it came down hard enough to blanket the ground. And that's when I knew. The tiny being that we had brought into the world was going to be special." My mom turned to look at me, her eyes shining and a wide smile on her face. "And I was so right. Every day with you, Max, is a blessing. Thank you for not only being who you are, but making me who I am as well. I love you, son."

I stood up to hug her, and she gripped me tightly. It always amazed me how much these people loved me. I wasn't wholly sure I deserved it most days, but I was thankful for it anyway.

"If anyone wants the unabridged version of that day, you come see me," my dad remarked, trying to lighten the sentimental mood that had taken hold of the room.

"Bill," my mom said sweetly, causing my dad to turn his head toward her. "Zip it," she added sternly.

The table fell into easy conversation as we ate and shared stories of growing up. Lily actively participated, drawing my family in with the same charm that had attracted me to her.

At one point, after dinner had been cleared and we were waiting for dessert, she leaned toward me. "Your family is really something else."

"You got that right." I chortled.

"They're great, Max. Really great."

"Yeah, they're that too." I looked into her eyes and enjoyed the happiness I saw there. Enjoyed how well she fit into my family. Enjoyed how at ease she looked. I swore to myself right then that I would do everything in my power to keep the stress out of our friendship. I just wanted this: easygoing and pure.

Once dessert was finished, we all stood and moved about the room. Lily talked to my parents while I made my way to the bar with a few of my buddies.

"So, who's that chick talking to your parents?" Matt, a friend from high school, asked.

I glanced over at Lily, as if I didn't know who he was referring to, and then turned toward the bar. "Just a friend," I said as nonchalantly as possible. I hadn't told them about Lily. Any of them. They knew I had banged a girl in an airport because there was no way I wasn't going to get credit where credit was due. That was a stud move, and I wanted acknowledgment for it. But I never told them her name, mostly because, at the time, I didn't know it. And then I mentioned running into my airport hottie again at Swift and partaking in some extracurricular activities, but again, withheld the name. Only that time, I didn't want them to know it because I knew they'd be assholes about it if they ever met her. And I also knew that she would be in deep shit if it ever got out that she was banging me on school property. After that, feelings got mixed in, and I didn't want my friends to see what a pussy she'd turned me into. So, I just stopped talking about her and they never asked.

"You, uh, tappin' that?" Brian asked in a hushed voice.

I shot a defensive look at him. "What? No. I said she was just a friend." I didn't like these pervs talking about Lily and making assumptions about her. I was getting agitated. Fast.

"So you don't mind if I make a play for her?" Trevor asked.

I stared at him like he had seven heads. *Is he fucking serious?* If I couldn't have Lily, I sure as fuck wasn't going to let one of my friends have her. Especially since I knew what kind of pricks they really were. "Yeah, I mind," I replied gruffly.

"Why? You said she was just your friend," Brian interjected.

"Because she's too good for you douchebags. Stay away from her." My posture shifted. Tension radiated through every muscle in my body, and I was close as hell to punching one of these fuckers out.

"Ha, friend my ass. He's totally nailing her," Matt scoffed.

I was up in his face the second the words left his lips. "Do you really think pissing me off is the best idea?" I threatened. Matt was a tall, lanky guy who I could put in the hospital with one hand. And he damn well knew it.

"Calm down, man. I'm just playing around." Matt held up his hands and backed away from me.

"Let's just get this straight right now. Lily *is* just my friend, but that doesn't mean she's not important to me. So back the fuck off." I spun away from them and nearly plowed right into someone. I grabbed the person's biceps to try to keep us both upright. When I looked down, I saw a familiar pair of hazel eyes. *Of course she's standing right behind me.* "Lily, I just . . . Shit."

"You just shit?" she asked, her lips twitching slightly.

I stared at her for a second and then shook my head to clear it. "Uh, no . . . gross. No, I meant sorry. For all of that." Unsure of how much she'd heard, I decided that keeping things vague was my best option.

"You're sorry for defending me?" Her eyes were twinkling, and I knew she was fucking with me.

"No, I'm sorry for . . . How much did you hear?"

"Enough. I always thought your friends were dicks. They certainly didn't prove me wrong."

"You thought they were dicks? Why? You've never even met any of them." I was intrigued by her assumption about them. Though it was more than an assumption. She was completely correct.

"Exactly. Where the hell have they been? You've been going through a ton of shit in the past few months, and who does your mom call to help you? Not them. They're clearly assholes." She spoke loudly enough for the guys to hear her, and she didn't seem the least bit intimidated.

I stared curiously at Lily, loving this protective instinct, but wondering where it had come from at the same time. "This may surprise you, Lily, but I'm a pretty private guy," I said with a smirk. She rolled her eyes in response and I continued. "I don't need them to know my business. That's why my mom didn't call them."

"But they're your *friends*. Friends should be there for one another."

"I didn't say they were *good* friends." I laughed, but Lily remained stolid. I couldn't figure out why this bothered her so much. Was it because if I had better friends, she wouldn't have had to get involved? I felt sick just thinking of that as a possibility.

"Max, this isn't funny. When I struggle, I have people to support me, to help me through it. You just have a bunch of dickheads who want to see what they can squeeze out of you. I hope they all get Ebola and die." She said the last bit a little louder than necessary while she stared directly at them. *When did she become so feisty?*

"Hey, I have people who support me." I placed my hand under her chin and tilted her head to look at me. She looked . . . sad. I had just promised myself that I would never cause her to be brought down by our friendship, and I hadn't even been able to make it an hour.

She gently swatted my hand away from her face. "You need more than just your parents to be there for you. You deserve better than those . . . parasites."

"I have more than my parents." Gazing down at her, I tried to convey with my eyes all the things I hadn't been able to say—*wouldn't* be able to say. How sorry I was for being so selfish. For ruining things between her and Adam. For almost ruining them between us. And how fucking thankful I was that she was there with me now. That she could be the friend she knew I needed even before I did.

She looked back at me for a moment before rolling her eyes again and smiling. "Okay, I guess you have me too."

"Good. Now that that's all settled, can we please have some goddamn fun at this party? I'm thirty for Christ's sake. This is a big deal. *I* am a big deal. And I expect to be treated as such." I continued my rant about my greatness as we walked back toward the rest of the guests. But I left out how the thing that was the greatest about my life was that Lily was back in it.

chapter fifteen

a d a m

Lily and I had hung out a few times over the past two plus weeks. We'd done little things together that usually just consisted of grabbing a bite to eat after I'd finished work and before Eva got home from whatever activity she had that day. So far, we'd taken things slowly: a hug when we greeted each other, a quick peck on the cheek to say goodbye. But adults could only tolerate that pace for so long before someone took things further. And since neither of us had, the sexual tension between the two of us was palpable.

Eva had plans to sleep at a friend's on Saturday night and would be going to church with her friend's family the following day. So Lily and I spent Sunday morning together. The weather for late November had been unseasonably warm lately, so Lily suggested we go for a walk at a nearby state park.

With my hand locked around hers, I guided her through the paths in the woods slowly, impressing her with some of the dorky facts I still remembered from Boy Scouts twenty years ago. Or maybe she was more just pretending to be impressed. It made me feel good either way.

Eventually, the woods opened to an expansive field full of tall feather reed grass that came to just above our knees. I gazed at Lily as she made her way toward the middle of the field and looked up to the sky. "You look beautiful," I said, as the warm sun caressed her face and brought out the subtle highlights in her hair.

A goofy expression came over her as she glanced down, tugging at her cream-colored North Face jacket and motioning to her jeans and sneakers. "In this?" she asked.

I noticed, for the first time, a kind of humble shyness in her. She had no idea just how gorgeous she really was. "Not what you're *wearing*," I said, stepping toward her until I was close enough to stroke the smooth skin on her cheek with my thumb. "You."

The need to kiss her—really *kiss* her—had been unbearable in that moment. It was as if a physical pull was guiding our mouths to each other. I hesitated a moment before allowing my desire to dictate my actions. But once it did, I lost the restraint I'd fought so hard to maintain with her. And as our lips touched, that pull I'd felt seconds before had already grown stronger, urging our eager tongues to collide with one another. We lost ourselves as I licked the inside of her mouth until the taste of sweet mint and her mango-flavored lip gloss coated my own lips.

It seemed as if one kiss had brought us back in time to months ago, when our passion and need for each other had gone well beyond a physical one. I could tell Lily felt it too as she scratched my back through my sweat shirt, pulling me closer.

But before we could take the kiss any further, I broke it, pulling away slowly, my teeth tugging at her bottom lip before letting go. I stroked the small of her back and cradled her head in my hand, our foreheads touching and our mouths only millimeters apart.

A passionate moment that had been only that: a moment. And the brevity of our intimate encounter could only be attributed to my own insecurities.

I spent much of the next few days attempting to ignore my growing feelings for her. *I'd* been the one who'd wanted to take things slowly. But that kiss had given way to emotions I would rather have left untouched. I couldn't get a handle on myself and my feelings. Part of me was like a horny teenager excited just to be around her. And another part was a crotchety old bastard who'd been burned by the love of his life and was royally pissed about it. The worst of it was that I felt like a total pussy. I didn't want to be the guy who got involved with some chick who had already proved herself to be untrustworthy. If she could do that bullshit to me once, she could do it again. But...

"Fuck," I growled as I banged my palm on the steering wheel.

Thinking these things did nothing to help my mood, and sitting in traffic on the Schuylkill Expressway on Thanksgiving Eve wasn't making it any better. I looked at the clock on my dashboard. My fifteen-year reunion would be starting in twenty minutes, and I was stuck on the goddamn highway. Of all nights, why did they plan these fucking things for the most-traveled day of the year?

I was on edge and exasperated, but it wasn't just because of the traffic. I sank back into my seat a little and tried to examine the "But." *But* I didn't think she'd do it again. I had no idea why I thought that, but I did. I would've nearly bet my life that she wouldn't do it again. Would I have made that same bet seven months ago? I was so sure of my answer, it sent a thrill through my body. *No, I wouldn't have.* Because deep down, I knew something was shady. Not wanting it to be true, I ignored my instincts and trusted Lily when I shouldn't have. *But* I wasn't going in blind this time. I had a better grasp on what I wanted out of our relationship now. I wouldn't settle for less than all of her.

However, this brought on a whole list of other concerns, the biggest being that I wasn't fully sure I *wanted* all of her. When I was with her, I was consumed by her: enamored by her beauty, captivated by her personality, and desirous of her body. But when we weren't together, I wasn't sure that we actually fit all that well together. I could see a life with Lily, but I couldn't see her in *my* life. Or maybe it was more that I was afraid that I'd let her back in just to have it all go to hell again. It was all this baffling bullshit that had kept me from really pressing our relationship beyond friends-who-make-out status.

There had been quite a few occasions where it had been impossible to keep from wrapping my arms around her as I stood behind her nuzzling her neck, or grabbing her hand and pulling her to me so that I could feel her chest swell against mine as I grazed her lips softly. But I hadn't taken it further, and it was killing me. I had jerked off more in the past two weeks than I had in the previous two months. But I didn't want to be a prick and bang her only to realize that I didn't want to pursue anything with her. Even though part of me felt like that would serve her right, I didn't want to sink to that level. I wasn't an asshole. And I sure as shit wasn't going to be a casual fuck to her like that cocksucker Max Samson had been. *God, I fucking hate that douche.*

I pulled into the parking garage across the street from The Pitchfork forty minutes later. *Why did we need to have our reunion in Philly when we went to school almost thirty minutes outside of it?* Deciding that the organizers were clearly morons, I parked my car and headed toward the bar. As I walked in, I tried to remember why I had even agreed to go to my reunion.

"Yo, asshole, where ya been?"

Oh, yeah. That was why. "What's up, Frank? How long have you been here?"

"About twenty minutes. I got here right at eight. I got a drink with some guys from work closer to the office and then caught a cab over here."

"Huh," I replied as I scanned the room. The reunion was for graduates only, so there were no husbands, wives, or significant others around unless they had also graduated with us. "How did Claire take the news that you'd be coming alone?" I asked with a smirk. Claire didn't trust Frank in the least, mostly because he acted like a pig. But that was all it was: an act. To my knowledge, he had never fucked around on Claire. Probably because she had threatened to reenact the movie *The Burning Bed* if she ever found him with another woman.

"She got over it."

I let out a brief laugh, knowing damn well it had probably taken an act of God and a ton of sexual favors for her to get over it. As we stood there surveying the room, a redhead I didn't recognize slunk past us as she eyed me suggestively. I held her gaze and licked my lips. *Man, do I wish I could remember her.*

I heard Frank grumble beside me. "Come on, ladies' man. Let's mingle." Then he wrapped an arm around my shoulder and led me away from the hot redhead. Though I couldn't resist one last look over my shoulder. And damn if she wasn't still staring at me.

❤

Two hours later and I was having the time of my life. Being around people from high school had successfully catapulted my maturity level back to that of a teenager as we told lame jokes and laughed hysterically at the petty crimes we had committed fifteen years ago. It was great.

I had just finished regaling the crowd with my tale of the time a few other buddies and I had put the principal's tiny two-door car in the stairwell when I felt a tap on my shoulder. I noticed Frank's brows raise as I turned slowly. *Jesus Christ.* It was the redhead.

She watched me curiously for a moment before saying, "You don't remember me, do you?"

Shit. I really hated conversations that started that way. I quickly racked my brain for any hints as to who this woman could be. Coming up empty, I shrugged and stammered, "Uh, no, I, umm ... sorry, I ..."

She eventually took pity on me and reached her hand toward me. "Carly Stanton."

I had hoped that a name would ring some kind of bell for me, but it didn't. "Uh, hi, Carly. I'm Adam—"

"Adam Carter," she finished for me. "Yeah, I know."

This was going from bad to worse. "I'm so sorry, Carly, but I'm drawing a complete blank here."

She shrugged. "I'm not totally surprised by that. After all, we only spent about seven minutes together in the four years we knew each other." Her eyes twinkled a little as she revealed this tidbit.

And then it hit me. *Seven minutes.* "Holy shit, Carly Stanton." I smiled broadly at her as the memory of our time together in Brad Holbrook's basement while we played Seven Minutes in Heaven flowed through me. She had moved onto my street in ninth grade, and though we had seldomly interacted, I had often admired her from afar.

Needless to say, the seven minutes we spent together had been one of the highlights of my high school days. I took in her body and felt my pulse throb a little harder. *The years have definitely been good to her.* She was only about five-foot-five, but her stiletto heels caused her legs to seem endless. Her frame was thin, with average but perky tits, and she had the most mesmerizing blue eyes I had ever seen.

"I thought that might jog your memory." She giggled.

"It sure did." What guy didn't remember awkwardly fumbling boobs in a dark room? The smile on my face was too big, but I couldn't rein it in. "How have you been?" It was such an unoriginal question, but my brain was only working at half capacity since most of my blood was currently pumping in the opposite direction.

"I've been good. I work at an advertising firm in the city, been there about five years now."

"Five years? What were you doing before then?" *Who cares, Adam? Get to the good stuff, like if she wants to suck your dick in the back seat of your car.*

"Ugh, I was a teacher. I spent four years teaching high school math before I finally admitted to myself that it just wasn't for me. I figured if I was going to be forced to do something I hated, I at least wanted to make good money doing it. So I transitioned to advertising and actually found that I liked it."

I nodded, still smiling, though it was strained now. *Why did she have to say she had been a teacher?* I hadn't thought about Lily since I'd arrived, but now I couldn't think of anything else.

Silence fell between us, and I found myself unable to fill it. Thankfully, Carly picked up the slack. "What about you? What have you been up to?"

Get it together. You aren't dating Lily and, if memory serves, this woman gave you some of the best seven minutes of your life about seventeen years ago. I cleared my throat and gave her the rundown: architect, daughter, single. I *might* have emphasized single.

We continued to talk for a long time. The remainder of the reunion actually. I found out that she was also single. She had been engaged, but broke it off four months ago because her fiancé didn't seem passionate about her anymore. I paid rapt attention to her, especially her mouth. I was just getting involved in a daydream about those lips on various parts of my anatomy when I heard a throat clear behind me.

"Sorry to interrupt."

Fucking Frank.

"Adam? Most of us are heading out. You staying or going?"

The old Adam probably would have left, uncomfortable with having a meaningless fling with a woman I hardly knew, especially when I *did* want my relationship with Lily to progress. But as of that moment, we hadn't put a title on what we even *were.* Though we both felt something for each other, that *something* had yet to be defined.

Besides, I wanted this. And as I looked over at Carly, who merely raised an eyebrow and took a sip of her drink, I realized that she wanted this too. It seemed ironic that I had just been thinking in the car on my way there how I didn't want to be that guy to Lily. The guy who had sex with her only for the relationship to go nowhere. But the way Carly was looking at me made it seem like she wanted me to be the type of guy who did exactly that. And it was sexy as hell. *I can do this. Tonight's the night to take charge—see how the other half lives.*

Evidently there's something inherently attractive about assholes. Lily thought so. If I had been one then, maybe I wouldn't have taken the breakup so hard. I turned back to Frank. "I think I'm going to stay for a bit longer."

"Okay. I'm going to grab a cab back to my car. I'll catch up with ya later." Frank was clearly trying to refrain from applauding me openly in front of Carly. He clasped his hand on my shoulder before he headed toward the exit and disappeared out the door.

Carly and I sat quietly for a few minutes, sipping our drinks and trying to figure out how to get back to the easy conversation we'd been having before Frank interrupted our flow. Finally, Carly brought her attention back to me. "You wanna get out of here?"

It took me a minute to register what she had said, but when it finally sank in, I slammed my drink down on the bar and stood up. "Absolutely."

I led her to the coat check, helped her put her jacket on, and followed her outside into the freezing night.

"My apartment building has a garage beneath it, and since I don't need a car in the city, my spot is open. It'll probably be easier for you to drive there than have to worry about getting a cab back here later."

"Sounds like a plan," I said as I grabbed her hand and pulled her toward the parking garage.

♥

We were quiet for most of the ten-minute drive to Carly's apartment. Other than to give me directions, she was silent, which unfortunately gave me time to think about what I was doing. As I pulled into the parking lot Carly directed me to, I had reached a conclusion: I wasn't doing anything wrong. Lily and I had made it clear that we were just friends.

Maybe we would take it beyond that, maybe we wouldn't. And even though we had done a lot of flirting and even some kissing, that didn't mean that we weren't able to see other people. We'd had no such conversation, and for all I knew, she was out with some other guy right now. And even though this thought made me want to put my fist through a wall, I had nothing to feel guilty about.

Except, as I followed Carly up to her apartment, I did feel a little guilty. But as she opened the door and we walked into her apartment shrouded in darkness, my guilt ebbed. And as she pushed me back against the door, roughly bringing her lips to mine and applying the perfect amount of pressure to my hardened cock, any guilt that remained disappeared altogether.

We were frantic. All hands and mouths as we tore clothes from one another's body while breaking our kiss only when absolutely necessary. I quickly pulled the zipper down the back of her tight green dress and let it drop to her feet. My breath caught as I took in how gorgeous she was, especially wearing nothing but underwear and heels.

Withdrawing slightly, I ripped my polo shirt over my head while she fumbled with my belt. I kicked off my shoes and worked my socks off with my feet as she pushed my pants down my legs so I could step out of them.

I dipped my head to kiss down her neck and work my hands down to her ass. Then I gripped her ass tightly, lifting her off the ground so that she would wrap her legs around my waist.

She tangled her hands in my hair as I gruffly uttered, "Bedroom?"

"Straight back," she replied breathily.

My mouth reclaimed hers as I started walking us down the hall. She pointed toward the door that led to her bedroom, and I nudged it open with her body. She moaned as I nipped and sucked along her jaw. She gyrated against my cock, and I could feel how wet she was even through the fabric.

I lowered her onto the bed and pulled her bra straps down her arms, yanking the black lace down to expose her perfectly round tits. Pulling her nipple into my mouth and stroking it with my teeth, I massaged her other breast with my hand, rubbing my thumb over the sensitive flesh.

Carly arched her back off the bed, causing her to rub deliciously against me. I was suddenly extremely thankful I was going to get more than seven minutes with her this time. I pulled her matching lace thong down her legs as she unclasped her bra and threw it to the ground beside the bed.

"Beautiful," I whispered as I slid a finger inside of her, feeling her juices coat my hand, making me even harder than I already was. I lowered my head to kiss along her taut stomach as I pushed a second finger inside of her and began circling

ELIZABETH HAYLEY

her clit with my thumb. She nearly bucked off the bed at the stimulation, and I knew I was going to take her hard once I was inside her. There was no way I'd be able to control myself and take it slow. She was too responsive, too vocal, and too fucking sexy to hold back.

She slid her heels up my thighs and hooked them onto the waistband of my boxers to push them down. It was so erotic, I probably could've come from the thought alone. I leaned back on my knees and took my cock in my free hand, stroking it with one hand as I worked her with the other. Then, I remembered that my pants were in the hallway.

"Shit, I'll be right back. I have to go get a condom out of my wallet."

"No, wait, here." She reached up and opened a drawer in her bedside table. Withdrawing a condom, she tore it open with her mouth and pushed up on her elbows to slide it over my length.

As odd as it might seem, I was calmed by the fact that she had condoms readily available. Clearly, she wasn't new to this kind of encounter, so I didn't have to worry about her wanting to make more out of it than it was. Not to mention the fact that just feeling her roll the condom over my shaft was euphoric. This woman clearly knew how to fuck.

I positioned myself at her entrance and raised my eyes to her face briefly before pushing into her, hard and deep. It had been a while since I'd felt the warm, soft feeling that only a woman's pussy could provide. And I briefly wondered if I'd overestimated my original prediction of lasting longer than seven minutes. Her eyes fluttered closed as she groaned in pleasure. I intertwined her fingers with mine and held them above her head as I began to pound into her. Her slickness allowed me to slide in and out of her with ease, but she was tight enough to give my dick the pressure it needed.

"You like that? You like the way my cock feels inside you?" I couldn't believe those words had just left my mouth, but it was too late now. Knowing that this would most likely be the only time I would have with Carly, I didn't intend to hold back. I would say and do whatever came to mind, and from the whimpers leaving her mouth, she wasn't complaining.

"Harder, Adam. Please. I need it harder."

I complied, thrusting into her with such force, my balls slapped against her ass and the bed began to sway with our movement. "Feels so good," I groaned. As I rocked into her over and over, I felt her tighten around me, her body preparing for an imminent climax. *It should be fucking illegal for anything to feel this good.*

"I'm so close. Oh, please."

I released her hands so that I could reach between us and stroke her clit as I continued to pump into her. "Play with your tits for me." She immediately complied, rolling her nipples between her thumbs and index fingers.

I gazed at her ministrations of her hands against her hardened nipples. The sight had my balls drawing up, a tingling starting at the base of my spine. I continued to brush my thumb over her clit and pumped wildly in and out of her. Just when I thought I wouldn't be able to hold out any longer, I felt her body tense and then shake.

She screamed my name as her pussy pulsated around me. I released her clit as I thrust into her three more times, enjoying the steadily increasing sensation before my own orgasm shuddered through my body, jetting come into the condom.

I continued to slowly pump into her, bringing us down softly from our climaxes. Lowering my head to her chest, I pressed a gentle kiss between her breasts before lifting off and pulling out of her. I shivered at the loss of her warmth from around my cock.

I ran my hand down her thigh before getting up to dispose of the condom. When I returned to the bedroom, Carly had already dressed in a tank top and sweatpants. She stood beside the bed as I pulled on my boxers and then turned to collect the rest of my scattered clothing.

She followed me toward the door as I put my clothes back on as I found them. We didn't speak, but it wasn't awkward. We both knew what this was, and we'd both enjoyed it immensely.

Once I was dressed, I turned around to face her, gently grabbing the front of her tank top and pulling her to me. She brought her hands to my chest and then slid them up around my neck as I covered her mouth with mine. When we broke apart, we looked at each other for a moment, smiling.

"Your ex is a fucking idiot," I said huskily.

She laughed softly as I pulled away, opened the door, and left her apartment.

❤

My drive home was quiet and smooth. A smile played on my lips as I thought about the night. I was surprised by how uncomplicated it had all been. Just two people who were attracted to each other and wanted to get off. Nothing more.

But as I thought about how easy it had been to walk away from Carly afterward, I finally understood why my relationship with Lily would always be more complicated. Lily wasn't someone you walked away from.

chapter sixteen

l i l y

"It's about time all of us finally got together. I feel like we've been saying we were gonna have a night out forever." Tina poured herself some more white wine and grabbed a marker from the counter.

"So what exactly do we *do* at one of these parties?" Trish asked. "I can't believe I let you talk me into hosting this."

"Well, for starters, you have to come up with a sexy name for yourself. And it has to be alliterative. Mine's gonna be Lickable Lily," I said as I stuck my name tag to my chest.

Trish's expression looked to be stuck somewhere between completely horrified and utterly impressed. "Lickable Lily?" Trish said, drawing out each syllable. "You're serious?"

"Yeah, she's serious," Amanda replied. "It's a sex toy party. What the hell did you think we were gonna do? Drink tea and talk about classic novels? Besides," Amanda said, "that's a fucking awesome name! I'm not sure mine has the same ring to it."

"Aroused Amanda." I laughed, gesturing to her name tag. "I love it. It's definitely...you."

"Damn right it is. And I have Shane to thank for that. He does the hottest shit sometimes, I swear to God. The other day he started jerking off while he was fingering me. So fucking hot. Not kidding." We both glanced over at Trish, knowing her reaction would be priceless. I couldn't be sure, but I thought she might pass out. "Anyway," Amanda continued, "I told him to stop and fuck me, but he just said no. You believe that shit?"

"God, I'm so jealous. Dan would never do that," Steph said. "He barely makes any sound at all when we have sex. Sometimes I don't even know if he's alive. When we first got together, I had to ask if it was even good."

"Ask if it was *good*?" Amanda furrowed her brows incredulously. "Even *bad* is good to guys."

For once, I kept my comments to myself.

Trish had finally decided on the name Trashy Trish, and she stuck the name tag to her shirt. I watched her eyes widen at the possible consequence of attaching such a name to herself. "So what happened next, Amanda? Are you gonna finish your story?"

Maybe the name was actually starting to loosen Trish up a little.

"Hell yeah, I'm gonna finish my story," Amanda said enthusiastically. "He climbed on top of me and kept one of his hands between my legs and the other around his dick. He got me off and then came all over my stomach."

Trish had taken a seat on her couch to steady herself. "He did what?" *On second thought, maybe the name hadn't loosened her up after all.* "Why would he do that?"

Lately, I had resorted to living vicariously through Amanda

and Shane's sexcapades, and this one was exceptionally great. "What do you mean, why? 'Cause it's totally hot, that's why," I answered for her.

"I'm just . . . I don't know. I don't usually talk about this stuff. I think I need a drink." Trish ran an anxious hand through her dark hair and headed for the kitchen.

"You're probably gonna need more than one," Amanda yelled behind her.

Once everyone had their drinks and snacks and were settled into their seats in the living room, the "sexpert" began her introduction. "I want to thank everyone for coming. I'm Deviant Dana," she said, pointing to her name tag, "and you're in for some fun tonight."

"Hell yeah we are," Amanda yelled as Steph and Danielle cheered like drunk fans at a football game. They were all so crazy. It baffled me that they all worked for an accounting firm. Who knew number nerds could be so rowdy?

Deviant Dana continued her speech, pointing out all the benefits Trish would get for hosting, including a percentage of all sales to put toward her own purchases, as well as special clit cream, which was only available for the host—making it that much more intriguing to the rest of us. Dana passed around a few innocuous items: some lotions, massage oils, and shaving cream. We smelled, rubbed, and even tasted.

"Okay, Dana," I said. "These are okay, but we didn't come here for this. Where's the good stuff? I want that," I said, pointing to a vibrator with moving metal balls inside it.

"We'll get to that," Dana said. "I promise. First, I'll give you a chance to try out the clit cream I was talking about earlier, and you can all look through the catalog while we take a break." She pulled out a tiny bottle that had what looked like an eye dropper inside it and explained how to use it in a sanitary way so that we could all try it if we wanted to. "Only use one drop, though, no more. It's really strong," she warned us. "Now, who's up first?"

Danielle's hand shot up as she rose and snatched the bottle from Dana's hand, heading upstairs enthusiastically.

The rest of us took some time to peruse the toys in the catalog and make a wish list. "I definitely need a vibrator. That's for sure," I said.

"I told you that last year," Tina pointed out.

"Yeah, well, I certainly didn't need one *last* year," I countered.

"Why? What happened last year?" Trish asked.

How do I explain this without sounding like a complete slut?

"She banged two guys at once," Amanda blurted out.

Nope. Definitely not the way I would have explained it. "Well, not at *once*," I clarified. "I mean, not at the same time . . . together. I was kind of dating both of them. Well, maybe not *dating* both of them. Dating one, and just having sex with the other." *Shit, Lily, just stop talking.*

Trish's eyes had grown wider as I spoke. Clearly *my* explanation was no better than Amanda's. "*Two* guys?" Trish asked incredulously.

Had she known me last year, she wouldn't have been so shocked. "Well, yeah, but it's not as bad as it seems." I thought for a moment about what I'd just said. "Actually . . . maybe it is. But I learned my lesson, trust me."

"What happened?" she asked, concern in her voice.

"I screwed up," I said simply. "I hurt them both. And hurt myself." I could feel the sadness moving through me. "That's why I'm here. I've been in one hell of a dry spell, and I could use a little relief," I added in an effort to lighten the mood as I flipped through the pages quickly. "What are you guys getting?" I glanced over at Amanda's list, which already had about fifteen items on it.

"What am I *not* getting?" she replied. "Shane's gonna fucking love *this*," she said as she snapped a picture of a vibrating cock ring with some sort of contraption that went around his balls. "I'm gonna text it to him. You should get one too, Lil."

"Me? What the hell am *I* gonna do with that?"

"Well, you started seeing Adam again, right?" She shrugged. "Spice things up a little."

"Adam was one of the guys from last year. We just started seeing each other again," I explained to Trish before turning back to Amanda. "You know we're taking things slowly. I can't just show up with a bunch of sex toys like some kinky nympho. We haven't even slept together yet. Well, since last year. You know what I mean. Besides," I added, "I don't think Adam's really into that sort of thing." As hard as I tried—and believe me, I tried damn hard—I just couldn't picture Adam sliding that cock ring onto himself before we made love. But I had to admit, the image was definitely a turn-on. "Looks like it's my turn for the clit cream," I said as Steph pranced down the stairs. "Be right back."

I entered the bathroom and studied the bottle closely after washing my hands. *Only one drop*, Dana had said, and the directions on the bottle confirmed that. But with the sexual frustration I'd been feeling lately, I figured one more drop couldn't hurt. Especially since I planned to bring home a new toy to try out. I put two drops on my finger and rubbed them on my clit slowly. At first, I didn't feel much of anything, but by the time I'd washed and dried my hands, closed up the bottle, and descended the stairs, I began to feel a distinct warm, tingly sensation.

"You're up," I said to Amanda as I settled back into the couch. Within a minute, Amanda bounded back down the stairs.

"I didn't feel anything after the first drop, so I put on two more," she said excitedly. "How many did you put on, Lil?"

"Two. And that's enough, believe me," I said, shifting on the couch to find a position that didn't turn me on more than I already was. *God, I have to get off tonight.*

A few minutes later, Trish had seated herself back on the couch and Dana was ready to continue. "Now you'll get a look at what you've really come here to see," she said. "But first, I have to go over the rules. Well, there's actually only one rule: don't judge. People are going to ask about things that you might think are weird. Don't judge them. If you do, you get hit with this," she said, holding up a leather paddle. "Who's gonna be tonight's Christian Grey?"

"Right here," Tina yelled, and Dana gave her the paddle. "I'll keep these bitches in line."

She gave us each a few practice swats, and when Trish squirmed uncomfortably and began to turn red, I exchanged looks with Amanda.

"Do you have to pee or something? Why do you keep moving around like that?" Amanda asked.

"Uh..." Trish began, looking like a kid who'd just got caught shoplifting. "I think I put too much of that cream on."

My eyes widened. "I didn't know you put *any* on. How much did you use?"

"Five drops. I feel like my vagina's on fire."

"Well, no shit. You're supposed to just put one on," I replied. At my judgment, I felt a sting from Tina's paddle. "Ouch!"

"I know, but I figured if one was good, five would be five times better."

I opened my mouth to reply, but I couldn't argue with her logic. In most sexual scenarios, five always trumped one.

Eventually, Trish calmed down a bit, and Dana began passing around a few of the smaller vibrators: discreet ones that looked like lipstick, small egg-shaped ones meant to stimulate only the outside of your body. When it got to her, Amanda dangled one of those in between her breasts by the cord.

I looked over the tiny vibrators disguised as everyday items and shook my head. "This is like foreplay," I said to Dana. "You're teasing us. I need one that's like the real thing. I haven't gotten myself off in like a month, and these baby ones aren't gonna do the trick."

"In a *month*?" Amanda said, shocked. "Why the hell not?"

"She said she hasn't slept with Adam yet," Trish answered for me.

"So what?" Amanda said. "That doesn't mean anything. What, are you playing hard to get with yourself? If you can't get *yourself* off, it just means you aren't trying hard enough."

"It's not for lack of trying," I assured her. "And believe me, I'm plenty sexually frustrated these days. Not sure why it isn't happening."

"Wait, how are you supposed to do that *without* one of these?" Trish asked, holding up one of the larger vibrators, completely confused. The poor girl was so innocent.

"With your hand! How else?" Amanda said quickly, shaking her head in a way that let Trish know how stupid her question was.

"Hey, that's not nice," Tina said sternly as she swatted Amanda on the thigh with a sharp smack.

"Well, seriously," Amanda continued, "what kind of question is that? So you don't...?" Amanda's voice trailed off. "And you don't have a vibrator? *Or* a boyfriend?" Trish shook her head silently in response. "So what the hell do you do then?"

Another hard blow stung Amanda's thigh, courtesy of Tina. "Ouch!" Amanda yelled. "Stop that!"

"Nothing. Guess I just have good self-control," Trish said. "I mean, I used to have a boyfriend about five months ago, but we broke up. We never slept together, though. I'm waiting until I'm in love for that, and I didn't love him. We did everything else." Trish bit her lip, clearly having more to say. But she seemed to be contemplating whether or not to say it. "He played the piano," she added. "I can't compete with fingers like *that.*"

"I think it's good you're waiting 'til you're in love, Trish," I said. "Sex complicates things." I knew that firsthand. But somehow the "no sex" relationships seemed equally complicated, just in a different way. I couldn't deny that spending time with Adam and not doing anything more than kissing him had gotten increasingly difficult emotionally and physically.

"Bull*shit* you can't compete with that," Amanda said, shocked. "The only person who's never let me down is *myself.* It might not feel as good if I'm the one doing it, but I can beat Shane on time any day of the week. Three minutes tops, start to finish. Shane can't do that to me on his *best* day."

Trish looked like we had just told her Santa Claus actually existed. "For real?"

Steph nodded and Danielle shrugged, confirming Amanda's statement.

"Used to be the case for me too," I added. "And hopefully it will be later. This cream's really kicking in. I need some alone time." I crossed my legs and enjoyed the feeling of my jeans rubbing against me in just the right way. *Maybe tonight's the night*, I silently prayed.

My not-so-subtle movement caught Amanda's eye. "Yeah, you *do*."

"Do you have like a floor model I can buy?" I asked Dana.

She laughed at my desperation and then shook her head. "Unfortunately, no. Orders usually take about ten days to come in."

I threw my head back in utter frustration at the thought of another night completely turned on with no release. But that didn't stop me from spending over a hundred and seventy-five bucks on vibrators of different shapes and sizes. *Better late than never.*

❤

After the party, Amanda went straight to Shane's to spend the night. I guess all the sex talk had gotten her a little worked up. I had to admit it had done the same to me. But as turned on as I was, the thought of getting myself so close without finding release would be even worse than what I felt right now. And what I felt right now was pretty bad. Or good, depending on how you looked at it. *To try or not to try? Shit, shit, shit.* I felt like I was making a life decision. *Jesus, Lily. You're not getting married—you're just masturbating.*

I washed my face, brushed my teeth, and got changed for bed. It was already past midnight, and I was tired. But as much as I tried to close my eyes and relax, I couldn't stop the tightness in my core. The prospect of a much-needed release was just too tempting to pass up. I could do it if I put my mind to it. I was no quitter.

My hips flexed as I began to work my hand down my skin to the area that was still so sensitive from the cream I'd put on hours ago. I slid one hand beneath my underwear to feel the wetness that had probably been there for most of the night.

My mind raced with images of Adam's hands claiming every inch of my body during our first night at the hotel together. I felt my insides clench and my legs tense at the thought. I could feel myself get closer and closer to a long overdue orgasm as I slid my fingers more rapidly over my clit. *Come on, come on. Don't give up. Fuck, I need something else.* With my other hand, I let my fingers travel over the wet fabric, pushing gently on my opening as I imagined the full sensation I'd feel with Adam's cock sliding inside me.

Then I pictured him standing above me, waiting for me to take him in my mouth. Me waiting for him to climb on top of me or pull me against him as he lay beside me. I let my mind go, allowing it to wander to thoughts of the dirty words he'd texted me while he had been at the beach last spring. But still that didn't push me over the edge. And God, I needed to be pushed over, to feel my body pulse with the pleasure I'd been missing for what seemed like forever. And it didn't matter how I got myself there.

With that realization, Adam's dirty words faded, and

someone else's took their place. *The way I see it, you have two options.* I swore I could feel his hips push against mine. *Touch yourself while you think about my thick cock . . . over and over again while I make you come. Or . . . actually let me do it.* Then my lips were on his, his hard chest against my aching breasts.

And that was all I needed. I felt my insides clench uncontrollably at the memory as my body writhed against my own hands. But it wasn't until my orgasm had ceased entirely that I realized what had actually caused it.

Oh, shit.

chapter seventeen

m a x

When I'd agreed to meet Jack for dinner at a steak house in the city, I hadn't anticipated being so anxious about it. But as I buttoned up my shirt and took a look in the mirror, the enormity of our meeting's importance finally set in. Jack hadn't told me the specifics of the job opportunity—mostly because I hadn't given him the chance to until then—but I knew it had the potential to turn into something more permanent. And that knowledge was enough to keep me on edge.

I ran some gel through my hair and played around with the strands until I created a perfectly messy look. *You're meeting your agent, not a potential lay, you asshole.* But if I were honest with myself, I knew why the knots in my stomach had been growing steadily since I'd made reservations to meet up with Jack: I found the prospect of permanently living there incredibly appealing. I told myself it was because Philadelphia was where I'd grown up, the place I called home. My family was there. My friends.

But I knew what the real reason was. Or rather *who*. Lily had let me back into her life, and I wanted to keep it that way. I was done fucking things up. Done *being* a fuckup. The good things in life weren't going to just find me while I sat at home in bed hungover with last night's blowjob sound asleep next to me. If I wanted to make something of myself, *I'd* have to be the one to do it.

This realization was what had finally led me to call Jack back and arrange a meeting with him. Well, that and the fact that Lily called me out on my lack of initiative. It didn't take her long after my birthday dinner to ask me what the hell we were really doing with one another. She had been trying to help me get my shit together, but I was being a stubborn ass, as usual. Here she was putting effort into our friendship, and I had still been shittin' around, making no progress at all. When we'd first agreed to meet up a few months ago, it had been under the pretense that I'd start making some changes. And up until now, I'd made none. If I didn't start getting my shit together soon, I had a strong feeling I'd lose her. And I couldn't let that happen twice.

❤

"Well, it's about damn time," Jack said when I took a seat across from him in the brown leather booth. "I feel like I'm seeing a fuckin' ghost. What the hell have you been up to?"

"Uh . . . not a whole lot. That's kinda why I'm here, right? But we have all night to talk business. How's Gretchen? And the kids?" Though I was anxious to know about the job, I felt guilty for not keeping in touch with Jack. He'd looked out for me more times than I could count. I'd known him for nearly ten years. He was more than just an agent. I could count on him to be a friend.

"Eh, you know . . . the wife's good. She's still a nurse. I keep telling her she should retire soon, but she loves it. Megan's in her second year at Penn State. She's probably at some party as we speak. I don't even wanna think about it. And John graduates in May. He got a pretty good internship in DC this year. They're gonna hire him on after graduation. Some political shit I know nothin' about."

"Nice. Who knew your stupid ass could produce such intelligent offspring?"

"Well, the brains come from Gretchen. That's for damn sure," he said with a laugh as he lifted his glass and took a swig of the dark liquid. "And probably their *looks* too, now that I think about it. As you can probably tell, I rarely miss a meal these days." He patted himself on his stomach, which had gotten slightly rounder since the last time I'd seen him over a year ago. "Now let's eat."

Once the small talk—along with our steamed seafood appetizer—was out of the way, the conversation turned to the real reason for our meeting. "So listen," Jack said. "It's pretty simple. You know the show *On Thin Ice*, right?" he asked without waiting for me to answer. "Well, they want some former players to do a couple of guest spots during the next few months. You know, interview a few players, give your opinion on a game here and there . . . that kinda crap. Nothin' to it. At the end of the season, they're gonna pick one guy to stay on permanently."

"Nothin' to it," I repeated, though I wasn't so sure.

"Yeah, just go in there and be you," he said, gesturing at me with his free hand and taking a sip of his drink with the other.

"Well, maybe not the *you* of late. That one's been a fuckin' moron recently. But you know that." Pausing for a moment, he seemed to be deciding whether to continue or leave the topic alone. Unfortunately, he didn't. "What happened anyway? You started gettin' your shit together toward the end of last season when you were with that cute girlfriend of yours. You know, the one you took to your Atlantic City gig."

"She was never my girlfriend." My voice sounded as strained as I *felt* having to say that. "And it should come as no surprise that I managed to fuck *that* up too."

Jack let out a sigh, and his voice softened. "Hmm, that's a shame. She seemed good for ya."

"Yeah, she was." I couldn't argue with that. "*I* just wasn't good for *her.*"

"Well, listen, whatever happened with you guys is in the past. I've known you since you were practically a kid. You're like a son to me. You *know* that. You gotta do this for *you*, Max. Whatever needs to happen for you to get this job, you better make it happen. None of your bullshit excuses. Ya understand?" Jack's voice held the urgency I wish I'd seen in myself lately. "This is yours for the taking. You just gotta *take* it. You're not gettin' a fourth or fifth chance. This is it. You got it?"

"Yeah, I got it, Jack." I tried to sound upbeat, but even a brief conversation about Lily had affected me in a way that I knew Jack would pick up on.

"I know losin' that girl did something to you, Max, but ya gotta move past it. You sound like someone just shot your dog. Just go in there next week and be that charismatic son of a bitch who always knows just what to say and how to say it. Sometimes you just gotta know how to get outta your own way and stop bein' such a pussy."

It seemed what was left of Jack's filter had disappeared with some of the hairs on the top of his head. "Well, you know what they say, Jack. You are what you eat." I laughed, holding out my arms confidently.

"See"—Jack pointed at me—"now that's the kinda shit I'm talkin' about. That's funny. People like funny. Just say some crap like that." I could see Jack second-guessing his advice immediately. "Well, maybe not *exactly* like that. It's a family show." I noticed his eyes appraising me. "And for Christ's sake, lighten up on the hair gel and put on a fuckin' tie when you go in there. You're interviewing for a job on a sports network, not auditioning for the cast of *Jersey Shore*."

♥

By the time I'd entered the television station the following Tuesday night, I felt ready. The previous week had given me plenty of time to prepare. Despite the fact that I still followed hockey religiously, especially the Flyers, I had felt the need to brush up on my knowledge anyway.

I'd spent countless hours online researching current players' stats from across the league. And I'd watched every pre- and postgame show I could catch for the sole purpose of studying how the hosts conducted themselves. When did they look at the camera? Did they give a candid opinion, or was it more of a political comment aimed to please the masses? All of it was exhausting.

I arrived at four thirty for the seven thirty game against the Capitals and immediately began prepping for the pregame show. I studied my notes in the dressing room while some chick brushed my hair back and sprayed it with something to hold it in place. Nothing could break my focus. Well, almost nothing. I'd have to be blind or gay to ignore this woman's tits as she positioned herself in front of my face so she could dab some makeup on my cheeks. *I could get used to this shit.*

The evening ran relatively smoothly. I answered direct questions when asked by the other hosts and gave a truthful, yet tactful opinion. I even managed to make a few off-the-cuff remarks that elicited a laugh from a few of the guys. I felt that, overall, it had gone as well as could be expected, and I couldn't be happier.

"I think they liked ya, Max," Jack said when he called later that night. "You did good. Keep this up, and you got a shot."

"Really? You think so?" I could hear the excitement in my own voice at the thought. It was the first thing I'd done right in . . . well, in a really long fuckin' time. And it made me pretty damn proud.

Jack and I discussed my next audition, and I knew when I hung up I had a stupid ass grin on my face. I needed to share the good news with *someone*. I couldn't just let the excitement I felt linger in my body overnight. I might combust.

So even though it was already late, I called my parents to tell them the news. I mean, there really wasn't a whole lot to tell other than the fact that I didn't fuck something up for once, but my mom couldn't have been prouder.

"Oh, Max, I knew this would happen. I'm so happy for you." I could hear the pride in her voice when she spoke. "Let me go wake up your father."

"No, Mom, if Dad's asleep, I'll just talk to him tomorrow."

"Don't be silly, sweetheart. When you tell him you're going to be on a television show, he'll be happy I woke him."

"Mom, no, not permane—"

My voice was cut off by hers. "Bill, wake up! Max is on the phone. He's gonna be the host of a hockey show."

I heard the click of another phone pick up, and my dad's voice bellowed across the line. "Hey, buddy, is that true? See? I told ya, doll," he said to my mom, "we just needed to give him a little time."

"Uh, I'm not on a hockey show *yet*. I mean, I'll be on TV here and there, but it's nothing permanent. I won't know 'til the end of the season if I got the job."

"Oh, don't be so pessimistic," my mom replied. "You'll get it. I just know it. Did you tell Lily? She's gonna be so happy for you."

❤

I'd thought that sharing the news of my audition with my parents would assuage the excitement coursing through my veins. Like I would experience some sort of magical transference of energy from my body to theirs.

It didn't work.

And with the mention of Lily's name, my heart raced a little bit more and my already fidgety hands began to visibly tremble. But my mom was right.

Lily would be ecstatic.

So why was I so nervous to tell her? She'd be happy for me, if for no other reason than I had *tried* to do something to better myself. I'd finally *tried* to take a few steps in the right direction instead of sitting around on my ass, waiting for life to come to me.

But the more I thought about how unconditionally

supportive she'd been of me lately, the more I realized why I was so anxious. Though *trying* might be good enough for Lily, it would never be good enough for *me*.

I didn't come in second place. To anyone. I wasn't some fucking seven-year-old who'd gotten a trophy for participating. I was Max fucking Samson. And I was a fucking winner.

❤

My restless night had afforded me time to decide whether or not I wanted to tell Lily about the audition. If I told her, I knew I'd have to get the job or risk being embarrassed that she'd know I'd lost it to someone else. And I couldn't let that happen.

If I tell Lily about the job possibility, I won't fuck this up. I can't *fuck this up.* So I used that as my motivation when I'd texted to ask her if she wanted to meet for lunch the following day. I said I had big news to share, and I'd wanted to share it in person.

At ten forty-five the next morning, I arrived at a diner across from Swift Middle School. Seated facing the door, I waited, not so patiently, for Lily to arrive. Her lunch period was from ten fifty to eleven forty. I briefly wondered who could eat lunch that fucking early on a daily basis, before I remembered that last year I had done exactly that. Though I'd been free to come and go as I pleased at the school, I'd chosen to eat lunch fifth period so I could eat with Lily.

And for some reason that thought calmed me, comforted me even. That ten months ago at nearly this very minute, I could have been doing this exact same thing: eating lunch across from Lily as we talked to each other about how our day had been so far. *Or at least we would be doing this exact thing if she ever friggin' got here?*

I had just looked down at my watch for the twentieth time when I heard the jingle of the bell on the door. And as I watched Lily stroll confidently toward me, I felt a stupid grin creep across my face. Her black pants fit tightly to her legs, and my gaze traced the length of them before it made its way up to those eyes that I always loved so much. Eyes that I loved even more on days like today, when the sunlight brought out the specks of gold in them that I was sure she'd never even noticed herself.

"Hey, Max," she said as she pulled the silky strands of chestnut hair around the back of her neck to rest on the front of her shoulder. The sweet smell of her coconut shampoo washed over me, waking me from my trance. "I'm happy you asked me to meet."

"You are?" Not only was I excited to tell Lily about the job opportunity, I was even more excited at the idea that she seemed eager to see me.

"Yeah, I haven't seen you in a few weeks, and a lot's happened."

She paused for a minute or so to peruse the menu, and I motioned for the waitress to come take our order once Lily seemed ready. I knew she had to be back in about forty-five minutes and didn't want her to be late. "So what's up?" I asked. I could tell she was in an unusually upbeat mood, and I was eager to find out why she was so happy.

I didn't know what I expected her to say. Maybe she'd won the lottery. Or she'd gotten a new puppy. Was it possible that she'd just found out Christmas break was starting a week early? Whatever it was, I hadn't seen Lily that excited in as long as I could remember. I only wished that when she started to speak, I could have maintained my excitement for her. Or at least faked it better than I had.

But the moment I heard Adam's name leave her lips, I felt my face drop. Trying to think of anything else than what she was saying, I did my best to tune her out. Unfortunately, my best wasn't good enough. As hard as I tried, I couldn't help but hear at least some of the words. *Adam and I ... dating again ... a few weeks ... seems to be going well.*

I felt my eyes glaze over as I tried to maintain eye contact. Every word out of her beautiful mouth was like a nail across a chalkboard, making my blood run cold. And my visceral reaction surprised me.

I knew I should be happy for her. She'd lost him because of me, and we were only *friends* now. What right did I have to think the thoughts that ran through my head—that pussy's hand across her cheek as he kissed her, his words making her smile? I wanted her to smile at what *I* said.

"Enough about me, though. What news did *you* have? You seemed so excited when you texted."

"Uh ... yeah, I do have news." I bit my lip to keep from saying what I'd gone there to tell her, though I wasn't entirely sure why. Maybe I didn't want my moment to be tainted by the sound of that douchebag's name as it hung in the air between us. Or maybe I just didn't think she'd give a shit about what I had to say. But most of all, I think I just didn't give a shit about it *myself* anymore. "My dad got a new fishing pole the other day," I said.

"That's the big news?" she replied. "You're becoming more like him every day. Should I alert the authorities?"

I savored the sound of the subtle laugh that escaped her and focused on the smile that played on the corners of her mouth. It was the best thing I'd seen all day. Because *I* had been the one to put it there.

♥

Despite the fact that I managed to fake my way through enjoying the rest of our lunch, inside I felt like something was missing. Like the part of herself Lily had been sharing with me for the past few months would now be suddenly shared with *him*. I didn't even know what part that was. I just knew I didn't want that asshole to have *any* of her.

But I could never tell her that.

So I told her I was happy for her. Happy for *him* even. And happy for the two of them. Together. God, those words tasted bitter as I said them.

So by the next day, I was in desperate need of a night out with the boys. I wanted something to wash the thoughts of Lily and Adam from my cluttered brain. And what better way to do that than with alcohol?

chapter eighteen

l i l y

My relationship with Adam had been progressing…slowly. Up until about two weeks ago, that was. It was as if Adam had experienced some kind of epiphany over Thanksgiving that had prompted him to kick our relationship up a notch. He had begun to call me every night, made an effort to see me as often as possible, and the sexual tension between us was palpable.

I looked in the mirror as I applied my makeup, gearing up for a hopefully hot date with Adam. We were going to a new steak house that had just opened near us. The place was trendy, and I wanted to make sure I looked the part. Drawing back from the mirror slightly, I took in my deep blue wool dress that hugged my toned body. I paired it with a pair of patterned black tights that added a touch of naughtiness. Topped off with four-inch black stilettos, even *I* had to admit that I looked smoking hot. Putting the cap back on my lip gloss and giving my lips one last pop in the mirror, I walked out of my room and into the living room to wait for Adam.

I looked around the apartment and took inventory of what was missing. As Amanda spent more time at Shane's, she had been slowly removing items from our house and taking them to his. I was bracing myself for the conversation where she told me she was moving out and tried to take half of my stuff with her when she went. We had already gotten into it earlier in the week because I noticed her walking out with our blender. That *I'd* bought.

"But I need it," she had whined.

"Tough shit. And Shane's a friggin' nutritionist. There's no way he doesn't have a blender."

"His makes my smoothies taste weird," she had continued as she clutched the blender like I was trying to steal her firstborn.

"It does not, you blasphemous liar. Now put it back."

"Is 'blasphemous' a real word?"

I looked at her with irritation, partly because she dared to question my vocabulary and partly because she was a conniving thief.

"He always puts gross things in his blender. Like kale. Who the fuck drinks kale? I can't share a blender with him. All the healthy stuff will seep in."

I just continued to stare at her, making it clear that I wasn't going to back down.

"Fine," she huffed as she turned to return my property to its rightful place. "You need to get some," she muttered.

"What was that?" I asked with an edge to my voice that I didn't really feel.

"Bitch, you heard me."

I'd let loose a deep laugh, shaking my head at the craziness that was Amanda.

I'd started keeping a mental inventory of my shit after that. But as I glanced around at the empty spaces scattered throughout our living room, I couldn't help but let a little sadness creep in. I was going to miss that crazy bitch.

Just then, the buzzer rang. I walked over to the intercom and held down the button. "Hello?"

"Hey, Lily. It's me."

I could hear the smile in his voice. It made me melt a little. "Me who?"

"Uh, hopefully the only guy you're expecting tonight."

Even though his voice was playful, I immediately regretted teasing him when I heard his response. I wondered if his mind had traveled where mine did: to the fact that there had been times when he hadn't been the only guy who had made visits to my apartment. Dropping my head slightly, I tried to compose myself quickly before I replied. *You're not that girl anymore. You won't fuck up this time.* I lifted my head and interjected happiness into my voice. "I'll be right down."

Throwing on my coat, I hurried from the apartment and descended the stairs to meet Adam. He was waiting in the foyer, his blond hair gelled to messy perfection, a black pea coat stretched over his solid arms, his hands shoved into his dark jeans. His back was to me, giving me a moment to eye-fuck the shit out of him through the glass door that separated us.

Adam and I had done our fair share of making out and allowing our hands to roam each other's bodies, but we hadn't been intimate yet. And God did I *need* to be intimate with Adam. It was all I could do to keep myself from throwing open the door, tackling him to the ground, and straddling his face. *Keep it in your pants, Lily.* Inhaling deeply, I pulled open the door.

Upon hearing me, Adam spun around, a wide smile lighting up his beautiful face. I felt the familiar slickness between my legs as he appraised me from head to toe, spending a little extra time on the good parts.

I sauntered over to him with my sexiest strut. "Hey," I breathed as I wrapped an arm around his shoulders and lifted my lips to his. My intention had been to simply share a quick kiss, but as soon as our lips met, the need spilled out of us. We intertwined our tongues, invading each other's mouths roughly, wildly. He ran his hands up my body before pressing firmly into my lower back, pulling me tighter to him.

I had no idea how long we stood there, and it didn't matter. I could've stood there forever wrapped up in the moment, in him, in us. He eventually pulled away, letting a low growl escape from his throat. *Just when I thought I couldn't be more turned on.*

"Hi," he said breathlessly. We laughed softly as we both backed up slightly. "You ready to go?"

"Yup," I said as I looped an arm through his and let him lead me outside.

❤

It only took us about ten minutes to drive to the restaurant. Adam and I fell into easy conversation about who-cares-what. I would've happily talked about knitting, as long as I got to be near him while I did it.

Once inside the restaurant, we were shown to a table nestled in a corner. The lighting was dim, and it instantly made me think of how hot it would be to make love to Adam by candlelight. Attempting to push this thought from my mind,

I opened the menu and studied it. But I couldn't focus on the words. *Jesus Christ, the man's sexiness has made me forget how to read.*

"What looks good to you?"

My eyes snapped up and drank him in. *Oh, I know what looks good to me, all right.* "Uh, the New York strip maybe." *Shit, is there even a New York strip on this menu?*

"Hmm, that sounds good. I'm thinking of going with the prime rib, though."

As I contemplated whether or not I could stealthily finger myself under the table and relieve some of the desire that had settled there, our waiter appeared.

"Hi, folks. How are you both doing this evening?" He filled our water glasses as we replied that we were fine. "My name is Chris, and I'll be your server this evening. Can I get you started with something from the bar?"

"Want to share a bottle of wine?" Adam asked me.

"I'd share anything with you," I blurted out dreamily before realizing what I had just said. My eyes widened as Adam tried to suppress a smile and Chris shifted his weight slightly.

"We'll take a bottle of your house Chianti."

"Certainly, sir. I'll be right back with that."

I watched Chris hurry away before turning my attention back to Adam. He was staring at me intently, a sly smile playing on his lips.

"So, you'd share anything with me, huh?" His tone was teasing, but there was a heat in his eyes that caused warmth to spread over my body.

I figured I could play this one of two ways. I could either be embarrassed by what I had said and try to change the subject, or I could embrace my words and set about my primary goal for the evening: seducing Adam Carter. Needless to say, I chose option B. "Pretty much. Why? Are you offering?"

He leaned back, allowing his cream sweater to pull deliciously over his taut body. I wanted to unravel it with my teeth. "Well, you know me. I like to know all the specifics about the person sitting across the table from me before I entertain an offer."

Chris returned with the wine and poured a little in Adam's glass so he could taste it. But instead of taking a sip, Adam handed the glass to me.

"Taste this and see if it's the one you want."

My eyes jerked from the glass to him. He was gazing intently at me, and I knew his words carried weight beyond the wine. I wrapped my hand around the glass and brought it to my lips. I let a small moan escape as I let the wine fill my mouth. Handing the glass back to him and looking directly into his eyes, I replied, "Yes, this is definitely the one I want."

His eyes gleamed as he set the glass down and settled back against the chair. Chris realized that he was intruding on a private moment that was about much more than a simple bottle of Chianti. He asked if we had any questions about the menu and took our order swiftly before leaving us alone.

Adam sat up straight and placed his forearms on the table. His eyes never left mine as he seemed to be trying to work something out in his head. Finally, he spoke. "I meant what I said. I need to put everything on the table before this goes any further." He watched me warily, clearly unsure how I would react.

I also straightened up then, mimicking his body position and leaning closer to him. "This looks like a pretty sturdy table. I bet it can handle whatever strain we put on it."

I watched the tic in Adam's jaw. He looked uncomfortable. And I knew there was only one thing that could make Adam feel this way. "Is it Max that you want to talk about?"

He hesitated briefly before releasing a sigh. "Yes," he said simply.

"What do you want to know?"

"I haven't wanted to ask this, mostly because I'm not sure I really want to know the answer, but... do you still see him?"

Now it was my turn for a simple answer. "Yes."

His posture sagged just slightly, but it was enough for me to notice. "How... uh, when... um..." He ran his hand roughly over his face, instantly making me feel guilty for making this such an issue between us.

I reached over the table and grabbed his hand. "Adam?" I waited for his eyes to meet mine before I continued. "You need to ask me whatever it is you want to know. Nothing is off limits. I want this." I motioned between us with my free hand. "More than you could ever know. But it'll never work if we don't clear the air. So ask."

Adam eyed me cautiously as he got his thoughts organized. "In what capacity do you see Max?"

"Strictly as friends." My eyes never left his in the hope that he could see the truth that resided there.

"Friends?" he scoffed quietly and pulled his hand back from mine, lowering both to his lap. "I seem to remember being told that before."

I took a steadying breath. "You're right. You were."

"And it was a lie then."

"Yes. It was," I answered, though I knew it wasn't a question. I kept my voice low and neutral. Everything was riding on this conversation, and I didn't want it getting muddled in a haze of emotions.

"But I'm supposed to believe that it isn't this time?"

"I don't expect you to believe me at my word. I've given you a lot of reasons to doubt me. But . . . I don't know what else I have to offer you other than that." I couldn't help but feel a sliver of defeat crawl through me. I had no other way to assure him of my feelings other than to say them. But my words weren't credible to him. If he gave me time, I was sure I could prove it to him. Was he willing to take the risk and give me that time? That was the million-dollar question.

"Here you are."

My head whipped toward the source of the intrusion. *Fucking Chris.*

Chris lowered the salad plates in front of us and backed up a little. "Anything else I can get for you right now?"

We shook our heads.

"Okay. Your dinner should be ready shortly."

We stared at the food in front of us for a minute before picking up our forks and starting to eat. The silence that descended upon us was heavy and constricting.

Chris came back and cleared our plates before returning with our main course. Adam and I made small talk about how good the food was and what other restaurants the chef owned. It was brutal.

Once we had both eaten the bulk of our meals, Adam cleared his throat and set his fork down. "I don't know if I can do this, Lily."

Tears sprang to my eyes, and I tried to regain my composure before any of them fell. I played with my napkin on my lap, trying to think of something, anything, that I could say that would fix this.

"Hey," Adam said gently. "Look at me."

I slowly dragged my eyes to his.

"I don't want to hurt you, Lily. But I don't want to get hurt either. What happened last spring...it ripped me apart. I can't go through that again." He continued to look at me and I could see his struggle. "I think we could have something truly amazing. But it would take a lot of work to get there, on both of our parts. And I just don't think I can put that kind of effort in if you still see Max."

I looked down at the table, unable to hold his gaze any longer. Max was coming between us again. But this time, things between Max and me were different. I knew that. Though Adam didn't. And I couldn't blame him. If the roles were reversed, I wouldn't want Adam to keep in contact with his side action. What he was asking me for wasn't unreasonable. But, for some reason I couldn't quite figure out, telling Adam that I would expunge Max from my life felt...wrong.

I couldn't get logic and emotions on the same page. A relationship with Adam was the one thing I wanted more than anything. But when it came time to prove it, I hesitated. *Why the hell is this decision so difficult? It should be a no-brainer.*

Adam was everything I wanted. Everything I needed. I had dreamed about the possibility of him taking me back for the past eight months. And now that it was finally here, I was going to risk it all for Max? Why was I doing this? Again?

"I know I can't ask you to stop seeing him. The decision is clearly yours. But...now you know where I stand. So think about it and let me know what you decide." Adam gave me a stiff smile, and I immediately felt unworthy of even that small act of kindness.

I was failing him already. By taking time to think about

something that should have been an automatic response, I was telling him all he needed to know. I would give anything for him. Anything except Max.

We managed to hold a casual discussion for the remainder of dinner, but it was awkward and loaded with unresolved issues. When we returned to my complex and Adam walked me to the lobby, I didn't even bother asking him if he wanted to come upstairs. Our relationship felt like it was starting to dissolve before it had even had a chance to form. And as Adam pulled me to him for a hug goodbye, I held him tightly and inhaled deeply into his shoulder, wanting to commit his scent to memory.

As I walked into my apartment and locked the door behind me, I lost all control. I slunk down against the door and cried for the first time in months.

❤

Once I pulled myself together, I stood and made my way to my bedroom. I walked in, threw my purse onto my bureau, and caught a glimpse of myself in the mirror in the process.

"Who are you?" I asked my reflection. I stood in front of the mirror, looking at myself. *Really* looking. I felt like I was the Lily of eight months ago: desperate for approval from the man I wanted, but still fucking it all up. Weak and vulnerable, the glimpse of the old Lily was sobering.

I straightened my spine and lifted my chin. This pathetic little girl wasn't me anymore. Ultimately, it was *my* approval that I needed—no one else's. And as I continued studying myself, I realized why I hadn't agreed to stop seeing Max. It was because, even though I wanted a life with Adam, I didn't want Adam to *be* my life. I worried that if I gave in on that, then I'd give in on other things. Independence was something that took me a long time to find, and I didn't want to throw it away the first time it was tested.

While losing Adam would be a decision that would haunt me, possibly forever, casting aside a friendship that was, for whatever reason, important to me could be damaging. What would I be willing to give up next time simply to put Adam at ease? I unzipped my dress and unclasped my bra, allowing both to fall to the floor before reaching to my bed for the tank top I slept in.

But I didn't put it on. I gazed at myself, bare. No pretenses, no illusions, no hiding. I needed to ask the tough questions. And I needed to answer them. Did Max still arouse me? Yes. Did my eyes sometimes go to him and linger there, unable to look away? Yes. Was I happy when I was with him? Yes.

Did I love him?

I lowered my head to stare at the carpet. I took some deep breaths before forcing my head up again. Did I love Max? Yes. In the way a girl would always love the dangerous boy she grew up with. He might not be her future, but he was instrumental in making her who she was as an adult. I'd only truly been an adult for a matter of months, but I had no doubt that Max had shaped this person I now saw reflected back at me. And now it was my turn to be that person to Max.

Pulling the tank top over my head, I gave myself a nod before turning and walking toward the bathroom to get ready for bed. If Adam and I were meant to be, then we'd be. I wouldn't compromise who I'd become—and who I still might grow to be—because that wouldn't be fair to me. And I'd never be able to live with Adam if I couldn't even live with myself.

chapter nineteen

l i l y

Things in my life were tense, and I had never been more thankful for Christmas break. I had spoken to Adam a few times since our date on Friday, but our conversations had been stilted and pregnant with the things we weren't saying. Eventually I knew we'd have the talk we'd both been clearly avoiding, and that it would either be a beginning or an end for us. I wasn't in a hurry to find out which.

I was sitting at my kitchen table eating a bowl of oatmeal and enjoying a cup of coffee when my phone rang. I looked down at it: *my parents.*

"Hello?"

"Lily, honey, Merry Christmas."

"Thanks, Mom. You too. What are you guys up to?"

"Oh, nothing really. We wanted to give you a call before we exchanged our gifts and started getting ready for dinner." It was my parents' turn to host Christmas for family and a few friends in Chicago. My mom was disappointed that she wouldn't get to spend the holiday with me, but I really wasn't interested in having a repeat of last year. Even though my relationship with my parents was much stronger, I didn't want to tempt fate. "What are your plans today?"

"I'm going with Amanda to Shane's for dinner. He's cooking for his family and Amanda's mom." I had already told her all of this, of course, but something told me she didn't quite believe me. Ever since my breakup with Adam, she worried about me a lot more. I kept trying to reassure her that this wasn't an episode of *Intervention* and I wasn't sitting alone in my apartment huffing computer duster.

"That's good. I'm glad you're going somewhere."

I rolled my eyes. "Where's Dad?"

"Right here. I'll put him on."

I heard muffled voices before my dad came on the line. "Lily! Merry Christmas, princess."

"Merry Christmas, Dad. So, you guys ready for the Hamilton and Tasker invasion tonight?"

My dad let out a grunt. "There's no getting ready for that. Hey, you wanna place a bet on which of your mother's relatives gets drunk first?"

I laughed as I heard a slap through the phone and my mother's irritated voice. He was right, though. The Taskers were a rowdy bunch and usually couldn't make it more than a couple of hours without verbally or physically assaulting one another.

"Don't encourage him, Lily," my mother scolded as she came back on the phone. She must have ripped it out of my dad's hand, since I could still hear him laughing in the background.

"Have a great day, Lily. I love you," my dad yelled.

"Tell him I love him too."

"She says she loves you too. Now go make yourself useful and start peeling potatoes," my mom ordered. I heard her sigh before she spoke again. "I miss you, Lily. Christmas isn't the same without you here."

I dropped my head to the table and started banging it against the wood softly so my mom wouldn't hear it through the phone. No one knew how to lay a guilt trip on me like my mother. "I know. I miss you guys too. But I hate traveling over the holidays. And work has been stressful, so I really want to just relax." Most of what I had said was true. I did hate traveling over the holidays and I was feeling a lot of stress, though it wasn't because of work.

"I understand. But I still wish you were here. With all of this snow we've been having, I didn't get a chance to mail your gifts. I'll send them out tomorrow."

"Mom, we talked about this. You sent me to Europe over the summer. That definitely takes care of all gifts for at least the next five years."

"Oh, stop. They're just a few small things."

I shook my head but didn't pursue the matter further. "I mailed your gifts out two days ago, so you should be getting them soon."

"You shouldn't have gotten us anything. Save your money."

"They're just a few small things," I mocked.

"All right, all right. We'll call you when they arrive. Have a great day and be safe, okay?"

"Always. Love you."

"Love you."

I disconnected the call and set my phone down on the table. It was only eight in the morning. I didn't need to be at Shane's until three. Amanda had spent the night at his place so she could help him get ready for dinner, though she spent most nights there anyway. Rinsing my bowl and mug, I put them in the dishwasher and made my way to my bedroom. *May as well go back to bed.*

I put my phone on my bedside table and climbed back under the covers. I thought about shooting a quick text to Adam to wish him a Merry Christmas, but I had already done that when we spoke last night and I also knew he'd most likely be opening gifts with Eva right now. However, this knowledge didn't stop me from hoping it was him when my phone beeped with an incoming message.

> *Merry Christmas, Lily. Hope*
> *Santa was good to you. Give me*
> *a call later if you get time.*

Max. I stared at the message for a minute before setting it back on the table without typing a reply. I hadn't spoken to Max much since Friday, and the irony wasn't lost on me. I wasn't willing to stop talking to Max when Adam asked me to, yet I was pulling away from him anyway. Though my intentions weren't to ignore him forever. I just . . . needed a break. At least this was what I told myself as my eyes closed and I drifted off to sleep.

❤

I pulled up to Shane's house at two thirty, thinking that they could probably use some help getting everything ready, and also because I was tired of sitting around by myself. I knocked as a courtesy but didn't wait for anyone to let me in. I entered

Shane's home that had been tastefully decorated and was filled with delicious aromas.

"Amanda? Shane?" I called out to alert them to my presence. I didn't want to accidentally walk in on them having sex somewhere.

"Lily, thank God! I'm in the kitchen."

"Hey," I said as I walked in and gave Amanda a quick hug. "Merry Christmas. What's going on?"

"Merry Christmas. And nothing, unless you count the fact that I'm about to slaughter my boyfriend and serve him for dinner."

I let out a laugh. "Why?" I scanned the kitchen. Every available surface was covered with food. "Are you guys doubling as a soup kitchen tonight? Why is there so much food in here?"

"Exactly."

I looked at her questioningly.

"Shane cooked all this healthy Paleo shit that no one's gonna touch. Then he had the nerve to accuse me of trying to poison his family with all my 'processed bullshit,' as he called it."

I couldn't contain my smile. "Where is he now?"

"Who knows. He probably caught me eyeing the knives and decided that it was best to leave me alone."

"Amanda, what do you expect? He's a nutritionist and a CrossFit coach, for Christ's sake. Of course he's going to give you a hard time when you cook a ton of fattening food."

Amanda raised the knife she was holding and pointed it in my direction. "Listen, you are going to have to pick a side here, and if I were you, I'd choose wisely."

"You're ridiculous." I laughed. "So what can I help with?"

"You can hold the trash bag while I throw half of this junk away," I heard from behind me.

I turned to see Shane standing in the doorway. Even though he was Amanda's boyfriend, I couldn't help but drink him in. He was really quite a specimen. Not quite six feet tall, he was built like a fucking tank. But his blond hair and light eyes gave him a gentle quality that offset his imposing stature.

"If you touch my food, they will need bloodhounds to locate your body," Amanda threatened without looking up.

"Do you have any idea how hard I had to work to get your body to look as good as it does right now? How much of your bullshit I had to endure? And you're just going to throw it all away on macaroni and cheese and sweet potatoes coated in syrup." Even Shane had a hard time keeping a straight face as he spoke. Amanda could gain two hundred pounds, and Shane would still be head over heels for her.

"Shane, if you ever want to see this body naked again, you will shut the hell up."

I propped my elbow on the island and rested my head on my hand, settling in for the show. These two fighting was truly a spectacle.

Shane walked to Amanda and pressed his body up against hers. "That threat goes both ways, sweetheart."

Amanda stiffened at the feel of Shane behind her. If I had an ounce of shame, I might have felt uncomfortable witnessing their exchange, but I didn't so I stayed where I was, riveted.

Amanda quickly regained her composure and continued chopping vegetables, though I saw her grind backward into Shane slightly. "Does it now?" she asked coyly.

"Absolutely."

"Why don't we just let everyone else decide? We'll put all

the food out and see what people enjoy more."

"Fine by me." Shane smiled and gave Amanda a light kiss on the cheek before he started toward the dining room. But he stopped and turned back toward us before he left the room. "Oh, and Merry Christmas, Lily."

"Back at ya," I yelled after him. Once I was sure he was gone, I leaned toward Amanda. "The poor bastard doesn't stand a chance."

Giggling, Amanda replied, "I know. Now let's discuss more important things. Like what my mom will be wearing."

❤

Amanda got the answer to her question about an hour later when her mom showed up "fashionably late" as she called it, wearing an oversize green sweater with appliqué candy canes and gingerbread men.

"Hi, Mom," Amanda said, leaning in for a quick hug. I was surprised that she initiated anything that resembled affection. She must've been really overcome with the Christmas spirit. It's not that she didn't love the woman. She did. But Amanda also didn't have the greatest patience when it came to her mom, and I couldn't blame her. As well-intentioned as Angela was, she was a total flake. "I see you're still keeping the local Salvation Army in business."

There's my girl.

"Oh, I didn't get this one from the Salvation Army. I found it in a lost-and-found box at the mall."

Amanda actually looked stunned. "You mean you're wearing a complete stranger's crusty old Christmas sweater?"

"Would I have somehow magically known the previous

owner if I had gotten it at the Salvation Army?" Angela questioned.

"No, but at least that person probably would've cared enough to wash it. A hobo could've been wearing that for Christ's sake. And even *he* didn't like it enough to keep it."

"You're ridiculous," Angela scoffed as she walked toward the living room.

"I'm ridic ... never mind. Why do I even bother?" Amanda threw up her arms in mock indignation but couldn't hold in the laughter as she walked back toward the kitchen.

I couldn't help but giggle as they both walked off. *This is going to be one helluva Christmas.*

By four o'clock, we were sitting down to dinner. Well, two dinners would be more accurate. Shane's dining room table had developed a sort of nutritional divide. They had agreed to serve turkey and a round roast as the staple dishes of the meal, so these were in the center of the table, flanked to the left by Amanda's side dishes and to the right by Shane's.

We all eyed each other warily as we stood around the table, afraid to show allegiance to either side. Amanda and Shane sat on opposing ends of the rectangular table, Amanda in front of her food, Shane in front of his. Choosing a seat became akin to choosing gang colors. Suddenly, I felt a shoulder bump mine. I looked to see who had tapped me.

Shit.

"Where you sittin', shawty?" Shane's eleven-year-old nephew, Henry, was going through some sort of bizarre identity crisis. *Hate to break it to ya, kid, but you're not Eminem.*

I smiled sweetly at him. "Where are you sitting?"

"Uh ... I guess ... I guess right here," he stammered as he pointed to a chair next to Shane, clearly thrown by what he interpreted as me flirting with him.

I immediately dropped my smile and said curtly, "Then I'm sitting over there," as I pointed to a chair beside Amanda. I began walking toward my chosen seat when I heard him mutter behind me.

"I love it when a chick plays hard to get." He pulled out his chair and plopped down in it.

I swung my head toward Amanda and raised my eyebrows.

"Ignore him. Everyone else does," she offered as she took a sip of her wine. Her eyes never left Shane.

Angela sat down on the other side of Amanda. "You use very interesting language, Henry. Is it, oh, what's it called, umm . . . oh, yeah, ebonics?"

"Jesus Christ," Amanda murmured.

"Nah, it's just me, baby."

"Henry," Talia scolded, "that's enough."

"Haters gonna hate, Mom," Henry muttered.

"And idiots gonna get grounded if they don't learn how to show some respect," Talia countered.

Henry immediately shut up, which caused me to fall slightly in love with Talia.

"Everything looks wonderful," Shane's mom, Katherine, interjected, probably hoping to steer the conversation in a more positive direction.

"Looks can be deceiving," Amanda said under her breath, which earned her a kick from me. She hadn't been around Shane's mom that much since they got together, and the last thing she needed was to make a bad impression.

"So, are we all going to stare at the food, or are we actually going to eat it?" Shane's brother, Ben, asked loudly.

"We should say a blessing," Katherine suggested.

"Well, who's going to do it? And can they hurry? I'm starving." Ben received an irritated glare from Talia, but simply shrugged and added, "We were all thinking it."

"It's Shane's house. He should do it," Amanda suggested with a smirk.

"What a great idea," Katherine gushed.

Shane stared daggers at Amanda. "Sure, I'd be honored to give the blessing."

We all joined hands, bowed our heads, and Shane cleared his throat. "Dear Lord..."

Amanda let out an extremely unattractive snort, and I squeezed her hand tightly. "Sorry, something was stuck in my throat."

Shane let out a long, agitated breath before he started again. "Dear Lord..." He hesitated a moment and looked up at Amanda, as if daring her to interrupt him again. She smiled coyly and he went on. "We thank you for this food we are about to eat, even though some of it has been stripped of any nutritional value during its preparation."

I tried to bite back a smile as Amanda's head shot up.

"We also thank you for allowing all of us to be here today. Even though some of us are difficult and pigheaded, we appreciate being able to celebrate this day together. In Jesus's name. Amen."

"That was... very nice, Shane," Katherine commented.

"Yeah, Shane. Very nice," Amanda added. Her voice sounded sincere, but anyone who knew her could recognize the gleam in her eye. Tonight was about to get very interesting.

"Why thank you, Mom. Sweetheart."

To my knowledge, Shane never referred to Amanda as "sweetheart" and meant it sincerely, which led me to believe the gauntlet had not only been thrown, but also accepted.

"Mommy, can I have some turkey?" I looked at the sweet little girl beside me. I'm not sure how Talia and Ben had created an abomination like Henry and then something so adorable like Mackenzie.

"Sure, baby. What else do you want?" Talia asked.

"Ummm…"

"Kenzie, how about some fresh tomato with basil?" Shane interrupted.

Amanda scoffed. "Why would a six-year-old want that? I have some macaroni and cheese over here, Mackenzie. How does that sound?"

"Why would she *want* this? Maybe because she wants to live to see her teenage years. Trust Uncle Shane on this one, Kenzie. Amanda is trying to kill you."

Our heads all flew toward Shane when we registered his words. Then Mackenzie started to cry. "Why would she do that, Uncle Shane?"

A look of horror swept over Shane's face as he realized what he had just said. "Oh no, Kenzie, I didn't mean that."

Kenzie was all-out sobbing now as Talia wrapped her arms around the young girl and tried to soothe her.

"Nice job, Shane," Amanda quipped.

"Shit, I'm so sorry, Kenz."

"How come when I talk, Mom threatens to ground me, but Uncle Shane can curse?" Henry accused.

"Because, like Mom said, you're an idiot."

Katherine looked appalled at her oldest son. "Ben, you shouldn't call your son names. That's twice his parents have called him an idiot at the Christmas table. I never spoke to you boys like that."

"Well, Mom, maybe if you had, your other son wouldn't be traumatizing my daughter over Christmas dinner."

Then Angela decided to offer her own pearl of wisdom. "Don't worry, Ben. Shane probably didn't cause any real damage. I mean, you should hear some of the things I said to Amanda over the years. And she turned out just fine."

"Thanks for helping, Mom," Amanda said dryly.

"My pleasure," Angela replied happily as she spooned some sweet potatoes onto her plate.

The dinner table was in complete chaos, with everyone talking at once and arguing with one another. *And to think, I almost went home to Chicago for Christmas and missed all this.* Suddenly, I started laughing. An uncontrollable belly laugh that echoed through the room. Eventually, all other conversation ceased as everyone stared at me. Even Mackenzie stopped her crying to look at me quizzically.

"Did I miss a joke?" Amanda asked, amusement evident in her voice.

I couldn't even stop laughing long enough to answer her.

"I think she's drunk, dear," Angela volunteered.

This little gem from Angela only made me laugh harder, which I hadn't even thought was possible. Finally, I tried to form some kind of coherent speech. "You two . . . are such . . . assholes. You're utterly . . . perfect for each other."

Amanda pushed her tongue into her cheek to keep a serious countenance, but it was no use. She was soon laughing just as hard as I was. She looked up at Shane, smiling the first genuine smile she'd worn all night. "I love you immensely. You know that, right?"

"I do," Shane replied simply, his lips tilted up in a boyish smile that showed just how in love with Amanda he was.

"Good. Then let's eat. Mackenzie, you know I love you too, right?"

The little girl nodded.

Amanda smiled. "Then, you know that I'd never hurt you. You can eat whatever you want. Nothing bad will happen."

The little girl sniffled a few times, but visibly relaxed.

The rest of dinner passed without incident. We enjoyed easy, lighthearted conversation and no one else cried or threatened physical harm. Once we had finished dessert, which Shane had thankfully not even tried to prepare something for, we got up to clear the table. But Shane and Amanda quickly told everyone to go into the living room to relax. They'd clean up and be in so that we could all exchange presents. Even though we all repeated that we'd help, the offer was halfhearted and proved insincere as we all walked toward the living room without giving the dinner table a second look.

However, as Henry sidled up next to me and tried to hold my hand, I quickly thought better of my decision and started toward the kitchen to offer some help. As I walked through the doorway of the kitchen, I stopped short and quickly drew back so that I was hidden behind the corner. I poked my head forward just enough to watch Shane and Amanda.

Shane was scraping uneaten food off plates into the trash can and putting away leftovers as Amanda rinsed dishes and loaded them into the dishwasher. But it wasn't what they were doing that captivated me. It was *how* they were doing it. They worked silently, but cohesively, moving around each other as though it were a dance they had practiced to perfection. I watched as they exchanged loving glances and quick kisses. I saw the light touches Shane gave Amanda as he moved around her, as well as how her body leaned into every graze of his fingers.

And as I stood there observing them, I knew I was witnessing a special moment in time that I'd always remember. It would be a moment I would hope to recreate in my own life. A moment that I would lean on when things in my life weren't going as planned. A moment that would always reassure me that true love did exist.

♥

Two days had passed since what would probably go down as the most memorable Christmas dinner in history, and by nine o'clock Friday night, I was becoming sufficiently bored. Adam and I had texted back and forth a few times about nothing in particular. Amanda was busy staying glued to Shane's ass, Tina was visiting family upstate, and the rest of my girlfriends sucked. That only left Max, but I didn't want to hang out with him either.

Well, that wasn't *entirely* true. I did *want* to. But I just wasn't sure where I stood with him. I'd been giving a lot of thought to our friendship, and I was starting to think that maybe it wasn't worth everything I was sacrificing for it. I enjoyed hanging out with him, but was that enough?

I had already lost Adam once because I was wrapped up in having "fun" with Max. And I just couldn't justify losing who was potentially the love of my life for someone who was just a good time once in a while. In fact, I was pretty sure doing so would make me the dumbest motherfucker on the planet.

But this is Max we're talking about here. I tried to envision my life without him in it, and I just couldn't. He was like a dejected little kitten who lived in the alleyway behind your house. Once you fed him and showed him a little kindness, he laid claim to you, whether you wanted him to or not. And while being Max's wasn't as important to me as being Adam's, it was still something I couldn't just throw away. *Could I?*

This shit was like a bad soap opera. I needed to stop harping about it and do something productive with my time. But as I pulled the covers over my head and drifted off to sleep, I decided that being productive could wait until the next day.

Though I didn't expect the next day to begin with my cell phone blaring at three in the morning. The caustic ring echoed through my quiet bedroom and jolted me awake. I fumbled for my phone and glanced at the name on the caller ID. *Max Samson.*

"Someone had better be dead. Preferably you," I grumbled into the phone.

"Well, look who finally decided to talk to me," Max slurred slightly.

"Are you seriously drunk dialing me right now?" I was suddenly wide awake and completely exasperated.

"Ummm, no?"

"Max, what the hell? Do you have any idea what time it is?"

"Late enough for all the bars to be closed," he quipped, sounding quite pleased with his answer.

"Where are you?"

"Wouldn't you like to know?"

"Max," I warned.

"Okay, okay, don't get your titties in a twist. I'm at Mulvaney's."

"Isn't that in West Chester?" My voice was getting louder as my irritation grew exponentially with every passing second.

"Aren't you quite the little tour guide? How did you know that?"

"Because I went there..." I started to explain, before realizing he was getting me off track. "Does it really fucking matter? How did you get there? Or, more importantly, how are you getting home?"

"I'm not sure what matters to you anymore," he said sadly.

My heart dropped a bit at his words and I realized that, no matter what decisions I made concerning Max and Adam, I'd be hurting someone. *Well, ... shit.* I took a deep breath and calmed down before I spoke again. "Max, how are you getting home?"

His voice was brighter when he replied. "Well, it just so happens that I have this coupon..."

Goddammit. I knew those coupons were a bad idea. I sighed heavily. "I'll be there in forty minutes. Don't go anywhere."

"Thanks, doll," he said before the call disconnected.

And even though I knew he was drunk and would probably never remember most of our conversation, I couldn't help feeling a little thrilled when he called me "doll."

❤

After throwing on a sweat shirt and jeans, I drove to West Chester like a bat out of hell. Thirty-five minutes later, I pulled up in front of Mulvaney's to see Max half sitting, half lying on a bench out front of the bar. I beeped my horn at him and his eyes flickered open. He registered me and then got up slowly and staggered toward my car.

"You look like shit," I said as I pulled away from the sidewalk.

He chuckled. "Nice to see you too."

"So what happened? Did your friends ditch you, or did you ditch them?"

"You know, I'm really not sure."

I shook my head but let it go.

Max leaned his head back and closed his eyes. I thought he had fallen asleep when he spoke again, never opening his eyes. "So, you going to tell me why you didn't call or text me back?"

"Are you even going to remember this conversation tomorrow?"

"Only one way to find out." He had swung his head toward me, looking directly at me.

"Adam doesn't want me to see you anymore." I figured the best way to tell him this news was to treat it like removing a Band-Aid. It was best to just rip the sucker off.

Max straightened up in his seat. "And you agreed to that?" His voice was emotionless, which betrayed just how hurt he really was. Max only bothered to cover up the feelings that affected him the deepest.

"No."

Even from my periphery, I could tell he was confused. "Then, I guess that brings us back to my original question. Why haven't I heard from you?"

"I just . . . need time to get my head on straight. I feel like I'm starring in my own version of *Groundhog Day*. And mine isn't nearly as funny as Bill Murray's."

Max didn't respond, and we drove the rest of the way to his house in silence. I was surprised by his lack of a response. I wasn't sure what I had expected him to say, but I sure as hell had expected *something*.

A short time later, I pulled into his driveway. Max started unbuckling his seat belt before I even had the car in park, but he fumbled with the door handle.

"You need help getting inside?"

"No, I got it," he replied gruffly as he opened the door only to have it immediately swing back closed.

"Sure ya do," I grumbled as I got out of the car and walked around to the passenger side. Pulling the door open wide, I reached down to hook my arm under Max's and began to hoist him up. *God, he's a heavy son of a bitch.*

He leaned back against the rear door, while I closed his. But before I could turn back toward him, I felt his hand roughly grip my bicep, twirling me around and pressing my back against the door I had just closed. He then moved both hands to grip the car behind me, caging me in.

I almost called him out on his rejuvenated sense of coordination but decided to let it go. My skin prickled at his proximity, and memories of what it felt like to have his body pressed against mine flooded my brain. But these were the wrong thoughts to be having right now.

"What the hell do you think you're doing?" I spat.

He gazed at me for a long time, not saying a single word. Eventually, my body started to relax from the lack of conflict, and he noticed it immediately. "I'm reminding you," he finally said.

"Reminding me of what?" I tried to pack my voice with annoyance, but I couldn't hide the genuine curiosity that resided there.

"What it feels like. What *we* feel like."

"*We* don't *feel* like *anything*, Max. We're just friends. And I'm not even so sure we're that."

He moved one hand to tuck a piece of hair behind my ear. The feel of his icy hand reminded me that it was freezing out, but I didn't feel cold. I wasn't sure what I felt.

He replaced his hand on the car. "You're right, Lily. We're not friends. We'll *never* be friends. Because, deep down, you know we're so much more." He leaned in, his lips on a crash course toward mine.

And I wanted it. I wanted his lips on mine so badly, I was nearly consumed by the thought. Until I remembered that this was how Max operated. He took. Whatever he wanted, whenever he wanted it. He had taken my common sense last year, he had taken Adam, he had taken every ounce of friendship I had offered him, and now he was trying to take even more. And I might not have had such a problem with that had it not been for the fact that Max never *gave* anything in return.

So, just as his lips were about to connect with mine, I turned my head away from him. The realization of just how one-sided our friendship was filled me with such unfathomable rage, it made me shake. I had been so fucking blind. All this time, I had been making the effort, trying to be a good friend, to help him get his life together. Then I tell him what *I* need: time. And instead of respecting that or discussing it with me like a normal person, he decides to ignore my needs and take what he wants. Again.

"I'm done with this, Max."

He pulled back from me and hung his head. "I'm sorry, Lily. I know. We're just friends. I'm drunk and got a little carried away. It's fine. We'll—"

"No, I mean I'm really done." I turned my head and waited for him to return my gaze. "With the friendship. With you. With all of it. I won't risk my future on someone who clearly cares so little about me."

His eyes narrowed, and his voice was barely above a

whisper. "How can you say that?"

"Because it's the truth. Everything you do, you do for yourself. The rest of us are merely players in the all-consuming story that is your life. But I'm done being in your story, Max. It's about time I started starring in my own." With that, I pushed his arm out of my way and walked around to the driver's side. Just as I was about to get into my car, I hazarded a look at him. He had backed away from my car, his head bowed, his hands fisted in his pockets. "Goodbye, Max."

I jumped in my car, turned the ignition, and sped away from his house. And even though I was determined not to look back, that was one battle I was never going to win. My eyes darted up to my rearview mirror before his house was out of sight. And there he was, still standing in his driveway just as I had left him.

And I realized why I needed this clean break from him. He was too busy standing still, while I was desperate to move on.

chapter twenty

m a x

I reached up to adjust my tie one last time before entering the reception. *A few more hours and I can get out of this thing.* I liked being in a suit about as much as my dogs liked when I'd get drunk and put them in my old hockey jerseys. As I strolled toward the open bar, I took in my surroundings.

The ballroom was expansive with floor-to-ceiling arched windows along one wall. And the decor matched the feel of the historic hotel: deep gold striped wallpaper wrapped around the room, and dark wood trim accented each doorway.

On the round tables sat centerpieces of red and white roses, and tasteful white Christmas lights created a soft glow in the otherwise dim room. "Who the hell has a wedding on New Year's Eve, anyway? That dumbass ruined an awesome holiday for the rest of his life by agreeing to make it his anniversary."

"No shit," Brian laughed, before turning away for a moment to order two beers for us. "But Gary's been a dumbass since elementary school, and Yasmine has him completely pussy-whipped." Brian paused to take a drink. "At least the worst part's behind us, though. I hate ceremonies. And the fact that it was a Catholic one didn't help. They're so fuckin' long, and since I'm Jewish, I have no idea what the fuck's even happening."

"Well, I'm Catholic," I said, "and I didn't know what the fuck was happening either, so don't feel too bad. Of course that could've been because I was paying more attention to the bridal party than to anything the priest was saying. I mean, did you see the tits on the maid of honor?"

"Did *I* see the tits on the maid of honor?" Brian raised an eyebrow in disbelief and stretched his arms out confidently as he leaned against the dark wooden bar. "Come on, Samson. This is *me* you're talkin' to. That's why I love winter weddings: cold air and low-cut dresses. It's like a Christmas miracle in my pants." A devious smile came across his face, and I braced myself for what might come out of his mouth next. I knew that look well. "Hey, you think if I tell her I still breastfeed, she'll let me suck on those fuckin' things?"

Somehow Brian always managed to cross the line I didn't even know existed until he sprinted over it. "That's sick. Even for you." But I couldn't help but laugh.

"What?" He shrugged. "You act like I'm the only one who says shit like that. Remember that time you asked Trevor's older sister if you could feel her satin pajama bottoms to see how soft they were?"

I smiled at the memory. My first pickup line. "Yeah, I fuckin' remember. Because she let me do it. That was the highlight of my seventh-grade year."

"Well, tonight we're gonna relive those days, my friend. Good call on the no date thing, by the way. It's way easier to pick up chicks if you don't bring one with you."

"Can't argue with sound logic," I said. Even if I'd wanted to bring a date when I'd mailed in the response card over a month ago, I wouldn't have known who to take, so I'd opted to pass on the "plus one." My first instinct would have been to ask Lily—as friends, of course—but now I was definitely thankful I'd gone solo. *Fuck. Come to think of it, I've "gone solo" a lot lately.* "I definitely need to bag someone. I haven't gotten my dick sucked in over a month, and it's killing me," I said. "The only action I've gotten in a while is from Jill."

"Jill? Who's Jill?" Brian asked, intrigued.

"You know Jill," I said, holding up my left fist. "J." I raised my index finger and stuck out my thumb to form the shape of the letter J. "I, L, L," I added as I raised my three other fingers one by one.

Brian nearly spit his beer out as the meaning of my joke sank in. "That's good. Never heard that one before." Then I could practically see the light bulb go on over Brian's head. "You're right-handed, though. What the hell are you doing that with your *left* hand for?"

I shook my head and let out a subtle laugh. "I don't know. I do all the shit I'm not supposed to do with my left hand: drink, smoke, jerk off . . . the list is endless."

"Interesting," Brian replied. "I didn't know you still smoked."

I rolled my eyes. "I don't, asshole."

♥

Dinner dragged as we were seated with some strangers—a heavier woman named Becky, who'd grown up with Yasmine, talked for an hour about how her cat was still throwing up the stuffing from a pillow he'd eaten over a week ago; a couple who didn't speak a single word throughout dinner, even when we spoke to them; a woman in her late fifties who ate everything on her plate, including the decorative flower; and a guy Gary worked with who had just gotten married for the third time. I wondered why his wife hadn't come with him to the wedding. But as I watched him get drunk and start dirty dancing with one of the groomsmen, my guess was that wife number three was filing for divorce at that very minute.

How the fuck did Brian and I get stuck with these losers, especially when we know some of the other people here? Gary would be hearing about this when he got back from his honeymoon. But as we downed our sixth beers and I told a few stories of some memorable games I'd played years ago, the appropriateness of our seating assignment became as clear as the thick lenses in Becky's glasses. We were seated with these losers because, well, we were losers too.

By ten o'clock, I'd had enough of *The Breakfast Club*'s ten-year reunion. If the party wasn't coming to me, I'd have to go to the party. So I stripped off my jacket, loosened my tie, and unbuttoned two of my shirt buttons. It was time to dance.

I didn't make a habit of dancing at weddings. I usually preferred to relax at the bar and then take off early with whoever I'd brought with me. But it was New Year's Eve, and I was shit-faced. I sure as hell wasn't leaving early, especially when I had no one to leave early *with. May as well make the most of it.*

The band played a mix of classic rock, current pop, and modern country mostly, so there was something for everyone. The alcohol coursing through my system made it impossible for me to care how I danced or who I danced *with*. And for a while, I was pretty sure I was dancing with no one at all.

Until I felt a pair of hands slip around my torso and up my chest from behind me. I enjoyed the feeling of her fingers teasing my stomach so much that I almost didn't turn around to face her for fear that I wouldn't like what I saw. Luckily, when I finally did turn, a wave of relief washed over me. She couldn't have been more than twenty-three and was come-in-your-pants gorgeous. Solid Cs, smooth porcelain skin, and the type of hips that begged to be grabbed. So I did, pulling her so that her tight abdomen was against mine and I could feel the graze of her breasts on my chest.

As she moved deliciously to the beat of the music, she ran her hands through her long copper hair, revealing the soft skin on her neck that was glistening with a hint of sweat. My tongue swept across my lips as I imagined sucking her salty flesh. With her eyes closed, she used my body as a pole, sliding up, and then back down again until her face was in line with my crotch. *Fuck, this girl knows how to move.*

With one sharp movement, I spun her around so the crack of her ass in that tight burgundy dress pressed perfectly against my cock. I moved my hands to her stomach, rubbing along the smooth fabric until they made their way down to her thighs and back up again, where they came to rest on the sides of her round ass. She reached around to tangle her fingers in my sweaty hair, and with every gyration, I could feel myself hardening steadily. I got lost in the feeling of the alcohol, the vibration of the music, and this chick's body grinding against mine.

And just when I thought I couldn't have been more right about the whole "coming in my pants" prediction, I felt another set of hands massaging their way up my back. *Oh, fuck yes!* I reached behind me to feel the mysterious body, and I liked what I felt: her toned thighs, the soft curves of her hips. She put her own hand on mine as I teased the hem of her short dress, and I thought I felt her moan against my back at the touch.

In the moment, I was oblivious to the people around me as I pushed on the woman's neck in front of me to bend her over. I rolled my hips against her ass to create the perfect amount of friction I craved. I would have been content to do this all night: rub myself against *one* girl while another rubbed herself against *me*.

It wasn't until Yasmine's horrified gaze locked on mine from across the room that I remembered that I was at a wedding and not in the back room at a strip club. Of course, I would have preferred the latter. But there was no mistaking the judgment in her stare, and I couldn't deny she'd had a right to judge. I was basically having a public threesome during the most magical day of this woman's life, and I hadn't even thought twice about my behavior until then.

I spun Burgundy Dress to face me and pulled her in close as I turned slightly so I could see the girl who had been behind me too. *Thank fuck.* She was just as hot as the other one. "You ladies wanna take this somewhere else?" I asked over the music, though it was more of a demand than a request. I was so fucking hard, I thought I might explode. And I was pretty sure I could get one of these chicks to at least give me a hand job in the bathroom. But convincing both of them to have a little fun would be ringing in the new year with quite a bang, so to speak. The last time I'd had a three-way was the night I'd gotten drafted to the NHL. *God, chicks'll do anything for professional athletes.*

But it occurred to me that I wasn't one anymore. So, when the two agreed to my proposition, I couldn't contain my excitement. With an arm around each of their waists, I led us past my table, where I picked up my jacket and said goodbye to Brian, who could barely hold his head up enough to lick cake off his plate like a puppy. "Don't wait up, sweetheart." I winked as I slapped him hard on the back and then strutted past him out the ballroom doors.

I walked us briskly down a hall to our right that looked like it might have some discreet locations available. I pulled on a few door handles, but was disappointed to find them all locked. Briefly, I thought about getting us a room, but I wasn't sure if these girls were worth four hundred dollars a night. I silently cursed Gary for not picking a seedier neighborhood to get married in.

After trying every possible door with an urgency normally reserved for people attempting to hide from a serial killer, I finally came across an unlocked room, opened the door for the girls, and urged them inside with a playful slap on each of their asses. Closing the door behind me, I let my back rest against it and pulled both girls toward me. My mouth found one of theirs, our tongues mingling in the darkness, while the other one bit my bicep through my shirt and fumbled with my belt. I searched clumsily for a light switch. With the door shut, I couldn't see a thing, and I definitely wanted to witness whatever would be happening here.

At last I found the switch and flicked it on, revealing the mystery room we'd been in. *The fucking bridal suite.* Clothes were strewn across the couch to our right, and makeup and hair supplies cluttered the mirrored dresser to our left. "Why don't you girls get on the couch?" I said. "I'll be right over."

Giggling, they pushed some of the clothing aside and sat side by side on the sofa. "I'm Hallie," the one in the burgundy dress said. "And this is Beth," she said, gesturing to the blonde beside her who had already started caressing Hallie's thigh.

I turned on a lamp on a nearby table and switched off the overhead lighting to dim the room. The music from the reception could be heard coming through a speaker on the wall.

Thanks to Hallie, I think, my belt was already unbuckled. So I pulled it off and let it drop to my feet. "This isn't the first time you've done this, is it?" I asked. These two were way too comfortable with one another for it to have been their first time kissing each other.

Already nibbling on each other's ears and neck, they let their tongues tangle outside their mouths for my viewing pleasure. And it made me as hard as I'd been in recent memory. I didn't know how I wanted to relieve the pressure I felt building inside me. My eyes went to their mouths and soft lips, the insides of their thighs as their dresses crept even higher up their legs. *God, do I love having options.*

"What makes you think that?" Beth asked in a low whisper. I immediately wondered how her breath would feel against my eardrum as she said my name when she came. *My name.* I hadn't told them what it was, though I was pretty sure they probably already knew.

"All of this," I said, gesturing between them as I removed my shirt. "And don't stop. I'm enjoying the show." I settled myself on the chair across from them. "I'm Max, by the way."

"Yeah, we know who you are," Hallie replied, stifling a moan as Beth pulled at her nipple through the fabric of her dress.

"Oh, you do, do you?" I asked playfully, as I palmed myself over my pants to alleviate my need to be touched. I didn't know how long I could hold out before I'd have to ask one of them to do that *for* me. But it was so hot just watching them. "You a fan?"

"A fan of what?" Beth looked confused. "I'm Yasmine's cousin. She just warned me to stay away from you." A devious smile crept across her lips. "But I don't usually do as I'm told. Come on. You gonna come join us?" she asked, shifting to make room for me as she patted the cushion.

I moved to sit between them, closing my eyes and letting Hallie's hand take the place of my own as she slid it beneath my pants and boxers. With every long pull of her warm hand, I felt myself get closer to the release I'd craved since our time on the dance floor. I didn't know how much longer I could last like this, but I would enjoy every fucking second of it.

Ever the gentleman, I thought it was only polite to reciprocate the favor. So I slipped one hand up Hallie's thigh, tickling her skin lightly on the way to my destination. Her breath halted at my touch, and she let out a soft moan as I pulled the lace fabric to the side. Gently, I teased her opening, enjoying the bucking of her hips in response.

Two fingers slid inside easily. This chick was fucking soaked for me. As I stroked the warm insides of her pussy and my thumb swirled with pressure around her clit, I watched as Beth did the same to herself. "Oh, shit. This is like a fucking race," I said. Though I was certain I could win without much effort if I wanted to.

"Oh, Max," Hallie moaned in response, "make me come. Now!"

Yes, ma'am. On cue, I traced a free finger up the crack of her ass, rubbing softly until the pressure became too much and she let go, her cunt clenching in hard spasms around my slippery fingers. I imagined it was my cock inside her, plunging deep as her insides gripped around me tightly. That image, combined with her heavy breaths and soft whimpers, almost pushed me over the edge, but somehow I managed to bring her down slowly from her orgasm while holding off my own.

Then without warning, the girls attacked my mouth with theirs. I could taste the sweet lip gloss one of them was wearing. Strawberry maybe. And my tongue swept across their swollen lips, biting and pulling until my own were sore from the exertion. Then resting my head against the wall behind me, I enjoyed the moment, listening to the urgency of Beth's cries as I tugged hard on her nipple with my fingers.

When she finally came, her moans mixed with the soft music coming from the speakers: "Hard to Love" by Lee Brice. Opening my eyes to gaze into the mirror across from us, I let the girls' mouths and hands devour me as the meaning of the lyrics stared me right in the face: I was selfish, impulsive, and incredibly irresponsible. I couldn't be upset that Lily never loved me the way I loved her. *I* had been the one to sabotage that. And I knew I'd never get her back. I was pretty sure I'd never even had her to begin with. But if I could ever get *anyone* worth loving to love me back, I knew I had to change.

These girls had no clue who I used to be. They didn't know I was once a hockey player. They only knew me as an altogether different type of player now. And nothing I was doing presently would do anything to change their preconceived notion. I watched the proof of that in the mirror as Beth moved her tongue across my chest and Hallie continued to work me until I finally exploded with hot spurts into her palm.

It was nearly midnight after the girls cleaned up in the bathroom. They left before I'd even gotten up to put my shirt back on. And I couldn't say I was disappointed. They knew as well as I did what this had been: three strangers having a little fun for the sake of sexual gratification—nothing more.

Nothing more. The words bounced around my mind like a racquetball in an empty room. And as hard as I tried, I couldn't escape their echo. Nothing in my life had ever been anything *more.* I'd lived thirty years never putting anything into any relationship except for the bare minimum.

But as I stared at my reflection and listened to the countdown to the new year through the speaker, the realization hit me: it didn't matter who I used to be. It only mattered who I *could* be. In 2013, I'd been an egocentric asshole who'd made it impossible for anyone to love him.

But in 2014, I planned to be someone else entirely.

I spent much of the next week rehashing what had happened during the past year. Two thousand thirteen had begun as a year full of hope, full of promise. I'd started it with the opportunity to clean up my image and start fresh. But now, there I sat, one year later, thinking the same exact fucking thing as if nothing had changed at all.

What had gone so wrong that an entire year had passed without any progress at all? It seemed like for every step I took forward, I took two more back. And I had no one to blame for that but myself. I'd been the one walking backward.

I'd been the one to try to kiss Lily a week ago when she'd been selfless enough to pick me up in the middle of the night.

I'd been the one to fuck everyone with a beating heart and tits since Lily had said she'd never wanted to see me again last spring. *I'd* been the one to leave Swift Middle School without any sort of job opportunity. And *I'd* been the one to let Adam know about my relationship with Lily in the first place.

The irony was that I was about to give him that same news again.

But this time, I hoped it would bring them together instead of tear them apart. Lily's relationship with Adam would suffer, or disintegrate completely, if he didn't know I was out of the picture. If I had any hope of making *my* life and the lives of those around me better, I had to own up to my mistakes, no matter how difficult that would be.

Surprisingly, as I waited for Adam to get home from work and a light snow began to fall, I had no reservations about my decision to talk to him. It was the right thing to do. And I so rarely did what was right.

At just after five, through my snow-speckled windshield, I saw Adam's SUV pull in. As he made his way to the end of the driveway toward the mailbox, I exited my car, careful to maintain the distance between us. I had already interfered in his life, and I didn't want to intrude any more than necessary by stepping onto his property.

"Adam," I said, my voice even and steady as I stood on the sidewalk. Through the darkness, I could see him turn to face me, but I knew he didn't recognize the voice. "It's Max." I paused to see if he'd respond. When he didn't, I continued. "I was hoping I could talk to you for a minute."

As he took a few steps toward me, I couldn't help but be thankful that my history as a hockey player would help me take a punch if Adam decided to throw one. It wouldn't have been the first time.

He didn't get close enough to hit me. Though his clenched fists were a good indication that he was probably fighting the urge to do so. I tried to read his expression through the darkness. His open posture, and the fact that he'd come toward me instead of immediately going inside, made me think that he might listen to what I had to say. But his eyes held anger. They had a right to.

And when he spoke, his voice held it too. "You've got some nerve coming here. To *my* house. When my daughter's inside," he said, gesturing toward his home. "You just can't stay out of my life, can you?"

Something told me Adam's question was rhetorical, so I let it pass unanswered.

The soft snow that had coated the ground created a silence so obvious that it was, strangely enough, almost audible. Adam seemed to be making every effort to be quiet, probably so his daughter didn't hear us. But despite the fact that he spoke each word in a whisper, I could tell he was screaming them inside. His lips barely moved as he spoke in a clear effort to restrain himself. "You've got two minutes to tell me why the fuck you're here, asshole, before I beat your ass on my fucking front lawn."

Since I'd gotten out of my car, my eyes hadn't left Adam's. It was almost as if we were two wild animals staring each other down to intimidate the other. I let my face soften before I spoke, allowing myself to be the first to back down for the first time in my life. I hoped that Adam would hear the sincerity I *felt* as I said the words. "I came here to tell you she's yours."

chapter twenty-one

a d a m

"Mine? I'm sorry, I didn't know I needed *your* fucking permission to date someone." I shook my head, keeping my eyes locked on his. *Arrogant prick.* "When was she *yours* to give away? Did I miss something?" I stepped closer, ready to make good on my promise of pummeling him in my yard. My eyes darted quickly toward a few of my neighbors' houses as I wondered briefly if I could pull an Edward Norton and curb this asshole without anyone noticing.

"Look, you have every reason to be upset. I—"

"I'm not 'upset.' I . . . I don't know what I am." I could feel the anger building inside me as I ran my other hand through my hair, exasperated and unsure of what to do next. "You know . . . I don't even know why I'm trying to explain my emotions to *you*. You deserve *nothing*." My teeth clenched, and I suddenly found myself two inches from that douchebag's face in an effort to keep my voice down. "You . . . You're . . . God, you're not even worth it," I growled as I waved my hand toward him dismissively.

"I'm not gonna argue with you about that. What happened was *my* fault. But I still want you to know why I did it." Max's initially guarded posture softened slightly, and it was clear he wouldn't fight me even if I wanted him to, so for some reason— chalk it up to pure curiosity—I let him continue. "I loved her. We're more alike than you think, Adam ... me and you. I loved her. Just like you did. But she didn't love me then, and she doesn't love me now. I know nothing I can say will make you change your opinion of me. But I was hoping"—he hesitated— "that it might make you change your opinion of *her*."

"You don't know shit about my opinion of her."

"No? Well, I know you asked her not to see me anymore because you don't trust her."

The fact that he knew all this only proved that Lily had been talking to him about me. About *us*. And the thought sickened me. "How the fuck do you know all this?"

"She told me." He shrugged. "And I also know she didn't agree to it. At first," he added.

At first? Did that mean that she'd eventually told him she wouldn't see him anymore? She hadn't told me any of that.

"A few days after Christmas, I called her for a ride home, shit-faced and acting like an asshole. I know, right? What else is new?" He rolled his eyes at his own recklessness. "She told me she was done with me ... that all I do is *take* from her. And she's right. I'm selfish. So for once in my fucking life, I'm trying to do something for someone other than myself." His eyes shot toward the ground, as if he were submitting to the truth of his next words. "She loves you, Adam. And I can't stand in the way of that." Finally, he raised his gaze, and I actually thought I saw a spark of sincerity in his eyes. "Not again."

♥

I hadn't been prepared to believe anything that came from Max's mouth. So it surprised me when I took his words seriously. He'd told me he was done with her. He was bowing out of the race. And he seemed to think that made Lily mine.

But she wasn't mine. And I knew the only reason that wasn't the case was because *I'd* been the one to maintain the emotional distance between us. And I'd done that to protect my own feelings. But now I wondered if I was hurting myself *more* by *not* allowing our relationship to progress the way a typical adult relationship should.

The one thing I did know was that I couldn't protect my feelings forever. At some point, if I wanted anything more to develop between us, I'd need to go all in. Even if that meant getting hurt again. I had only two choices: I could believe that Lily and Max were done with each other, or I could continue on this inevitable course to nowhere.

And only one of those choices had the potential for a happy ending. And fuck if I wouldn't do almost anything for one of those lately.

The decision had been made before I'd even realized I'd made it. I popped my head into my front door and yelled up to Eva, "I need to run out for an hour or so, honey. I forgot something at my office. I'll pick up dinner on the way home." I briefly felt guilty for lying so easily to my daughter. That was until I reminded myself that she probably lied way more to *me*.

♥

"Who is it?" Lily asked when I buzzed her apartment.

Shit. Suddenly it occurred to me that she could be busy. And here I was, showing up at her apartment like a desperate boyfriend. What if she didn't give me the invitation I'd hoped for? "Uh, it's Adam. Sorry, I—"

"Adam?" She clearly seemed surprised it was me. But if I wasn't mistaken, she seemed surprised in a good way.

Leaning against the doorframe of her apartment, wearing nothing but black yoga pants and a tight gray V-neck T-shirt, stood the most beautiful woman I'd ever seen. "Hey," she said, confused. "I don't mean to be . . . but what are you do—"

"I can do this," I cut her off. "This." I motioned with my hand between us. "I can do it."

chapter twenty-two

l i l y

In a split second, I'd analyzed Adam's expression. His stare was unmistakable. It was the same stare I'd seen during our first night in the hotel together; his eyes held desire, trust, and undeniable urgency all wrapped up into one solid package. My eyes scanned down his body until they stopped just below his waist. *Speaking of nice packages.*

I wasn't looking at his face, but I didn't need to. His actions spoke for him. Before I could eye-fuck Adam's "package" any longer, I found myself pressed up against it, as his lips parted mine with a determination he hadn't demonstrated since we'd started dating again. Gone was the hesitation and uncertainty we'd felt together. In its place was a longing and need for each other. And I knew Adam could feel it too.

My back found the wall as Adam kicked the door shut, not missing a beat as he worked his mouth swiftly down my neck and chest. I'd forgotten how much I missed the feel of his soft lips on my skin. And as he tugged gently with his teeth on my taut nipples through my shirt, I ached to feel them inside his warm wet mouth.

I gasped as his tongue traveled up my chest, his lips planting soft kisses along my collarbone on the way to suck hungrily on the flesh of my neck. And an unexpected shiver ran through me at the feel of his breath blowing tantalizingly against my wet skin.

His name was barely a whisper as it left my mouth. And a low growl vibrated against my heart as it escaped his throat. "Touch me, Lily," he groaned. "Like you used to."

And like that, we were back to who we were almost a year ago. Moaning into his neck, I pulled at his messy hair, clawed his biceps, and slipped into the back of his jeans to knead his firm ass through his boxers.

Finally, he slid a hand under my shirt to feel the curve of my heavy breasts, and my body tingled with pleasure as I rubbed shamelessly against him. His hips pushed into mine, forcing me harder against the wall, and I relished the feel of his hard cock rubbing against my clit through my thin cotton pants. *Thank God I'm not wearing underwear.* The combination of that friction and his thumb circling my nipple was nearly enough to push me over the edge.

From the moment I'd seen Adam standing in the hallway—ripped jeans, a worn T-shirt, and Carhartt jacket—a slick wetness had gradually begun to pool inside my pants. And now, the slippery arousal between my thighs overwhelmed me, silently begging Adam to relieve the pressure building inside. Unable to control it, my breath escaped in rough bursts, and my heart pounded so loudly I could hear it banging against my chest.

Adam guided my leg around him forcefully, creating more

of the delicious stimulation I craved. "Arms up," he said sternly, and I did as I was told, savoring the feeling as he quickly tugged my shirt up past my neck and over my head.

"Feel how much I want you, Adam. Feel what you do to me," I said as I guided his hand down the front of my pants to tease my clit before he plunged two fingers deep inside me.

"I'm gonna get you so close. Because once I'm inside you, I don't think I can be slow. Or gentle," he added with a beautifully deep rasp that tickled my eardrum as he spoke. No wonder I'd had so much trouble doing this to myself. I'd lacked Adam's intimate touch and the feel of his body on mine. How could I forget about *those*? The combination of it all drove me wild. His long delicate fingers stroked me, played with me, and pushed me so close to the edge that I would have lost all control with one more tap of his thumb.

But luckily, Adam's intimate knowledge of my sexual responses hadn't faded with time, and he pulled out slowly, just in time to leave me empty and wanting. "Oh God, Adam, I've missed this," I moaned into his mouth. "I need you."

The unbuckling of his belt was his only response and was quickly followed by a tug to free himself. As much as I missed Adam's fingers slipping inside me, I thought I might come as he teased me through the fabric with the head of his cock. "God, that's so hot. Please," I begged.

"Please what?" he asked playfully.

My inhibitions had wavered the moment Adam had kissed me. And now, up against a wall, grinding onto the tip of his dick, the few inhibitions I had managed to hang onto left me the moment his fingers withdrew. My need for a release, my need for *him,* went beyond any coherent sentence I could string together. So I mumbled something that resembled

"Please fuck me," and hoped he'd interpret my message.

At my words, Adam reached into his back pocket and withdrew a condom. Then he pulled down his pants before yanking down mine as far as he could so I could take them off the rest of the way. Adam quickly put the condom on and pushed inside me, sliding me up the wall with his hard thrusts. My legs locked around his waist, pulling him deeper inside me as my shoulder blades scraped the drywall, the pain only making the pleasure more intense.

His pace was uneven and erratic, every drive like an urgent plea for me to take what he offered. And what he gave me not only filled me physically but emotionally as well. We'd been missing this—this closeness, this completeness that came with being part of each other even for such a brief moment. It seemed that with every sharp drive of his hips into mine, we became that much closer to where we were when our relationship began.

A few more strokes of his cock deep inside me and I was dangling on the edge. I clenched tightly around him, seconds away from losing control. His quickening pace and sharp breaths told me he was right there with me, ready to come at any moment, but he wasn't going to leave me behind. "I can't wait, Lily. Let go! Please! I don't wanna finish without you."

Adam's swirling hips created friction in just the right place, and when I heard his words, I lost all control of my body. My legs shook, and I spasmed uncontrollably as Adam drove hard into me, his thickness twitching inside me as my orgasm tapered off.

I relaxed my legs and let Adam slide me gently down the wall to my feet. "Jesus, Adam. That was incredible."

"Yeah," he said against my lips before pulling away. "It was."

I ran my hand across his cheek. "Your eyes are different."

He looked at me, confused. "Different? Like a different color?"

Smiling, I shook my head. "The way they're looking at me. It's different. What changed?"

Adam paused for a few seconds, seemingly contemplating what to say before speaking. "*I* did. I forgive you. And more than that, I trust you. I can't keep making you pay for what happened over eight months ago. It's not fair to you." Adam put his arms around me, pulling me in to a firm hug. "It's not fair to *us*."

❤

For the first time since we'd started dating, Adam and I had a serious conversation about our relationship, one that ended with both of us feeling at ease. We'd discussed sharing our new identity as a "couple" with people, even Eva, and Adam agreed that it was for the best. Letting friends and family know that we were back together would only solidify our relationship publicly.

Although I had already let some people know I had been seeing Adam, he hadn't told anyone. And truthfully, I could understand why: if it didn't work out again, he didn't want to have to explain it to everyone. I knew the feeling.

We'd made progress since the talk, making time to see each other when we could for coffee or a quick bite to eat. But I was ravenous with the need to spend more than a few hours together, though it seemed we'd soon have our chance. Eva had the Snow Ball—her first formal dance—on Friday and was having a slumber party at a friend's house afterward. Which meant Adam and I would have his house to ourselves.

With Eva gone for the night, I would finally get to spend a night with Adam. He had assured me last week that he'd discuss our relationship with Eva, and he thought she would handle it well. But seeing a former student the morning after you came on her dad's face was a whole other story. Talk about awkward.

❤

Adam came to pick me up around six o'clock, and when I saw him standing in the entrance to my apartment complex, I immediately felt underdressed in yoga pants and a sweat shirt. "Why are you so dressed up? I thought we were just gonna order Chinese and watch a movie."

"I'm not *that* dressed up. Just khakis and a sweater. I couldn't look like a slob to take Eva to her pictures before the dance."

Of course. I was such a moron. I should have known that Adam would have dropped Eva off and taken a few pictures of her and her friends. There would have been other parents there, and he would never just wear sweats to that. "Ah, pictures. I totally forgot. I would have gone with you. Of course, looking a little better than this," I added, tugging at my Ocean City sweat shirt. "I would've liked to have seen some of my old students dressed up."

When we arrived at the car, Adam shifted to put his seat belt on, started the car, and turned the heat on high. "It'll warm up in a few minutes," he said. "Just give it some time."

"I know how heaters work, Adam." The car was already warm since he'd just been driving it. Clearly, he was trying to avoid responding to my comment about seeing Eva and her friends before the dance, so I figured it was better I dropped it. "How'd Eva look? Was she excited?"

"She looked so grown up. It was so weird. Her date kept trying to put his arm too low on her waist for the pictures. I had to put him in his place a few times," he said, his voice intentionally stern as he mocked the way he spoke to Eva's date. "Is it wrong to punch a thirteen-year-old?" he asked with a laugh, though I could tell he was only partially kidding.

"Who *was* her date? I didn't even ask before."

"Uh . . . Christian Grey or something like that."

The laugh that burst out of me was the hardest I'd laughed around Adam in as long as I could remember. "Well, if that's the case, you better turn around and go get her," I said, still trying to catch my breath.

"Why," he asked sternly. "What type of kid is he?"

"He's not a kid, Adam. He's a fictional character from a book, and one who's into BDSM. I don't think you want him taking out your thirteen-year-old daughter."

"Oh," he replied, a little embarrassed. "I knew that name sounded familiar."

"I think you meant Chris Greyston, as in Christopher. He's a nice kid. He plays soccer, I think. He gets good grades . . . the responsible type. No need to be worried."

"Oh, okay. He sounds like my kinda guy, then."

"Yeah, though I'd probably pick a Christian Grey type over a nice guy any day. I like a little mystery and danger in my life."

"Danger, huh?" Adam asked, looking over at me with a slight twinkle in his eye. "I'm dangerous," he said, stepping on the gas until he accelerated to a few miles over the speed limit.

"You like that?" he asked. "I do that shit all the time. I've also been known to go swimming only a few minutes after I eat," he said with a laugh. "And I always hold scissors by the handle when I walk."

I shook my head and rolled my eyes. "Scissors, really? That sounds dangerous," I said, lowering my voice seductively and leaning in to put a hand on his thigh.

"Yeah, well, ya know...not *too* dangerous. I never run with them. Walk quickly at most," he said with a wink.

❤

As we pulled into his driveway, it occurred to me that the last time I'd been to Adam's house—the only time I'd been there actually—had been under very different circumstances. We'd hit a breaking point from which it seemed impossible to return. And now, here we were, months later, back.

After he unlocked the door, Adam held it for me to go inside. The act was just as symbolic as it was literal. Adam had opened the door to his life and, at last, let me in. Even when we'd dated months ago, we'd kept our relationship somewhat secretive. Or at least Adam had, and that was understandable because of Eva. But now, with our feelings for each other out in the open, we could finally begin to intertwine our lives into one.

"Make yourself at home," Adam said. "I'm just gonna hop in the shower. I didn't have time to take one after work before I had to take Eva out for pictures."

"Hmm...make myself at home," I said, glancing around the foyer and peeking into the adjacent room like I was deep in thought. I was. "Does that mean I can look through your medicine cabinet and lie around in my underwear?"

"Uh . . . not sure what you'd want to do the first one for, but the second sounds like a great option." He leaned in to kiss me gently, cupping my chin in his hand before heading upstairs.

Why the hell did I say the medicine cabinet thing? He probably thinks I'm some kind of a creepy voyeur, hoping to spy on his private life. As soon as the thought crossed my mind, the irony that I *was* part of his private life sank in. Adam had nothing to hide from me, and the thought put me at ease.

I shuffled from room to room, taking note of the home's decor. Modern touches adorned each room of the downstairs. Granite counters wrapped around the kitchen's perimeter and tall cherry cabinets stretched to the ceiling. Light hickory floors complemented the beautiful cool tones of the walls: deep cream in the living room, soft blue in the foyer spanning to the upstairs hallway, crisp white with a hint of gray to pick up the specks of silver in the black countertops. But the more traditional structural elements—archways between rooms, crown molding in the living room, wainscoting in the foyer and stairway—provided a nice contrast. Adam clearly had good taste.

I heard the shower turn on upstairs as I strolled from room to room, admiring the framed artwork and photographs that decorated his home. A picture of Eva as a baby in Adam's arms sat on an end table in the living room. He looked like a baby himself: only twenty years old, but forced to grow up so quickly. I picked up another picture of who I assumed were Adam's parents. Of course I had no way of knowing because I'd never met them. But seated at the head of the table in front of a huge turkey was Adam. And the age of the people on either side of him, as well as their striking resemblance, told me they were probably his mom and dad.

Without realizing it, I followed a mosaic of pictures up the stairs. I'd always wanted a stairway filled with photos when I "grew up." The problem was that I didn't have any stairs yet. Or any pictures worthy of being hung for that matter. But Adam's wall was full: pictures of Eva, other relatives, some photos of him playing baseball, hunting. I didn't even know he liked to hunt. Looking at how full Adam's life was only made me more aware of my own life's emptiness.

As I ascended the stairs, I heard the shower shut off, and a rush of adrenaline coursed through me at the thought of Adam stepping out of the shower dripping wet with a towel around his waist. Entering his room, I took a seat on the bed, quietly waiting for him to emerge from the steamy bathroom, hopefully just as I'd pictured. And when he finally did, the real vision didn't disappoint. His damp messy hair hung across his forehead, and as I let my gaze drift back down, my eyes stopped on the water that glistened off the soft hairs of his firm chest. I imagined catching a stray droplet with my tongue as it slid down his solid stomach.

But I didn't dare move yet—not until I took in the entire image standing before me. I bit my lip, silently admiring the way he gripped the towel in one hand, pulling it tightly enough to allow me a glimpse at the outline of his dick. I thought I saw it twitch as he spoke. "See something you like?" he asked, raising an eyebrow as an invitation.

As if by reflex, I rose from the bed and moved toward him, slipping my hands around him. His warm, damp skin smelled of aftershave and clean body wash. "I like *everything* about you. Especially this," I said, running my palm above the towel to feel his thick shaft get harder as I massaged it.

Adam let his towel drop, giving me full access to his hard cock. I stroked his length slowly, teasingly, skimming the head with my fingers to rub around the bead of fluid that had accumulated at the tip.

In one swift motion, Adam had me in the air, moving me toward the bed and stripping my shirt off within seconds of placing me on my back. With a rough tug, he removed my pants and tossed them aside. "No underwear again?" he asked. "I like this new habit of yours."

He kissed down my stomach, blowing teasingly on the way down to his destination. I moaned in pleasure as he kissed, licked, and sucked at my opening. With each lap of his tongue, I begged for him to make me come, feeling myself get closer with every groan against my clit. His fingers invaded me gently, then harder until I thought I would explode at any moment. "Oh God, Adam...please."

The sound of Adam's phone was the only thing that prevented the release I craved. To my surprise, Adam stopped to grab his phone off the nightstand to answer it. *Fuck.* I imagined I felt like a guy did when a girl stopped sucking his dick right before he came. I thought briefly about finishing myself off while Adam was on the phone, but I was too distracted watching him pace the room giving monosyllabic responses to his caller.

"It's Eva," he said suddenly after tossing the phone on his bed. "I gotta go get her. The douchebag she went to the dance with was a jerk to her. She's crying." He threw on sweats and grabbed his wallet and keys from his dresser. "I'll drop you off first."

Wait, what? Can't we finish what we started first? But I could never say that. "Adam, just get her first and then drop me off. The school's closer."

I could tell I'd caught him off guard with my comment, but I couldn't figure out why. Until he told me.

"Uh...Lily." He looked at me cautiously, as though he were trying to gauge how I'd react to his next words. "I haven't told Eva about us yet."

Huh? Did I hear him right? "What?" My voice was strained, angry. "You told me you'd told her."

"I will. I swear. It's just weird. I don't know what to say to her." His hurried tone told me he was possibly more annoyed than I was. And I didn't know how the fuck that was possible. "Can we talk about this later? Let's just go."

"Sure," I said, because I didn't know what else to say. I certainly wasn't about to say what I'd been thinking. Mostly because, at this point, I didn't know what to think. About anything.

chapter twenty-three

l i l y

The past week with Adam had been strained. I kept wondering when we'd stop making everything so difficult and just let our relationship unfold without all the bullshit. And even though we'd talked a few times, there was still an occasional awkward silence, some internal questioning of how he would interpret things I said, and a vague feeling like something was missing between us. I couldn't identify what that "something" was, but I felt its absence frequently enough to obsess about it. *Typical girl shit.*

And as I stood in front of my closet, trying to figure out what to wear, I decided to let it go. Whatever Adam and I were meant to be, we'd be. Things were bound to be a little weird. I'd essentially cheated on him with a professional athlete. That kind of shit would scar any relationship. I just hoped that the scars would fade with time.

Grabbing my Flyers jersey, I pulled it over my head. Shane and Amanda had offered us the two extra tickets they had for the game that night before Adam and I had our disagreement over his failing to tell Eva about our relationship. I hadn't seen him since and wasn't completely sure how tonight was going to go. *Guess I'll find out soon enough.* I was reaching for my jeans, the ones that cupped my ass perfectly, when my phone rang. I looked down at the caller ID and smiled. "Hey. Can't make it another hour without talking to me?"

Adam exhaled a loud breath. "Hey, baby."

My posture straightened and my brow furrowed with concern. "What's wrong?"

"Eva's sick. She came home from school complaining about her stomach, but I figured she was just being dramatic. Then the puking started. I can't leave her like this. I'm sorry."

Disappointment crept through my veins, even though I tried to stave it off. I knew I couldn't be pissed because he was a good father who didn't ditch his sick kid so that he could go to a hockey game with his girlfriend. But, for a shameless second, I kind of wished he was more of a scumbag. "No need to apologize, Adam. I completely understand that you need to be with Eva. No worries."

"You're not mad?"

"Mad that you're a responsible father who loves his daughter? I find it simply infuriating," I said with a laugh.

"Guess these are the downsides of dating a guy with a child."

"Will you stop? It's no big deal."

He hesitated a moment before continuing. "So, what will you do with the extra ticket?"

The slightly detached tone of his voice made me think that he was trying to unsuccessfully mask his clear interest in my answer. I couldn't help but feel like I was being tested.

And while I might have deserved to be tested, it still pissed me off. I took some relaxing breaths before responding. "They're Amanda's tickets. I'll call her and see if she has anyone else who wants to go. It may be a tough sell on a weeknight, but tomorrow's Friday, so maybe someone won't mind being tired for just one day." Despite my trying to rein in my emotions, I couldn't keep the coolness from my voice.

"Oh, okay. Sounds good. Listen, I better go, but have fun tonight. I'll miss you."

His sweet words thawed me enough to respond genuinely. "I'll miss you too. Let me know if you need anything."

We said our goodbyes and disconnected the call. I stared down at the phone in my hand, doubt crawling into me. When Adam and I were together, it felt so *right.* Even with the weird moments that passed between us and the sense of something lacking, I still felt like I was exactly where I was supposed to be. But when we were apart, I couldn't help but think about the negatives. Though, no relationship came without its issues. If we could get through last spring, we could get through this. Couldn't we?

"Time will tell," I muttered to myself. I quickly scrolled through my contacts and hit Amanda's name.

"No, you cannot fuck Adam on center ice. It's totally inappropriate."

I laughed loudly at Amanda's unorthodox greeting. *This is why I love this crazy girl.* "Are you really one to judge the inappropriateness of something?"

"Are you?" she countered.

"No, probably not."

"Definitely not. Now what do you want, hooker? We're leaving in about fifteen minutes to pick you guys up."

"Well, see, that's the problem. Adam isn't coming."

"Why not? Jesus Christ, you're not fucking one of the Flyers are you?"

"I truly hate you. Like from the depths of my being." I sighed. "Eva's sick, so he has to stay home with her."

"Damn kids. They ruin everything."

I shook my head at her insensitivity, but not without acknowledging that I had thought something very similar only five minutes prior.

"Do you know anyone else who'd want to go? It'd suck to lose money on the ticket."

"I dunno. Let me call around. We'll see you in a bit."

"Okay." I hung up and finished getting ready, hoping Amanda didn't invite some wacko just to fuck with me.

Twenty minutes later, my cell phone lit up with a text.

We're here.

I grabbed my clutch, locked the apartment, and made my way out to Shane's car.

My reticence at who Amanda would call to join us abated as soon as I saw the figure leaning out of the back window, waving at me like a lunatic. *Kyle.*

Kyle and Amanda were fuck buddies before she started dating Shane and Kyle started dating Shane's coworker Kate. Though, to my knowledge, the specifics of Kyle and Amanda's relationship were not common knowledge to their current significant others.

The door to Shane's Mustang flew open as Kyle yelled, "Ah, my princess has finally arrived. And she's wearing a Flyers jersey. Be still my heart."

"You're such an asshole." I giggled and drew him into a hug.

"What's up, Lily?" Shane greeted.

"Hey, Shane," I replied warmly before turning back to Kyle. "Thanks for filling in tonight. I was worried I was going to be the odd man out."

"Yeah, Amanda called and said your boyfriend had stood you up and you needed a big dick to cheer you up."

"He's got the big dick part down. And I'm not talking about his penis size," Amanda quickly retorted.

I saw the exact moment when she realized what she said. Her head snapped toward Kyle, who raised his eyebrows at her. They both looked stealthily toward Shane and then back to each other. *Nope, Shane definitely doesn't know about the sexcapades that went on between Amanda and Kyle.*

Shane either didn't register the comment or chose to ignore it.

I spoke, hoping to move us past the deafening silence. "Yup, I've been stood up in favor of a puking teenager. I must have really lost my appeal. I need to step up my game."

"You have no game," Amanda said.

"And you do?"

"Of course. How do you think I wrangled this sexy beast over here?" She roughly patted Shane's thigh to emphasize her words.

"By shoving your tits in my face," Shane countered.

"Bullshit!" Amanda yelled. "I never did that. I had you at hello."

"Had me agitated and contemplating homicide maybe."

"You don't value your life at all, do you?" Amanda threatened.

"Clearly not. Look at what I subject myself to." Shane waved a hand in Amanda's direction. When she didn't reply, he quickly looked over and saw her menacing glare before swinging his eyes back to the road. When, after a full minute, she still hadn't replied, Shane chanced another glance at her. Her eyes were still boring into his head as though she were trying to incinerate him with them. "Why are you staring at me like that?"

"I'm trying to figure out if you look better in blue or gray."

"What? Why does that matter?"

"So I know which suit to dress you in for your funeral."

"Oh," Shane said, relaxing. "Definitely gray."

"Blue it is," she replied as she slunk back into her seat.

"Just don't fuck up my face. I'd like to have an open casket." Shane was obviously trying to keep her talking in an effort to gauge whether or not she was really mad or just messing around. I couldn't blame him. Amanda could be a difficult person to read.

"I can't make any promises." Amanda tried to keep her voice serious, but I could hear the smile behind it.

Shane reached across the center console and grabbed Amanda's hand, pulling it back toward him so he could comfortably hold it.

"Lily?" Kyle asked sweetly.

"Yeah?" I replied.

"Would you hold my hand all the way to the stadium? I want to be totally lame like Amanda and Shane."

I burst out laughing as Amanda hissed out a "Fuck you" and Shane shook his head.

I finally managed to suck in enough air to reply. "I dunno. Won't that mean we're going steady?"

"Absolutely. I'll even give you my letterman's jacket to sweeten the deal."

"Groovy," I released breathily.

"All right, assholes," Amanda humorlessly interjected. "Unless you want to walk the rest of the way to the stadium, knock it the hell off."

"She's so snippy," I whispered loudly enough for Amanda to hear.

"I know. She must have gotten caught necking at the drive-in," Kyle added.

"Enough!" Amanda yelled, which caused Kyle and me to completely lose it in the back seat.

The rest of the drive passed with Kyle and me teasing Amanda and Shane, and Amanda pretending it pissed her off. It was the lightest I'd felt in weeks.

❤

Kyle and I were quite a pair. After skipping hand-in-hand into the stadium behind Amanda and Shane, begging "Mom and Dad" to buy us dinner, and asking them to take us to the bathroom, we made our way to our seats. When Shane led us onto the escalator, Amanda must have noticed the mischievous gleam in my eyes because she immediately warned, "If you start doing something stupid like running back down this escalator, I swear I will tell your principal about your deviant behavior in his school last year."

My eyes narrowed on her. *This traitorous slut did not just say that in front of Shane and Kyle.*

She propped her hand on her hip and threw me a smug look that said, "Oh yes, I did."

It took Kyle about five seconds to process Amanda's words, but I knew the second it finally clicked. He immediately whipped toward me, his mouth agape. "Please tell me that's true."

"I can neither confirm nor deny," I said coolly as I crossed my arms over my chest.

"Holy shit! In a school? Where there are children?"

I winced at his words. Despite obviously knowing that there were children in my school, I hadn't really *thought* about them being there. That might seem ridiculous, considering they provided the background chatter to one of my more illicit sexual encounters in the backstage of the auditorium, but I hadn't felt as dirty and creepy about it then as I did now. *Well, too late to do anything about it.*

Kyle took my silence as tacit agreement.

"Stop staring at me," I snapped at him, though my lips quirked into a half smile.

"I can't. You're like a unicorn. I thought this one had no shame," he said as he jerked a thumb in Amanda's direction, "but you're on a whole new level."

"As thrilled as I am to be a mythical creature, I'd like to move on now."

"I can't. It's like I'm a little kid who's met their hero. That's it! You're my sexual hero."

I shook my head as we got off the escalator.

"If I bought you a cape, would you wear it?"

I thought for a moment before enthusiastically nodding. *Who am I to turn down a cape?* I'd been so preoccupied by Kyle's adoration that it took me a minute before I realized where we were. "Do we have tickets in a suite?"

Shane turned his head slightly to answer me as he kept

walking. "Yeah. I got them from Tyler at the gym. His law firm has season tickets up here."

"Why'd he give them to *you*?" My tone was more condescending than I'd intended, so I tried to backpedal. "I mean...I didn't mean that in a bad way. Just... God, never mind. I'm an ass."

Shane laughed his easygoing laugh. "Well, you're definitely right about being an ass. I know this is hard for you girls to believe, but some people actually *appreciate* what I do for them at the gym."

"Fools," Amanda quipped as she scanned the signs for our suite number. "Here we are."

We opened the door and stepped into awesomeness. There was a waitress there who I instantly decided was put on this earth to make me happy. "Can I get you guys anything before the game starts?" she asked us warmly.

"You guys want a beer?" Shane asked, to which he received a resounding "Hell yes."

As Claudia, as her name tag read, walked off to get our drinks, I leaned forward and rested my forearms on the railing. "Where are the baskets?"

"Baskets? What are you talking about?" Kyle asked.

His reply reminded me of the last hockey game I had attended. I had met Adam at one of the Swift Middle School games and he had tried to explain the game to me. We had been having a lot of fun, until Max slipped up and called me "doll" in front of Adam and I had then lied and told Adam I loved him to cover my ass. *Ah, memories.* "Shouldn't there be baskets that the guys throw the balls in?"

I saw Amanda smirk in my peripheral vision. It was true that I knew next to nothing about hockey, but even *she* knew that I wasn't *this* dumb.

"Are you for real right now?" Shane added. I could see in his face that he suddenly regretted letting Amanda choose who came with them to the game.

"Do I have the wrong sport? Is there a goalpost instead?" The boys stared at me in disbelief.

Then the players emerged onto the ice, and I clapped excitedly "Ooh, look. They have ice skates."

"How are you friends with her?" Kyle asked Amanda.

"What do you mean?" I asked, feigning offense. "I was just your sexual hero five minutes ago."

"I'm seriously reconsidering giving you that honor right now."

"Lily, you really didn't know they wore skates in hockey?" Shane's tone reflected one he might use with his niece Mackenzie.

Finally, Amanda threw her arms up in exasperation. "Guys, really? She spent the better part of six months fucking a professional hockey player. Do you really think she didn't pick up *anything* during that time? Morons."

"You always ruin all my fun," I whispered to her.

"I couldn't take it anymore. It's a wonder they're able to dress themselves."

The game passed quickly, and before I knew it, I was hugging Claudia for making all my food and beverage needs come true. *I may be a tad drunk.*

We walked out into the mezzanine and toward the escalators. My eyes registered a commotion off to the left, and I innocently turned my attention in that direction. *Fuck, shit, motherfucking whore.* As if sensing me, his blue eyes shifted and locked on mine, effectively depleting all the oxygen in the room and causing all the people between us to fade into the backdrop. *What the hell is he doing here? And why is he holding a microphone?*

Amanda followed my gaze. "Oh, you've got to be shittin' me."

"What's wrong?" Shane asked, concern lacing his words.

"You'll see. It's heading this way," Amanda said, a little too amused for my liking.

I whirled my head away from her and back toward where Max had been standing. Only he wasn't standing there anymore. He was on the move . . . right for us. I took him in as he took deliberate, confident steps. He was wearing a white dress shirt, the top two buttons undone, sleeves rolled up, coupled with gray slacks. *God really outdid himself when he created Max.* I shook my head softly, needing to wipe those thoughts from it. I had to sober up. Fast.

Max sidled up to us and stuffed his hands in his pockets, making him look even hotter, which I didn't think was even possible. "Hey, Lily." A genuine, but tentative smile overtook his lips.

Ugh, this is bad. Not only was our meeting like this awkward in light of how we left things, but I was also fairly certain Adam would have a coronary when he found out. *Maybe I just won't tell him.* Though I knew I couldn't go down that road again. It started with one simple white lie and ended with me spread eagle in Max's bed. *Ha, in your dreams.* Wait. What the hell was I thinking? *Please rein in drunk Lily, please rein in drunk Lily,* I chanted over and over in my head until I realized everyone was staring at me. Oh, shit. I was supposed to be responding. "Hi, Max. What are you doing here?" *Very smooth.*

Max raked a hand through his hair and looked back toward the camera crew he left behind. "Uh, I kind of work here. Well, not work here yet. I'm doing a couple of guest spots at home games, interviewing the crowd, offering analysis, things like that. Hopefully it'll become permanent soon."

I watched Max intently as he spoke. There was something different about him. He looked almost...peaceful. "That's great, Max," I said sincerely. "I really hope it works out for you."

Max and I stood there and stared at one another, getting lost in the moment like only Max and I could.

"Ahem." Amanda successfully pulled me out of my daydream, or whatever you'd call it.

"Sorry. Max, you remember Amanda?"

He nodded and extended his hand. "How ya doin', Amanda?"

She offered him a small smile as I continued the introductions. "And this is Amanda's boyfriend, Shane, and our friend Kyle."

Max shook their hands and said to Shane, "So you're the CrossFit trainer?"

I couldn't even remember telling him this tidbit of information, so I was surprised that he'd remembered.

Shane looked like he was going to come on the spot. "Oh, uh, yeah." He took a deep breath as if to clear his thoughts. "Sorry, I'm just kind of awestruck. You were a great player."

Max's smile grew as I rolled my eyes. I knew all it took to get on Max's good side was to give his ego a little stroke. Shane had probably just made a friend for life.

"Thanks so much," Max responded coyly.

What a wanker.

Kyle must not have wanted to be left out of the ass-kissing, because he quickly added his two cents into the conversation. "It's the truth, man. You were a fucking force to be reckoned with on the ice. I remember when you broke that dude's nose and jaw with one punch. Epic."

Max tilted his head slightly, as if remembering a particularly fond memory. "Sal Perdone. That prick deserved everything he got. He high-sticked me throughout the entire first period."

"Well, you showed him," Kyle added.

Max released a hearty laugh. "You're damn right I did. So, Shane, I'm really interested in all this CrossFit stuff. I've done a little research. It looks really intense."

"Yeah, it's a great total body workout. You should come in and try it sometime. We'd be excited to have ya."

"That'd be awesome. You got a card or anything?"

"Absolutely."

Amanda looked shocked. "Wow, it took me months to get your phone number, but less than ten minutes with Max and you're giving up the digits. You whore."

"Hey, when ya know, ya know," Shane deadpanned as he handed Max his card.

"Great. I'll give you a call later in the week, and we'll try to set something up."

"Fantastic. Looking forward to it."

Max turned away from me slightly, pulled out his wallet, and put Shane's card inside. He then turned his attention back to me. "Well, it was really good seeing you, Lily."

"You too, Max."

Our eyes scanned each other, both of us not wanting to make the first move. Finally, he broke down and leaned toward me, wrapping one arm around my back. I reciprocated, placing one arm around his shoulder. His masculine cologne infiltrated my nostrils, and the familiarity of his embrace, as well as my tipsy state, caused me to melt into him more than I consciously meant to. We broke away from the hug both too soon and too late.

Max flashed me a boyish grin before he started back toward the cameramen, who had almost finished packing up their equipment.

"Christ, I feel like I need a cold shower after that," Amanda stated.

I darted my eyes to her. "Stop, it was nothing," I chided gently.

"Whatever you say." She sighed as she resumed our walk toward the escalator.

As I followed them, I couldn't help but turn back for one last glance at Max. I slowly turned my head and immediately connected with Max's eyes. *Guess I'm not the only one who can't resist looking back.*

❤

The ride home was quiet as sleepiness stretched through us. Kyle walked me to the foyer door, and I waved to Shane's car before heading up to my apartment, alone. I put my hand into my coat pocket to retrieve my door key that I had stuffed there after letting myself into the building. When my hand hit a piece of paper, I withdrew it and, unfolding it, read its message. I couldn't help the welling of emotions that coursed through me.

He must've slipped it to me when we'd hugged. Though the *how* wasn't all that important. It was what it had represented,

with simple words but a complicated message.
Good in the place of one apology.
Goddamn those fucking coupons.

chapter twenty-four

a d a m

Somehow, over a week had passed since Lily and I had spent any time together. And I wasn't exactly sure how to reconcile my epic fuckup from the last time I'd seen her. I'd claimed I was all in, only to tell her in the next breath that I'd kept our relationship from Eva. Although it wasn't so much that I'd *kept* it from her as it was that I just hadn't gotten around to discussing it with her yet.

I'd told Lily I was certain that Eva would take the news well. But the truth was, I'd been about as excited for *that* conversation as I'd been to tell her about the birds and the bees. That lovely chat had been a fucking blast. Saying the word "erection" to your twelve-year-old daughter ranked right up there with plucking out your eyelashes one by one.

Despite the fact that awkward conversations seemed to have become a part of my daily repertoire lately, I just couldn't seem to accept that having them was a part of life. But last Wednesday, after only speaking to Lily through a few short texts, it became abundantly clear that my conversation with Eva was not one I could avoid. Not if I wanted Lily to forgive me. And certainly not if I wanted her to *love* me. Which I definitely did.

So on Wednesday night, I decided to tell Eva that Lily and I had been seeing each other. Evidently, I repressed most of the conversation into the recesses of my memory because I'm not exactly sure what I said. I do know that I didn't mention that we'd dated the year before. That would only complicate things and put a strain on Eva's trust in me.

Surprisingly, it seemed I didn't completely lie to Lily: Eva *did* take the news relatively well. She respected Lily, liked her even. She seemed genuinely happy that I'd found someone I enjoyed spending time with. The conversation had been shockingly less awkward than I'd anticipated, and Eva had truly seemed okay with the situation.

But when that conversation had been followed by Eva puking her guts up for the next four days, I couldn't help but wonder if her illness had been at all related to thoughts of her father banging her former teacher. But as bad as the weekend had been, I'd found a strange *comfort* in it. The role of loving father was one I knew well. I could play it well with little to no effort.

The role of loving boyfriend seemed completely different, however. As hard as I tried, life kept interfering with my relationship with Lily. I'd canceled on her Thursday night to stay home with Eva. And though I knew she understood why I couldn't go to the game, a part of me felt guilty for ditching her.

I felt we needed to talk about everything that had happened, so I invited her out to lunch. I needed to be honest about why I'd led Lily to believe that I'd told Eva about us when I hadn't. And I needed to come clean about why I'd gone to her house unannounced the night Max had come to see me. I couldn't ignore the hypocrisy I felt knowing that I'd kept important information from Lily when I'd condemned her for doing the same to me.

This was different, though. *I* had a reason for keeping things from her. I had done it to protect her feelings.

Then why did I feel so nervous about talking to her? My foot tapped uncontrollably on the floor underneath the table as I waited for her to arrive. I'd already checked my watch at least six times since arriving at the restaurant. I knew she had her lunch break and should have been there by now.

But somehow, at the sound of the bell jingling on the door, I felt a wave of relief undulate through me. It was like some strange variation of Pavlov's dogs. Her presence alone set me at ease.

"Hi," she said quietly as she took a seat across from me. "Sorry I'm late. I had a student finishing a test."

My hand found hers, and I ran my thumb across her skin. The feeling soothed my nerves even more. "It's fine. I'm just glad you came." I thought I saw confusion in her eyes. She probably wondered why I thought she might not show up. I wasn't so sure why I thought that myself. "It's been a crazy few days," I said, as if that helped to explain my behavior lately. "I just had some things I thought we needed to talk about."

"I'm guessing one of them is why you didn't tell Eva about us." Her voice was flat, calm even. If she'd been angry, it didn't show now. "How's she feeling, by the way?"

Even though Lily clearly had a right to be angry, she still had the courtesy to ask about Eva's health. That only made me feel shittier. "She's doing a lot better. Just a bad stomach virus.

Thanks for asking." I sat back to allow the waitress to put our food on the table. "I hope you don't mind. I wanted to make sure you ate, so I ordered for us before you got here. Chicken salad's okay, right?"

"Yeah, perfect. Thanks." The smile that spread across her face seemed genuine.

I hadn't been sure if my gesture would have been seen as thoughtful or controlling. Thankfully, she seemed to appreciate it. "Anyway," I continued hesitantly, "I think I owe you an explanation . . . for why I didn't tell Eva about us."

Lily raised her eyebrows, waiting for me to explain.

"I'd planned to tell her. I just never did. I mean, I did, but not until the other day." I shoveled a few fries into my mouth, along with a bite of my burger to give me time to gather my jumbled thoughts. Lily's eyes remained locked on mine. I wasn't getting out of this easily. "It's just . . . weird. You know . . . telling your daughter that you're sleeping with her teacher."

"Well, I hope you didn't use the sleeping together line as an icebreaker. I don't think details are necessary."

I thought I saw her crack a smile, which thankfully served to lessen the tension. "I didn't give her *all* the details. Or any really. I just told her we'd been dating for a little while." I'd hoped that Lily would be relieved that I'd finally told Eva, but she looked agitated. "What? What's wrong?" I studied Lily's face for an answer that I didn't find. "That's what you wanted, right? For Eva to know?"

She shook her head, clearly disappointed. "I wasn't upset you didn't tell Eva. I was upset that you told me you *did*."

"Well, I didn't exactly tell you I *did*. Just that I'd take care of it." I was grasping at straws, and I knew it.

"Jesus, Adam. That's semantics. You know what I'm

saying. Lying by omission is still lying. You of all people should know that."

"I'm sorry. You're right." It was all I could think to say. "I should've told you." She'd stopped eating, and I took her hand in mine as I focused my eyes on hers. I hoped she would see the remorse behind them. I was trying my best to be honest. Well, almost my best. "There's something else," I said quickly. "I told you I'd be truthful."

"What?" I could hear the fear in her voice.

"It's not anything bad," I blurted out, hoping to ease her nerves. I took a deep breath. *Here goes nothin'.* "That night… when I showed up at your apartment and you asked me what had changed…I said *I'd* changed. Well, I left out the part where Max came to talk to me."

"Max?" Her voice raised as she said his name. I didn't like hearing her say it at *all.* "Came to talk to *you*?" She shook her head and clenched her eyes as if she was trying to shake the thought of him from her brain. "Why?"

I figured the best option in this situation was just to be direct. "He told me he'd leave us alone."

"What does that mean?"

"Uh… I'm hoping it means exactly that… He'll stay out of our lives. Because, I swear if he doesn't—" I stopped midsentence, trying my best to remain calm. I silently added *talking about Max Samson* to the increasingly long list of conversations I'd rather not have. Although truthfully, it had probably been at the top of that list the whole time.

"Relax, Adam. We don't have to talk about him," she said, nearly reading my thoughts. She swept a stray lock of hair from her face and tucked it behind her ear before grasping my hand in hers. Relief washed over me simply because she'd been the one to initiate physical contact this time.

Did that mean she forgave me for not telling Eva about us? For not telling her Max had been the reason I'd decided to finally take our relationship to the next level? The look in her eyes told me she'd already let it all go. There was no icy stare. No intense line of questioning. I'd apologized, and she'd forgiven me. Just like that.

But it shouldn't have been just like that. Because I knew that I had more to come clean about. More to confess: my night with Carly. Gazing at her, watching the forgiveness seep from her, I couldn't bear to ask for any more. In that moment, it was all about moving forward, and I didn't want to jeopardize that by telling her about a fling that had meant nothing. I knew what it was like to realize the person you cared about had been with someone else. And I didn't want her to feel that pain.

So I took the coward's way out and remained silent in order to not doom us before we ever even began. Sitting across from me, Lily radiated strength. Strength in her conviction that we could work. That we *would* work. And as I lowered my head to her neck, kissing her softly, I let her strength be enough for the both of us.

I could probably learn a thing or two from her.

chapter twenty-five

l i l y

As I climbed the stairs to my apartment, I couldn't help the anxious feeling I had. I had spent extra time at work, trying to immerse myself in correcting papers and lesson planning to get my mind off Max. But when that didn't work, I went to the gym to blow off some steam.

Unfortunately, none of it did jack shit to lessen the nagging feeling I had in the back of my brain that told me I had to see him. I had to know why he'd done it. And I couldn't risk asking him over the phone, where he could easily lie to me. Only his eyes could assure me of the truth. No, I was going to have to do it in person.

I unlocked the door and walked tiredly into my apartment. I heard Amanda and Shane bickering in the kitchen, so I started in that direction. I had been surprised when Amanda had told me she'd be there tonight when we spoke earlier since they spent most of their time at Shane's. I leaned against the doorjamb, listening to their latest squabble without them realizing I was there. *Seriously? Who fights about popcorn?* After making my presence known, I headed off to my room to get ready.

I walked out of my room twenty-five minutes later, wearing a pair of dark rinse skinny jeans and a black boatneck sweater that hugged my thin frame. It was the fourth outfit I had tried on in my quest to capture the right look. I wanted to be casual, but appealing. I tried to convince myself that I wanted to look appealing just because that's what all women want. It had nothing to do with the man I was on my way to see. A man who would definitely appreciate the way this tight sweater cupped my ample breasts. *Nope, not thinking about that at all.*

I entered the living room to find Amanda and Shane on the couch. They were still arguing about the fucking popcorn. *These two are certifiable.*

But the mood in the air quickly changed as Amanda's hand hit something at the bottom of Shane's popcorn bowl. Next thing I knew, Shane was down on one knee and Amanda was yelling, "Yes, I'll marry you," as she hugged him tightly.

Shane stood with Amanda still in his arms. They deepened the embrace as Shane lifted her off the ground and hugged her fiercely. It was in this moment that I realized I was crying. And that I shouldn't be there. No wonder Shane had seemed unhappy to see me. I was crashing his proposal. So, as much as I desperately wanted to congratulate them and get a good look at the rock he'd bought her, I didn't. I almost made it to the door when Amanda spotted me.

"Oh my God, Lily, I totally forgot you were here."

I smiled. "I really shouldn't be. Congratulations, you guys. I'm just . . . I'm so happy for you both. I'll let you guys have your privacy."

Amanda pulled slightly away from Shane as she asked, "Are you coming home tonight?"

Even during one of the most important events of her life, Amanda couldn't help but let her suspicion get the better of her. She knew I wasn't going out with Adam tonight, since I had told her as much when we'd talked earlier, and this was her way of asking who I *was* seeing tonight.

She'd been subtly probing me for information about Max ever since the hockey game. I felt bad that I still hadn't come clean to her, but I just couldn't. I wasn't ready to make her understand why I was seeing him again. *I* didn't even know why I was seeing him again. Our meeting at the game had been a chance encounter, but I couldn't say the same for tonight. And a part of me felt guilty for not only seeing him, but for also knowing that I had no plans to tell Adam about it.

And though I knew he'd have an issue with this kind of dishonesty, I was confident that my decision to see Max was the right one. I couldn't put my relationship with Max behind me until I got the answers I needed. But dragging Adam into this served no purpose. In this instance, what he didn't know really *wouldn't* hurt him.

"Of course," I said, finally answering Amanda's question. "Why wouldn't I come home? I'm just going to meet up with some friends," I replied innocently, hoping to dissuade her curiosity. It didn't work.

"I just wasn't sure what kind of *friends* these were."

"Since you pluralized 'friends,' and asked me if I was spending the night elsewhere, are you insinuating that I'm engaging in recreational sex with multiple partners?" I pretended to be affronted as I put my hand on my chest for effect, hoping humor would stop her from grilling me so I could get the hell out of there.

"Well, ya never know with you," Amanda replied with a smirk.

Damn. I walked right into that one. "Well, it's been lovely chatting with you crazy kids, but I've taken up enough of your night. Besides, I have places to be and evidently tons of people to bang." I pulled the front door open and looked down at them. "You guys are really great together." I started to close the door behind me, but popped my head back in quickly. "Oh, and don't fuck on my couch." And with that, I slammed the door and made my way downstairs, smiling broadly.

♥

Once in my car, thoughts of Amanda and Shane drifted away. Instead, my thoughts were consumed with what I was doing. I was walking a delicate line and had to be careful not to sway too far one way or the other. *Why was I putting myself through this?*

The situation I currently found myself in caused nothing but stress. And it was a huge distraction. I had just learned how to handle my own shit when I had *his* foisted upon me. And his shit was *way* heavier than mine. Then I freed myself from all the Max-centered drama, only to willingly walk back into it. And for what? I really didn't need this aggravation when I had just gotten myself back on track with Adam.

But, ultimately, I knew why I was doing it. I just couldn't leave things on bad terms with Max, especially not now that I knew what he had done for me. And I knew that he still needed me. Yes, it was twisted and confusing and more than slightly insane, but none of that really mattered. Not when you had the power to help someone put the pieces back together again. Even if his life would never be perfect, at least it could be whole. After all, I had been the reason he had shattered in the first place. I had to try to make it right.

As I parked my car and walked up his driveway, I thought about how far our relationship had come in the past four months. He had gone from flat out refusing to see me, to yelling at me, to calling me late at night when his depression hit him hardest, to finally starting to let me back into his life. And I did want to be in his life, even if it had disaster written all over it.

I rang the doorbell and took a deep breath. I wondered if I would always experience this hesitation when I saw him. Despite how much progress our friendship had made before I'd ended it, I still felt butterflies at the prospect of being in his company.

As he pulled the door open, my eyes surveyed him briefly, and I quickly tried to steel my resolve. I was there for noble reasons. I was there as a friend. I would *not* fall back into the same old pattern with him. He deserved better than that. But goddamn, was he sexy.

"Hey," he said quietly, a shy smile playing on his lips. His coyness only made him more attractive. This man in front of me was different from the one I knew so intimately nine months ago. I wasn't sure which I liked more.

He stepped back so that I could enter. As I moved closer to him, I felt the familiar jolt of electricity that crackled between us whenever we were near. The feeling both terrified and titillated me. I looked up at him as I passed, our gazes locking instantly, and I spoke the only word my mind could formulate.

"Hi."

chapter twenty-six

m a x

Am I fucking dreaming? What the hell is she doing here? My mind was rapid-firing expletive-filled questions as I watched her walk into my house and greet my dogs. *Why do I feel like my heart is going to beat out of my fucking chest?* I closed the door and tried to regulate my breathing. And my emotions.

I wasn't sure how I felt about having her there. On one hand, I was more excited than a six-year-old on Christmas. But on the other, I felt like an inmate peering out of the prison fence, looking at the life he would never have. I turned around to see her bent down on one knee, petting my dogs as they licked her lovingly. I'd never been more jealous of an animal in my life. "I'm surprised to see you. Everything okay?" My voice was soft, quiet, unsure. All the things I normally wasn't.

She straightened, dropped her shoulders, and turned around to face me. "I'm not sure." Her face contorted into a genuine look of confusion.

"That sounds . . . ominous."

She laughed, and I was overcome with the depth with which I loved that laugh. Part of my road to self-discovery over the past few weeks had involved me coming to terms with my feelings for Lily. And as I finally accepted how deep they were, I knew that I had to also accept that they'd never be returned. But with her there, in my house, a slight flicker of hope radiated within my chest. And I almost hated her for putting it there. This unannounced visit would set back the progress I had made in trying to get over her. And since there had been virtually no progress to begin with, I knew I was totally fucked.

She looked down at her hands clasped in front of her before jerking her eyes up to me sheepishly. "I have to ask you something, and I need the truth."

"Am I known for lying to you?" Though I'm sure she hadn't intended it to, her comment stung. Between the two of us, I was definitely *not* the bigger liar.

Reading the irritation in my voice, she dropped her hands and lifted her face so that I could see her fully. "I'm sorry, I didn't mean to insult you. I just meant that I don't want you to spare anything. I want to know it all."

My arms were crossed over my chest, and I leaned against the nearest wall. "Go ahead."

"Why did you talk to Adam?" She wasted no time asking the question, almost as if she needed to hurry up and put it out there before she lost the nerve.

My body jerked slightly at her words. Of all the things I thought she'd come here to ask me, this wasn't one of them. I had expected an inquiry about the coupon I'd slipped in her coat or my not telling her about the broadcasting gig, but definitely not this. *What the hell kind of fucked-up mind games is Carter playing?* I lifted myself off the wall and dropped my hands to my side before raising my shoulders in a small shrug. "If he told you about our conversation, then I think it's clear why I did it."

"It's not."

I stared at her for a moment, willing her with my eyes not to do this. The talk with Adam had been one of the most difficult things I'd ever done in my life. Ceding defeat to that prick had been gut-wrenching. I'd replayed the night in my mind at least a hundred times: sometimes with regret, sometimes with sadness, and sometimes with rage. "I don't want to stand in the way of anyone's happiness anymore. That's all."

"Oh, come on, Max. First I find the apology coupon, and then Adam tells me that you went to him and promised you'd stay away from me. I—"

"A promise you're making me break by being here, I might add. What do you want from me, Lily? To admit that I'm a dick? Fine, I'm a dick. Everything you said to me that night in my driveway was the truth. I'm a taker, a user, a spoiled brat who's only out for himself. But I don't *enjoy* being that person, especially not when it comes to you. So I finally try to be a decent person for once in my life and fix something that *I* broke, and I get fucking interrogated for it in my own goddamn house."

The more I spoke, the more my anger flared. She was always fucking with my head, calling me out on things that were best left the hell alone. Why couldn't she just go have her happily ever after with that asshole and leave me to try to figure out my own shit?

"Stop being a drama queen. I'm not interrogating you; I'm just trying to figure out"—she flailed her hand in my direction—

"you." She took a deep breath and seemed to try to organize her thoughts before she spoke again. "I feel bad."

I started to speak—to tell her that I didn't need her fucking pity—but she rose a hand to stop me.

"I feel bad because I've placed a lot of blame on you for everything that's happened in my life during the past year. And even though I've said over and over again that I accept responsibility for my actions, I really haven't. It's easier to lash out at you, to make you the bad guy, to point out all your flaws and shortcomings than to take ownership of my own. When I called you in September, I acted like I was doing some noble thing: helping out poor, sad Max. But we both know I'm far from noble, don't we?" She smiled sadly. "Part of me needs you. And whether it's because you'll willingly play the bad guy so that I don't have to, or because you so adeptly play the victim while I get to be the savior, or because we have some kind of fucked-up codependence, I'm really not sure. But whatever it is, I can't let you feel that you need to keep paying for some sin that you never committed." Suddenly, her face lit up into a genuine smile. "I'm here to help ya down off the cross, Samson. You don't need to pay for my mistakes anymore."

I stood there for a second, trying to process what the hell had just happened. Then, my lips twitched into a sardonic smile as I said, "Did I just get saved?"

Lily released a throaty laugh and shook her head. "You're such an ass."

I let the smile fade slowly from my lips. Then I looked at her seriously. "So where does all this leave us?"

"I don't know." She rubbed a hand over her face. "My life is beyond complicated." She looked at me hopefully, clearly wanting me to pose a solution that could make this all better.

But there was no such solution.

"I think that we both only complicate things further for each other."

Her brows lifted in surprise at my words, but then she cast her gaze downward, accepting the truth of them all the same.

She stayed silent, so I continued. "We both have a lot to figure out. And while I don't plan to actively *avoid* you, especially since I was serious when I told Shane I wanted to see what that CrossFit bullshit is all about, I don't think it's a good idea for us to try to have any kind of meaningful friendship right now. We're people with a history that we can't ignore, but I don't think that necessarily means we can have a common future. We're just not heading in the same direction."

Lily looked at me thoughtfully. "You're doing it again."

"What?"

"The whole new I'm-selfless-and-I-want-to-do-what's-best-for-everyone-else thing. It's kind of endearing," she teased.

I blushed at her words, but tried to cover it with a laugh. "Let's not get crazy. I'm pretty sure I'm still an asshole."

Then she grew serious, closing the distance between us as she placed her hand on my cheek. "But an endearing asshole all the same." She leaned into me, raised up on her tiptoes, and placed a soft kiss on my cheek where her hand had just been. "See ya around, Max."

And with that, she walked around me, opened the door, and disappeared behind it.

I stood there, looking at the door that had just led her away from me. After who knows how long, I reached beside me on the wall and flicked off the foyer light. "Goodbye, doll," I whispered before heading upstairs and going to sleep.

chapter twenty-seven

l i l y

There was a reason February was shorter than the other months: it sucked. It was cold and dark, and there weren't nearly enough days off from work to compensate for its negative qualities. Other than the potential for a snow day—which we were blessed with on February seventh, resulting in an unexpected three-day weekend—and Presidents' Day, February was all but void of anything to look forward to. Especially when you threw in the Hallmark money grab known as Valentine's Day.

For so many years, Valentine's Day had just been another holiday I didn't celebrate. It ranked right up there with Boxing Day and Day of the Dead as holidays I couldn't give a shit less about. So it was strange to think that for the first time in probably six years, I would actually get to have someone wish me a happy Valentine's Day. Well, someone legal, that is. I was obviously not counting the handful of adolescent boys who asked me to marry them each year.

This year was something different. *This* year I'd get to spend Valentine's weekend with my *boyfriend*. I said the word aloud softly without even realizing it.

"What'd you say?" Adam reached across the center console to squeeze my thigh. Since he had apologized for not being a hundred percent honest, Adam had made a conscious effort to be especially loving and attentive. During the last few weeks, I'd felt closer than ever to him.

"I just said 'my boyfriend.'" I leaned over to snuggle into him as he put his arm around me. I inhaled the smell of his fresh body wash and spicy aftershave—an intoxicating combination. I wanted to lick it off him. "I just like the sound of it, that's all. My *boyfriend*," I said again, enjoying the feeling of it on my tongue as it rolled off it.

"I like the sound of it too," he said. "And I like the thought of having you all to myself for an entire day and night. I can't wait to show you the beach house. You're gonna love it."

"When do I get my gift?" I asked with an excitement equivalent of a child waiting at the top of the stairs on Christmas morning.

"Didn't anyone ever teach you that it's better to give than to receive?" he asked playfully.

A warmth radiated inside me as the double meaning of his words sank in. "Mmm... I guess not. I *am* very giving, but there's something about being on the receiving end that just can't be trumped." I squirmed in my seat as I felt the wetness seep into my underwear. I couldn't wait to jump out of this car and onto Adam. It'd been over a week since we'd slept together, and I was definitely feeling the side effects of our lack of sexual encounters.

Though I understood the reason for the week-long dry

spell. With Eva around most weeknights, it was difficult for Adam to get out of the house, even for an hour or so. We'd seen each other on my lunch break a few times, but with my days of an afternoon quickie long over, we'd used my lunch break to do just that—eat lunch. And though any time spent with Adam was enjoyable, I desperately needed the release that could only be triggered by hot, passionate sex. Abstinence was still abstinence, no matter how unintentional, and that only made me that much more thankful that Adam's parents had agreed to stay with Eva so we could have the weekend together.

"You seem fidgety," Adam said after I shifted in my seat again.

"Just trying to get comfortable." I couldn't decide if I wanted to be in a position that caused my jeans to rub against my clit at just the right angle to keep me turned on, or sit in a way that had the opposite effect and hope that my arousal would die down enough that I could concentrate on something else. Anything else. Ultimately, I opted for the former. I was a glutton for punishment.

The car ride was filled with easy conversation and so much sexual tension I didn't know if I could make it to Adam's house without slipping a hand down my pants to relieve the pressure that had been building inside me. Whether it was *his* hand or my own would have made very little difference.

"Do you want lunch before or after?" Adam asked as he unlocked the door to his house.

"Before or after what?" I asked, confused.

"Before or after I do whatever it was you were thinking

about in the car," he said, closing the door and caging me against it with his arms.

Holy shit. I swept my tongue across my dry lips to wet them. My legs wobbled and my breathing grew ragged as Adam's green gaze penetrated me. I hoped another part of him would penetrate me soon. "After, please," I whispered.

In one rough motion, Adam scooped me up, urging my legs to wrap tightly around his waist, both for stability as he carried me down the hallway and also to achieve the stimulation that I'd been craving for the last hour and a half. *Fuck, I want him.*

My head lolled back to allow Adam access to my neck. Tossing me onto a bed, he bore his weight down on me as he nibbled, kissed, sucked, and licked my sensitive skin. He kept up this tantalizing routine, grinding his hips so I could feel his stiff cock straining against his jeans until I was writhing beneath him. I rode him shamelessly from below, creating the friction I longed for. And I couldn't think of anything else but having his thick hard-on buried inside me as I came apart around him.

Eventually, he put a stop to the torturous pleasure, just long enough to undress us both before resuming his position above me. But this time, he straddled me, pressing his legs against mine to limit my movement. With my thighs restrained, the pressure inside me built quickly, especially as Adam reached down to stroke my clit with his thumb and swirl his fingers around inside me.

I massaged Adam's balls, stroked his length up and down, and ran my palm across his slick tip. I didn't think it was possible for me to be any more turned on than I already was with Adam leaning against me, kissing along my jawline, fucking my mouth with his soft tongue. But ever since our sexting experience during spring break last year, the image of him—in this very room—pretending his own hand was mine as he made himself come had been my go-to fantasy on more than one occasion. And now, my fantasy and reality could quite possibly merge into one. "Is this where you touched yourself that day when we were texting last year? In *this* room?"

His thick cock pulsed in my hand at my words, and I could sense him struggling to control himself. "Yeah, baby, right here. Just like you're doing now." His breath came out in sharp bursts against my mouth as he kissed me and thrust slowly into my hand. In the midst of his own pleasure, he withdrew his fingers from me, leaving me hollow and even more needy. "You gotta stop, Lily." He let out a low growl before continuing. "I'm not gonna be able to wait much longer."

I knew the feeling. I ached to be touched, and feeling Adam's warm, pulsing erection in my hand did nothing to help quell the urge inside me.

"Show me what you do to yourself when I'm not around to do it *for* you." His voice was low and deep, a raspy groan escaping as he continued to fuck my palm. "Show me what you do to yourself when you think of me."

Jesus Christ, that might be the hottest thing anyone's ever said to me. With my other hand, I reached down to rub myself in slow, deliberate circles as I tightened my grip around Adam's hard length with my free hand, pulling quicker. My hips bucked slightly against my own fingers, and I moaned with pleasure at the touch and the sight of Adam's dick sliding through my clenched fist.

Adam's eyes stayed down as he watched me bring both of us closer to orgasm. Instead of feeling embarrassed that I was doing this in front of him, I felt liberated that he enjoyed watching me. My pace quickened, and I no longer cared about having Adam inside me. I just needed to find the release I'd been craving, and I would take it any way I could get it.

Again Adam leaned down to kiss me as I worked us both with my hands. "Lily, I really can't wait if you keep doing that." He moved his hand to mine to push it away. That's when I knew if I didn't stop, he would come on me.

And I wanted nothing more. So I kept my hand firmly on his shaft as I pumped him faster, urging him to let go as I felt his deep moans against my mouth. He struggled to concentrate on kissing me as his warm cock twitched in my hand. The rapid bursts of hot semen that shot onto my stomach matched the pace of his rough, quick breaths. I milked him slowly, draining him of every last drop he had to offer as I enjoyed the feeling of his climax on my skin.

Finally able to concentrate on my own, I quickened the speed of my hand, gearing up for my much-needed release. Adam leaned back to watch me, his cock still semierect. "Make yourself come for me, Lily."

His words were all I needed to push myself over the edge, and I relished the feel of my own orgasm as it tore through me, making me shake below him until I brought myself down gradually. I lay there for a few moments, admiring the sight of him above me and feeling the warm sensation of the trail of come on my abdomen.

"I'll get you a tissue," he said. "Sorry. Though seeing me all over you is a huge fucking turn-on."

"Don't be sorry. That was seriously one of the hottest things you've ever done."

His eyebrows raised in excitement. "Really?" he asked playfully, his cock twitching slightly. "How about I wash you off in the shower instead?" He extended his hand to me to pull me to my feet.

"I don't think I'm dirty enough yet."

He pulled me toward him, sliding two fingers down the come on my stomach before slipping them inside me. "How's that for dirty?"

Holy hell, this is gonna be a great fuckin' day.

❤

I'd been spot on with my prediction. Once we were appropriately cleaned up, Adam and I relaxed in our sweats and enjoyed a lazy day of Chinese takeout and movies. A week ago, I'd made the mistake of admitting that I'd never seen *Animal House*, *Field of Dreams*, or *Heat*. I thought I'd actually seen the last one until he informed me that I was thinking of *Heat* with Sandra Bullock and "that manly chick from *Bridesmaids*," as he so kindly referred to her. I guess he thought Valentine's Day was the appropriate time to rectify my limited knowledge of classic guy films, so he'd come prepared with all of them.

Despite the fact that watching three back-to-back movies of your boyfriend's choosing was not the romantic night every girl hoped for on Valentine's Day, I couldn't help thinking that the gesture was sweet. Not to mention I found a certain enjoyment in letting Adam feed me lo mien with chopsticks. Every now and then he'd recite a line or two from one of the movies, and I could appreciate the excitement he felt when he watched his favorite parts. It was the same enthusiasm I had when I watched the riff off in *Pitch Perfect* for the thirtieth time. *Those bitches can sing.*

Finally, when the last movie ended, I couldn't take it anymore. "I wanna give you your gift," I whined.

He let out a loud laugh in response and pulled me closer to him on the couch to stroke my hair. "*You* wanna give me *my* gift? I thought it was the other way around. I thought you wanted to get *yours*?"

"I do," I said, "but I really *am* looking forward to seeing you open yours. Maybe there's some truth to that whole 'giving' thing."

"Okay, okay," he said, feigning apathy about our upcoming gift exchange. "I guess we can do gifts now. Wait right here. I gotta go get it."

I watched him walk down the hall and into one of the two bedrooms at the end. Once he was out of sight, I got up to grab his gift from my purse on the kitchen counter and plopped myself back down on the plush off-white couch, concealing his present behind me.

A few moments later, Adam returned to hand me a red envelope. "You go first," he said, a wide smile sweeping across his face. He seemed excited for me to open it.

In the seconds I had before I opened the card, my mind involuntarily guessed at its contents. *Tickets to a concert or comedy show maybe?*

I couldn't contain my enthusiasm, so I tore open the envelope, barely stopping long enough to read the card: some lighthearted poem with two cartoon bears on the front. Inside was a gift certificate for a spa near my house. *Three hundred dollars.* "Wow, Adam. Thank you. But . . ." I bit on my lower lip. "It's too much."

"It's not too much," he said with a shrug. "I thought you could take off from work and spend the day there sometime.

Get a massage or pedicure or something. Do whatever girls do when they wanna relax."

Wrapping my arms around his neck, I pulled him into me to give him an innocent kiss on the cheek. "Thanks, Adam. Really, I can't wait."

"You're welcome. I'm happy you like it. I wasn't sure what to get you."

"It's great! I hope you like yours too," I said, handing him the small box I had behind my back.

"I'm sure I will." He took it from me, unwrapping it carefully like he wanted to savor the moment. He pulled every last speck of paper off the box before opening it to see what was inside.

"Do you like it?" I asked nervously.

"I love it," Adam said, taking out the watch to study it closely. "I like that you can see the gears inside."

"I was hoping you'd like that kind. I figured since you're an architect, you'd like to see how things are built. Flip it over."

Unsure of why I said that, he looked at me curiously and then turned the watch over to see the inscription underneath. "To make up for lost time," he said quietly. He took my hand in his, his eyes thanking me more than his words ever could. "It's perfect."

chapter twenty-eight

m a x

After Lily's visit, I knew that I needed to start moving on. Even though I had been pissed to hear that Adam had told her about my conversation with him, in retrospect I was glad. If she could know what I had sacrificed for her and *still* not want me, well, then I guess she never would. And while I accepted that she'd never love me like she loved *him*, there was still a part of me that hoped maybe one day she might feel something close.

It was thinking like that that only fucked me up more, though. It made me question whether my conversation with Adam had really been as selfless as I had initially allowed myself to believe. Maybe I had hoped that he would tell her all along, and that it would cause her to see me in a different light. But I hadn't *wanted* that holier-than-thou jackass to actually *tell* her I'd talked to him. Did I? *Fuck.*

Thinking like this was getting me nowhere. I wasn't a man of deep reflection and pondering. I was a man of action. *What the hell does a man of action do to get over the love of his life?*

Getting drunk was out. Been there, done that, and it didn't fix anything. Well, at least not in the long term. A mindless fuck could relieve some tension, but past history had taught me that it would ultimately only make me miss Lily more. *What would make me* not *miss Lily?*

I paced my living room like a caged tiger, ready to pounce on any viable option that popped into my head. Finally, a thought so foreign to me—so out of my comfort zone that I nearly pushed the idea away due to the anxiety it filled me with—stopped me dead in my tracks. I shook my head as I ran a hand roughly through my hair. *Maybe it'll be good for me.*

"I guess anything's worth a shot at this point," I muttered under my breath. I snatched my phone from the coffee table and began scrolling through my contacts. I finally found the name I'd been searching for and called before I could think any more about it. She picked up before the second ring.

"Hello?" the surprised voice asked.

"Hey, uh, Alison, it's Max Samson. I was, ahem, I was wondering"—I took a deep breath, willing myself to stop sounding so pathetic—"would you like to go out with me tonight?"

♥

As I sat at Lorenzo's restaurant, I quickly began losing my nerve. Maybe I needed baby steps toward getting over Lily, like settling for a hand job in a bathroom as opposed to actually fucking somebody. A date suddenly seemed like a gargantuan leap for me to be making.

I tried to calm down by reminding myself that Alison was a serious piece of ass. I met her at a photo shoot I had done a few months back. Jack had insisted I get some headshots to take with me for my interview, and she'd been the makeup artist who had worked the shoot, though she definitely belonged *in front* of the camera. She was stunning with her jet-black hair, fair skin, lean body, and tall stature. I had readjusted myself at least ten times as she leaned over me to apply my makeup, thrusting her perfectly round tits in my face.

She had given me her number in case I ever needed someone for another shoot, but she had also flirted with me incessantly. Not in a tacky, hey-I'm-super-easy kind of way, but in a coy, I'm-interested-in-more-than-one-night kind of way. So when I had decided to take this drastic course of action, she had been the obvious choice.

But as I sat there waiting for her, I felt like this whole thing only served to further demonstrate that I would never get over my impulsive nature. I hadn't thought any of this through. Alison had seemed like a really sweet person, funny and charismatic. What kind of fucked-up asshole chose a girl like that as his rebound? I was probably going to crush this girl's heart when I moved on. How was that fair to her?

I tried to reassure myself: maybe I wouldn't move on. Maybe I'd really hit it off with her and we'd have a whirlwind romance that resulted in eloping to a tropical island. Or maybe she'd lock herself in her garage with a car running after I went out with her twice and never called her again. *Stop it, Max. You're being ridiculous. She probably doesn't even have a garage.*

I had just started rocking in my chair like the guy in *Rain Man* when I heard her.

"Max, hi. How are you?"

Her voice was so happy, her smile so genuine as she leaned

down to give me a hug, that I swore Satan was carving my name on a seat in hell at that exact moment.

"Alison, so great to see you," I said with as much enthusiasm as I could muster as I returned her hug.

She giddily plopped herself in the chair across from me and slipped her purse under the chair. I quickly took her in. Her long, straight hair fell past her shoulders and spilled over a cream-colored shirt. She was beautiful.

It took me a moment to realize that she was staring at me, clearly waiting for me to say something. "Didn't you wear a coat?" *Smooth, Max.*

She let out an awkward laugh and narrowed her eyes, as surprised to hear my words as I was. "Yeah, I checked it at the front."

"Oh, yeah. Sorry. Stupid question. So…" I took a long drink of my water, trying desperately to think of something to say. "How have you been?"

She crossed her arms on the table and leaned forward, putting those tits I loved a little more on display. "I've been pretty good. Work's been steady. How about you?"

I started to reply, but was interrupted by the waiter. After he had read us the specials, taken our drink orders, and stared adoringly at Alison's chest, I had totally forgotten what we were talking about. We sat in silence for a minute, both releasing a strained chuckle before she finally picked up the conversation.

"So I was really surprised to hear from you."

"Yeah, well, I'd been thinking about you"—*for about ten seconds before I called*—"and finally decided to ask you out."

"I'm glad you did." She smiled sweetly. "You've been on my mind quite a bit since we met."

"Oh yeah?" I asked, hitting her with my signature smile

that girls usually couldn't resist. *Tone it down. You're on a date, not ho hunting.* I relaxed my lips into a slight grin before continuing. "Thinking all good things, I hope."

"Definitely good things."

The waiter arrived with our drinks, and we continued with casual conversation. The more we talked, the more I liked her. She was down-to-earth, easygoing, and even funnier than I remembered. All my reservations had nearly slipped away. That is, until I watched her reach for her wineglass midway through dinner.

"Uh, Alison, this is probably a weird question, but"—I lowered my voice slightly—"are you married?"

She set her wineglass back down and eyed me curiously. "Why would that be a weird question?"

"Because I ..." *What the fuck am I supposed to say to that?* "I don't think women usually wear rings on their left ring finger unless they're married."

"I don't think they do either."

I waited for her to continue, but she didn't. *What the hell is going on here?* "So that means you *are* married?" *Why is she still fucking eating? This chick is out of her mind.*

"Yeah, I'm married. I thought you knew that."

"Why the hell would I know that?" I couldn't believe this. I mean, for all I knew, I'd banged dozens of women who were married, but that was all one-and-done type of shit. I was actually trying to *date* this girl, and here she was, somebody's goddamn wife. It suddenly occurred to me why I'd had that image when she first showed up. Satan really *had* been carving my name in a chair. Too bad I was already fucking sitting in it.

"I was wearing this ring when we met, Max. I'm left-handed and was putting makeup on you. I figured you saw it."

I wanted to defend myself by screaming that my attention hadn't exactly been on her hands, but I didn't think that would help this nightmare. "Well, I didn't." I was appalled, and that almost *never* happened.

"Why are you making such a big deal out of this?" She looked genuinely confused, and I suddenly had an overwhelming urge to take her to the nearest hospital for a psych eval.

"Why am I—? Because it *is* a big deal, Alison. You're cheating on your husband. With me. I have enough bullshit going on without your marital drama adding to the pile."

"The only one creating drama is you." Her tone was clipped and annoyed.

Is this bitch seriously pissed at me?

"And I'm not cheating on my husband. He knows exactly where I am."

I opened my mouth to retort, but her words sank in and caused me to slump back in my chair before I could utter a sound. I just sat there and stared across the table at her. This night had been going so well. How had it gone so wrong so quickly? Alison glared at me, waiting for me to say something. Finally, I did. "So let me get this straight. You're not only married and out on a date with me, but your husband is aware of this and is, what, okay with it?"

"Yes, Max. It isn't that uncommon. We both have our individual needs, and we allow the other to satisfy those needs elsewhere. It keeps our marriage fresh and drama-free."

"How does dating other people keep drama *out* of your relationship? You guys don't mind sharing each other with other people?" I didn't want to ask, but curiosity got the best of me. I mean, in theory this was the kind of marriage that would appeal to a guy like me. But I couldn't imagine another dude boning my wife. *It would probably hurt as much as it does when I imagine Lily with Adam.* I lurched forward and rubbed my hands over my face. Like I really needed *that* fucking thought right now. Just when I thought the night couldn't get worse, my brain had to prove me wrong.

"Well, we have certain rules," Alison said, answering the question I'd forgotten I'd even asked.

"Rules?" I asked in disbelief. Why was I still having this conversation? Part of me didn't want to know, but part of me *had* to know—the degenerate part, of course.

She leaned in and smiled conspiratorially, like she was about to share a national secret with me. "Yeah, rules. Like the spouse has to approve of the other person. My husband was almost as excited as me when I told him about you," she said with a wink.

I wanted to throw up.

"We need to be safe. Condoms, birth control, no drugs or heavy drinking, stuff like that."

"And we always get to watch the other have sex."

I lifted my hand at the waiter and yelled across the restaurant, "Check, please!"

Alison reached across the table and dragged her talons across my hand seductively. "Excited to get out of here now, huh?" she purred.

I yanked my hand away from her. "Yeah, excited to get the fuck *away* from you." I gave the waiter my credit card and begged him to hurry back with it. I tried to avoid Alison's glare as I took a large gulp of my scotch. The waiter returned quickly, and I signed the receipt and stood. But I couldn't resist one parting comment. "You know, Alison, I want to thank you.

It's people like you and your husband who reassure me that I'm not nearly as screwed up as I think I am. Have a good one."

As I turned to walk away, I heard her hiss, "Fuck you."

"Not in this lifetime, sweetheart," I replied with a smirk, never breaking stride. "Not in this lifetime."

chapter twenty-nine

a d a m

Ever since Valentine's Day, Lily and I had spent as much time together as possible. It was like we were finally back to where we had been last year, and it was incredible. I wasn't sure I'd ever be able to love her with the same completeness as I had before, but my doubts about that were slowly slipping away.

I also knew that I owed it to her and our relationship to begin fully incorporating her into my life. So, when Frank called and said that Claire was *dying* to meet Lily, I accepted his invitation to dinner and drinks with them and a few of our other friends.

"Claire's literally salivating to get her hands on your girl. And she started clapping like a seal when she realized that now you'd get to be included in our couples' nights. It'd almost be cute if it weren't so annoying." Frank chuckled. He could call Claire annoying all he wanted, but we all knew that she was the best thing to ever happen to him. And he knew it too.

"Well, would you try to reel her in a little? I don't want her coming on too strong and scaring Lily away."

"Ah, so you've got yourself a shy one, huh?" Frank asked.

I hesitated before replying. *Was Lily shy?* I hadn't interacted with her much around other people. She didn't seem shy; she certainly hadn't come off that way when I had met her. The Lily I knew was outgoing and friendly, but would she be that way with a table full of strangers? It seemed odd that I didn't know, even though the answer didn't really matter. I couldn't blame her if she were reserved when she first met my friends.

"Nah, she'll be fine," I finally answered, hoping it was the truth.

❤

I pulled up in front of Lily's apartment at five minutes to seven. We were meeting the rest of the crew at seven thirty, and while the restaurant was only ten minutes away, I thought it would be easier if we were the first ones there so that Lily got to meet everyone gradually as they arrived. I pulled out my phone and called her. "Hey, I'm downstairs," I said when she answered.

"Okay, be right down," she quickly replied and hung up.

I watched her exit her building and walk toward me. She looked beautiful, as always. Her hair flowed over her shoulders and down her light blue top that accentuated her slim figure, even though it was partially obscured by a khaki jacket. Her dark rinse jeans and black heels made her legs look incredible, and I quickly wondered if I had time to take her upstairs before dinner.

"Hey," she breathed as she sat down beside me and turned to pull her seat belt around herself.

"Hey, gorgeous." I leaned in to give her a soft kiss on the lips. "You look great."

She smiled warmly at me, her eyes sparkling. "You too."

I ran a hand down my green cashmere sweater. "Glad you approve."

"Always." She gently brushed her hand along my cheek.

We just sat there and stared at one another for a moment, letting our adoration for each other fill the car. Finally, I shook my head. "We better get going before I make us very late."

"You know, there is something to be said for being fashionably late."

I smiled. "All good things come to those who wait."

She giggled. "Well, when you put it like that, let's get this show on the road."

I laughed as I pulled the car onto the road and drove to the restaurant, holding Lily's hand in mine the entire ride.

We talked about trivial things: how Lily was sad that February was almost over and she hadn't gotten another snow day, what Eva had done recently to show me what an inconvenience it was to have me for a father, Amanda losing her mind over her upcoming wedding.

"Why the rush?" I asked her. "Why didn't they just pick a date a year from now so they could've taken their time planning?"

"I think Shane's worried that Amanda will change her mind if he gives her too much time to think about it," Lily said, laughing.

I didn't see the humor. "Should they really be getting married then?"

Lily's face sobered, and confusion seemed to set in as she silently asked me to explain what I meant.

"I mean, if she's that likely to change her mind, are they sure this is the right move for them?"

"Well, first of all, I was kidding about her changing her mind. Mostly." When I eyed her skeptically, she continued. "Amanda's skittish, and when left to think too much, she's prone to overanalyze everything. She could poke holes in the sturdiest foundation. But I don't think that's really why they're rushing." She sighed. "I just think that they're ready, ya know? They know what they want and can't see a reason to wait for it."

I thought for a moment. "So you don't think they're making a mistake?"

She whipped her head toward me. "Why would their marriage be a mistake?"

I let out a breath. *Why did I have to bring this up?* "Lily, come on. They've only been dating a few months. That would've been like me proposing to you last spring. We both know what a disaster that would've been. We barely knew each other."

She sat still, facing forward, her eyes unwavering from the windshield. After a few silent, tense moments, she turned her head toward me. "I think—" She stopped and cleared her throat, causing her voice to be stronger, surer. "I think that when you meet the person you're meant to be with, your heart just knows, even if it takes your brain a while to catch up. You can deny it and fight it all you want. God knows Amanda did. But it's ultimately no use. There is no living without that person, Adam." She turned her head to face the passenger window. "Shane is the air Amanda breathes. To walk away from him would be like never taking a deep breath again. And she damn well knows it. Anyone looking at them does."

I glanced over at her, wishing I could read her mind. I reached over and grabbed her hand that I had just realized I must've let go of at some point. "I know what it's like to feel like you'll never take a deep breath again. Believe me." I gave her hand a squeeze, and she turned to face me, a shy smile on her face. She squeezed back before looking out her window again.

"Me too," she whispered.

I pulled into the parking lot, wishing I could've been convinced that she was referring to me.

❤

When I told the hostess Frank's name for the reservation, I was surprised when she told me that the rest of our party had already arrived. *Is anything going to go the way I'd planned tonight?* I put my hand on the small of Lily's back as we followed the hostess through the restaurant toward our table.

"There he is," I heard Frank bellow.

We approached six smiling faces, and I felt Lily tense slightly. But her face was all smiles as we walked up to the table.

"Hi, guys," I said. "Lily, this is Frank and his wife, Claire, Troy and his wife, Kelly, and Doug and his wife, Shannon. Everyone, this is Lily."

Lily reached around and shook everyone's hand before I pulled out her chair and she sat down.

"So how is everyone?" I asked, trying to delay the impending inquisition I knew was coming. Everyone nodded and murmured that they were good, fine, and so on.

Claire was the first to strike, as I knew she would be. "Lily, that's such a pretty name. Where did you get it?"

"From my parents," Lily deadpanned. Quickly, her eyes

widened as she realized she'd replied before considering her answer.

I covered my mouth with my hand to hide my smirk.

Claire looked momentarily flustered. "Oh, no, I meant is it like a family name or anything?"

Lily smiled. "No, I know. Sorry, I have kind of a sarcastic sense of humor. I apologize. Uh, yes, it was my paternal grandmother's name."

Claire smiled, but it didn't reach her eyes.

This is going well. Lily had her head practically buried in her menu. I swung my knee under the table to bump hers. When she looked up, I shot her a reassuring smile, which she returned as she visibly relaxed.

"What's everybody having?" I asked in an attempt to get a conversation flowing again.

Once we discussed our dinner choices, the waiter came over to take our drink orders.

"We're ready to order our dinner too," Kelly said impatiently.

Of all my buddies' wives, Kelly was my least favorite. She was snobby and cold. I wasn't sure what Troy saw in her. Other than her obvious physical appeal, she was a bitch.

"Yes, ma'am. Would you like to start?" the waiter kindly asked her.

"Wouldn't it be easier to start at one end of the table and work your way around? I don't want my order getting messed up."

And here we go.

"You can start with me," I heard a soft voice next to me say. I turned to see Lily smile at the waiter before giving him a wink. "I'll have the—"

"He really should start with Frank or Doug. They keep the order straight if they start at an end." The look on Kelly's face showed that this was no longer about our order. It was about the *new girl* learning her place in the female hierarchy.

"Oh, I don't know." Lily leaned slightly toward the waiter to read his name tag. "Kevin here looks pretty intelligent. I think he can take eight orders without too much difficulty. Right, Kevin?" She directed her question toward the waiter, but her eyes remained locked on Kelly.

"Yes, ma'am," Kevin replied, discomfort lacing his voice.

"Great." Lily snapped her attention back to him. "Then I'll have the tortellini Alfredo."

"Would you like a soup or salad with that?"

"Salad. With Italian dressing, please." Lily handed him her menu, smiling brightly at him.

Kevin smiled gratefully at her. "Sure thing, ma'am."

The waiter moved on to Claire, and as I watched Lily's victory sink in around the table, I hoped that her need to defend our server was worth potentially ruining our evening.

❦

The women decided to abandon their questioning of Lily after her pissing match with Kelly. I talked sports with the guys, and eventually the mood at the table warmed and we all fell into our usual bantering. Well, all of us except Lily. She seemed to be content to listen, rather than participate.

"So, Lily, Adam told us you're a teacher?" Shannon, probably the sweetest of them all, asked.

"Yes, seventh-grade English."

"Wow, that sounds difficult. We have two boys who are

three and five, and they're tough enough. I can't imagine a room full of teenagers," Shannon said sincerely.

"It's interesting, that's for sure," Lily replied.

"Lily's great at it, though. She's even a mentor to a new teacher this year." I knew that Lily didn't want to be the center of the conversation, but I couldn't resist. If she wasn't going to willingly interact with my friends, then I'd have to prompt her to.

Lily shot me a tight smile before speaking. "It's really not that big of a deal. They hired someone at the last minute, so the principal asked if I would help her get her feet wet."

"Where do you teach?" Doug asked.

"Swift."

"Oh, isn't that where Eva goes, Adam?" Claire asked, even though I knew she was already aware of the answer. Claire and Frank lived in the same school district.

"Yeah, Lily taught Eva last year. That's how we met actually." I leaned in and wrapped my arm around her, knowing this was about to get awkward and wanting to physically show her my support.

"Is that allowed?" Kelly bit out.

"Is what allowed?" Lily asked evenly.

"Dating the parents of your students. That seems like a breach of some ethical code of conduct." Troy fidgeted uncomfortably as he listened to Kelly.

"Eva isn't currently one of my students, so I don't really see an issue with it."

I couldn't help but be thankful none of them knew we'd dated last year.

"Of course you don't," Kelly scoffed.

"What does that mean, exactly?" Lily tensed, and I knew

that this was about to get ugly. It was like watching a pit bull circle a pretentious poodle.

"Adam's a very eligible bachelor. It's not surprising that you wouldn't see a problem with getting your hooks in him any way you could."

"Kelly, that's enough," Troy muttered.

Way to take a stand, Troy.

Everyone at the table began to shift nervously, unsure of where to look or what to say.

"You're right." Lily sighed. "Adam is an eligible bachelor. Any woman would be lucky to have him. But not because of his money, as you're clearly suggesting, but because of who he is. So yes, I do recognize what a catch he is, and I did maybe ignore that he was the father of one of my students in order to be with him. But that's because I love him." She turned toward me, looking deeply into my eyes. "Just like I knew I would when I met him."

I leaned in and gave Lily a deep kiss, so happy to hear her publicly verbalize what we'd both hidden for so long. And to show her, and them, that I felt the exact same way.

Thankfully, we had all nearly finished eating by the time Kelly and Lily had gotten into it, and we all graciously declined dessert. It was definitely time for this nightmare to end.

We all said our goodbyes, and Lily and I made our way to the car.

"So, have fun?" I asked with a wide smile, knowing she'd sense my sarcasm.

"Yeah, a fucking blast," she retorted dryly.

I laughed, though I couldn't ignore the heavy feeling in the pit of my stomach that she hadn't fit in with my friends as I'd hoped she would.

chapter thirty

m a x

In the spirit of my New Year's resolution, I'd managed to make it over three months without pissing anyone off. I tried to focus all my energy on the positive elements in my life: family and my job auditions. I'd made it a habit to go to my parents' once a week for dinner, and my television tryouts had been going fairly well. I'd had more than a few pregame spots, while some of the other guys only had one or two before they weren't asked to come back again.

But other than that, there wasn't much going my way. Especially when it came to my love life. For some reason, I hadn't considered that being so selective about who I bang would cut down on my sexual activity. And out of all the things that I'd recently been trying to change about myself, abstaining from fucking and chucking had been by far the hardest. I hadn't hit a dry spell this long since puberty hit. And it was killing me.

As it turned out, being an unemployed ladies' man was an unbearable combination. It led to long stretches of boredom

that could only be sufficiently filled with a little "self-love."
Surprisingly, using a cheesy euphemism didn't make what
I was doing seem nearly as lame. But it didn't matter what I
called it. When it came down to it, flogging the log, giving
myself a one-gun salute, making stomach pancakes, or using
some other name coined by an imaginative middle schooler
didn't make a damn bit of difference. It all meant the same
thing. If I were being honest with myself, I was a thirty-year-
old man sitting around on a random weekday watching porn
and masturbating.

My rock bottom had arrived a few weeks ago when I'd
caught myself Googling home remedies for carpal tunnel
syndrome. Then I started debating whether to continue my
search or fill my day with porn again. When I decided that porn
was always the better option, I knew it was time to take my
mom up on her offer to go on a date with her friend's daughter.

Months ago, when my mom had suggested that I go out with
Mary, I'd been too busy banging randoms and being a selfish
prick to even entertain the idea. Mary and I had gone to grade
school together, and though our moms stayed close friends, I
hadn't seen her since eighth grade when her family had moved
to Atlanta for her dad's new job. A few months ago, the idea of
dating the lanky, awkward girl I remembered from seventeen
years ago could not compete with stickin' it in a drunk blonde
with a perfect rack.

But now that the most action I'd seen in months had been
from myself, lanky and awkward seemed preferable, hands
down. Literally. And when I almost didn't recognize the dark-

haired beauty that tapped me on the shoulder at the bar, I couldn't have been more pleasantly surprised. *Hell yes.* The color of her eyes matched her silky hair: a gorgeous shade of midnight that, when combined with her tanned skin and perky breasts, created an erotically exotic look.

Before I realized it didn't matter, I briefly wondered why I hadn't ever picked up on the fact that she was probably partially Hispanic. I'd probably do just about anything to get those plump soft lips on my mouth. And I'd *definitely* do anything to get them around my dick, which was already perking up at the thought.

"Max?" she said shyly, her soft voice pulling me out of my erotic daydream.

"Mary?" I knew my voice revealed my shock at her changed appearance.

She wrapped her arms around me, pulling me in for a hug so tight her breasts squeezed against my chest. I momentarily wished I'd gone to church more regularly so that God would answer my prayer that there'd be more to her than just her physical features. That would at least make me feel less like a man-whore if I wanted her for more than her body. *I don't ask for much, God.* After that, I did a cursory check for a wedding ring. *All clear.* I wasn't making *that* mistake twice.

As we got reacquainted, I found out Mary and I had a lot in common. She had spent a few years as a sports writer before deciding to move back to Philadelphia to start a sports-themed magazine. "A friend of mine from college had the idea," she explained. "It's nothing major yet, but we're hoping in time it'll take off. I have a few connections in the area, so that should help." She tucked a few stray hairs behind her ear as she spoke, and I wondered what it would be like to pull on that hair.

"Luckily," she continued, "I had a great job out of college at a Dallas paper. It paid well enough for me to save some money so I could pursue my dream." She took a sip of her wine and licked a stray drop from her lips. "I've always wanted to be a part of something big."

"I know the feeling," I said. I told her a bit about my hockey career, leaving out the less flattering parts, and jumping to my current job opportunity. She seemed impressed and, judging by her hand resting comfortably on mine on the bar, at least somewhat attracted to me. *Thank you, God.*

We spent much of the next hour and a half catching up on how our families had been and reminiscing about when we were little and life was so much simpler. "Remember that time you sledded right over the creek and hit that tree on the other side?" she asked. "I can't believe they just let kids sled down that hill with nothing to stop them from falling into the creek or hitting rocks. That would never happen today."

"No kidding. They put up one of those orange plastic fences a few years after you moved. Not nearly as much fun." I laughed at the memory. Even back then I had no fear.

We never even made it to a table. Instead, we just shared a few appetizers and another drink at the bar before I suggested we take dessert to go. I figured that would be a good way to gauge her interest level. If she was willing to take me back to her place, then she was probably interested in more than a walk down memory lane. And while I didn't want to be presumptuous, I was pretty sure if I could get her alone, I could at least get her partially naked. Hell, even a heavy make out session would be preferable to jacking off all night.

"We can," she said hesitantly. "But I should tell you . . . this won't be what you think." For the first time since I'd greeted her, she seemed a little bashful, and I wasn't sure why. "It's just that I don't have meaningless sex. I want to be in love first."

What the hell? Did I just hear her right? I am on a date with the fucking Virgin Mary. "So you're a...you're like a thirty-year-old virgin?" *Real smooth, asshole.* I heard my voice crack as I said it, and I knew she could hear the shock in my voice.

Her laugh told me I'd made more of a fool of myself than I'd originally thought. "No, Max, I'm not a virgin. But that doesn't mean I sleep around. I've been with two people, but I loved them both. It's just kind of a thing with me, I guess." She shrugged and bit down on her bottom lip in the sexiest way.

Confusion spread across my face. "So what are you saying?"

"I'm saying...we can see what happens tonight. But no sex. Is that okay with you?"

Well, only a complete douchebag would say no. And oral sex doesn't actually count as sex, does it? "Sure, who said anything about sex?"

❤

Mary's apartment was only a few minutes away from the restaurant, so I decided to follow her in my car. Staying true to my resolution, I'd cut down on my drinking significantly, and only had two beers at the bar. I was happy I wouldn't have to call a cab and worry about coming back to get my car in the morning, especially since I clearly wouldn't be spending the night at Mary's.

Somehow, in the few blocks we had to travel to her apartment, I'd managed to nearly hit a cat, forcing me to slam on the brakes. And in an effort to save the dessert in the passenger's seat like I would a small child in an accident, I reached my hand across to catch it, only resulting in the tiramisu covering most of my hand and the sleeve of my sweater, along with the dashboard and floor mat. *Real fucking smooth, jackass.*

By some miracle, I was able to parallel park my car on Mary's street without getting any of the tiramisu on the wheel. She parked her car across the street and started toward me.

"Uh...could I grab a few paper towels from your apartment?" I asked, holding up my right arm. "There was a fatality on the ride here."

"Sure," she laughed. "Is it all over your car too?"

"Pretty much." I smirked.

"Oh no. Come up, and you can clean up and then bring down some wet paper towels for your car. It's probably not good to leave it on the leather too long."

I followed Mary up the two flights of stairs to her apartment and into the kitchen, glancing around her apartment as I strolled through. For someone who had just moved in, her place was well put together. The living room was furnished tastefully: neutral furniture with a few splashes of reds and oranges to give it a less sterile feel.

"Here," she said, grabbing my sweater at the bottom with both hands. "Take your shirt off, and I'll throw it in the wash for you."

I didn't really care what she planned to do with my shirt once it was off me. When a hot woman told me to take off an article of clothing, it usually took very little convincing for me to do so. I set the Styrofoam container on the counter and lifted my arms above my head, enjoying the feel of Mary stripping my shirt from me.

As she stretched to reach up, her body inched closer to mine so that when she finally peeled my sweater over my head, our faces were nearly touching. Immediately, I felt the tension between us. Me: resisting the urge to pull her against me and inhale the scent of her flowery shampoo. And her: resisting the urge to let me.

She swallowed hard and took a step back, but the physical distance did nothing to alleviate the electricity between us. "Uh," she stammered, "I'm just gonna throw this in the wash." She pointed toward the stackable washer and dryer behind her, but her eyes never left mine. "You can wash up, and then we can clean your car out."

My right hand was still covered in mascarpone, pudding, and cocoa, so I made a move toward the sink to my left before stopping. "We should at least taste it first, don't you think?" I asked, lowering my voice softly in that seductive way I knew most women couldn't resist. I slid my index finger inside my mouth, licking off the sweet dessert before pulling my finger out slowly. "You want a taste?" I asked.

I heard only the gasp of a sharp inhale before Mary let her mouth fall open just enough that I knew her answer. Stepping toward her, I extended my thumb, letting her suck gently. The feel of her soft wet tongue around my finger made my already semierect cock stiffen fully against my jeans as I imagined her mouth around it instead. There was no amount of jerking off that would satiate the need I felt for her.

I slipped my thumb out, tugging slightly on the corner of her mouth on the way. My hand came to rest around the back of her neck as I leaned in to push her lips against mine. Quickly, I spun her, slamming her up against the fridge, causing her to drop my shirt. I worked my mouth urgently down her neck to her collarbone, and the moans that escaped her made me harder than I'd been in weeks. "We don't have to do anything you don't want to do," I promised her. Despite the fact that I would have one hell of a case of blue balls if we stopped now, I respected Mary. I liked her even. And I didn't want to make her feel uncomfortable.

I rubbed shamelessly against her, enjoying the friction of her body stroking my cock through my jeans. There was only one other time that I remembered being so turned on that I thought I might actually come in my pants, and I quickly pushed *that* thought from my memory. The last thing I needed was to think about *her* right now.

Mary's moans told me she didn't want me to stop, but I needed a respite from the stimulation. So I slid her away from the fridge, picking her up with one fluid movement and sitting her on the counter. I positioned myself between her legs, spreading them farther apart as I pulled her ass closer to the edge.

I stroked the inside of her thigh to see if she'd shy away. When she didn't, I moved my hand above the hem of her dark gray dress to the lace of her underwear. I pulled roughly on the fabric, causing the back of her thong to slide up the crack of her ass. It seemed to startle her at first, but this was a Samson Signature Move, and I anticipated her response perfectly.

After a few moments, she enjoyed the feeling of the taut fabric rubbing against such a private area, and she leaned back to allow me access to her slippery cunt. "I bet I can make you come just like this," I said, massaging her clit with my fingers as I pulled roughly on her thong to stimulate her ass.

Her only response was a whimper as she reached for my

belt, fumbling for a few moments before slipping her hand down my pants to grasp my pulsing hard-on. *God, yes.* "You don't have any boxers on," she said.

Why are girls always surprised by that? "Nope. Does that bother you?"

"No, I just didn't know guys did that." Her breathing hitched slightly as I sped up my deliberate strokes against her clit, and I could sense her struggling to concentrate on my cock in her hand. "Like this?" she asked, sliding her hand up and down my length.

This girl's innocence was as big of a turn-on as the hand job itself. "I like it pretty hard and fast."

"Show me, then."

Shit, that's hot. With my free hand, I gripped myself hard, pulling in long quick strokes as she watched me. "Like this," I said, removing my own hand and replacing it with hers. "That's it, baby," I said when she gripped it tightly in her fist and began pumping roughly. I was beginning to rethink my hard and fast request as I felt myself get dangerously close to coming on Mary's countertop.

I tried to take my mind off my own orgasm and concentrate on hers, stroking with my thumb in teasing circles. "Is this how you do this?" I asked. "When you're by yourself?"

"Yeah, push a little harder. And I want your fingers inside me."

Well, if there's one good thing about abstinence, it's that it does wonders for people's masturbatory skills. Mary knew what she wanted as much as I did. And she continued to work my cock, tugging in rapid strokes as I swirled two fingers inside her, massaging the insides of her slick pussy with my fingertips. And she wasn't kidding about wanting my fingers inside her.

I could feel her clench tightly around them as she rode my slippery palm.

"I wish it was my cock inside you," I whispered, "that was about to make you come."

"Oh God," she muttered. "Keep going. Just like that."

She moved her hand faster in response to her own pleasure, and I could feel my orgasm building quickly. "If you don't stop, I'm gonna come," I said. Not that I wanted her to stop. That was actually the *last* thing I wanted. But I thought it was only polite to give a fair warning in case she wanted to grab a napkin or paper towel first.

Surprisingly, she sped up, circling her hand around my slick tip when she got to the top. "Ladies first," I said, biting my lip as I tried to hold back my own release.

My fingertip found that spot inside that could make any woman come almost instantaneously, and I pressed hard against it as my thumb tapped against her clit. Within seconds, I had her convulsing around my hand, riding my fingers until I felt the last of her orgasm die down.

Her warm palm continued to move faster, and I thrust my hips in quick jerks until I knew I couldn't last any longer. My hand clamped over Mary's as semen came out in long hot spurts into her palm. I groaned with a release I hadn't felt in months as she milked every last drop from me. *I can't give myself a hand job like that.*

When Mary removed her hand from my pants, I gave her a paper towel to clean up. *Who ever thought I'd like not having sex that much?*

And as I fixed my clothes and accepted the cleaning products she handed me for my car, I couldn't help the smile that played on my lips as I thought how I'd definitely be calling Mary for a second date.

chapter thirty-one

l i l y

It had been a few weeks since our own public version of *Dinner for Schmucks*—otherwise known as a night out with Adam and his friends—and neither one of us had brought it up since. Both of us seemed content to pretend that the uncomfortable horror show hadn't even happened. And surprisingly, that feat came fairly easily. We'd gone on a few more dates with just the two of us and, as always, things had gone smoothly.

However, as much as I enjoyed having Adam all to myself—and Jesus, did I enjoy that—I couldn't shake the feeling that it would have been nice to have some other couples to hang out with. I had seen his friends once or twice since then, but unfortunately the epic fail had been strikingly similar to *The Butterfly Effect*. And after a careful analysis of what could have gone wrong, I could only come up with one explanation: all his friends were complete fucking assholes.

But despite the fact that I would rather suffer a slow death by hanging myself with the elastic of a stranger's underwear than spend more time with Adam's friends, my gut told me they were the problem, not us. So I figured it was time to test this theory by arranging a night out with some of *my* friends. I saw it as my duty—a public service—to show Adam what *normal* people were like.

And for some reason I decided that *normal* was Amanda and Shane. When I invited Adam to come to Shane's house on Friday night for a double date, I figured it would be the best of both worlds. Adam and I could spend time together while I enjoyed the comfort of familiar friends and surroundings. No strange questions. No one patronizing the waiter. Just the four of us relaxing and eating whatever health-conscious crap Shane decided to cook for us. Who *couldn't* have fun with the two of them?

Work dragged on Friday because Mr. Murdock scheduled me to proctor the standardized test that the school had been giving. For three days in a row. One day was more than enough. Two days was nearly unbearable. And by day three, I considered writing a letter to the Department of Homeland Security that suggested they use this shit as a form of torture for suspected terrorists.

By the time five thirty rolled around, I desperately needed a drink. Or maybe two. Luckily, Amanda took it upon herself to get me slightly liquored up while we got ready to go to Shane's. She also agreed to drive us. It made the most sense since Amanda would most likely be sleeping at Shane's anyway, and I could catch a ride home with Adam.

"Enjoy it," Amanda said, gesturing up and down the length of my body with her hand.

"Enjoy what?" I'd become used to having to ask Amanda

to explain things, but she had me completely baffled. *What the hell is she talking about?*

"The tights," she said. "It's your last year in them. You're twenty-nine now. Once you hit thirty, you can't wear 'em anymore."

"What? Why not? They're comfortable, and as long as my ass is covered by a long sweater like this one," I said, pulling my striped gray shirt down a little lower, "there's nothing to worry about."

Amanda's expression remained incredulous. "Uh-huh. Hey, speaking of you turning twenty-nine, what did Mr. Wonderful get you? I never even asked. Wait, let me guess," Amanda said, squinting her eyes together as she plopped herself on the bed, pretending to be deep in thought. "I know it's gotta be good. An all-expense paid trip to some tropical island where everyone's beautiful and the orange juice is made each morning from freshly squeezed fruit off the trees near your private villa?"

I stared at her blankly.

"No? Huh. I thought I had it. Okay, let me try again." She thought for a few more seconds before answering. "A diamond-studded unicorn."

"Seriously?"

"Okay, those are all the imaginary gifts I can think of right now, so why don't you just *tell* me what he gave you?"

I turned around and kept my eyes glued to the mirror as I put in earrings, refusing to look at her. "Nothing."

"Don't tell me you told him not to get you anything. That's a waste of a good boyfriend, Lily."

"I didn't tell him not to," I said simply. "He just didn't."

In the reflection of the mirror, I could see a wave of

confusion sweep over Amanda's face before she spoke again. "Wait, what? Adam Carter forgot your birthday? What kind of boyfriend does that?"

"The kind who doesn't know when it is."

"What do you mean 'doesn't know when it is'? He knew when it was last year. You practically kicked me out of the house so he could have dinner with your parents."

"Well, a lot's happened since last year, Amanda."

"A lot's happened? Like what? You stopped aging? A person's birthday is vital information. If he didn't remember it, he should've asked."

I let out a long sigh, hoping that would show her how much I did *not* want to talk about this right now. "It's not that big a deal."

"Yeah? When's *his* birthday?"

May twenty-second. And though I didn't say this out loud, my silence told her I knew the answer.

"Uh-huh, I rest my case. You absolutely know when his is. And what's more, I bet you remembered it without having to ask him again. I don't know why you're acting like this doesn't matter. This is a huge—"

"I'm acting like it doesn't matter because it doesn't. It's just one day." I could hear how defensive I sounded, but for some reason, I felt it necessary to come to Adam's rescue. Everyone forgot birthdays and holidays at one point or another, and when I forgot his birthday or our anniversary years from now, I didn't want to be chastised for it. "And you're not gonna act like it matters either. He doesn't even realize he forgot it, and he'll feel awful if he knows."

Amanda's face softened slightly, and she backed down. "Okay, okay, I'll be nice. I promise not to say anything," she huffed. "Now finish your drink and put on some pants so we can go."

I looked down at my tights again. "Should I change? Really?"

"Nah, I'm just fuckin' with you. You look great. And I'm sure Adam will think so too," she said, plastering an overly exaggerated smile on her face. "Let's get going. It's time to go eat some dry salad and oats or whatever appetizing delicacy Shane has prepared for us this evening."

❤

By the time we arrived at Shane's a little after six thirty, I was famished. I hadn't eaten anything since lunch, which had been around nine thirty because of the amended testing schedule. And I'd barely eaten anything because it had been so early. Now, with two margaritas and little else in my stomach, I desperately needed food.

"Do you have any rolls or something, Shane? I feel like I need something in my stomach."

"Rolls?" Amanda's voice deepened, clearly trying to imitate Shane. "What do you think this is? Bertucci's? We don't eat empty carbs in this house," she said sternly.

"Yeah, that sounds *just* like me." Shane rolled his eyes and poked Amanda in the stomach, making her squeal like a child. "How's this, Lil? Flatbread okay?" Shane handed me a plate with some hard, grainy breads.

"That's great, Shane. Thanks. What are these?" I asked, pointing to a few of the homemade spreads.

"This one's a bleu cheese and fig glaze, and the other's roasted peppers with chopped kalamata olives and sage."

"Are you speaking English right now?" Amanda chimed in. "What happened to butter? Or oil and spices? The only fig I eat is in a Newton."

Refusing to give Amanda the satisfaction of seeing his expression, he kept his back to her and continued to chop some vegetables. "Yeah, well, *I* don't eat cookies, dear, remember?" he said, emphasizing the term of endearment. "So I gotta get my fig from other sources."

"It's not a cookie. It's a cake, Shane. Haven't you heard the commercial?"

Shane's body shook, unable to control his laughter. "What am I gonna do with her, Lily?"

"I don't know, but you better figure it out soon. She's all yours in less than two months."

Shane turned to face the two of us, reaching his arm around Amanda's waist to pull her quickly against him and plant a soft kiss on her forehead. "Hmm," he said, exhaling a sharp laugh through his nose, "I thought she was *already* mine."

"Well, duh," Amanda said as the doorbell rang.

I shoved the last bite of flatbread in my mouth and hopped up from my barstool to head toward the front door. Watching how cute Shane and Amanda were together made me even more eager to see Adam.

As always, Adam was the perfect gentleman, arriving with a bottle of wine and an appetizer. "You didn't have to bring anything," I said, taking the wine and bowl of spinach and artichoke dip from his hands. He took a moment to smooth any wrinkles out of his navy-and-white plaid shirt and slipped a hand in his pocket casually. "You look great," I said, leaning up to give him a peck on the cheek. And he smelled even better. I'd never get tired of inhaling his fresh aftershave.

"Thanks. I wasn't sure what to wear."

"Yeah, me neither." Adam followed me toward the back of the house to the kitchen. "Shane, this is Adam. Adam, Shane," I said.

"Hey, Adam," Amanda said, a wide grin across her face. "Glad you could come."

Adam nodded toward Amanda and smiled politely.

"Good to meet you, Adam," Shane said, wiping off his hands with a towel and extending one toward him. "I've heard a lot about you. Nice to finally put a face to the name."

"Likewise. The girls talk about you all the time."

"Not too much, I hope." Shane shot a glance at Amanda. He knew as well as I did that she had no filter. I knew more about their sex life than Shane probably did, and I guessed he was hoping that Adam hadn't been present for any of those conversations.

"They told me a lot about CrossFit. Lily's been dying for me to go. I guess I have you to thank for getting her in such great shape."

Shane's eyebrows furrowed in confusion at Adam's remark. "Um, yeah, I guess. Lily was always in great shape, though. Can I offer you something to drink?"

"Um, yeah, thanks. A beer would be great if you have one. And I didn't mean Lily wasn't in great shape before. I mean, she always looks beautiful. I just meant... I know CrossFit's different from a regular gym."

Shane laughed as he handed Adam a beer from the fridge, and I could see in his eyes that he was gearing up for a CrossFit explanation. Adam listened silently as Shane explained the origins of CrossFit and why people preferred it to a traditional gym. "You should really take Lily up on her offer and come by sometime," Shane suggested. "You look like you're in great shape. I'm sure you could handle it."

"I'm sure I could too," Adam countered. "I'm just not sure it's for me. Too much structure or something. And Lily mentioned that sometimes you do workouts as teams... I don't think I want other people depending on me like that. I kinda just like to do my own thing."

I sensed Shane debating whether or not to continue the conversation any further. "Well, the invitation stands if you'd like to come by sometime. You should give everything a shot at least once," he said. "And I think you might be surprised. Don't be so quick to think other people will be relying on *you*. It might be the other way around, you know. Okay, who's hungry?" he asked quickly, allowing Adam no time to respond.

❤

Thankfully, the battle of the gyms had ceased as soon as we'd sat down. And strangely enough, so had the conversation. I wasn't even sure Amanda and I were this quiet in our sleep.

"More wine?" Shane asked Amanda and me, presumably in an effort to break the noticeable silence that had settled over the table.

"Please," we both said at the same time as we raised our glasses toward Shane.

"You good, Adam?" Shane asked, still holding the wine bottle.

Adam glanced at his half-full glass and nodded. "I'm good for now. Thanks."

Shane placed the bottle back on the table and silence descended again. It was deafening.

"The food is really excellent, Shane. You're quite a cook," Adam said between bites.

"Thanks. It helps in my business to be able to cook well. Sort of like practicing what you preach."

"Do a lot of the people at the gym ask your advice on their diets?" Adam asked.

"Some do. But I'm a nutritionist by day, so that's when I give most of my advice."

Amanda snorted. "By day? What are you, a superhero?"

Adam's face contorted slightly at Amanda's comment. He hadn't been around her enough to understand that she showed love through sarcasm.

"Ignore her, Adam. I do," Shane said simply.

"You couldn't ignore me if you tried," Amanda balked.

Shane sat up straighter in his chair.

Challenge accepted. I grabbed my glass of wine and sat back in my chair, awaiting the fireworks.

Poor Adam looked like he had just stumbled upon a den of rattlesnakes. He clearly knew that a war had been waged, and he didn't want to give allegiance to one side and risk pissing off the other. And I didn't blame him. He'd get verbally bulldozed by either of them.

"Lily told us you're an architect?" Shane was trying to get the conversation rolling again. He couldn't make a show of actively ignoring Amanda if she didn't have an opportunity to speak.

"Uh, yeah." Adam's eyes were darting between Shane and Amanda. He might not have known either of them well, but he knew enough to understand that this was far from over.

"That's interesting. What do you build?"

"Houses mostly. My crew is currently putting up a housing

development about an hour from here."

Shane nodded. "Guess we have that in common." Adam looked perplexed so Shane continued, "Building. You build houses, and I build muscles. I imagine both are equally gratifying." Shane's lips twitched, and I wondered if anyone else noticed. His response sounded fairly douchey, and I guessed from his attempt to suppress a smile that it was intentional.

Well played, Shane. Amanda wouldn't be able to resist a smartass comment after that pompous display.

"He's also working on building quite an ego, Adam. I'd tell him to show it to you sometime, but, well, he just did."

There's my girl, right on cue. I almost felt bad for taking such enjoyment in watching Shane play Amanda like a violin. But it wasn't often that she found a worthy opponent, and I reveled in it.

"Umm, yeah, it's pretty gratifying. I guess." Adam picked up his wine and took a large drink.

"Oh, so you're going to ignore me too, huh, Adam?" Amanda charged.

"No." Adam sounded horrified. Exactly what he'd been trying not to do had happened. He'd made an enemy. "I didn't ... I mean, I wasn't ignoring you. I just didn't know how to respond to what you said."

Adam looked to me for help, but I just shrugged. I figured he should get the full experience that my friends had to offer. That's what *I'd* gotten from his flock of assholes. Plus, I thought of it like immersion therapy. I'd immerse him in the crazy, and eventually he'd get used to it.

"So respond now. Shane here has quite an ego, don't you think?"

I looked at Shane and watched him roll his tongue around

his mouth. He'd underestimated Amanda. If he was going to ignore her, she'd have to outsource and drag someone else in who Shane couldn't ignore. And Adam was that someone. *Poor bastard.*

"I don't . . ." Adam looked around helplessly. "I don't know him well enough to make that assessment."

"Please," Amanda said as she batted a hand in Shane's direction. "Don't be worried about hurting his feelings. He doesn't have any. Answer the question, Adam. First impression of Shane and his ego: what was it?" Amanda was leaning on her arms, which were crossed on the table.

"I . . . I . . . Jesus Christ, you people are driving me insane," Adam blurted out as he ran a hand over his face.

Shane and Amanda looked at each other and then burst out in howls of laughter. I couldn't resist chuckling along with them, though I tried to tone it down for Adam's sake. He looked completely frazzled.

Adam stared at the two of them for a minute before finally sighing deeply. "Glad you two find me so amusing." One side of his mouth was turned up into a slight smile, which was appropriate because I could tell he was only half kidding.

Shane held up one of his hands and tried to rein in his laughter enough to respond. "Sorry, Adam. I know Amanda and I take a little getting used to."

"Yeah, sorry, Adam. We get a little carried away sometimes," Amanda added.

"Sometimes?" I asked skeptically.

"Okay, all the time," Amanda conceded.

Shane served dessert, and we chatted a bit more about nothing much in particular. Adam was nearly silent, obviously spent from his ordeal with the two of them. I figured I'd put him through enough, so after we helped clear the table, I spent a second talking to Shane, announced our departure, and we said our goodbyes.

Once we were tucked safely in the car, Adam turned to me. "Are they *always* like that?"

I shrugged. "Pretty much."

"I don't know how you hang out with them so much. I'm exhausted just from *watching* them argue."

"You'll get used to it." I smiled.

"I doubt it. I'm going to need a month to recuperate before we hang out with them again. I should be good by the wedding." He huffed out a laugh.

"You don't have that long."

"What do you mean?" He looked alarmed.

"I told Shane and Amanda we'd see them Wednesday. At CrossFit."

"Why the hell would you tell them that? I said I didn't want to go there."

I patted his knee lovingly. "I know what you said." I smiled sweetly as he groaned and started backing out of Shane's driveway. Even though I had told Amanda, and myself, that Adam's forgetting my birthday was no big deal, it did sting a little. So I felt there was no harm done if he stung a little too. Plus, maybe he'd let me ice down his muscles afterward. What girl would pass up that chance?

❤

Monday rolled around and I was already counting down the days until I got Adam to CrossFit. But, at least for today, I'd have to settle for going by myself. I had brought a bag with me to work so that I could head for the gym as soon as I left, but Amanda had asked me to go to a later class so we could go together. She'd spent the rest of the weekend at Shane's, so I guess she was going through Lily withdrawal.

Since I had extra time before the gym Monday night, I was able to get there a few minutes early. I plopped my belongings on the ground against a side wall and waited patiently as the previous class finished up the last of their exercises.

I kept my eyes fixed on the door, knowing that if Amanda was late, Shane wouldn't hesitate to make her row just like any other CrossFitter. When I saw her breeze through the entrance, I let out a sigh of relief—for her sake—and glanced over toward the other class, who had just finished up and was coming this way to get their things.

I began to make my way over to the workout space to get ready for our warm-ups, when I stopped dead in my tracks. *What. The. Fuck? What is he doing here?* Though he was leaned over tying his shoe, his face obscured by his own body, there was no mistaking him. His broad shoulders and tanned muscular arms were showcased by his snug sleeveless Under Armour shirt. My breath hitched as I ran my eyes down his body to appraise his firm ass in dark mesh shorts. And as he stood, the small speck of doubt I had about his identity disappeared entirely when he ran a towel across his sweat-glistened neck and dark messy hair.

Max fucking Samson was there.

I couldn't figure out why I'd been so shocked. He'd told Shane he'd take him up on his offer to try out CrossFit. I knew that. But there was something about having him there— in a place I almost considered a second home—that felt too invasive. *Jesus, Lily. He's just in your gym, not your vagina. Get a fucking grip.*

I'm not sure if it made it better or worse that Max didn't seem fazed at all by *me*. He strolled confidently over to where I stood, picking up his keys from the floor on the way. "Thanks, Shane." *Oh, shit. When did Shane come over here?* I'd been so involved in my shock at seeing Max, I hadn't even noticed that Shane had come over to talk to Amanda. "You weren't kidding. This is a killer workout. I appreciate the opportunity to come by," Max added.

I could tell Shane was tempering his excitement. "Yeah, man. Anytime. We'd love to have you back."

The two shook hands before Max shifted his eyes toward me. "Nice to see you again, Lily," he said tentatively. "Enjoy your workout."

"Uh, thanks. Nice to see you too." We both hesitated for a moment, unsure of how to finalize our uncomfortable goodbye. *Will it be weird if we hug? Will it be weirder if we don't?*

"I'll make sure Shane goes a little easier on you next time," Amanda said to assuage some of the tension. "He likes to ride people pretty hard sometimes."

I saw Max smirk at the sexual connotation of her comment. Would there ever be a time when his mind *wasn't* in the gutter?

"I never heard you complaining," Shane fired back at Amanda with a wink.

"Looks like you've got your hands full with this one, Shane," Max said, pointing at Amanda. "Thanks again. I'm sure I'll see you before the bachelor party. Ladies, it was nice seeing you both again," Max added politely before heading toward the exit.

"Sounds good! I look forward to it," Shane called out over the blaring music as Max made his way to the door.

"Jesus, Shane, you might wanna adjust your broner. People can see it through your shorts."

"My what?" Shane asked, only half listening as he looked over Amanda's head toward the door where Max had just exited.

"Your broner. It's a boner for another dude."

"Oh, shut up. That's not a real thing. You just made that up."

"It is too a real thing. I may have made up the term 'broner'—which is awesome, by the way—but your man crush on him is totally real."

"I don't have a man crush on him. He's just a cool guy who likes sports and is in great shape. We have a lot of the same interests."

"What would those other interests be? Gazing at each other longingly and lying on his back as he does push-ups? I can't believe you invited him to the bachelor party. You know it's gonna be a joint party. Lily will be there. And she sure as hell isn't gonna feel like hanging out with Max Samson for a whole weekend."

"That's why you had me come later, isn't it?" I asked. "You knew he'd be here." I appreciated that Amanda had stopped me from going to the exact same class as him, but it was *more* awkward that she hadn't prepared me to see him. I wasn't sure where he and I stood, so a little heads-up would've been helpful. And now I'd have to spend an entire weekend with him in Atlantic City for Shane and Amanda's party. I thought back to the last time Max and I had been in Atlantic City together. *Shit, I'm really fucked.* Even though this time I was sure we wouldn't have another almost-sexual encounter, Adam wouldn't be so sure. "If Adam knows Max is going to the party, he's gonna lose his shit."

"What's the worst that Adam thinks could possibly happen? Yeah, never mind. He'll probably be pissed if he finds out."

"You don't have anything to worry about, Lily," Shane tried to assure me. "He's bringing his girlfriend to the bachelor party weekend. Now I gotta start class. We can talk about this later."

Girlfriend? I wasn't sure why, but this news filled me with more dread than my impending conversation with Adam. I blew out a breath. "Today sucks," I muttered before starting my jumping jacks and contemplating running away from home.

chapter thirty-two

a d a m

"Today is the day, Adam. Let's go." Lily was positively giddy.

"I know, I'm ready." I was behaving purposely reluctant, though was actually feeling the opposite. Not that I was *excited* to go with her to CrossFit, but seeing her so happy was contagious. I started shuffling papers on her dining room table.

"What are you doing?" she accused more than asked.

"Just making sure my will is in order before I let you drag me to my death."

"You're so dramatic," she murmured as she rolled her eyes. "Now, come on. If we're late, we have to row, and I prefer to not *begin* my workouts exhausted."

I followed her out of her apartment and used my key to lock her door. As I looked down at her house key on my key chain, I shook my head slightly, smiling. Who would've ever thought that we'd be here when we got back together in December? It still didn't seem real.

"Old man, what the hell are you doing?" Lily's shrill yell pierced through my happy moment.

I ran to catch up with her, barreling into her from behind and wrapping my arms tightly around her. "Letting you drag me to your gym."

She wrapped her arms around mine as we moved awkwardly, but lovingly, down her hallway. "I let you drag me out with your friends, so you're going to CrossFit with me and you'll damn well like it," she said with mock seriousness.

"You don't like it when I make you go out with my friends, so why do I have to like it when we go to your gym?"

"Touché, Mr. Carter. But I do *pretend* to like them. At least to their faces. Most of the time."

I laughed into her shoulder. She was right—she did try to put on a good show. We'd been out with my friends a few times since their disastrous first meeting, and Lily always went in with a smile and a good attitude. That's not often how she left, but at least she tried. It still bothered me that she didn't get along with them, but at least the effort was there.

I had tried asking her what it was that she didn't like about them, but she didn't really have a solid answer. "We just have nothing in common," she had finally responded.

"But you and I have things in common," I had said. "And I have things in common with them. So, I don't get how that works."

"They have different things in common with you than I do."

"Wow, I must be pretty common," I had joked.

She'd swatted me on the arm but then turned serious. "They don't like me either, Adam. Did you question them too?"

Truth was I had, and I received similar answers. They

just didn't mesh, and I doubted they ever would. It was kind of how I felt about her friends actually. Granted, there wasn't a palpable tension between me and the Lily Brigade like the one that existed between Lily and my crew, but my interactions with them were stilted and forced all the same.

Lily and I finally made it down to her car and started for her gym. I had been actively avoiding this trip for months now. It's not that I didn't want to participate in something she clearly enjoyed, but I, well, I just didn't want to participate. I was fine at my own gym where I was able to do my own thing. The class structure to CrossFit didn't appeal to me. But she had been hounding me about it, so I finally agreed to go and see what it was all about.

I regretted it instantly.

I walked into the warehouse-converted gym and was greeted by blaring rock music and twenty people dripping sweat everywhere, while about fifteen more watched and waited for their class to start. We stood there for a couple of minutes while the previous class ended and the drenched exercisers limped toward their belongings. I saw Shane walking toward us and plastered a smile on my face.

"Hey, guys," he greeted us as he stretched his hand out toward me. "You ready for this?"

"Ready as I'll ever be."

"Shane, I swear to God, I'm going to kill you for the mess you've made in that office. Lily, Adam, is it six already?"

We all spun toward Amanda as she walked up to us and gave us each a quick hug.

"Yeah, it's six. I didn't think you were going to be here tonight?" Lily inquired.

"Me neither, but I'm still trying to get this doofus's books in order. Did you know he has all of his accounting in *ledgers*?" She uttered the last word as though it were dirty. "Ledgers, Lily. It's going to take me weeks to get that shit all sorted out."

"Oh, stop," Shane admonished. "It's not that bad. And you offered to do it."

"Not that bad? Have you been huffing your creatine? It's a train wreck in there." Her voice elevated as she thrust an arm toward the office. "And *excuse me* for wanting to get our finances in order before we get married. I should've never encouraged you to take over partial ownership of the gym. 'Go for your dream,' I told him. Well, this shit is no dream; it's a fucking nightmare. I don't even know how you can be sure these people are paying you every month for their memberships." Amanda was ranting a mile a minute. I actually found it hard to keep up.

"They're probably not." Shane smirked.

I couldn't understand what he got out of goading her all the time, but it seemed to work for them . . . if fighting all the time really *worked* for anybody. Lily tried explaining it to me once how this banter was fun for them, but I couldn't understand how that was possible. To each his own, I guess.

"Oh, so this is like a charity, then? Kind of like what you are to me." Amanda's lips quirked up at the corners.

These two are so fucking weird.

"Exactly like that," Shane replied, moving toward Amanda and wrapping his arms around her. He leaned down and pecked a kiss to her cheek. Then to her nose, then her other cheek.

"Stop pecking me. You know I hate chickens." But she couldn't hold in her laugh as he kept up his assault.

"Okay, dirty birds, can we get class started? Some of us would like to exercise." Lily started pulling on Shane's T-shirt.

"Really? Who? Surely you aren't talking about yourself because I don't think anyone would consider what you do here exercising."

"Fuck you, Shane. Come on," Lily whined. "I wanna see Adam cry."

Everyone thought that was hysterical. Everyone except me. "Very funny, Lily. It can't be that bad. You act like I don't work out regularly."

"Aww, did I hurt your feelings?" she said as she put her arms around my waist and looked up at me with pouting eyes. "Well, get used to it, Carter. It's not the only thing that's going to be hurting today." She placed a quick kiss on my lips and darted toward the mats to join the stretching that Kate, Shane's coworker, was leading.

What followed was the longest hour of my life. The workout really hadn't seemed so bad when Shane had previewed it for us, but hearing about it and enduring it were two different things. After finding my back squat max, Shane informed us that the workout of the day—WOD—was about to begin. I turned to Lily. "That wasn't the workout?"

She laughed. "No. We always start with muscle building, and then we move into the actual WOD."

"Shit," I muttered. I had felt good on the back squats, managing to build up to three hundred and thirty-three pounds. But if I had known that there was still more to come, I might have taken it down a notch.

The WOD consisted of three power cleans, six push-ups, and nine air squats. We had to cycle through this as many times as possible in three minutes. Then, we would rest for a minute and repeat. Five times!

What made it even worse was that Amanda had taken

a break from bookkeeping to elect herself my own personal cheerleader. "Come on, Adam, dig deep. Deeper," she grunted animalistically during my squats. This was followed by her yelling "Up, down, up, down. Faster, Adam. Oh yes, faster," while I did the push-ups. Thankfully, she evidently had a difficult time thinking of any sexually charged comments to accompany the cleans. Until the fourth round when she commented, "Wow, you must be really used to bringing things up to your face," and winked suggestively at Lily.

I had hoped Shane would drag her away from me so that she would at least stop distracting the other people in the class. But, since he was clearly enjoying her one-man comedy act even more than she was, he never said a word.

Lily also seemed to be having a great time at my expense. But I was so winded from the workout, the only retort I could muster was sticking my tongue out at her as she laughed like a hyena when Amanda tried to lie beneath me for my last round of push-ups.

It was sweet in a way, how they were trying to include me in their jokes and gibes. I just wasn't into it. I didn't know them well enough to enjoy being ridiculed by virtual strangers. Maybe Lily and I just weren't meant to hang out in a group. Or maybe we both just befriended assholes.

By the end of the fifth round, my legs were quaking and my arms were hanging lifelessly at my sides. I slid down against the wall and tried to catch my breath.

Lily sat next to me. "Did you like it?" she asked hopefully.

"Who in their right mind would *like* that?" I wheezed.

"Look around. Lots of people." She giggled.

"You're all nuts," I said as I struggled to my feet.

"Agreed."

I looked over and saw her smiling as I threw my arm around her shoulder. "Carry me out of here, beautiful."

We headed for the exit, but Shane intercepted us. "How was it?"

"Brutal. I give you guys a lot of credit. You're way fitter than I am if you can do that every day."

"It gets easier," he replied. "So, Amanda wanted me to ask you guys if you wanted to stop for dinner. I have a few things to finish up here, but I'll meet you guys in fifteen minutes."

Lily looked up at me. "We're all sweaty and gross," I complained.

"That's no big deal. There's a little place around the corner a bunch of us go to all the time. It's supercasual," Shane explained.

Lily was still looking at me, the pout coming back to her face. But I couldn't do it. It was bad enough I had just let Shane torture me for an hour. I just wasn't up for hanging out with him afterward too. "Why don't you just drop me off back at my car and then you guys can go?"

"But I want to hang out with you more before you have to go home to Eva."

"That's not very long from now anyway. I told my mom I'd be home by eight. And I'm beat. It's fine; I'll see you this weekend."

"Okay," Lily relented, though she definitely wasn't happy about it. "Tell Amanda that I'll come back and get her in fifteen minutes," she said to Shane as we walked out.

"No problem. Oh, and Adam, if you want to join our little family here, just come on back in anytime."

"Thanks, Shane," I said as I continued to shuffle toward the door, "but I'm not sure this is for me."

chapter thirty-three

l i l y

It had finally arrived: spring break. I had been longing for it since Christmas, and now here it was. There was only one thing standing in the way of complete and utter elation. And that *thing* was the Swift Middle School Spring Concert. There were really very few things that were worse than a bunch of puberty-stricken boys trying to sing. And one of them was a bunch of hormone-fueled girls thinking they were all Kelly Clarkson. *This is going to be straight-up hell.*

The concert was set to start at six the Friday night before my week of freedom, so I decided to corral Tina and Trish and drag them to happy hour. Maybe a slight buzz would make the kids seem more talented. Though it was more likely that it would get me fired because I'd probably be unable to prevent cackling at their vocal abominations.

Trish was hesitant at first. *What else was new?* But I was ultimately able to break her, and we all made our way to Flanagan's.

"I'll get the first round. What do you hos want?" I asked when we had settled at a high-top table by the jukebox.

"Just water for me," Trish declared. "I don't want to drink before the concert."

I stared at her. "Are you fucking with me right now?"

She drew back in her seat a little at my abrasiveness.

"Trish, the concert is the *reason* I'm drinking. Are you really going to toast to our spring break with water?" I was incredulous. Had I taught this girl nothing?

"But we're going back to the school in a couple hours. I don't want to smell like alcohol."

"So pop in a Tic Tac and keep it moving," Tina interjected. "I'll take a vodka and cran, by the way."

"No one's telling you to get plowed. But you're off the clock; you can have a drink or two if you want one. So, what'll it be?" I leaned my hip against the table, daring her to say the word *water* again.

"Okay fine, you win," Trish released with a breath.

"I normally do."

"I'll have an appletini."

"Now you're talking. Be right back." I went to the bar and ordered our drinks, deciding on a Tequila Sunrise for myself, in honor of not seeing another sunrise for ten days. When I arrived back at the table, I saw Trish gesturing wildly with her hands while Tina seemed to be taking calming breaths. "What's up?" I asked cautiously.

"Why don't you tell your mentor what you were just explaining to me, Trish?" Tina said patronizingly.

Thankfully, Trish was either too awkward to appropriately register tone or was too caught up in her own brain to notice it. "Ugh, I was just talking about my parents. They're so unsupportive."

"Oh, parent bashing. I can get down with this."

Tina raised her index finger. "Wait for it."

"They wanted me to go with them to St. Thomas for spring break. I mean, can you believe them? It's like they have no idea how much work goes into being a teacher. Like I really have time to go on a vacation right now. I have essays to grade, lesson planning to do, materials to create. And then they had the nerve to get mad at *me* for telling them no. They're so ridiculous." She huffed as she finished her last words and picked up her drink.

I sat there in shock before slowly turning my head to Tina, who simply nodded, affirming that I had heard this crazy broad right.

"Just in case you were wondering," Tina said as she lifted her drink to her lips, "you failed at your job as a mentor."

"What do you mean?" Trish shrieked. "Lily's a great mentor." She look at us, trying desperately to figure out what we were talking about.

"No," I finally said in a hushed voice. "Tina's right. I've failed you, Trish. And I'm just . . . so, so sorry." I looked at Tina. "Where did I go wrong?"

Tina shook her head and cast her eyes to the table. "I wish I knew."

"What are you two talking about? You're scaring me."

I reached over and grabbed Trish's hand. "It's okay, Trish. I'm scared too. Scared for your fucking sanity," I yelled as I dropped her hand. "What the hell's the matter with you? You never, I repeat, *never* pass up a trip to a tropical island to mark papers and do lesson plans. Jesus Christ!"

"I . . . I don't understand," Trish stammered.

"That's the problem. You don't get it. Trish, you need to

have a fucking life outside of teaching or you're gonna burn yourself out. It's great that you love what you do, but you need to love other things in your life too. Like yourself for starters. Not going on an awesome vacation because of your job is ludicrous. Ask me what I brought home from my classroom today?"

Trish sat there, scared, meek, and silent.

"Ask me!" I yelled.

"Fine, what did you bring home from your classroom?"

"Not a goddamn thing. And you wanna know why? Because I'm not doing anything work related over *my* break. I work hard all year. I've earned this break as much as the kids. They didn't leave with work today, so why the hell should I?"

"Well, actually my kids did leave with work today," Trish whimpered.

"Bah, no wonder they hate you," I screamed before really processing the words. Trish looked about ready to cry. *Shit.* "Trish, I got carried away. They totally don't hate you. I was on a roll and couldn't rein it in."

Trish picked up her glass and took a gulp. "No, you're right. They do hate me." She propped her elbows on the table and buried her head in her hands. As her body began shaking, I reached over to rub her back, and Tina and I began talking over her head like Trish wasn't even there anymore.

"Smooth move, Ace," Tina said dryly.

"Oh, what do you want from me? You know I have a flair for the dramatic. I couldn't help myself."

"Now what are we going to do? She looks seconds away from twisting the table napkins into a noose."

"Move the napkins?" I offered with a smirk.

Tina rolled her eyes before leaning across the table

toward Trish. "Hey, come on. Relax. Don't listen to Lily. She's heavily medicated."

I threw one of the napkins I'd collected at her as she snorted. "Seriously, Trish, this isn't the end of the world. The first year sucks for everyone. And you're really good at your job. I just want you to find a balance is all. You'll be so much happier when you do that."

Trish lifted her head and sniffled. "How do you two do it? Find a balance?"

"We just have lives outside of here. Friends, boyfriends, husbands, hobbies. What about you? Are you seeing anybody?" I wasn't sure that last question was a good idea, but I'd asked it anyway, hoping we could steer the conversation in another direction.

Trish shook her head.

"Nobody at all?" I asked, sensing there was something Trish wasn't telling us.

"Well, there is one guy, but I dunno, I've kinda been blowing him off. I just don't have time for a relationship right now."

"You need to make time. You'll feel so much better when your life doesn't revolve around your students. I promise."

She was still for a few minutes, seeming to weigh my words before she nodded. "Maybe you're right."

"I am."

Trish picked up her glass and drained the rest of her martini. "I'm gonna go for it. When I see him next, I'm gonna tell him I'm interested."

"Good girl," I squealed.

Trish stood up. "I'm going to get another drink. You guys want one?"

I looked down at my nearly full glass and shook my head, as did Tina.

Trish merely nodded and walked off toward the bar.

Tina and I watched her for a second before turning our attention to each other. At which point we both completely lost it. Through hysterical laughter and tears streaming down her face, Tina sputtered, "What the hell is wrong with that girl?"

"She needs to get laid. Like, yesterday."

"What are you two laughing at?"

Shit. Trish.

"Lily almost fell off her stool," Tina offered as she clutched her sides and started to calm down.

"Yeah, I'm a total klutz."

Trish seemed to accept that answer. She took another large drink from her glass before walking over to the jukebox and sliding in a dollar. And as "I Will Survive" started blaring through the speakers, I knew the night was going to be interesting.

❤

"Dude, we shouldn't have let her drink so much," Tina whispered as we followed a swaying Trish up the driveway to the school.

"How were we supposed to know? One minute she was fine and then she was annihilated. I've never seen someone go from sober to shit-faced so quickly."

"Well, we have now. She's a mess."

"You heard me try to talk her into letting us take her home. She threw a fit. What else can we do?"

Tina simply shrugged.

"What are you two whispering about back there?" Trish demanded.

"Nothing," I replied.

"Yeah, right," Trish said, clearly able to read my tone.

"She's a sassy drunk." Tina chuckled.

"Stop. We have to get her under control or she's gonna get into trouble."

"Maybe a little trouble wouldn't be bad for her," Tina muttered.

I yanked my phone out of my purse as we walked into the school and headed toward the auditorium. Adam had said he'd text when he got there. Eva wasn't singing in the concert, but she was part of the stage crew. I gave Adam credit, even supporting his daughter when her sole job was to push a set of bleachers aside and roll a piano onto the stage. He really was a good man. *Hmm, nothing yet.* It was almost six and it wasn't like him to be late.

Just as I walked into the auditorium, a couple of students ran toward me. "Miss Hamilton, you came." Their parents walked over behind them, and I readied myself to kiss some parent ass.

"Hi, guys. Of course I came. I told you I would."

One girl, Tessa, turned toward her mother and gushed, "Mom, this is Miss Hamilton. She's my favorite teacher."

I heard a loud "humph" next to me and cast a sideways glance at Trish, who avoided my gaze.

As I made small talk with some of the parents, Trish kept muttering under her breath like a lunatic. Finally, Tina grabbed her by the arm and led her to the other side of the auditorium. I heard her say something along the lines of, "What do I care if these little assholes hate me?" as she stumbled to keep up with Tina. The parents looked at me inquisitively, but I quickly changed the subject.

"Looks like they're getting ready to start the concert. Have a great time, everybody, and enjoy your breaks." They all said their goodbyes, and I started to rush toward Trish and Tina when a familiar voice caught my attention. I scanned the crowd, my gaze finally landing on him. I walked over to him and waited for a break in his conversation before speaking. "Hey, Adam."

He turned and looked surprised to see me. "Oh, uh, Lily, hi. Umm, Carl, it was good seeing you. I'll catch up with you later."

The men shook hands and Adam began walking away, so I followed. He finally came to a stop at the back of the auditorium where there was a small alcove and looked at me expectantly.

I narrowed my eyes. *Why is he being so weird?* "You said you were going to text," I finally said.

"Oh, shit, yeah, I got caught up talking to Carl. Sorry." His eyes were darting around and his hands were in his pockets. To say he looked uncomfortable would have been an understatement.

"Adam, what's wrong with you?"

His eyes found mine briefly. "What do you mean?"

"I mean, you're acting weird as hell. What is it?"

He sighed heavily and rubbed his hand against the back of his head. "I just . . . Look, Lily, I'm sorry. I just don't want this to be awkward for Eva. I can only imagine what these parents and their children would say if they knew about us, and I just . . . I just don't want to hurt her."

"So we're back to this, huh, Adam? You're telling me one thing while another thing is the real truth?"

"What do you mean? What did I tell you that was untrue?"

My voice dipped dangerously low to prevent myself from screaming at him. "You said we'd meet here. You acted like it was no big deal to be seen here with me. I get that you have to think of Eva's feelings, and I don't fault you for it. But be *honest* with me. Tell me it makes you uncomfortable, so I can be prepared for it and we can avoid all of this. God, please, Adam, just be up-front with me."

Adam was staring at the floor, his posture rigid. He was clearly fuming, but I couldn't for the life of me figure out what he had to be pissed about.

"You're really gonna stand there and lecture me about being honest?" His voice was crisp, and when he finally looked at me, his eyes were penetrating, angry. "Seems a lot of things could have been avoided if you'd been as honest as you expect me to be."

His words were like a slap in the face. But they didn't make me sad. They made me fucking furious. "Is this what it's always going to come down to, Adam? I'm going to call you out on something and you're going to go back to that? Your *trump* card? I guess you win, then. Because I know that what you did tonight doesn't beat what I did to you last year. It's not even close. But the fact that I can't tell you what I'm feeling, that what you're doing hurts me, is basically telling me *not* to be honest with you." I felt the anger slipping as the tears rose. *Don't do it, Lily. Please don't cry in front of him.* But my emotions wouldn't listen. And as the tears started to fall, Adam's posture slackened.

"Lily, I—"

"Save it, Adam." I started to walk away, but then spun back toward him. "It can't be like this. We'll never work if it's like this."

Before I even registered his movement, he had me in his arms and was holding me tightly. "Baby, I'm so sorry. God, I'm so sorry. I love you, Lily. I just don't know how to be everything—the father Eva needs and the boyfriend you need. I just wanted to protect you both. I don't want people to talk about either of you because of me. And then, when you questioned me, I got angry, and I'm such a dick for that. Please, Lily, I didn't mean that shit. I'm sorry that my first reaction was to go there, to hurt you with our past. I won't do it again. I swear."

My body instinctively leaned into him, even though my brain scolded me for it. I didn't want to depend on him. Not right now. But I did. Because he was Adam. My Adam. And even in the worst moments, I knew I'd always be able to count on him. He'd always catch me, even when he was the one who caused me to stumble. It's why I loved him. Why I needed him. Why I chose him. I wrapped my arms around his neck and hugged him back, hoping that hugs like these would always be able to hold us together.

"Lily, there you are."

The voice caused Adam and me to jerk apart. I sniffled and turned my head to see Tina, slightly panicked.

"Tina, what's wrong?"

Tina clearly registered that she'd interrupted something important, but she couldn't take it back now. "Uh, sorry, guys. But I lost Trish."

I whirled around fully. "What do you mean you lost Trish?"

Tina shrugged, raising her hands in front of her, and stared at me.

I turned to Adam. "Hey, I gotta go. Trish got a little drunk earlier, and we gotta find her before she does something stupid."

Adam tucked a piece of my hair behind my ear. "I understand." He lowered his face so that he could look more clearly into my eyes. "Are we okay?"

I pressed a chaste kiss to his lips and smiled slightly. "Yeah, baby. We're okay."

A relieved smile spread across his face. "Good. I'll call you later tonight. Maybe we can Skype," he added with a wink.

"Don't be a tease, Mr. Carter."

"I'm not a tease if I intend to follow through, Miss Hamilton." He gave me another kiss on the cheek, and I left with Tina to fucking find Trish.

❤

Tina and I did our best to locate Trish, but the lights had been dimmed some time ago, and it was nearly impossible to see as we stood at the back of the auditorium.

"I don't know what to do. We're never going to find her in here," Tina said.

"Yeah. I mean, how much trouble could she get into at a middle school concert?"

As soon as those words left my mouth and I heard children's screams and cymbals crashing from backstage, I made a promise to myself that I would *never* ask a question like that again.

Tina and I hoped that the kids were just messing around back there or that a rabid dog had been let loose, anything but the actual cause. But our worst fears were confirmed when we heard Trish yell, "Stop screaming. You act like you've never seen two people kissing before. How do you think you all got here?"

"Oh. My. God," Tina whispered.

"Come on," I said as I grabbed her arm and yanked her backstage.

There we found Trish, her clothes thankfully still on her body, though they were clearly rumpled. She was surrounded by kids and behind her, rubbing his face with his hand, was the school's band director.

Tina leaned in to me. "Don't you have some advice for a situation like this?"

I knew she was referring to my romp with Max in nearly the exact spot Trish had just been caught by a flock of choir nerds. "Yeah," I muttered. "Don't get caught."

❤

Tina and I took Trish home and consoled her as best we could. Unfortunately for her, the principal and the superintendent had been attending the concert. Trish was immediately suspended without pay. I told her I'd contact a union rep on her behalf, but I had a feeling that the next time I saw Trish, it'd be when she was clearing out her classroom.

"Maybe it's for the best," Tina remarked as we walked out to my car. "I don't think she was really cut out for teaching. She would've broken under the stress eventually."

I thought about Tina's words for a second. "Don't we all?" I sighed as I climbed in the car and left Trish behind.

chapter thirty-four

m a x

Surprisingly, the Virgin Mary and I got along incredibly well. So well, in fact, that I was beginning to feel a little guilty for putting the words "the Virgin" in front of her name every time I thought of her. She was sweet, kind, and unbelievably generous to every*one* and every*thing*. She was the kind of person who would take home a doggie bag of scraps from a restaurant to give to stray cats and squirrels. Correction: She wasn't the *kind* of person who did that. She actually *did* do that. On several occasions.

We did our best to get together when we could, but with her new magazine just getting off the ground, her time was limited. Though somehow, with what little time she had, she still managed to give back to others. *Volunteer work. Why the fuck hadn't I thought of that when I'd been jerking around—literally—for the past four months?*

The truth was, Mary's philanthropic nature only left me feeling like more of a loser than I already thought I was.

If someone so busy could find the time to give back to the community, surely I could at least *help* her give back. Maybe we'd go pet some puppies at a local SPCA or organize a beef and beer somewhere. *That's charity, right?*

So when I expressed my newfound desire to be Philadelphia's Mother Teresa, Mary said she was more than willing to show me the ropes. In the middle of April, she planned to go to The Children's Hospital of Philadelphia to help with an Easter egg hunt. When I arrived with her for our "date," and laid eyes on the patients, I couldn't decide if I wanted to stay or turn around and take the elevator back down to the lobby and run through the streets screaming. I knew that was a douchebag thing to even *think*, let alone give serious thought to actually *doing* it.

But despite the fact that a thirty-year-old man shouldn't be shocked to see a few sick kids, I hadn't been prepared for what I'd encountered. All the children on the floor required long-term care. Most of them had already been there for months and probably had the same amount of time—if not more—ahead of them. Some, Mary had told me, would never come out at all.

The hospital had sufficiently set the wing up to feel more like a home than a hospital. With brightly colored murals painted on most of the walls, several game rooms for kids of all ages, and nurses who treated the children like their own sons and daughters, it was almost easy to forget you were in a hospital.

Almost. What I couldn't ignore were the IV poles that these kids had to pull with them when they walked down the hall to the game room, or the wheelchairs that needed to be pushed by someone who was bigger and not as weak as they were.

I did my best to have some fun with them, playing PlayStation with a few of the older boys and speaking in a horrible British accent after inhaling the helium from some of the "get well soon" balloons. Though I did manage to elicit some genuine laughs from those around me, I clearly didn't have the natural connection with these kids that Mary had. *One day she'll make a damn good mother.*

With no more than a smile and a slight hug, she could make anyone around her feel loved, including me. Just when I thought I was impossible to love, Mary was slowly changing my mind.

The only problem was, I couldn't figure out if I'd ever be able to love her back.

❤

A week passed, and so did Easter. I spent it stuffing my face with ham, macaroni and cheese, and scalloped potatoes at my parents'. And The Virgin Mary spent hers doling out ladles of soup at a homeless shelter in the city. *Sounds about right.*

I was beginning to think that the reason our relationship felt so unbalanced was because it was. Mary had so many things going for her. She and her friend had gotten the magazine up and running, and it was gradually beginning to take off. She'd landed a few solid interviews with some pretty big sports names in town, and her connections in the business were steadily growing.

I, on the other hand, filled my time with random guest spots and hoped that showcasing my skills as a television personality would land me what had now become my dream job. Lately, I felt like I was one step above picking up someone's dry cleaning and asking if they wanted extra sugar in their grande latte if it would get me in front of the camera full-time.

Okay, that might have been a slight exaggeration. But the time was approaching when I'd find out whether this audition was going somewhere or nowhere fast. Recently, I felt like all the progress I'd made might have just been an illusion, a mirage to string me along as I searched the desert hopelessly for water I'd never find.

That only made Jack's call that much more nerve-racking. "Hey, Jack," I said tentatively when I answered.

"Maxi Boy," he answered. "How the hell are ya?"

I ran a nervous hand through my hair before answering. "I don't know, Jack. *You* tell *me*. And you know I hate it when you call me 'Maxi.' It reminds me of a girl's period. Fucking disgusting," I blurted out quickly. "I mean, unless you thought she might be pregnant. Then it's a good thing." *Why the hell am I talking about periods?* I was rambling and I knew it. "Sorry, Jack. Ignore me. I'm just nervous. Tell me you have good news."

"Okay," he said simply, "I have good news."

"Really?" My heart had already been beating so loudly, I was sure Jack could hear the pounding through the phone. "Or are you just saying that 'cause I told you to?"

"Well, which is it, jackass? Do you want me to say it or not?"

"Jack, come on. I'm fuckin' dying over here. Did I get the job or not?"

"You got the job, you fuckin' asshole." Jack laughed. "As if there was ever any doubt."

A wave of relief washed over me. "What do you mean 'as if there was ever any doubt'? All I *had* was doubt."

"Well, that doesn't surprise me. If you had half the faith

in yourself that other people have in you, you'd be a lot better off. You know, that's really gonna put a dent in that arrogant facade you have going for ya."

"Ha, yeah, I guess so."

"Anyway," he continued, "they're sending over the contract tomorrow morning. Stop by my office around noon, and we'll look it over together. You don't have any plans tomorrow, do you?"

"What? Uh...no, noon's good. I'll see you then." My lingering shock caused my voice to falter a bit. "And thanks, Jack," I added.

"What are you thanking *me* for? *You* got the job. You're a big fuckin' deal. Go brag to some people or somethin'." Jack let out a breath of feigned disappointment. "For Christ's sake, this humble shit really doesn't suit you."

I hung up with Jack, but over a minute later, I found myself still staring at my phone, unsure of who to call. He'd said to brag to some people, but "bragging" just didn't seem like the appropriate word for what I planned to do.

I agreed that I needed to tell people: my parents, for starters. I knew my mom would be ecstatic, but just as Jack had said, she wasn't at all surprised that I got the job. "I knew you'd get the job, honey. That ice show is lucky to have you."

"It's not an ice show, Mom." I laughed. "That makes me sound like a figure skater or something. It's a pregame show called *On Thin Ice*."

"You know what your mother's trying to say," my dad chimed in. *When the hell had* he *picked up the phone?* "Don't be such a wiseass."

"Well, you know where he gets *that* from," my mom joked. "Certainly not me."

"Are you insinuating that he got the smartass gene from me?" my dad asked, doing his best to act shocked.

"Okay, well, I'm gonna leave you two alone to bicker about my inherited traits. I just called to tell you the good news."

"Well, thank you, sweetheart," my mom said. "You know who else will be excited to hear the news? Did you call her yet?"

It had more than crossed my mind to call Lily. When I'd hung up the phone with Jack, my first instinct had been to call her. I knew, despite the fact that we hadn't really spoken, she would be proud of me. I'd waited so long to have Lily's approval, I knew hearing her say she was proud of me would be like an orgasm to my ears. But, I just couldn't. "I can't call Lily, Mom," I said, finally answering her question. "I haven't told her much about the auditions."

The momentary silence on the other end of the phone told me I'd said something wrong. "I meant Mary, honey. You know, that sweet girl you've been dating for the last month and a half."

"Oh, right...her." *Fuck.*

chapter thirty-five

l i l y

I knew there was no getting around telling Adam that Max was going to Shane's bachelor party. Though I did manage to put it off for two weeks. I hadn't intended to wait that long, but I found that the time was just never right to have that conversation with him. Instead, I spent a ton of time thinking about all the things I'd rather do than discuss it with him: donate a kidney without anesthesia, go trolling for johns on the streets of Philadelphia, develop a crack habit, all sorts of things.

But I had to tell him, and delaying it only made my anxiety worse. So I finally decided to come clean as we sat at a local pizza joint sharing a pepperoni pie. I figured he wouldn't kill me in public. Too many witnesses.

"Amanda's bachelorette party is in two weeks," I said shyly, looking at the slice as I put it to my mouth.

"Yeah, I know. That'll be fun."

"It definitely will. I haven't been to Atlantic City in a long time." I hadn't anticipated using that as my segue into coming clean, but once it had tumbled out of my mouth, I decided to go with it.

Adam tensed, clearly remembering the conversation we'd had where I revealed all my indiscretions. That had been one of the most difficult discussions we'd ever had. Until now.

"Well, I hope this trip turns out differently from that one." He was smiling, but it didn't reach his eyes. I knew that masked behind his attempt at a joke, he was asking me for reassurance.

Guilt crept through me, causing my face to heat. I wasn't going to be able to set his mind at ease, and I felt horrible about it.

"Well, it will definitely be different, though not as different as you're probably hoping."

Adam halted all movement, his slice of pizza hovering inches from his mouth. He stared at me curiously for a moment, before dropping the pizza back to his plate and resting his arms on the table. "What does that mean?"

"Shane invited Max to his bachelor party."

"You're joking, right? You really need to tell me you're fucking joking, Lily."

I shook my head, but kept my eyes on his. I needed him to see that I had nothing to hide this time. "I'm sorry, Adam. I didn't know he was going to ask Max to go. He just did it."

"And you're still going to go?" His eyes bored into me with a rage that I hadn't seen since that day in my classroom almost exactly a year ago.

April is not a good month for us. "I have to go. I'm the maid of honor."

Adam stood abruptly. "That's perfect," he said sardonically. "Have a great time. I ... need some air. I'll meet you at the car."

And with that, he turned and walked out.

I was stunned still for a second before I rose and rushed after him. *Good thing we already paid for the pizza.* I flung open the restaurant door and silently cursed the jingling of bells that sounded. How dare they sound so happy at a time like this? "Adam," I called as I ran after him. He was almost to the car and didn't bother turning around when he heard me. I ran and caught him by the arm just before he opened his car door. "Adam, please." He allowed me to spin him around and ended up standing mere inches from me. I could feel the anger radiating off his body, his posture tight and coiled. If I hadn't known him better, I would've been intimidated. Actually, I was still slightly intimidated. "What am I supposed to do?" I choked out. Even though I willed them back, the tears were coming anyway.

"That's a great question. I'm asking myself the same one. What the hell am I supposed to do? My girlfriend tells me that she's going to Atlantic City with a guy she had an intimate moment with while she was dating me, and I'm supposed to . . . what? What, Lily? Tell me. What am *I* supposed to do?" He was yelling, his voice thick with all the emotions that were running through him.

I hated knowing that I was the cause of his pain. Again. Looking down at the pavement, I racked my brain for a solution. There was only one. It was the same one I'd contemplated for the past two weeks, and I knew he'd never go for it. But maybe suggesting it would be enough. "You could always come with me."

He scoffed harshly. "Yeah, that's a fabulous idea. Everyone can take bets on how long it takes Max and me to end up in jail for trying to kill each other."

I raised my head so that I could look at him again. "Then I guess you'll just have to trust me."

"What?"

"You heard me, Adam. This is where you decide whether or not you trust me. Because if we don't have that, then we aren't going to last anyway. And I'm not letting Amanda down for a relationship that has no longevity. I've done everything I can to assure you that I'm all in. So now I need to know—is it enough? Am I enough, Adam?"

He slumped back against his car door and turned his head away from me, seemingly trying to mull over my question in his head. When he finally looked at me, his internal battle was evident in his eyes. "It's not a question of you being enough, Lily."

"Isn't it? I'm either what you want or I'm not. The time for hypotheticals is over. There's no room for could-bes and maybe-one-days anymore. This is the proverbial fork in the road." I smiled to ease some of the overwhelming tension. This wasn't a decision I wanted him to make in the heat of the moment. I wanted him to be sure because I didn't intend to ever have this conversation again.

He ran a hand roughly through his hair and exhaled. "Then I choose the road that leads to you." His eyes locked on mine, and I threw myself at him. He wrapped his arms around me and rested his head atop mine. "I love you, Lily. So much that it scares the hell out of me sometimes. You've always been what I wanted. I just wish I was the only one who felt that way."

I pulled back and brought a hand up to cup his cheek. "He's bringing his girlfriend with him. I think it's safe to say that he wants something different now. I know I do."

He smirked. "Oh, yeah? And what is it that you want?"

"You. Just you." I leaned into him as he lowered his lips to mine and captured them in a kiss that expressed everything we felt for one another. It was the best kiss we'd ever shared.

"Let's get out of here," he whispered against my lips.

"Good idea," I responded breathily as I pulled back from him. I walked around to the passenger side of the car, but Adam's voice stopped me before I actually got in.

"And, Lily."

I looked at him expectantly.

"If you think he doesn't still want you, then you don't know him nearly as well as you think you do." And with that, Adam lowered himself into the car and turned the ignition.

I hesitated a second, taking a deep breath of the cool night air before climbing in beside him, hoping to hell that he was wrong.

❤

I drove to Atlantic City with Amanda, Steph, Danielle, and Kate. The boys were all driving together, except for Max, who was coming separately with his girlfriend. We pulled up to Bally's and checked in. We had reserved one Premium Suite for the girls and one next door for the boys. It would be tight cramming us all in, but we didn't plan to spend much time in the room anyway.

Once we made our way up the elevator to the thirtieth floor, we located our room and proceeded to drop our stuff inside and inspect it. It was large, with one king-size bed and a huge armchair that someone could easily sleep in, and we'd asked for a cot to be delivered. The five of us could definitely make it work.

Amanda plopped herself on the bed to relax.

"Not so fast," I scolded. "We have reservations at the spa in thirty-five minutes. So don't get too comfortable over there."

"What are we having done?" Amanda asked.

"The works," I replied with a wink as I walked into the bathroom to drop off my toiletries.

"Well, it better include a happy ending or I'm gonna be pissed," Amanda called after me.

"You're getting your happy ending in seven days when you become Mrs. Shane Reed," Danielle interjected.

Amanda flipped over onto her back and stared at the ceiling. "That's so sappy." As a smile slid across her face, she couldn't help but add, "But totally true."

❤

Two hours later, we were massaged, pampered, and ready to blow the roof off Atlantic City. We all put on the sluttiest clothes we owned, did our hair and makeup, and headed over to the guys' room so we could head to dinner. I had made us all reservations at Arturo's, which was in the hotel. Then, we would all go our separate ways and see who made it back alive.

I knocked on their door and heard someone yell, "Our wenches have arrived."

Great, they're already wasted.

The door swung open, and Ben stood there in a magenta button-down shirt with the top three buttons undone. He held a bottle of Tanqueray in his right hand as he waved us in. "Come on in, ladies. Feel free to remove your clothes and make yourselves comfortable."

Amanda stopped in front of him and fixed him with a

deadly glare. "Just so you know, if you get my fiancé arrested, raped, or murdered tonight, I will make your children fatherless. I can't believe Talia let you come down here alone."

"I know, right?" He laughed.

Talia had opted to stay home with the kids instead of coming to the bachelorette party. Shane's mom had offered to babysit them, but Talia declined. We all had a strong suspicion that a night away from Ben was too strong of a temptation for her to pass up.

We walked the rest of the way in and were greeted by catcalls, whistles, and bottles clanking.

"You guys are pigs," I stated.

"Tell us something we don't know," Kyle retorted as he made his way over to Kate, kissed her cheek, and whispered something in her ear that made her blush deeply. *Lucky bitch.*

"You ready? I'm starving," Amanda said as she leered at Shane. I couldn't blame her; he was quite a sight. He was wearing a black polo shirt that hugged every last one of his rock-solid muscles and light jeans that looked like they had been specially designed for his body.

He looked back at her, letting his eyes graze over her body as if he were deciding which part of her to eat first. And since her black shorts and black corset top accentuated everything she had to offer, he had quite a bit to choose from. "You really going out in that?" he asked, pretending not to care, though it was clear from the way he stared at her that he was *very* interested.

"Yup." She popped the last letter as it left her mouth. She really was a masterful flirt.

He walked over to her and ran his hand down her bare arm as he leaned into her. "Just remember that I'm the only one who gets to take it off you," he said loudly enough for us all to hear.

"Trust me, baby. That's one thing that you never have to worry about me forgetting."

"Okay, let's get out of here. We're going to be late for our reservations," I said, to keep Shane from fucking Amanda right where they stood and giving us all the show of our lives.

Shane grabbed Amanda's hand and started for the door. Kyle wrapped an arm around Kate's shoulder and followed them. I took a quick inventory of the rest of Shane's friends. He had brought his other three groomsmen, all guys he'd grown up with and who I'd met only a couple of times: Mark, Luke, and Matt. I was always stunned how hot guys seemed to flock together. Their group would definitely be attracting some serious female attention tonight. Though, as I looked around at the girls, I knew we'd be turning some heads ourselves.

The only person missing was Max. I wanted to ask Shane where he was, but I worried how it might look. So I kept my mouth shut and silently hoped he'd decided not to show.

I had chosen Arturo's, an Italian restaurant, for one specific purpose: I knew it would be fun as hell to watch Shane try to find something to eat. And since he had insisted on at least beginning our night together, I felt I was owed my own sick form of revenge. I mean, seriously. Who wanted to have a joint bachelor-bachelorette party? Shane Reed, that's who. And while I knew it mostly had to do with his not wanting guys hitting on Amanda all night, he'd just have to get over that shit. We had all bickered about it for three hours one night until

Shane finally relented under one condition: we'd at least all go to dinner together. So here we were. One big happy friggin' family.

I walked up to the hostess and told her the name of our reservation.

"Oh, the rest of your party is already here. I'll show you back."

So much for Max deciding not to come. I motioned for everyone to follow, and we made our way into the restaurant. I might have noticed how cozy the restaurant was, how it seamlessly combined a homey feel with a touch of elegance. I might have noticed that, if I hadn't noticed Max's girlfriend first. *Damn, did she have to be so pretty?*

Max stood when he saw us coming, but I barely registered him beyond this. Well, this and the fact that he was wearing gray slacks that were tailored to perfection and a crisp white button-down with the top two buttons undone. *Yup, barely noticed him at all.*

My eyes were, however, all over his girlfriend. She was stunning. Tall, thin with a tan complexion and dark features: every ex-fling's worst nightmare. A trump card. And while I knew that it shouldn't matter—that I was over Max and who he dated was none of my concern—I couldn't help my instant hatred of her. It didn't help that she was so hot. Even *I* wondered what she looked like naked.

"Hi, guys," Max said in greeting.

"Hey, Max. Been here long?" Shane called.

I shot a glare over my shoulder at Shane, who probably got hard just at the sight of Max.

"No, maybe five minutes ago. Uh, let me introduce everybody. Mary, this is Lily."

Mary extended her hand toward me with a large, genuine smile. "Lily, it's so nice to meet you. I've heard a lot about you."

"God, I hope that's not true." My eyes grew as big as saucers once I realized I had just spoken those words out loud. I quickly grasped her hand and shook firmly, laughing off my verbal diarrhea as a joke and hoping like hell she bought it.

She laughed with me, but her smile was tight. *Christ, I sure know how to make a first impression.* I moved off to the side so Max could continue his introductions.

I felt Amanda bump my shoulder with hers. "You are fucking smooth. You know that?"

"Shut up." The retort was weak, but it was all I had at the moment. We moved to sit down and I all but ran to the other end of the table to avoid ending up anywhere near Max and his Victoria's Secret model. Shane and Amanda sat next to one another, and I sat to her left. Next to me were Steph and Danielle, and across the table sat Matt, Mark, and Luke. Ben sat beside his brother, with Max next to him and Mary across from Max. That left Kyle and Kate to sit directly opposite Shane and Amanda. Comfortable as I was going to get with the seating arrangements, I relaxed slightly.

"Good evening, my name is Melody, and I'm going to be your server for this evening."

I tuned Melody out as she ran through the specials, especially since she had chosen to stand at the opposite end of the table, but my ears perked up when she asked if she could get us anything to drink. "I'll take a Stoli Vanilla and Coke," I nearly yelled. When everyone turned to glare at me, I shrugged. "May as well get this party started, right?" Then I slunk back in my chair and hoped to disappear.

"No redheaded sluts for you tonight, Lil?"

I knew who said it without even having to look. Though I did anyway. He wore that cocky smirk that had irritated me over a year ago when I met him, and it was causing the same reaction now. I knew he was joking, trying to lighten the mood, but I wasn't up for it. He was crashing the party that *I* had worked hard to organize. And on top of that, he brought some chick with him for *us* to entertain all night. Same selfish Max. "No, I learned my lesson with those. They only attract a bad element."

His jaw ticked slightly, but his smile never wavered. Though it didn't matter. I knew I'd gotten to him. I just wished I had felt better about it.

Melody took everyone's drink order and then took off to get them. A weird silence descended on the table. I never knew thirteen people were capable of being that quiet.

"So what are you girls doing tonight?" You could always count on Shane to break an awkward silence. I suddenly regretted putting him through carbohydrate hell. Well, almost.

I wasted no time in responding. "Well, I hired a few male escorts. They should be arriving at the room in about an hour and a half. Then I thought we would head to the center of town and buy some meth. Smoke that for a while, and then, see where the night takes us."

"Amanda prefers heroin, Lily. Don't you know her at all?" Shane said, beating me at my own game. *Sly devil.* He really was perfect for Amanda.

Our drinks arrived as we all discussed our plans for the evening. Ours involved a new club called Swanky that had opened two blocks away from Bally's, and the guys' involved an upscale nightclub called The Last Out. Melody said she'd give us more time to look over the menus and then be back to take our order.

"Max got us VIP access in the club," Shane gushed.

What a girl.

"That's nice, sweetie," Amanda said to Shane before smiling sweetly at Max's date. "So, Mary, you ready to run with the big dogs? We've been known to get pretty wild."

"I think I'll be able to keep up," Mary answered, matching Amanda's smile.

"I hope so. Amanda is a total nutcase. Remember when you jumped into the Delaware River from the back deck of that bar?" Kyle was starting to look a little tipsy and was definitely a talker when he drank. He was probably gearing up to tell a whole bunch of wild Amanda stories. I couldn't wait.

"Do *I* remember it? You weren't even there." Amanda's tone was accusatory, but her face held only confidence. And maybe pride.

"No, but those three were." Kyle pointed at me, Steph, and Danielle. "Just ask them if you don't believe me."

Shane looked over Amanda at me.

"Hey, what happens in the Delaware, stays in the Delaware," I replied, taking a long sip of my drink.

"That's right," Danielle added. "Besides, it wasn't her fault. The cops were chasing her."

Amanda's and my eyes flew to Danielle, shocked by a betrayal from someone in our own ranks. Danielle put her hand over her mouth. "Shit, sorry."

"Snitches wind up as drug dealers' bitches, Danielle," Amanda warned before directing her attention back to Mary. "Don't listen to her. She's a lush. She has no idea what she's talking about."

"How come I never heard this story?" Shane asked, amused.

"Because there's no way to spin it so that I don't look like a complete asshole."

"How'd you hear it?" Shane asked Kyle.

"Oh, she tells me everything. Lily may seem like her best friend, but she's got nothing on me and Amanda. Right, princess?"

"Kyle, maybe you should quit while you're ahead," Amanda warned.

Kyle held up his hands in a defensive gesture.

"Ah, so maybe Kyle should've been your maid of honor," Shane teased.

"Nah, it's against the rules to choose a maid of honor you've slept with," Kyle blurted out.

Once the words were out, there was no taking them back, even though Kyle looked like he would've moved mountains to do exactly that. Everyone at the table stilled.

Shane was the first to speak. "What the fuck did you just say?"

Every muscle Shane had visibly coiled, and I knew that this might be Kyle's very last moment on this earth. I tried desperately to think of something to say to redirect the conversation. "So, Matt, Mark, Luke, where's John? Writing an addendum to his Gospel?" I laughed awkwardly at my own joke as everyone turned their blank faces to me. "What? No one else thinks it's weird that Shane's groomsmen all have names from the New Testament?"

Shane rose quickly and threw his napkin onto the table. "I'm suddenly not hungry. Maybe we should start our night, guys. What do ya say?"

The men all murmured assent as they began to get up. Well, everyone except Kyle. He knew better than to go anywhere with Shane and his closest friends.

"Shane, wait. Let me explain." Amanda grabbed his arm, but he shook her loose.

"There was a time and a place for that. This isn't it. Ready, guys?" And with that, they left.

"Kyle, you are such a fucking prick. What the hell is the matter with you?" Amanda hissed.

"I don't... Shit, I'm... God, I'm so sorry, Amanda. It just slipped." He turned to look at Kate, who sat like a statue beside him. "Kate, baby, just hear me out."

"I've heard enough from you, Kyle." Tears began to slip down her cheeks as she stood. "I'm suddenly not feeling very well, girls. I think I'm going to call it a night." She didn't meet any of our eyes as she walked off.

"You better go after her, dumbass. Fix it before she draws her own conclusions." Amanda sighed.

Kyle got up awkwardly. "Fuck, Amanda, I'm sorry I ruined everything. I never wanted that. I've never felt like a bigger dick."

"That's because you've never *been* a bigger dick. Now go get your girl." Amanda looked away from him, effectively dismissing him.

As Kyle strode off, I stared at Amanda in amazement. Kyle had just jeopardized her marriage, and she still cared enough about him to want him to go after Kate. Underneath that scathingly sarcastic, brazen shell was a real softy.

Amanda looked over at me, sadness written all over her face. "Well, we're off to a great start."

I glanced around the nearly empty table at Steph, Danielle, and Mary. *Fuck... Mary!* Max had left her behind? He was almost as big of a dick as Kyle.

Mary could evidently read my face because she explained. "I told Max to go. The guys won't be able to get into the club without him."

I smiled at her, though I knew it was grim. But it was all I had, so I hoped she took it for what it was worth. She was obviously a good person, way better than me. That was for sure.

Mary started to stand. "I'll just go up to my room."

"No way," I interjected abruptly. "This is Amanda's bachelorette party, and it's going to be a fucking awesome one if I have to hire every hot male stripper in Atlantic City to feed you caviar with his man meat. Now let's eat something small, and then go get our freak on."

The girls all cheered except Amanda. She simply sat there looking at us: her three best girlfriends and one virtual stranger, who were determined to give her the night of her life. "I'm probably going to regret this, but I'm in." Her voice lacked the conviction I was used to, but still, I could work with it.

"Atta girl." I leaned in and hugged her before turning to locate Melody. "Melody," I yelled to our server, who was currently about twenty-five feet away waiting on another table, "we're going to need some pasta and a *lot* of alcohol."

"I'm on it," Melody called back.

I nodded firmly. "Now that everyone's on board, let's get this ho train moving."

❤

Two hours later, I was sitting beside a very drunk Amanda in a back booth at Swanky. We'd lost track of the other girls on the dance floor at some point. As soon as I saw the waterworks coming, I knew to get Amanda somewhere secluded. The only thing she hated more than crying was crying in front of people.

"He's going to call it off, isn't he, Lil?"

"No, Shane would never do that. He's crazy about you."

"But I lied to him. He'll never forgive me."

"You didn't lie to him. You just didn't tell him. They're very different things." I instantly recognized my logic. I'd used it on myself quite a few times. The aftertaste of the words was bitter as I remembered how untrue this advice actually was. A lie of omission was still a lie. But saying that to a completely obliterated Amanda wasn't going to help her situation.

"No, I should've told him. It wouldn't have mattered if I'd been up-front about it. But it looks fucked up that I didn't, like we were trying to be sneaky about it."

"You weren't being sneaky. You just didn't want to dredge up awkward shit that had no bearing on your relationship. Shane will understand once the shock wears off. He's a great guy."

"He is, Lily. He really is. And he fought so hard for me. All I did for so long was push him away and make him feel like he wasn't good enough for me, when really it was the other way around. *He's* the one who's too good. I don't deserve him. But the kicker is, he wants me anyway. After everything I've done to him—how bad I made him feel—he still wants me." Her head dropped. "Now he'll see. I'm not worth all this bullshit. He could do so much better."

My heart twisted at her words. And as I tried to soothe her, I couldn't stop my mind from internalizing what she'd said. Maybe that's why seeing Mary with Max was so hard for me. He finally realized he could do better than me. And even though I had Adam—had declared that *he* was *my* version of doing better—the sinking feeling in my stomach left me hollow. I'd never even realized how much I liked the idea of Max fighting for me until now—when I realized he'd stopped.

chapter thirty-six

m a x

I'd felt like a prick for leaving Mary with the girls after Kyle's epic fuckup. She'd been all for a little girl bonding when I'd mentioned the weekend to her, but I was pretty sure riding through a category four emotional meltdown was not what she'd envisioned. But still, when Shane had announced he was ready to leave, she'd leaned over to me and told me to go, knowing that it was my name on the VIP list.

So I'd whispered for her to call me if she needed me, given her a soft kiss on the cheek, and trailed after the boys. And as I'd cast one look over my shoulder back at the table before we exited the restaurant, I'd thought about what a great girl she was. And I wondered what the hell she was doing with *me*.

I'd arranged for a limo to take us where we wanted to go, mostly because I didn't know how these guys partied and I didn't want to get stuck somewhere I didn't want to be. As we approached and I explained that the limo was for us, some of the excitement for the night stirred. *Maybe this won't be so bad after all.*

"Are there strippers inside? Tell me there are strippers," Ben pleaded.

"Sorry to disappoint ya, buddy." I grinned as I would at a four-year-old, clapping him on the shoulder for added support. *This guy was a fucking frat boy reject.*

I wasn't quite sure how Ben and Shane had emerged from the same parents. Granted, they looked similar, but that's where the commonalities ended. Ben made *me* look mature. And that was really fucking saying something.

The rest of the guys murmured their gratitude as they climbed inside. Shane was the last one to the car, and he stuck his hand out as he reached me.

"Thanks, man. For everything. This is all . . ." He gestured to the limo. "Incredible. And I'm sorry the night started out so awkwardly. You think your girl's gonna be okay with them?" He threw his head back toward the hotel, even though his meaning was clear without the gesture.

"Yeah, she'll be fine. Mary's impossible not to like, and Lily'll watch out for her."

"Lily? The same Lily who was staring daggers at you about ten minutes ago?" Shane looked skeptical.

"Yeah, that's the one."

"I don't know, dude. She didn't seem in the friendliest mood."

"Lily's only capable of being genuinely rude to me." I laughed, as though I were joking. We both knew I wasn't. "I know that girl better than I know anyone else in the world. She'll pull through for me."

Shane raised his eyebrows at me. "If you say so." He shrugged and joined his friends in the limo.

And as I lifted one leg into the car, I took another second to look back at the hotel. It surprised me that Shane doubted that Lily would include Mary in their evening. I briefly wondered if maybe I was wrong. But as I sat in the limousine and shut the door, I knew I wasn't.

The Last Out was new to Atlantic City, though its New York City counterpart had been open for five years. It had been founded by a few former Major League Baseball players and catered to a wealthier crowd. It was a nice diversion from the throng of twenty-somethings thrashing around to techno music that most of the other clubs attracted. This one, while definitely a nightclub that encouraged drinking and dancing, did so in a way that made you feel like you didn't have to keep touching your back pocket to make sure your wallet hadn't been stolen.

We'd been there for about two and a half hours, and the throbbing of the bass was starting to make my head pulse with it. The three Gospel writers, as Lily had called them, were much wilder than their namesakes. And teamed up with Ben, they were like kids strung out on POP ROCKS trying to attract girls by being as vulgar as possible.

"You wanna place a bet on which one gets slapped first?" Shane twisted his head toward me so that I could hear him over the music.

"They're your friends. You have me at a disadvantage on that one."

"Sometimes I have a hard time believing that I used to be out there with them."

I raised my eyebrows at him, which caused him to bark out a laugh.

"Okay, well, maybe I was never quite on the level they're currently operating on, but I was still in the general vicinity."

I smiled as I toyed with the beer bottle in my hands.

"I just... I dunno, man. One day I looked at Amanda and everything changed for me. I didn't want to be *that* guy anymore." Shane gestured toward his friends.

"You didn't want to be a skank magnet anymore?" I smirked.

"Exactly." He grinned, the first full smile I'd seen on him since we'd left the hotel.

"I get that, man. Wanting to change for a girl. Wanting to be better. I had a similar conversion not too long ago."

"Oh, I bet ya did. Mary seems like the kind of woman who would make any guy wanna get his shit together."

I huffed out a small laugh before responding seriously. "Yeah, Mary." I took a drink of my beer. "Straightened me right out." I didn't bother to correct him. To tell him that Mary hadn't caused my conversion. That there was only one woman who held that kind of power in my life.

"I can't say Amanda straightened me out, but she caused me to... I dunno, want to be a better person, I guess. God, I had to fight so hard for her to give me the fucking time of day. Every time I felt like I'd made some progress with her, she'd shut me out. And just when I thought I didn't have an ounce of fight left in me—that I was better off just letting her go and moving on—I decided to give it one last shot." As he looked over at me, his face lit up like the strip of casinos outside. "And she shut me out again." He started laughing at the memory like it was one of his childhood favorites.

I was about to ask him how much he'd had to drink because there was no way getting rejected should ever be remembered quite this fondly. But before I got the words out, he returned his focus to me, his face growing serious.

"I got to lay it all out, though. That last time, I told her exactly what I wanted, what I knew we could be together. She was honking her horn like a lunatic outside my gym less than twenty-four hours later." He smiled again at the memory, but it was softer this time. More emotional. "I almost didn't go to her that night. Thought of a million and a half reasons why I should just leave her be. But then I finally thought of a reason to go. And that was the only reason that mattered."

I looked at him expectantly, needing him to finish the story he'd started.

"I loved her. And that was more than enough reason for me to risk my pride, my sanity, everything. There's no happiness for me without her. Because she's the only thing that makes me truly happy." He sat there for a moment, contemplative. Finally, he pulled out his phone and started texting wildly.

I didn't need to ask who he was writing to. After a few minutes, he stood. "Hey, umm, this is going to be a total dick move, but I gotta go."

I shook my head and slapped him on the shoulder. "I get it, man. Go get your girl."

"Thanks, Max. Tell the guys I'll catch up with all of you tomorrow."

I nodded. He made it three feet from me before I called out to him. "Shane!"

He turned and looked at me, his entire stature lighter than it had been in hours.

"The love? It got you past all the bullshit? Made enduring all of that . . . worth it?"

His grin widened. "For the right one, it'll always be worth it."

I slunk back into my seat and nodded at him. Watching him race out of the club, on his way to the one person, the only person, who could make him happy, I wondered *what the hell do I do now?*

♥

I had been up for over an hour, just staring at her. She had already been in bed asleep when I got back to the room, and she had barely moved a muscle all night. She was gorgeous, even rumpled from a long night and a deep sleep. I knew that Mary would do everything in her power to make me happy. That together we'd try to carve out a life that we could be proud of.

We hadn't been dating long, but I saw her and our future with an acuity that was unparalleled—definitely different from the murky image I had when I tried to envision a future with Lily. Mary was all white picket fence and flower gardens. She was comfort and stability. She was willing to build a life with me.

But as I got out of bed and pulled some clothes out of my suitcase, I knew that, no matter how long I sat and stared at her and pictured our future together, it would never be the future I'd want.

♥

I caught Lily coming out of the girls' hotel room twenty minutes later. It had been difficult to pass off the meeting as a coincidence, but she seemed to buy it. And when she said she was going down to get breakfast, I quickly said that that had been my destination as well and invited myself along.

We were silent as we walked down the hallway toward the elevator. Lily pushed the down button, and we waited... in more silence. Finally, the doors opened and we climbed aboard, each settling against opposing walls.

We hadn't descended much when Lily cleared her throat. "Mary said she'd heard a lot about me. What exactly did she hear?"

I inwardly smiled at her question. *So she does care what I have to say about her.* But this really wasn't the conversation I wanted to have. "She was just being nice," I replied with a wink.

"Whatever," Lily huffed and threw some of her hair behind her shoulder.

She's such a damn child sometimes. "Do you talk to Adam about me?" I knew the answer to this, but I wanted to prove my point. Why should I stroke her ego when she pushed me to the deepest recesses of her mind on a daily basis?

"I don't need to talk about you. Adam already knows you."

I lifted off the wall and took a large step toward her before I had even processed the movement. "He doesn't know the first *thing* about me." My voice was tight, trying to mask the anger that simmered beneath it.

We stared at each other for what seemed an interminable amount of time. Then the doors slid open and Lily bolted off the elevator. "I'm gonna go for a walk instead."

I watched her rush away from me before my brain remembered its mission. *Pride doesn't have a place here, Max. This is your last shot.* I caught her around the arm just before she reached the sliding doors that led onto the boardwalk. "I told her you helped me. That you were a great friend when I needed one the most. But that our friendship was just..." I let out a sigh. "Too difficult to maintain."

She looked at me for a moment before she changed course and began walking toward the hotel restaurants. I fell into step beside her.

"She seems great. Fun and smart. Perfect for you."

I looked over at her to see her peering up at me shyly. "Yeah, she's really amazing." We made our way to the hotel's buffet and were shown a table. After placing our drink orders, we tackled the buffet separately.

I returned to the table to find Lily already there, a bowl of fruit and a bowl of cereal spread out in front of her.

"That's all you're eating?"

"It was kind of a rough night. I don't want to go too hard on my stomach."

I nodded my understanding and started in on my plate that was overflowing with waffles, bacon, and countless other breakfast favorites.

"Hungry, fella?" Lily asked sarcastically, though I could see the amusement in her eyes.

"Yeah, well, I tried that horrendous Paleo diet Shane's always going on about. I've never been so hungry in my life. I'm still trying to reclaim all the carbs I lost."

"How long were you on it?" she asked as she lifted a spoonful of cereal to her mouth.

"About five hours," I replied casually.

Lily burst out laughing, and the sound was like a punch to the gut. I hadn't heard the sound in months, and I knew that, after today, I might never hear it again.

We ate and chatted about what we'd been up to. I finally told her about my job, and she gushed just as I knew she would.

"I'm so happy for you, Max. Really. Everything seems to be

falling into place. You deserve that." Her words were sincere, but there was another emotion lingering in her eyes. Sadness? "Well, I think I'm going to go check on Amanda. Shane showed up at Swanky last night and they went to talk. She never came back to the room, which I assume is a good sign." She smiled warmly. "But I'd like to make sure anyway. It was good seeing you, Max."

Just as she was starting to stand up, I blurted, "Lily, can I ask you something?" I watched her settle back in her chair, preparing herself for what I might ask. Too bad I had no fucking idea how to say what I wanted to know. So I just let it fall out of my mouth and hoped for the best. "How do you do it?"

She looked confused. "Do what?"

"Pretend to be in love with someone you're not."

Her face hardened and her entire body tensed. "I wouldn't know," she ground out.

I looked deeply into her eyes and whispered, "I find that very hard to believe."

"Who the hell do you think you are?"

I struggled to retain my sense of calm. "I'm a man who needs to know."

"Why?" she spat.

I was thankful for her intensely curious nature, because I knew that it was the only thing keeping her in her seat. "Mary is everything I could ever want. Successful, driven, beautiful, kind. We haven't been together long, but she loves me. Or at least she *could* love me, probably one day soon. And as much as I try to tell myself to, I can't return even a fraction of the affection that she has for me. So as much as I want to hold on to her, to see if something grows with this person who you even said yourself is perfect for me, I'm not going to. Because

I know that keeping her with a lie will only hurt her more in the long run. So that leads me to wonder. If even *I* can't do that to someone," I said, looking deeply into her eyes, "how can you?"

I watched the storm brew just beneath the surface of her skin before she unleashed it. "Fuck you, Max. Our relationships aren't the same. I love Adam, more than someone like you could ever possibly understand."

"I didn't say you didn't love him. I said you weren't *in* love with him. There's a big difference."

She scoffed. "So who am I in love with then, huh? You?"

"I don't know." I deflected my eyes toward the table, unable to stand the uncertainty in my voice and the venom in hers.

"What else is new? The man with no answers, no solutions, rears his ugly head. Why don't you tell me something you do know then? Since you evidently have so much insight into my life, let's hear what else ya got?"

"I may not know how you feel about me, though I think I could guess." I lifted my eyes to hers, needing to find strength now more than ever. "But I do know how I feel about you. I've been in love with you since you dropped your bag at my feet in that airport. And instead of diminishing with time like I hoped it would, my love for you just keeps fucking growing. It consumes me. I can't love a *perfect* girl like Mary because I'm too hung up on this infuriating, stubborn, beautiful woman sitting in front of me."

Her posture was rigid, but her features had relaxed. She was at least listening. That was all I could have hoped for.

I resumed, my eyes blazing into hers, revealing the biggest truth I'd ever told. "You don't want me, and I don't want anybody else. So I'll just be . . . left behind. Left to pick up the pieces of my dreams and my heart when you get up from this table and walk away, shattering them both because the girl who means *everything* never even gave me a chance to mean *something.*"

I sat back in my chair, drained, and watched as Lily brought a hand to her eyes and wiped the tears from them. I gave her the moment she needed since she had given me mine.

When she finally looked back at me, my heart fell. The look on her face was sheer . . . determination. And I knew right then that I'd lost her. I'd put it all out there, and it hadn't been enough.

"I know that . . . God, I'm such a bitch, Max."

"No, doll. You're not."

Her head jerked toward me at my term of endearment. I hadn't said it to her in over a year. At least not so she would hear it. But I wasn't going to miss my opportunity now, when it would be the last chance I'd have.

"I am. I've been intentionally cold and distant because you scare me. The way you see me, it's so . . . accurate. Except for one thing. I am in love with Adam. Our relationship isn't always easy or perfect, but it's real. And I can't walk away from it just because you want me to. *I* need to want to. But I don't. I'm so sorry, Max. I'm sorry I can't be what you need, or what you hoped. I'll always be sad for that." She hesitated slightly. "But I think you're wrong. I think you love the idea of me: the crazy, uninhibited version of Lily. But that's not who I really am. It was an illusion. Give things with Mary a chance. A real chance. I think she'll be good for you."

She got up to leave, but I couldn't let her go thinking that I didn't see her. The real her. "I know the difference between reality and illusions. And I know that the Lily I was close to was much more real than the one who's standing in front of me right now. There's nothing about you that I don't see. And you damn well know it."

I watched her jaw set as she turned on her heels and started walking away. I wasn't surprised. Lily leaving me was an image I was all too familiar with. What did shock me was when she stopped.

Without turning around, and in a voice so low, I wasn't sure I heard her correctly at first, she asked, "Do you know when my birthday is?"

"Of course. March twenty-third. Why?"

Her breathing deepened and her shoulders crumbled slightly. She turned her head to look partway over her shoulder at me. "Nothing. It's not important."

"Everything about you is important, Lily."

Her face scrunched as if she were holding back tears. Then she turned quickly away from me and was gone.

chapter thirty-seven

l i l y

I allowed myself the drive home from Atlantic City to think about what had happened between Max and me. He'd told me he loved me. He'd opened up to me in a way he hadn't ever done before. It wasn't done out of anger or frustration, or in the heat of the moment, like he'd done in the past. He'd said those things when he was calm, self-assured, and completely sober.

And despite the fact that his analysis of my relationship with Adam had been off base, I could respect it. Regardless of what he thought my reaction might have been, he'd had the confidence to express his feelings. And part of me loved him for that, for how truthful and vulnerable he'd allowed himself to be. Mainly because I knew how difficult those two traits could be to show.

But once we were home, I forced all Max-centered thoughts from my brain. I figured all cities with casinos should be treated equally. What happened in Atlantic City, stayed in

Atlantic City, I told myself. And not surprisingly, I was able to focus on other things fairly easily, especially with the wedding coming up.

When Amanda had asked me to be her maid of honor, I'd anticipated the agonizing responsibilities that went with the title: planning the shower and bachelorette party, shopping for dresses, and making sure all the little necessities were accounted for. But luckily, Amanda had done most of the planning on her own, which meant I was just along for the ride.

The months leading up to it seemed relatively calm compared to other weddings I'd been a part of. No screaming matches among the bridesmaids since Steph, Danielle, and I were all friends. And Shane's sister-in-law, Talia, was also extremely easy to get along with. I'd imagine being married to Ben had given her plenty of practice when it came to putting up with bullshit.

All in all, I'd breezed through the last several months without much trouble at all. Unfortunately, the same couldn't be said for the wedding day.

"Amanda, calm down." I put my palm on her back and began to rub in what I thought were soothing circles. "Just relax and take deep breaths." Amanda had been gasping, wheezing and, according to her, on the verge of vomiting for the past twenty-five minutes.

"How am I supposed to take deep breaths when you bitches have me breathing into this goddamn paper bag? And why is it so hot in here? It's only May tenth. This church feels like a third world sweatshop." She crumpled up the bag and thrust it into my chest. "Someone open a fucking window."

I nodded to Danielle, who rushed toward one of the two small windows and flung it open. "You'll be fine, Amanda. I swear. You want this, remember? You love Shane."

"I'm not talking about *love*, Danielle. I'm talking about *marriage*."

Oh God, here we go.

"You realize I'm gonna have to spend the rest of my life picking up the socks and dishes that Shane leaves all over the house? And his socks are always sweaty." She jumped up, pacing back and forth between the organ and the brown couch. "I can't do this. You've all got the right idea staying single."

"Right idea?" Was this girl delusional? "It's not *our* idea, you nutcase. No one *wants* to marry any of us. And when someone finally does"—I gripped Amanda's shoulders firmly and guided her down to sit on the couch again—"I'm sure you'll be telling us the same thing we're trying to tell you: that you're doing the right thing."

"Yeah," Talia spoke up. "Believe me, being married to Ben definitely isn't a chapter out of some fairy tale. He swears constantly, passes gas at dinner, and has converted half of Kenzie's playroom into a home brewery." Talia sat down next to Amanda and leaned over to put her arms around her. "But I love him. And between the two Reed brothers, you definitely got the more refined one."

Amanda relaxed a bit for a moment and let out a soft chuckle at Talia's last comment before she jumped right back on the crazy train. "But remember what that psychic said, Lily?"

Ever since we'd gone to a tarot card reader at a local bar the other night, Amanda had been hung up on what the psychic had said about Amanda being sure that she was with the right person and that she didn't have "eyes for another," as the psychic had called it. "Amanda, I told you not to put any stock into what that woman said. She reads cards on Friday nights for twenty dollars at a seedy bar. Don't believe any of that shit."

Just as I checked my phone to see that the ceremony was about to begin, I heard a knock at the door. Henry's voice cracked slightly as he yelled, "You girls decent?" He waited a few seconds before continuing. "I mean, it's okay if you're not. It's not like I haven't seen a little T and A before."

"Come in, Henry," Amanda huffed.

"The only *T* you've seen is when you were breastfeeding from these about eleven years ago," Talia said, cupping her breasts. "You must have a pretty good memory."

Henry pretended to shiver at the thought. "Yo, that's so gross, yo. Why's it gotta be like that? Anyway, I came here to tell you that Uncle Shane said the wedding's about to start."

"Thanks, Henry. We'll be right out," I said, shooting Amanda a look that told her it was now or never. She shot me a look back that told me it would probably be never. For someone who barely feared anything, she looked scared shitless.

"Lily's right, honey. I think you're overreacting just a bit." Amanda's mom had been patiently waiting for the right time to speak. She probably knew her history with men didn't make her much of an authority on the subject of love. "Psychics are kooks, dear," Angela said. "You can't make life decisions based on one comment from a crazy woman. And Talia, I just have to tell you, Henry is so cute. He reminds me of this guy Flap Jack I just started dating, only taller."

A flood of disbelief washed over Amanda's face as her eyes fixated on her mother. "Okay, that's it," she finally said, knowing that her future could either involve Shane and some sweaty socks or a midget named Flap Jack. Quickly rising to her feet, she made her decision. "I'm ready. Let's get this shit show started."

❤

Standing next to Amanda as she and Shane took their vows had elicited a response in me I hadn't anticipated. Mesmerized, I watched as Shane brushed his thumb across Amanda's cheek to wipe a runaway tear as he promised to be there for her for their lifetime. He put a hand on the small of her back as they each picked up their separate candles and lit the one in the middle to symbolize the unity of their lives together.

It amazed me that two people could be so wrapped up in each other with an audience focused on their every movement and word. Not wrapped up in each other in a conceited, egotistical way that so many couples experienced on their wedding day. Not a hey-look-at-us-this-is-our-day kind of way. Rather, they gazed at each other as if they were the only ones in the room, their eyes having a silent conversation that only they could hear.

As happy as I was for her, I'd never been so envious of anything in my life. I wanted that: what Amanda and Shane had. Whatever *that* was. What they had was more than attraction, it was more than compatibility, and it was even more than love. I couldn't put my finger on what they felt as their lips touched, but a part of me felt it too. And I didn't want to let it go.

Sadly, that moment was only that: a moment. A fleeting, vicarious glimpse into whatever true love felt like. I felt like a drug addict coming down from a high, willing to do anything for her next fix.

And in an effort to get that feeling back, I surveyed the guests for Adam, spotting him a few rows away almost instantly. Like my own had been, Adam's attention was solely focused on Shane and Amanda, until he must have felt me silently urging him to look my way. When his eyes locked on mine, I made out the subtle movement of his lips. "I love you," he whispered.

I felt a calm overtake me, and I returned his sentiment with a sheepish smile. *I love you too.*

❤

I'd ridden in the limo with the bridal party from the church to the reception, and with all the chaos of the morning, I hadn't seen Adam much at all. So when I stepped out of the car, I took a moment to let him envelop me in his strong arms as I breathed him in, slipping my hands around his waist.

"You look beautiful," Adam said when we finally got a few minutes alone.

"Thanks. You don't look so bad yourself," I teased, keeping my hands on his hips while I pulled back a bit to admire him. His broad shoulders filled his jacket nicely, and the soft pink of his shirt created a nice contrast to his dark gray suit. "It was a beautiful ceremony, wasn't it?"

"Yeah, good weather too."

"It was crazy. We almost didn't get Amanda out there in time. She was a little panicked."

"Sounds about on par for Amanda." He laughed as we held hands up the escalator. "Well, I'm glad everything turned out well. And this place is incredible." Adam stopped in his tracks as we arrived at the entrance of the reception area. "I had no idea they had rooms like this here," he said, pointing to the two-story venue. "What a great idea."

When Shane and Amanda had decided to have their

reception at Lincoln Financial Field, I knew that it would be perfect for them. The Eagles stadium provided a flawless combination of their tastes. Casual with a bit of class, the long rectangular industrial-style room showcased floor-to-ceiling windows along one wall, looking out onto another stadium and the parking lot.

The venue had a loft feel with exposed ductwork and a modern color scheme of gray and deep reds. The main floor held the dinner tables, which were elegantly decorated with black tablecloths, cream napkins, and small green-and-white bouquets.

The DJ was stationed in front of the windows, and a long bar lined the opposite wall below the second-story balcony. At either end of the expansive space were various buffet stations: salmon, lobster risotto, and shrimp cocktail at one; cheeseburger sliders, buffalo chicken egg rolls, and a taco bar at another, along with a few assorted soups and a salad bar.

There was no formal sit-down dinner, no strict schedule to adhere to. People could eat, dance, snap pictures, and relax at their leisure. I laughed at how appropriate the whole setup was for Shane and Amanda. Neither one of them was ever any good at being told what to do or when to do it.

Upstairs, on the balcony overlooking the main dining room, were several flat-screen TVs tuned to local games, high-top tables near the railing with a view of the main seating area, and tall red velvet semicircle booths along the outside wall.

Adam and I took our time strolling through the facility, reading about various athletes on the plaques and photographs that hung on the walls, and munching on a few of the appetizers. "I can't believe Shane agreed to have bar food here," Adam said, taking a bite of his egg roll. "Not that I'm complaining."

"No kidding. And I can't believe Amanda let anything *healthy* in here. I mean, arugula salad and tilapia? I'm not even sure she knows what those are."

"I'm sure she knows what they *are*," Adam added. "She just knows she hates them. And I can't really blame her. Arugula belongs in a field somewhere, not on people's plates."

We made our way past the cozy booths upstairs and through the outside exit, which led to the stands in the football field. A few of the other guests had also decided to enjoy the fresh air or take pictures with the field as a backdrop.

Adam and I stayed outside for a while, until most of the guests had gone back in and the sun had almost set completely. Even though it was May, and Adam's arm draped over my shoulder to keep me warm, I couldn't help but feel a little cold.

"There the two of you are." Kyle's voice startled me. And I turned to see Kate smiling sweetly beside him. I was happy to see the Atlantic City drama was behind them. "We've been looking for you everywhere. Your best friend's celebrating her marriage and you're sitting outside being all antisocial and shit?"

"Be nice," Kate scolded Kyle in jest. "You really *should* come in, though. They're getting ready to do the first dance I think."

Adam and I rose to follow Kate and Kyle inside, making our way downstairs. Shane wasn't much for dancing, so it didn't surprise me to see him sitting to the side of the dance floor at one of the tables. He was probably working up the nerve to dance in front of over a hundred people.

I looked around, searching for Amanda and expecting to see her threatening Shane onto the dance floor with her glare. Instead, I found her stationed near the DJ holding the microphone. *God, please tell me she's not gonna sing.* Amanda leaned in to say something to the DJ, and as she backed away and moved slowly toward Shane, the DJ cut off the song that he'd been playing abruptly and replaced it with a low, soft song that I'd recognize anywhere: "(I've Had) The Time of My Life."

Amanda walked casually over to Shane, a devious spark in her eyes. But it wasn't until she spoke that I knew for certain Shane would undoubtedly kill her. "Nobody puts Shaney in the corner," she said, as she extended her hand down to take his. The look on Shane's face told me he was wondering if there were any Philadelphia judges who might be able to perform an annulment at a moment's notice.

With a look of horror plastered across his face, Shane surprisingly rose to follow Amanda to the center of the dance floor, watching her nervously. Amanda faced the audience and began to speak quietly. "Sorry about the disruption, folks. But I always do the last dance of the season." *She can't be fuckin' serious.* "Or in this case, the first," she said, smirking at Shane, who didn't seem at all amused. "But this year somebody told me not to. So I'm gonna do my kind of dancin' with a great partner."

Yup, she's definitely serious.

With that last comment, Shane made his first real attempt at utilizing one of the possible escape routes he'd probably been scoping out since Amanda had first grabbed his hand and ushered him onto the dance floor.

But as he made a movement toward the edge of the dance floor, Amanda grabbed him by the waist and pulled him against her before continuing to speak. "He's not only a terrific dancer," she said, "but also somebody who's taught me that it's worth it to take a chance on someone. Somebody who's taught me about the kind of person I wanna be. And what it means to really love someone." Amanda turned to look in Shane's eyes, and it finally became clear to me what Amanda was doing. She was expressing her true feelings for Shane publicly the only way she knew how: through a spoof of *Dirty Dancing*.

The music grew louder, and the guests cheered, urging them to dance. Amanda tossed the microphone to the DJ and moved behind Shane, who turned to look back at her as she ran a hand down his side and across his stomach just like Patrick Swayze did in the movie. The crowd grew wilder with every movement. "Do you think he's actually gonna try to dance with her to this?" Adam asked.

One look at Shane's face and I knew the answer. "I don't just *think* it," I said. "I *know* it. There isn't anything he *wouldn't* do for her."

And with that thought, Shane shook his jacket off and tossed it to the crowd before Amanda spun him out and pulled him back in, their hands locking and their hips and legs moving to the beat of the music. *Holy shit. It had all been an act.* Shane and Amanda had learned the choreography to *Dirty Dancing*.

Shane pulled her out and then in again, wrapping his arm around Amanda's waist as he led her toward the front of the dance floor, gyrating to the music as it grew louder. At least they had switched roles and Shane had now taken the male lead. The guests sang, and Amanda spun in circles, wildly tossing her hair side to side to the beat.

They continued their routine, their eyes locking at all the right moments as they paused to catch their breath together before the dance would pick up speed and they'd shake their bodies against each other. The audience seemed to anticipate the climax of the dance and hollered and clapped in encouragement.

When Shane jumped up and moved away from Amanda, the crowd that had formed near them backed away to make room for his solo. He spun around, snapping his fingers and moving his hips until he dropped his knees to the floor to shake in an overly exaggerated impression of Patrick Swayze. For someone who didn't like to dance, Shane could really move.

I couldn't wait for the part when he would pick Amanda up over his head, and when it finally happened, it didn't disappoint. As she ran toward him and jumped into his arms, Shane lifted her effortlessly above him, holding her firmly in his arms as they gazed at each other longingly. The crowd loved every second of it.

When he finally put her down, the two got lost in their own moment again, dancing with each other and inviting everyone else to join in. They'd both done the movie justice, each learning the choreography seamlessly. But as good of a dancer as each one of them was individually, nothing compared to how great they were *together*.

The excitement eventually died down, and Adam and I spent the next hour or so talking and dancing to a few slow songs. I enjoyed resting my head on his chest as he wrapped his arms around me and moved us gracefully to the music. After most of the guests had finished dinner, the wait staff set up an ice cream bar and brought out the cake for Shane and Amanda to cut.

We watched from a distance on the balcony above as Amanda slipped a piece of cake into Shane's mouth sloppily. "Make sure you get a video of this, people," Amanda announced. "Shane Reed's eating cake. This might go viral." Shane smirked and wiped a bit of the stray icing from his lips before sliding his fingers into Amanda's mouth so she could lick it off. Then he leaned in to whisper something in her ear. Her wide grin transformed instantaneously into another emotion entirely. Desire maybe? The whole experience seemed so intimate, despite the fact that they had an audience of over one hundred and twenty-five people.

Suddenly, Shane and Amanda's moment was interrupted by a loud voice coming over the DJ's microphone a few feet away. "I'd like to make a toast," Ben bellowed. *Oh God.* "I'm not really great with words. But I make up for it with my good looks," he quickly added. The guests chuckled a bit, and Ben nervously continued. "My brother'll probably kill me for telling this story." He glanced over at Shane, who seemed to be trying to figure out a way to murder him with his eyes. "So of course I'm gonna tell it." Ben focused his attention back on the guests. "When we were growing up, we had this chain link fence that wrapped around our backyard. Maybe about three feet tall or something. Anyway, we used to climb it all the time so we could cut through our neighbors' yards to get to different parts of the neighborhood faster. I usually had to help him get over it because I was so much bigger and stronger. That's still true today," he quickly added. "But one day when I wasn't there, he tried to climb it by himself."

I looked over at Shane, who was already red with embarrassment. Next to him, Amanda was grinning from ear to ear, waiting for Ben to continue. "I guess when he made it over the fence, his pants snagged on the top, flipping him upside down." Ben hinged at the waist and made a goofy face to imitate Shane dangling from the fence. Shane's mother was already laughing nearby. "And there he hung for almost six hours, screaming for someone to help him. Finally, our mom"—Ben pointed to her—"must've wondered where the hell he was. He was only six at the time. So she went outside to look for him."

"I didn't hear him screaming because I was doing the laundry all day," she called out in an effort to defend herself.

"It's okay, Mom, we all know you love me more," Ben corrected her. "Anyway, by the time she got outside and found him, Shane's face was beet red, his pants were so ripped that his Superman underwear was showing, and his face was covered in dirt because the neighbor's dog had taken a shit nearby and kicked mud on him."

"Does this story have a point?" Shane asked, embarrassment plaguing his voice.

"Does this story have a point? You believe this guy? Of course it has a fuckin' point. Why else would I tell it?"

"Oh, I don't know," Shane joked, "because most of your enjoyment comes from seeing me suffer."

"Well, yeah, that's definitely true," Ben admitted. "So I guess this story really has *two* points, then. The first time Shane stopped screaming was when he saw our mom finally coming to help him. She picked him up off the fence, carried him inside, gave him a bath, and put him to bed. My point is that he waited for what seemed like forever for the woman he loved to come along and make his world right side up again." Ben turned to his right to face Shane and Amanda. "And Amanda did the same thing for him twenty-four years later." Both Amanda and Shane smiled broadly at Ben. It had probably been the first time either of them had seen him this sentimental. "To someone I admire and respect," Ben said, raising his glass and prompting the guests to do the same. "And to my douchebag of a little brother," he said, smiling as he took a sip of his beer.

Shortly after Ben's speech, Amanda's mom followed suit,

recounting a tale about when she'd pulled down their street to find Amanda and her friend trying to pass off bags of sand as cocaine to sell in front of the church on the corner. "Even in second grade, Amanda was a firecracker," she said. "Now has anyone seen my shoes?" she asked, looking down at her bare feet on the dance floor. "I took them off when I got here, and I still haven't found them. Oh yeah, to Shane and Amanda," she quickly added as she threw back her champagne like a shot of tequila. There was a murmuring among the crowd, but they all followed Angela's lead, raising their glasses and drinking to Amanda and Shane's big day.

"What was that about?" Adam asked, practically doubled over with laughter. "That was a strange speech."

"I'm not sure," I answered. "I think she just wanted the microphone so she could ask where her shoes were. That story was funny as shit, though. Who the hell sells fake drugs when they're seven?" I hadn't even anticipated that anyone would give a speech because Amanda had told me not to prepare one. But if Ben and Angela could deliver, I sure as shit could. "Wait!" I yelled from above. "I'd like to make a toast too."

I hurried down the stairs, taking the few seconds I had on the way to decide what to say. Unfortunately, when I got to the microphone, I still had no fucking idea where to begin. "I didn't prepare a speech either," I said, "and I don't think mine will be as good as Ben's or Angela's. By the way, Angela, I saw a pair of blue heels over by the salad bar." The guests laughed, and I used the moment to catch my breath and compose my thoughts before continuing. "I don't have any funny stories like they do . . . or at least any that can be shared with the general public," I corrected myself. When people laughed again, I realized maybe I wasn't doing as horribly as I'd anticipated. I made eye contact with Amanda, who mouthed an appreciative, "Thank you," presumably because I'd decided to keep any embarrassing stories to myself.

I smiled sweetly at her. "I just want to say congratulations to the happy couple. Amanda and Shane are special people." I already felt a tear working its way out of the corner of my eye, but I made no attempt to keep it there. "And they're even more special *together*," I added. "Their relationship is one that many of us can only hope to have one day. I was watching them dance earlier . . . like all of you were. And by the way, Shane, you've got some killer moves," I said with a wink.

"Watch it, girl," Amanda hollered. "He's taken."

"Anyway," I continued, shaking my head and directing my attention to the guests, "when they were dancing, I finally realized what makes their relationship so unique, so able to withstand any hardship that they'll face in the future." Silence settled over the room, and I took the moment to look over to Shane and Amanda, who had their arms around each other tightly.

"It's what happens in the pauses," I said quietly. "When you're dancing . . . it's easy to let the choreography do the work because it tells you exactly where to go, exactly which steps to take. But it's the pauses that differentiate the *good* dancers from the *great* ones." I looked down for a moment, deciding how to best say what I wanted to convey next. "When the music stops, *great* dancers make even those small, seemingly insignificant moments special."

I wiped a few runaway tears from my cheek with my thumb, collecting myself before I spoke again. "And the same is true of life, I guess. When everything seems to come to a halt and you're in between steps, you have to find a way to come together and make even the mundane moments memorable." I turned to face Amanda and Shane, giving them a warm smile through my tears. "You both do that better than anyone I've ever met."

I raised my glass up to them, and the rest of the guests did the same. "Amanda and Shane, I wish you both many years filled with love, family, and unconditional happiness. But there's one thing I won't wish you. And that's luck. Because I know you won't need it." I shrugged. "You're already great at the pauses. To Amanda and Shane, everybody."

I took a sip of my champagne and held my arms out to hug Amanda, who had already begun to make her way toward me. "I love you," I said. "Congratulations to you both."

"I love you too, Lil." She wrapped her arms around me tightly and sniffled. "And that speech was badass, by the way," she said in an effort to lighten the mood as she pulled back. "Great at the pauses, huh?" She smirked. "That shit's fucking genius."

"Thanks," I laughed. "It's amazing what you can learn from *So You Think You Can Dance*."

Eventually, Adam made his way downstairs to congratulate Shane and Amanda. Then we took a slice of cake to share at one of the round booths on the second level. Alone, for the first time in a while, we fed each other small bites and chatted about the upcoming summer, our jobs, and how perfect the wedding had been. The entire night had been so Amanda and Shane. Sporty, but elegant. Comfortable, but still formal. The physical embodiment of their individual lives becoming one. It was so natural, so...effortless that I wondered how they did it.

Finally, it seemed that we'd discussed just about

everything there was to talk about, and despite the loud music, a noticeable quiet hung between us. "Guess it's almost over," Adam finally said as he swallowed his last bit of cake.

I shifted the last few crumbs around on the plate before looking up into his clear green eyes. "Yeah," I answered quietly. "I guess it is."

♥

"How many bathing suits do you think I'll need?" Amanda slung the contents of her top drawer onto the bed, covering it with bikinis, underwear, and bras.

"Um, I don't know. Maybe three? You'll be in Bermuda a week." I moved a thong off my leg with my fingertip and tossed it toward the edge of the bed. "I can't believe you still have stuff in the apartment. It seems like you've already moved pretty much everything to Shane's."

"I have. Well, everything except for my furniture and some leftover clothes. Oh, and that blender. Don't think I've forgotten about it. It's coming with *me*."

"No, it isn't," I said sternly, pausing just long enough to see the irritation on Amanda's face before I cracked a smile. "I bought you one of your own just like it. It's in my room. Brand-new, not yet tainted by kale."

"Aww, you're so sweet, Lil. What am I gonna do without you?" She threw a few more items into her suitcase haphazardly.

"Oh, I don't know. Cry yourself to sleep every night to thoughts of me, talk to photographs of me and pretend that they're real, spray your pillows with my perfume so my scent can comfort you—"

"Okay, okay, I get it." Amanda laughed. "You won't be nearly as sad to see me go as I am to leave."

"Oh, come on." I smirked. "You know sarcasm is my best defense mechanism. It's gonna be so different here without you. Whose clothes will I borrow when I get sick of my own?" Amanda shot me a look that told me it was time to stop protecting my feelings. "Oh, all right." I sighed. "The truth is I'm really gonna miss you. You've only been married two days, and I'm already going through withdrawal." I stood up to put my arms around her, rubbing her back to show her how much I cared. But the truth was, I held tightly onto Amanda more for myself than for her. Because even though I was glad she was moving on with her life, I was still scared of being left behind.

"We'll see each other all the time, Lil. Don't be upset. You can come over whenever you want." She gave me one last squeeze before letting me go. "Just make sure you knock first," she added quickly. "Besides, you'll probably be old and married soon enough too."

"Hmph, maybe," I said as I plopped back down onto the bed.

"What? What's that about? 'Hmph, maybe.' Why do you say it like that? You and Adam are so good together. Well, except for that whole birthday thing." She laughed. My expression must have told her to drop it. "But seriously, he's a great guy, and you both seem happy together. You love him, right?"

"Yeah. I love him."

"And he loves you?"

"Yeah."

"Then what's the problem?"

Uncomfortable with where this conversation might be

going, I picked at my fingernails, hoping Amanda would just forget that I'd had such a strange response to her marriage comment. But her silence told me she wouldn't let it go until I answered. "That's what I'm trying to figure out myself," I said. "I meant what I said at your wedding...how great you and Shane are together."

"Lily, don't do that." I shifted my eyes up to look at her, and she stopped packing to take a seat next to me on the edge of her bed. "Don't compare your relationship to ours."

Refusing to listen to her, I continued my train of thought. "Just tell me how you do it...not let things get old when you're in love."

Amanda breathed deeply and let her shoulders fall heavily as she exhaled, preparing to respond. "I don't really know how to answer that. We haven't been together that long. I'm no expert on love, Lil. I think you're expecting love to be this perfect fairy tale, and it just isn't. Every relationship has its issues, including my own."

"It's just...in the beginning, when things were still new, even when we were getting to know each other again for the second time, our conversations were so easy. Our time together never seemed long enough, especially when it was just the two of us." I paused to organize the jumbled thoughts in my head. "I don't know. It's like...when it's just the two of us, we fit together perfectly. But as soon as we try to incorporate the other one into our individual lives it's...awkward. Even at your wedding, our first instinct was to escape everyone and be alone. But I don't want to be that person who withdraws from her friends to be with her boyfriend. That just isn't me." I let my head fall as the realization of my revelation sank in.

"I think you're being too hard on yourself. Relationships take work."

"We've tried twice now." Although, I knew as I said it that it wasn't entirely true. The first time around I hadn't given my relationship with Adam my all. A part of me wondered if the reason it seemed so difficult now was because I'd made things so difficult the first time. I had a feeling that even though Adam assured me otherwise, he still harbored lingering feelings about my betrayal—feelings he might never get past. I shook my head, unsure of my own emotions. "It's like…we're so good at falling in love. We just don't know what to do when we stop falling."

"I think you need to talk to Adam about this. Chances are he's feeling the same way. It's perfectly normal. You guys just need to work through this *together*. *Falling* in love and *staying* in love are two completely different things."

"But for you and Shane, it was the falling you had a hard time with. The staying seems to be going great." I couldn't help the pout in my voice.

"I told you not to compare. Shane and I do everything backward. You can't use us as your benchmark."

"But you're the only truly happy couple I know." I spoke softly, knowing what my words meant, even though the veracity of them surprised me.

And as I watched Amanda's eyes widen, I knew she got their meaning too. "So you're not happy?"

I shrugged. "Sometimes I am. But sometimes I'm not."

Letting out a deep breath, Amanda took my hand in hers. "Lil, there is a ton of shit I know nothing about. Like what the hell Shane sees in me, or how I'm gonna survive on pine nuts and Paleo brownies." We both chuckled at her words, letting go of some of the tension of the moment. "But what I do know is that happiness should never be a part-time thing."

My whole body sagged. I knew she was right, but I had no idea how to fix it. Adam made me happy. But there were times, more often lately, that he made me unhappy too. It was like a puzzle with no solution.

"And, Lil," Amanda said, interrupting my internal wallowing. I brought my eyes to hers as she said, "Chances are, if you're not happy, he isn't either."

Burying my face in my hands, I willed our relationship to work. For everything to fall into place like it was supposed to.

That was when the tears came. And as they purged my system of the emotions I'd been carrying, I silently wished they could wash that thought from my mind too.

chapter thirty-eight

a d a m

Lily had been acting . . . strangely. I'd barely talked to her since the wedding, our phone conversations clipped and strained. When I'd called her out on it, she'd said she was just tired. That she just needed a few days to recuperate from the wedding. But it had been three days, and I was done waiting for her to tell me what was really bothering her.

So that's how I found myself at her apartment building Tuesday night, using the key she'd given me to let myself into her building. I walked up to her apartment, my legs feeling heavier with every step I took. It was like my entire body was trying to warn me that this wasn't going to end well. But as I rapped my knuckles against her door, not wanting to overly invade her privacy by letting myself in, I knew there was no disappearing now.

"Who is it?" I heard her voice ask tentatively.

At least she's home. Though that thought was quickly replaced by my hoping that she was alone. And as my mind snowballed into her having a guy in her apartment, I silently scolded myself. *Get it together, Carter.*

"It's Adam," I rasped. I heard the sounds of the chain dropping and the bolt clicking before the door flew open. I didn't like the look on her face. She looked...unhappy to see me.

"Adam, what are you doing here? Are you okay?" She was hugging the door, but moved back enough that I could enter. Closing it softly behind me, she turned toward me expectantly.

I took a seat on her couch, and she joined me. "I'm not allowed to come see my girlfriend?" I felt the shy smile on my face, hoping that my joking would set a more positive pace for our conversation.

"No, I mean, yes, no..." She sighed deeply and smiled. "Yes, you're absolutely allowed to be here. You just usually call. I'm surprised to see you."

"Is it a good surprise?" Despite my desire to keep the tone light, my words were tinged with a childlike curiosity. I needed to know the answer, and I needed it to be the truth.

"Of course," she replied with a tight smile. "When it's you, it's always a good surprise."

Her posture was rigid, and her eyes dropped as the words had left her mouth. *She's lying.* And with that, the feelings of betrayal started to wash in like the tide during a hurricane. *First she goes to Atlantic City with that asshole, then she becomes distant after the wedding, and now she's fucking lying to me.* I couldn't help the thoughts forming in my head or the words that were about to be released from my mouth. I was pissed.

"Do you have many people knocking on your door who *aren't* good surprises?" My voice was nearly a growl, so deep I almost didn't recognize that it had been me who had spoken.

She looked at me apprehensively. "No, I don't get many door knocks. None actually."

I exhaled heavily and dropped my head to my hands, pulling my fingers through my hair. "What the hell's going on here, Lil? I feel like I'm going crazy." I steeled my resolve and looked up at her. "You're avoiding me. I'm here to find out why."

She bit her lower lip, her hands fidgeting in her lap. "I don't know what you mean. I've just been tired."

"That's two," I boomed as I held up two fingers. "Two times you've lied to me since I walked in here. Now shoot straight with me." I waited for a few seconds, but when she made no move to speak, I filled the silence. "Are you seeing someone else?"

She rolled her eyes and scoffed as though she were disgusted. "Of course, that's what it always comes back to, huh? I need some space, and automatically it's because I'm screwing someone else. That's really perfect, Adam." She stood up and began to pace around the living room.

I followed her movements with my eyes. "You never said anything about needing space. You haven't said much of anything. What am I supposed to think?"

"So this is how it's going to be? I'm going to spend the rest of my life worrying that if I withdraw a little from you, you're going to immediately assume I'm fucking around on the side? I can't live that way, Adam. I shouldn't have to analyze everything I do for how it's going to affect you. Sometimes I need to do things because they're right for *me*."

"Ignoring your boyfriend is *right* for you?" I stood, her coffee table separating us. "Christ, you are still *so* selfish. You only ever think about what *you* want. Well, here's a newsflash: maybe you should spend a little time analyzing how things are going to affect me. If you'd done more of that last year, we wouldn't be in the mess we're in right now."

She just stared at me for a minute, her face contorting as if she were truly seeing me for the first time. And that was just fine, because as far as I was concerned, this was my first time seeing her as well.

When she finally spoke, her voice was low and calm, a complete contradiction to the fire and brimstone in her eyes. "You said you weren't going to do that anymore."

"Do what?" I ground out.

"Throw the past in my face. But you can't help it, can you? I wonder, is it the first thing that pops into your head whenever you think of me? Or just when I do something you don't like?"

"What are you talking about?" My voice was laced with incredulity, as if I thought she were crazy. But she wasn't. I knew exactly what she was asking, and she wasn't wrong for asking it. I had to get over these insecurities. And while I knew I put on a good front for Lily, I knew that the reality was I was *far* from over them. It sometimes felt like I was *waiting* for her to hurt me again. I resented myself for it, but I had to admit, a part of me resented her for it too.

"The pain, the betrayal, the bullshit. Can you even look at me without seeing it?"

The only sound in the room was that of our labored breaths, fuming like dragons. My mouth was suddenly arid, and my brain sputtered. I couldn't ask her for the truth and not give her the same courtesy. Still, I had to force the word from my body. "No."

Her shoulders sagged as though they were about to cave into her chest. I saw the glistening in her eyes, and both cursed myself for putting the tears there and celebrated that I had wounded her like she'd wounded me.

"Then why the hell are you with me?" Despite the fallen look on her face, her voice was steel.

"Because I love you." I stated the words simply because they were that simple for me. They were the reason I'd put my pride aside and given her a second chance.

"You really think that's enough?"

I couldn't tell if she was genuinely asking me or implying that I was naïve. "Yes." Was she really telling me that my love for her wasn't enough? After everything, was she saying that *I* wasn't good enough? *Where the hell does she get off?* "Listen, *you're* the one who broke us. What we had was perfect, and you ruined all of that."

"How can you possibly call what we had perfect? You basically hid me for the duration of our relationship. And I understand that you have a built-in excuse, not wanting to make things difficult for Eva, but that's what it was, Adam. An excuse."

Her words stung my ears as I heard them, and I hoped they hurt her just as much leaving her mouth. It was no secret that our relationship was anything but perfect now. But for some reason, I took comfort in believing that the problems we now faced were a direct result of *her* previous actions. That belief made our current struggles easier to swallow because I had somewhere to place the blame.

It was almost as if the idea that we *had* been perfect meant that we *could* be perfect again someday. It was that hope that had kept me going, kept me thinking that this was all worth fighting for. I had never even considered that maybe we were never that perfect to begin with. And the thought of what that could mean for our current relationship scared me.

She continued her verbal assault while I waited impatiently for the right time to strike. "We never went out with your friends, my friends. Hell, I've still never met your parents. You never went all in with me. You're quick to accuse me of being the only one who isn't invested in our relationship, but you've never given me all of you. It's always just been the pieces you were comfortable with. And I settled for that. First, because I thought that it was temporary, and then because I felt that I deserved it. But you're not the only one who deserves happiness. You're not the only one who should be forgiven unconditionally. I should get those things too. And you should want to give them."

I let her words sink in as I tried to formulate a coherent response that wasn't said completely in anger. "I admit, I've had a difficult time getting past what happened last year. But beyond that issue, I've done nothing that I need your 'unconditional forgiveness' for. I've been all in since January. I've done *everything* to try to make things right between us." I wasn't sure when I'd started raising my voice, but I willed myself to calm down. The last thing we needed was for the neighbors to call the cops.

"Really? You've done nothing that needs forgiving, huh?"

I shook my head, uncertain of what she planned to say.

A harsh smile crossed her face that looked more like a wince. "When's my birthday, Adam?"

I racked my brain, trying to remember if we'd been together for it last year. I didn't remember celebrating it. But, wait ... hadn't her parents come to town for it? Was it ... *Fuck.*

"March twenty-third. My birthday is March twenty-third." She crossed her arms over her chest and lowered her voice. "Don't tell me that you're all in." She shrugged. "Because you're not."

"But, shit, you never said anything."

"So it's my fault that you didn't remember?" She let out a bewildered laugh. "It's always someone else, isn't it?" She took a deep breath, closing her eyes. When she finally reopened them, she continued calmly, "Look, I'm not ten. It's not the end of the world that you forgot my birthday. It's just . . . it's a sign of just how little thought you really give me. I'm just part of the supporting cast in the movie of your life, Adam. You're so busy trying to forgive me, you aren't seeing me. We aren't together in this." She looked toward the floor. "We aren't equal. And I can't spend the rest of my life not being good enough. I love you. But I'm not sure that you love me."

I crossed my arms, mirroring her posture. I had shifted from feeling guilty to being irate again in a nanosecond. "You don't know if *I* love *you*?" I laughed, disgusted by the thought. "Shouldn't it be the other way around? What would make me think for a second that I should trust anything *you* have to say?"

"Ah, so blame finds its way back to me again. This is exactly what I'm talking about. You just can't let the past go."

My anger had quadrupled, and I tried unsuccessfully to keep my voice down. "Blame finds its way back to you because it's *your* fault, Lily. All this bullshit we're going through right now. You did it, not me. You act like I should just forgive and forget, sing kumbaya or some shit. Well, I've got news for you. It's not that easy. You ruined what we had for some fling with a piece of shit hockey player."

Her jaw ticked, her eyes the coldest I'd ever seen them. "Max is a lot of things, but a piece of shit isn't one of them."

My blood boiled at the sound of his name. "That's all you have to say? How can you possibly defend him at a time like this? Do you have any idea what that feels like?"

"He didn't force himself on me, Adam. How you feel about him, you should feel about me. And I think you do. You just won't admit it to yourself."

"You want me to forget what you've done just because you're sorry? Because you say you've changed? You hurt me, Lily. You hurt *us*. So don't act like you're not deserving of that pain."

Tears lingered behind her eyes, threatening to fall. But she spoke evenly. "I've *come* to terms with the pain I caused myself. I deserve every ounce of it. And you're right, Adam. I hurt you too. But I've served my time for that. I've apologized for it, and I've waited for you to forgive me. But you know who else didn't deserve the hurt I caused him? You know who never *once* asked me for the apology that he deserved?"

Don't even fucking say it.

"Max." Her eyes were acid on mine, burning through me as she spoke. "And you wanna know something else?" she said calmly, not waiting for me to respond to her rhetorical question. "That 'piece of shit' ... knew when my birthday was."

Her last comment struck me like a punch to the stomach, and I collapsed heavily onto her couch again, letting myself feel the full weight of her words before finally speaking. "This won't work, will it?"

My quiet words caused her expression to soften, and she took a seat on a nearby chair. "What won't?"

I buried my face in my hands as I tried to rub away the tension before making eye contact with her. "Us," I said. "No matter what we do, we'll never be able to fix what's broken."

She let out a sharp breath. "So what does that mean? You're giving up? Just gonna throw in the towel, call it quits, and walk out the door, Adam?" Disgust laced every syllable as she spoke. "Way to be all in."

"You said it yourself, Lily. I can't let the past go. As hard as I try to push Max Samson out of my mind, he just stays there." She rolled her eyes at the truth in my confession. "But there's one thing you haven't realized." I let her stare fixate on me before I spoke again, wanting to make sure that she heard what I had to say. "You're no better at leaving the past behind than I am. You'll always compare me to Max: who forgives you and who doesn't, which one of us remembers your birthday and which forgets. Because as hard as you try to push Max Samson from *your* mind," I said slowly, "you just can't do it either."

I stood up cautiously, not wanting to jar her any more than I just had. She watched me rise, looking at me as if she'd just seen a ghost. Maybe she had. I leaned down and planted a soft kiss on her forehead before turning toward the door to leave. "Bye, Lily," I said, stopping to put my key on the small table by the door as I gripped the doorknob. "And for what it's worth, I do love you."

I didn't wait to hear her response before closing the door softly behind me. Because while the thought of hearing her speak those same words scared me, the possibility of not hearing them scared me just a little bit more.

chapter thirty-nine

a d a m

Despite the fact that my love for Lily had been real, so had the feeling that our relationship had become strained beyond repair. When I'd closed that door to Lily's apartment, I'd effectively closed the door to that chapter of my life. And a part of me was devastated by it. For so long, I'd thought that if we just tried hard enough, we could go back to how we felt when we'd first met: that carefree newness and comfortable safety that we all take for granted until one day we realize we've lost it.

The truth was, I was sad. Not sad because I felt I'd made the wrong decision. I knew I hadn't. Lily and I could have never made our relationship work. But that's what saddened me: putting so much effort into something and failing miserably anyway. I mourned the loss of what I thought could have been.

Though the grief I felt for our failed relationship felt constricting at first, the more I thought logically about the situation, the more I realized that I felt like a weight had been lifted *off* me too. I'd put so much effort into trying to forgive Lily, to forget about what had happened in the past, I hadn't stopped to enjoy the present.

So when my thirty-fourth birthday rolled around a week and a half later, I couldn't wait to enjoy some time with family. My parents had invited Eva and me over for dinner and cake, and I was looking forward to the beautiful late May weather while I relaxed on their back deck.

❤

"Mom? Dad? We're here," I called, as I entered the front door.

"In here, Adam. Happy birthday." My mom's voice drifted out from the kitchen, where I could smell the delicious aromas coming from the oven.

"Thanks, Mom," I said, leaning down to give her a hug and a peck on the cheek. "I thought we were grilling today. What are you making?"

"We are grilling. Your dad's out on the deck making some grilled chicken and some sort of pork. Just making some homemade baked beans and roasted potatoes in here. Where'd Eva go?"

I turned around, thinking she'd followed me into the kitchen, but she was nowhere to be found. "Eva, where are you?" I called. *Teenagers.*

"In here!" she yelled from the family room.

"Well, come in here and say hi to your grandmother." The sound of Eva's exaggerated groan meant that she had enough sense to listen, but as she rounded the corner still texting, I rolled my eyes. "You know your friends will still be there if you remove your thumbs from your phone, right?"

"Yes, Dad." She returned my eye roll with one of her own before putting her phone in her pocket. "It's nice to see you, Grandma," she said sincerely as she hugged my mom.

"You too, sweetheart. Adam, why don't you go out and keep your father company? Eva and I will finish in here."

As I slid open the glass doors to the deck, I smiled sweetly at my mom and shot Eva a threatening look that let her know she needed to stay off her phone and help with dinner.

"Hey, Adam. Didn't even know you were here," my dad said, wrapping his big arms around me and squeezing tightly. "Happy birthday."

"Thanks. It's good to see you." I moved to the edge of the deck to take a look into the yard that was currently covered in mounds of dirt. "You're putting in a pool?" I couldn't believe my parents had finally decided to get an in-ground pool. I'd asked them for years when I was growing up, but they always said it'd be too much of a pain to keep up with. "What happened to it being too expensive and annoying to maintain? Did it suddenly get cheaper and easier now that I'm thirty-four?"

My dad let out a low laugh and his belly shook, reminding me of Santa in a grilling apron. "No, still expensive as hell. Just have the time for it now that we're both getting close to retiring. Plus, we know Eva and her friends would love it. And any other grandkids we might be getting in the future." He winked, elbowing me playfully.

I laughed, hoping that he wouldn't see how awkward his comment had made me feel. I couldn't shake the irony that plagued me after his not-so-subtle hint. Since I'd had Eva at such a young age, they were never quick to push me to have more kids. But now, with their son pushing thirty-five, I guess the realization had set in for them that I wasn't getting any younger. The realization had set in for me too.

Luckily, it wasn't hard to get my dad to switch subjects. One mention of the Phillies and he'd launched off into a critical analysis that would put any grad student to shame.

We spent the next fifteen minutes talking baseball before my dad asked me to go get some plates to set the table because dinner was nearly ready. I made my way inside to find my mom and Eva putting the side dishes on plates. Opening the cabinet, I removed four plates and set them down on the counter. But my mom quickly took out three more and placed them on top of the others. "What are these for?" I asked.

"We're having company," my mom replied simply.

I laughed. "Oookay, I thought *we* were company." I gestured between Eva and myself.

"You are, but I invited a few more."

Before I could call my mom out on her furtiveness, I heard voices coming from the deck. The "company" must have gone around back. I grabbed a few more essentials—napkins, forks, and knives—before heading back toward the door.

I'd just slid open the door and looked to my right toward the table when I saw her.

"You remember the Stantons, right, Adam?" my dad asked.

I felt my eyes widen, and for the first time since I was in middle school, my cheeks flushed with embarrassment. *Yes, this time I remember.* "Carly," I said, grinning awkwardly as I fumbled with the utensils and plates while I tried to shake her hand. "Nice to see you again." My tone was innocent, but my thoughts were anything but.

"Likewise," Carly replied with the same formality that I had exhibited.

My dad interrupted the staring contest Carly and I had found ourselves in. "I'm just going to take this cake the Stantons brought inside and let your mom know our guests are here." My eyes briefly followed my dad into the house before refocusing on the people in front of me.

Carly's mom stretched out a warm hand to me. "Good to see you, Adam. It's been so long. You're all grown up now." I briefly wondered if she might pinch my cheeks like I was ten. She had the same eyes as Carly and though the color of her hair was slightly darker than her daughter's, there were more similarities than differences between the two. It was like looking at Carly twenty-five years from now. And I liked what I saw.

I quickly pulled myself from my Mrs. Robinson daydream just in time to remember I hadn't even responded. "Nice to see you again as well, Mrs. Stanton."

"Please, call me Joanne. You're clearly not in high school anymore."

"So when was the last time you two saw each other?" Mr. Stanton asked, gesturing between me and Carly. I realized I'd been so shocked that I hadn't even bothered to greet him. I recovered quickly with a firm shake of his hand while I thanked him for coming.

Then I remembered that I still needed to answer his question: when was the last time I'd seen Carly? *Naked? In November.* "Um..." I shot a look to Carly to try to gauge her thoughts.

She looked equally as thrown by her father's question as I was, and she stumbled over her words. "At the ... at the reunion actually. We saw each other then."

"Just briefly," I added quickly. "We really didn't see much

of each other." *Idiot.*

Carly gave me a knowing smile, which I returned—I hoped—inconspicuously.

Finally, the awkwardness subsided as we settled into our chairs on the deck to enjoy our dinner. "It was so nice of you to invite us," Carly said to my mom with a sweet smile. "The food's delicious. I haven't had a home-cooked meal in what feels like forever. I've been working such long hours lately. Takeout has become my new best friend."

"Well, you're welcome anytime," my mom replied.

Joanne put her hand on Carly's arm and gave her a loving squeeze. "It's definitely nice to all get together like this. Ever since our youngest, Katie, has gone off to college, empty nest syndrome has set in. Since Carly's the oldest, we keep telling her it's time to settle down so we can get some little ones running around the house again."

Carly shook her head, but I could tell she wasn't as annoyed by her mother's comment as she pretended to be.

I couldn't help but laugh as I recalled the similar words my father had uttered not even an hour earlier. "They definitely grow up fast," I said, feeling the need to add to the conversation. "I can't believe Eva will be in high school next year." I looked up at Carly, who was paying rapt attention to Eva's reaction. "She'll be the same age we were when we first met."

"God, Dad, you're so embarrassing."

I shrugged as I lifted my drink to my lips. "What else is new?" I laughed before taking a sip.

Carly leaned closer to Eva. "That's what dads do best."

She glanced over at her own father, who simply shrugged. "Part of the job, I guess."

"See," Carly added. "They all do it."

The rest of the dinner flowed easily with conversations about our jobs, Eva, and the random reality shows that Eva and Carly both watched. I was shocked to learn that *Keeping Up with the Kardashians* now apparently had *two* viewers.

When it was time for dessert, Carly offered to go inside and get the cake they'd brought with them from a local bakery. And I decided to be a helpful son and clear the table while the rest of them relaxed on the deck. Not surprisingly, it didn't take much convincing to keep Eva outside. She was content to catch up on her tweets while the adults talked.

"So," I said when Carly and I were finally alone inside. "This was a . . . surprise."

"Good surprise, or bad surprise?" she asked.

"Good," I quickly assured her. "I just didn't expect it. That's all. When I first saw you, I didn't know what to say. I wasn't sure what you had told them."

She laughed, though I wasn't sure why until she spoke. "Well, I almost told them what a good lay you were, but I didn't want my mom to try to seduce you." She shrugged. "It was a long walk up the street. It was hard to not fill the silence with such juicy details."

A loud laugh escaped me, and I nearly dropped the glass I was getting ready to put in the dishwasher. "Wait, your mom wouldn't really try to seduce me, right?"

"Yes, Adam," she laughed. "I'm kidding. You should've seen your face, though. Priceless."

I rubbed my face to hide the embarrassment I felt at my own credulity. "A good lay, huh?"

"Yup," she answered, popping the P flirtatiously as she said it. "But I'm guessing you're good at a lot of things." She moved toward me, a seductive gleam in her eyes as she wrapped her arms around my neck, and I was momentarily stunned by how right they felt there. Then she planted a soft kiss on my lips that held just enough passion to make me want to throw her on the counter and take her right there in my parents' kitchen.

Christ, Adam, get a grip.

"What are you thinking?" she asked when our kiss finally broke and she pulled back enough to look at me.

I gazed into her eyes and brushed her soft red hair away from her face. "I'm thinking this beats Brad Holbrook's basement."

chapter forty

l i l y

Losing Adam felt like just that: a loss. When he broke up with me, walked out my door and effectively out of my life, I had been stunned. But once my senses had returned, I found that I wasn't angry. Because while there was the pain that came with losing someone of importance to you, there was also a loss of the weight I had been shouldering for quite some time. We weren't right for each other. I knew that for sure now.

In reality, I was pretty sure I'd known that for a while. But it became clearest at Amanda's wedding. Adam and I just didn't have the spark they did. And even though Amanda told me not to compare the two relationships, it was impossible *not* to when one had things that were fundamentally necessary to lifelong happiness and the other didn't: unconditional love and acceptance. Everything between Adam and me was conditional. And I suddenly realized that we always had an expiration date. That we'd actually allowed things to go on long past when they should have.

And these were the thoughts that had plagued me for the three weeks following my breakup with Adam. During this time, there'd been no contact between us. I had done a quick search of my apartment a few days after Adam left to see if I had any of his belongings that needed to be returned, but there was nothing. And I had nothing to collect at his house either. Other than a couple of pictures I had of the two of us, there was virtually no evidence that we'd ever even known each other, let alone dated. And as time passed, I became more and more sure that Adam had done the right thing by walking away. And I had done the right thing by not stopping him.

However, now I had nothing but time—time to think and obsess about what I wanted from life. I was driving myself crazy. When the soul-searching became too much, I often decided that CrossFit was the only way to escape from myself for a little while. That's what drew me to the gym on the Friday before school let out. I hadn't planned to go because I usually felt like a loser going to the gym on a Friday evening. But since that was what I felt like anyway, there was no real reason to keep up appearances of anything else.

I walked into the gym and my eyes scanned the room as I started to stretch. But my movement halted when my eyes settled on him. The blaring rock music thumped in time with my heart as my whole body reacted to seeing him. It had been over a month since I'd last spoken to him. And though I refused to admit it at the time, what he had said to me that morning at breakfast had shaken me to my core—had made me question every feeling I'd had in the past year and a half. Made me wonder...

"Hey," Max said.

I hadn't even registered that his class had ended and that

he currently stood directly in front of me. It took every ounce of willpower I had to resist scanning his body, to ignore the post-workout glow that emanated from him. *Goddamn, he's so fucking sexy.*

"Hey," I finally managed.

We stood there for a second, both struggling to find something to say. But what could be said? He'd laid it all out for me. Gift wrapped himself and dropped himself at my feet. And I'd refused him.

"How's Mary?" *Wow, Lily. Worst. Question. Ever.*

He looked at me curiously for a second before simply replying, "That's done. Like I told you, I just can't do that to her. She deserves better."

I wanted to disagree. Because if there's one thing I knew, there was no better than him.

"How's Adam?"

I shouldn't have been shocked by this question, but I was. "I'm, uh, I'm not sure actually."

He tilted his head, trying to read the meaning behind my words.

"He and I ... It didn't work out."

He was unreadable, except for the intake of a shaky breath. He quickly plastered on that cocky grin of his. "I wish I could say I'm sorry to hear that."

"Yeah, well, it's for the best. I think I just need some time. You know, to figure my shit out." My words were a cop out. Telling him I needed time was my way of brushing him off and avoiding having to face my feelings about him. Because while I was attracted to Max, and while a part of me would always love him, I wasn't sure we were what was best for each other. He represented everything I had tried to change about myself.

And while I didn't necessarily like the person I had morphed into, I didn't really like who I'd been back then either.

He nodded slowly, and watching him caused pain to ripple through my chest. *Why am I always hurting him?*

"Well, I hope you get it all figured out." His words were sincere, as was his heated gaze.

"Thanks."

"Bye, Lily."

And that's when something broke through. Adam had said these same words to me, and I'd barely flinched. But Max saying them caused panic to seize my body. His words held a finality that caused my stomach to bottom out, and I just couldn't let this be it.

So against all reason, against all the things I had told myself were for the best, I stopped him. "Max?"

He exhaled deeply, causing his shoulders to drop from the place of tension they had been. He slowly turned and looked back at me.

"There's talk of the teachers at Swift all meeting for happy hour next Friday at Flanagan's. We're going to be celebrating making it through another school year. If you're not busy, I'm sure all the teachers would love to see you."

He thought for a second before answering. "Would *you* love to see me there?"

Why couldn't he ever just let things be easy? I rolled my eyes, trying to downplay what he was asking. "Yes, I'd like to see you there." I couldn't keep the grin from my face, so I stopped trying.

"Then I'll be there," he said before turning away from me and walking out of the gym.

And as I watched his perfectly shaped ass go, I couldn't

help but wonder what the hell I was getting myself into.

❤

The next week was brutal. My emotional state swung like a hormonal teenager's. One minute, I was questioning if I'd tried hard enough with Adam, the next I was thinking about giving things a try with Max. And then I contemplated if a bigger slut had ever graced the globe. However, I quickly thought of some of the female twats I worked with and felt reassured.

But this was still wrong... wasn't it? Adam and I had been in a serious relationship for months. I couldn't jump into another one less than a month later. And did I even *want* a relationship with Max? I'd shunned the idea for a year and a half, and I see him sweat-soaked after a workout one day, and now all of a sudden I want to commit to the guy? That was ridiculous. Totally ridiculous.

And fucking appealing on so many levels.

And that's when my mind drifted to Atlantic City, and to the words Max had told me there. For the first time since that day, I allowed Max's voice to invade my thoughts.

I know the difference between reality and illusions. And I know that the Lily I was close to was much more real than the one who's standing in front of me right now.

He was right. This girl. She wasn't me. I had spent so much time forcing myself to grow up, to be the mature woman who wouldn't make stupid mistakes that hurt people just because I wanted to follow what felt good. But this Lily wasn't any better than that one. At least who I had been a year ago was real: the emotions, the mistakes, the chaos. It was all so much more real than this projection I was now. I was *alive* then. I was merely existing now.

I wanted to cry for that girl, the one I left behind last summer when I decided to "find" myself in Europe. But I couldn't. Or *wouldn't* maybe. This was the culmination of my decisions. There was no one to blame but myself. I couldn't go back. I couldn't unbecome who I was.

Could I?

And that's when it hit me. I had blamed my impulsivity on Max since I'd met him, telling myself that he brought these things out of me. But he didn't. They were part of who I was. He just let me feel safe enough to express it.

💔

By the time I plopped myself on a stool next to Tina at the bar, I had convinced myself that getting involved with Max beyond a platonic level was a mistake. I'd hurt enough men for one lifetime. I wasn't in a place to get involved with Max. At least not right now. Or maybe not ever. Or . . . who the hell knew? But definitely, unequivocally, beyond a shadow of a doubt, I was *not* getting involved with him anytime soon. *Nope, not gonna happen.*

Then I saw him—his faded jeans slung low on his waist, his tight gray T-shirt stretching over his tightly corded muscles, his intentionally messy black hair perfectly highlighting his electric blue eyes. My decision to wear a skirt had been a bad one because it didn't offer nearly enough protection from the flood of Biblical Noah proportions that was occurring in my underwear.

I had convinced myself that morning that my wardrobe

choice had been due to the extreme heat we were experiencing, and the fact that Swift's air conditioning wasn't turned on unless required by law. But seeing him in all his glory shot that lie to shit. I was dressed for him: an appropriate, yet formfitting skirt and a white pin-striped blouse hugged me in a way that made me feel attractive. And once I popped open an extra button or two, the look screamed "sexy teacher."

He scanned the room, looking for me, and tipped his head in my direction once our gazes finally met.

"Oh my God, look who's here."

I looked to my left to see where the voice had come from. *Ugh, fucking Crystal Hightower.* Even her name sounded like she should've been starring in porn, and the fake tits she threw in everyone's face did nothing to dispute the association. I wasn't exactly sure how Crystal had become a teacher. She was dumber than driftwood. She must've spent a lot of time on her knees in college. I vaguely remembered her lavishing her attention on Max last year, but I'd been too caught up in my own relationship with him to pay her much attention.

Max started making his way over, but was stopped by a few teachers before he got to me.

"I've just decided that Max Samson is going to be my summer fling," she purred to her gaggle of gremlins as she slid her drink onto the bar, pulled her shirt down, and shimmied her shoulders to get the girls ready for action.

My eyes widened as I listened while she told her creatures of the night entourage about her plans for Max, which were shockingly detailed considering she hadn't been expecting to see him. It seemed that she intended to fuck him senseless until he basically handed her his wallet and gave her free rein over his bank account.

"Kind of like an escort." Clearly my mouth possessed about as much of a filter as the water fountain at work. Tina nearly choked on her drink as she heard me, and I sensed Crystal turn in my direction.

"Did you say something to me, Lily?" Her eyes were glacial as she appraised me.

God, what I wouldn't give to mollywhop the shit out of this trick. "No," I said innocently. "Just talking to Tina."

Max finally appeared at my side. "How's it goin', Lil?"

"Good. You remember Tina," I replied, holding out my hand in her direction.

"Yup. How ya doin', Tina?"

Tina's eyebrows raised before she turned toward her drink. "Everything's fine with *me.*" I couldn't help notice the sly smile on her lips. She knew fireworks were coming, and she was looking forward to the show.

Max eyed her curiously for a moment before looking at me. "Man, it looks like the whole school is here. It's good to see everybody."

"Yeah, it's good to get out with everyone and talk about things other than school once in a while."

"Hi, Max." Crystal's voice was like nails on a chalkboard, and I wanted to beat her over the head with my stool for interrupting us.

"Oh, uh, hey." Max clearly didn't remember Crystal's name, and it thrilled me.

"Crystal," she said, smiling sweetly, though I thought I saw a slight wince of disappointment on her face. Or maybe embarrassment. I hoped it was both.

"Yeah, right. Crystal. Nice to see you." Max was polite, but he shifted closer to me.

"You too. Really nice."

The seduction in her voice made a laugh burst from my mouth. Everyone in our vicinity whipped their heads to gawk at me, so I quickly released a cough to cover my outburst. "Sorry. Wrong pipe," I lied.

"Anyway, Max, the bartender has been completely ignoring this half of the bar. Do you think you could get me a drink?"

I couldn't believe the balls on this skank. She'd been talking to him for all of two seconds, and she was already asking for him to buy her drinks. I was about ready to shank this ho.

"Um, sure," Max replied. He asked what she was drinking and then glanced at me. "You need anything?"

I shook my head, and he started off toward the other end of the long bar.

"He's really handsome, Crystal. Maybe you guys will really like each other," Dana, one of the meeker minions, chimed in.

"Who cares about any of that? I mean, don't get me wrong, it certainly helps that he's attractive. But I only have eyes for one thing . . . his credit card." Crystal cackled at her little joke and her hyenas all joined in. "God, athletes are so stupid."

"He's not stupid," I said quietly as I brought my drink up to my lips and took a sip through the straw.

"Excuse me?" Crystal asked as though I had offended her by addressing her at all.

"I said"—I paused, as I geared myself up to intentionally raise my voice—"he's not stupid. But you sure as shit are if you think he's falling for your bullshit." My eyes locked on hers, beckoning her to battle. Tina sat up a little straighter behind me, getting herself ready in case this turned ugly.

PICKING UP THE PIECES

"Please, by the time I'm done with him, he'll be so smitten he'll barely be able to see straight. And after I get him back to his place tonight, he'll be hooked."

"Better watch out for his whore-sniffing dogs," I muttered.

"What the fuck did you just say to me?" Crystal stood up taller and entered my personal space. *Bad move, Sybil.*

"I'm pretty sure you heard me. You stay the fuck away from Max. He's too good for you, so catch the next Greyhound back to Trampsylvania." I was off my stool in an instant, pushing back into the space we now shared.

"You're just jealous. I know all about how you tried to seduce him last year. And it clearly didn't work. Don't hate on me because I'm about to get what you couldn't." Her lips twitched into a cruel smile. She thought she had really zinged me with that one.

"I don't want to be with Max." My voice was low, but firm.

"Bullshit. It's written all over your face. You want him. But you can't get him." She backed away from me slightly and folded her arms across her chest, assuming the position of victory.

That's when I verbally launched on her. "I don't want to be with Max because he deserves better than me. And he sure as shit deserves better than you. He's a good man. A great man, actually. So if you think for two seconds that I'm going to sit here and let you hurt him, you've got another think coming. I will go to prison for murdering your skanky ass before I let you anywhere near him." My eyes bored into her, daring her to test me. And as I watched her face, I saw it change slightly. I silently began congratulating myself on the verbal lashing when I heard a throat clear.

"A great man, huh?"

My body tensed instantly at the sound of his voice. I turned slowly and gazed up into those blue eyes I knew so well. *Fuck. Me.*

"Uh, that ... that was ... Umm, how much of that did you hear?" I finally choked out.

"Enough," Max said, clearly irritated. "Outside. Now. We need to talk." He grabbed my hand and pulled me easily from the bar. His pace was difficult to keep up with. I would've been silently celebrating my success at getting Max away from Crystal if I hadn't been so nervous. He was angry, and there weren't many creatures in the animal kingdom that were more daunting than a pissed-off Max Samson.

"Max, wait," I pleaded as he pushed open the bar doors, still yanking me along behind him.

He turned right and guided me around to the rear of Flanagan's. It was pretty secluded there since the restaurant backed up to a bunch of trees.

This is going to be bad. Really bad.

Once we reached the back, Max used my forward momentum to spin me around and force me up against the wall in front of him. He then put two arms on either side of my head, caging me in. "Tell me what the hell that was."

I was in a state of shock. The dominance Max exuded was hot as hell. Pair that with his proximity and I was damn near orgasmic. "I was ... I was defending you."

"Don't bullshit me, Lily. That's not all you were doing. What you said, did you mean it?" His voice was stern, and it made me even wetter.

"Which part?" My brain was short-circuiting, and it was allowing incredibly stupid shit to come out of my mouth.

He bent his elbows and brought his body in tighter to

mine. His voice was a deep whisper when he finally spoke. "Do you really think I could do better than you?"

I met his gaze, though the way his eyes seared into me, I was finding it difficult to breathe. My chest rose and brushed against his hard body. My nipples puckered immediately, and my tongue darted out to moisten my lips. "I *know* you can do better than me, Max. You always could have."

He brought his hand up to cup my jaw. "Lily, when are you going to get it? There is no better than you."

I barely had time to process his words before his lips crushed against mine, the hand that had been on my face now twisting in my hair, holding me firmly in place. I couldn't hold back a moan of sheer bliss as he rocked his erection into me, making it clear that he still wanted me. In every way.

He moved both hands to cup my ass and lifted, causing my legs to instinctively wrap around him. His mouth was everywhere: my lips, my jaw, my ear, my neck. My skin was ablaze wherever he touched me. This was the feeling I'd been missing. I was finally alive.

"I want to make one thing very clear," he murmured, his lips against my skin. "You and I are going to have a do-over. I'm going to take you against this wall, just as I did in that airport a year and a half ago. But this time, when we're done, I get to keep you." He pulled back slightly to meet my eyes. "Do you understand? You'll be mine, Lily. Only mine."

I summoned all the strength I could and returned his gaze with passion equal to his. Maybe greater. "Under one condition." He looked at me expectantly, waiting for me to name my terms. I smiled at him, a smile meant to hold all the promise in the world. "You'll need to be mine too."

His eyes darkened with hunger and something else I

could only describe as love. "Doll, I've been yours since the day we met."

And with that declaration, we wasted no time picking up where we'd left off: all mouths, hands, and throbbing need.

"You wore a fucking skirt on purpose, didn't you? When you put it on this morning, you prayed it would end up around your waist."

"Damn right I did," I replied as I pushed one hand into his hair and dug the nails of my other into his shoulder.

Max slid his hand beneath my skirt, which had already been hiked up when I wrapped my legs around him. "This is in my way," he muttered as he ripped my thong from my body.

The warm air hit me at the apex of my thighs, and I briefly thought I would lose it right there. I needed him inside of me. Right then. So I pushed toward the ground with my legs, a silent plea for him to put me down. When he complied, I ran my hand down his stomach, toward his waistband, easily unbuttoning his jeans so I could pull down his zipper. I reached into his jeans and immediately found his straining cock. *No boxers. Glad some things never change.* I ran my hand over it, wanting to touch him freely, like I used to before I told myself he wasn't what I wanted. I couldn't have been more wrong.

Max suddenly reached into his pocket to withdraw a condom.

"Always ready, aren't you?" I jested.

"A guy can hope."

I took the foil wrapper from him, ripped it open with my teeth, and leaned back against the wall so I could reach down to sheath him with the thin latex. Once I had rolled it down his hard length, he lifted me back up into his arms as I guided him to where I needed him most.

He wasted no time thrusting inside of me. My back bowed and I stifled a loud groan by digging my teeth into Max's clothed shoulder as he stroked me steadily, forcefully from the inside.

"Look at me," he commanded.

I lifted my head.

"You're going to watch me so that you never forget who does this to you, who makes you feel this good."

I didn't respond, but did as he instructed, taking in his piercing blue stare that seemed to see right through me. The feel of him pushing into me was euphoric, and I hated that it would eventually have to end.

"Who do you belong to, Lily?"

"You," I hissed, barely able to get enough air into my lungs to respond.

"And why do you belong to me?"

"Because you love me," I answered, honestly.

His rhythm faltered slightly, letting me know that my answer had surprised him. "Who do I belong to?" His question was soft, almost unsure, like he wasn't certain what I was going to say and was rattled by the unsettling feeling.

"Me. You belong to me."

He continued to thrust, but his pace slowed as he looked at me as though he were trying to memorize exactly how I looked in that moment. "Why do I belong to you?"

My answer came without the slightest hesitation. "Because I love you."

"Say it again," he demanded as he thrust deeper, harder, causing me to cry out.

"I love you," I ground out as my orgasm built within me. Max rocked his hips into me hard, and I welcomed him every time.

"I'm so close. You don't know how much I've wanted to do this again, feel the warmth of being inside you." His pace increased, causing me to shiver with pleasure as his breath tickled my ear. "Come with me, doll."

I put my hands on his shoulders for some leverage and began to bear down on him, impaling myself on his thick shaft.

Max let out a guttural moan. "That's it. God, you feel so good. Just like that. I'm gonna come, Lily. You there with me?"

I mewled. "I'm there."

He found his release at my words. Then his head dropped to my chest as he pumped into me, filling the condom as his cock thrummed inside of me. I followed him over the edge, my body shaking with pleasure as I milked every drop of come from him. "Max," I sighed, knowing that there was probably nothing else he'd rather hear more. My body was limp in his arms, perfectly sated.

We stood there for a few moments, trying to catch our breaths and enjoying being wrapped in each other. Finally, Max lifted his head so he could look at me. "Say it again," he rasped.

I caressed his face. "I love you, Max," I said, hoping he could see the veracity of the words in my eyes.

"I know you do, doll," he said with a wink. "It's about damn time you realized it." He leaned in and kissed me. It was a soft, meaningful kiss—one meant to mark this moment as a time of firsts for us.

The first time we'd made love without all the bullshit in the way. The first time we were both completely honest with one another. The first time we accepted that this was what we had needed all along. This was what made us complete: each other.

"I thought I'd never see you again," Max whispered as he feathered kisses wherever his mouth could reach.

"What, after Atlantic City?"

He shook his head lightly. "After I left your apartment last April. After the fundraiser."

I pulled back, looking at him quizzically. *Does he need to be cryptic right now?* "I've seen you a bunch of times since then."

"I haven't seen you. Not the *real* you. Not the one I fell in love with in that airport." He sighed. "I thought I'd lost you forever. I missed ya, doll."

I felt my eyes water as I processed what he'd said. I finally got it. While I had needed to grow up over the past year, I also still needed that spark that made me who I was. Somewhere along the way I'd lost it. Max had made me realize that there was room for both. I could be this mature woman who made good decisions *and* still be that wild girl who let Max fuck her against a random wall here and there. In fact, being both was the only thing that would let me be truly happy. Well, that and getting Max somewhere more private so we could figure out where we went from there, and then see how many orgasms we could give each other in one weekend.

"What are you thinking about?" he asked as he lowered me to the ground.

I smiled. "About how similar this is to our airport escapade."

The smile he had been returning faltered. While that encounter had been mind-blowing, it hadn't exactly turned out the way Max had hoped.

I moved in closer to him. "And about how different the

rest will be." His smile returned as I continued, "Take me home, Max."

And he did.

chapter forty-one

l i l y

Once blood began running to the top half of my body again, rational thought came back to me. I didn't want a whirlwind romance with Max. I wanted something that would still be there when the winds died down.

So instead of fulfilling the promise I made myself about the multiorgasmic weekend that was ahead of me, I pumped the brakes. Max and I had needed to talk about so much, get on the same page, and sex would've been a hindrance to us.

But after two weeks of my denying him anything beyond a heated make out session on my couch, Max decided to play dirty. However, when even his expert fingers and roving tongue proved no match for my resolve, he tactfully reminded me that playing hard to get was usually reserved for those who hadn't already given up the goods. And after I'd leveled him with a lethal glare that was completely for show, I straddled him on my love seat and made it clear that he'd yet to see the best of my goods.

From there, we were inseparable. I tried to retain some autonomy at first, pretending like I actually wanted to sleep by myself in my apartment. But after Max knocked on my door at two in the morning on a Wednesday, complaining that he couldn't sleep without me hogging all the covers, we both decided spending time alone was overrated. My things slowly began taking over his house after that. *I* began taking over his house after that.

And that's how, two months later, I ended up on Bill and Marjorie's back patio, with Max casually holding my hand, and my parents talking about how great the food was.

"Really, Bill, everything is so delicious," my mom raved.

"Glad you're enjoying it, Lynn. It's nice cooking for folks who appreciate a good meal." Max's dad sent a purposeful look at his wife and son as he said the last comment.

"If we ever got one, we'd appreciate it," Max retorted, not looking at his father, but rather staring at our intertwined fingers as he drew lazy circles on my skin with his thumb.

"So, Max, Lily tells me you're doing really well with the hockey commentating. Is there room for growth with that?" My dad was smitten with Max, and who could blame him? It wasn't every day that I introduced him to my famous hockey player boyfriend. But he was still trying to play the protective father role. It was cute.

Max tore his attention from our hands to look my father in the eye, giving him the respect Max knew my father expected. "Absolutely, Howard. The postgame interviews I'm doing now could easily lead to doing play-by-play analysis during the game. I just need to wait for an opportunity to open up."

"Could that require you to move?" I knew my mom's question was asking more than it seemed. Even though she always wished I'd return to Chicago, she also didn't want me traipsing all over the country in order to pursue someone *else's* dreams.

"I have no intention of moving. My family's here." His eyes skated to mine. "Lily's here." Refocusing on my mom, he sat back in his chair. "I'm not going anywhere."

I knew he was talking about more than just relocating for his job. He was letting me know that he was in this for the long haul. And I loved him for it.

Our relationship had progressed rapidly, but none of it felt rash or sudden. I knew it was because we'd actually been building up to this for over a year and a half. And once we finally arrived, it just felt . . . right.

Which brought me to one of the reasons we were all having dinner together. Other than us obviously wanting our parents to meet, we also wanted to discuss something with them. I had tried to think of the best way to broach the subject, but nothing had come to me. So I finally decided to say the hell with it and just come out with it. "Max and I are going to move in together," I blurted as I pushed food around my plate.

Everyone looked up at me and set their silverware down. *At least they no longer have weapons.* I knew Bill and Marjory would probably be okay with the news, but my parents were pretty old-fashioned. There was really no telling how they would react.

"Are you two sure you're ready for that? It's only been a couple of months."

I had been prepared for that sentiment, though I'd been stunned that it was Marjory who had voiced it. But, when I thought about it, I had to admit that I had a habit of hurting her son. Therefore, I really couldn't blame her reluctance.

"I'm sure that I'm done waiting for my life to work itself out," I explained softly. "I want to start putting the pieces in place for my future. *Our* future. And I don't want to waste another second of my life. We only get one forever. I want to make every minute count."

Marjory smiled, clearly satisfied with my answer.

"Well, if you're sure, Lily, then your mother and I support whatever decision you make."

I nodded and looked at Max. "I'm sure."

"Great!" Bill exclaimed as he slapped his knee. "Now that all that's out of the way, what's for dessert?"

"Classy, Dad."

"What? We were all thinking it," Bill defended.

"I'm pretty sure everyone else was thinking about how great Lily and I are together," Max replied as he lifted my hand to his lips and kissed it. "Until you completely bulldozed the moment, that is."

"I'm going to bulldoze this table if someone doesn't bring me a piece of cake or a brownie or something. I worked over a hot grill for you, and you can't even get me a piece of pie. With some ice cream. And maybe sprinkles."

"Ignore him, Howard and Lynn. He gets antsy without his postdinner sugar fix," Marjory explained.

"Don't let her change the subject. She's just trying to keep dessert to herself. I'm wise to your games, woman."

My parents were grinning widely, clearly amused by Max's dad. And I couldn't blame them. If Bill was any indicator of what Max would be like in twenty years, then I was in for a life full of laughs.

"Max and I brought dessert. I'll go get it." I got out of my chair as if doing so was a great burden, though I couldn't stifle my grin. "I'll be right back."

When I got to the kitchen, I pulled the apple pie we brought out of the fridge and grabbed a plate to serve it on. Then I spread the cookies I'd made earlier around the outside of the plate. I was reaching up to grab dessert plates from Marjory's cabinets when I felt two strong arms wrap around me from behind.

"What are you doing in here?" I asked as I rested my arms over his.

"I missed you," he replied as he started trailing kisses down my neck.

I tilted my head to the side to give him better access, though I said, "Don't start something you can't finish."

I felt a small laugh rumble in his chest. "Have you ever known finishing to be a problem of mine?"

I slapped his arm lightly. "You're bad."

He spun me around and lifted me onto the counter, stepping between my thighs. I wrapped my arms around his neck as he slipped his around my waist.

"Not bad for you." He said the words as a statement, but his eyes let me know that they were a question too. He was asking me, pleading with me, to tell him that he was good enough.

And just as I'd done every time he'd needed this reassurance from me over the past two months, I gave it willingly, knowing that I was the reason he needed it in the first place. I just hoped that, with time, I could relieve all the hurt I'd caused him. "No, you're the very best thing for me." I leaned in and kissed him sweetly.

"I love you, doll."

"I love you too. Now let me off this counter before I show

you just how much," I said with a wink.

He clamped his hands around my hips roughly as he slid me hard against his waist, as if daring me to follow through with my threat. He stayed there for a moment, giving me access to the feel of his steadily growing erection.

Finally, when he knew I'd been sufficiently teased, he backed up and I hopped down from my perch, missing the feel of him against me immediately. I was still amazed that I'd been able to ignore my feelings for so long because part of me had always known that no one fit me like Max did. We were two halves of the same coin, two adjoining pieces of the same puzzle. We just fit … in every way.

Max swatted my ass as I walked past him with the plate. He picked up the dessert dishes I'd retrieved before he'd come in and followed me out of the kitchen. "Just so you know," he said behind me as we approached our parents, "you will be showing me how much you love me as soon as we get home."

And I smiled. I almost corrected him, but decided against it. Instead, I'd spend the rest of my life showing him that I wasn't only interested in demonstrating my love in the privacy of our home. I wanted it to be on permanent display so the whole world knew that Max Samson was mine.

And I was his.

❤

The rest of the night passed by smoothly, and we made our exit soon after my parents headed back to their hotel.

Normally, Max never missed an opportunity to touch me in some way, no matter how small. But as the night had worn on, his touch was noticeably absent. And in the car, I couldn't help but notice the determination on his face, as if he were struggling with something. When I moved my hand to the center console to brush his, he jerked back before I made contact. That's when it dawned on me: the bastard was going to make me beg.

Max had perfected the art of driving me insane. Actually, I often thought he had been specifically built for that purpose alone. But this was a game that two could play.

When we arrived home, I followed him up the path to the front door. As he unlocked it, I pressed into him from behind, causing my chest to rest on his strong back.

He ceased all movement. "What are you doing?" he asked.

"Just a little cold," I replied, adding a shiver for good measure.

"It's August, doll." He turned slightly so he could see me.

I simply quirked an eyebrow at him in response. He finally opened the door, and as soon as we were inside, I started shedding clothes. It began innocently, me slipping off my red peep-toe pumps one at a time and dropping them to the ground.

But then came my halter top. And then my jeans. I sprinkled these up the stairs as I made my way to the bedroom. When I was about four steps from the top, I unclasped my bra and let it fall to the stairs. I didn't need to look back to know that Max hadn't moved from the foyer. I could *feel* his eyes on me, enjoying the show, yet trying like hell not to sprint up the stairs and carry me the rest of the way to our bed. Once I was upstairs and out of his eyesight, I took off my last remaining article of clothing: my black lace panties. I giggled to myself as I tossed them over the railing. When I heard his footsteps pounding against the floor in pursuit, I dashed toward our bedroom, laughing the whole way.

I stopped just before the bed and turned around, observing him as he slowly stalked toward me, as a predator would approach its prey. I watched him shuck his own clothing, so that when he reached me he was completely nude.

He laid his hands on my shoulders and then began to drag them down my arms, before moving them to my stomach, and back up so he could fondle my breasts.

"I love seeing my hands on you," he said slowly, my body instantly responding to the sound of his raspy voice against my ear.

"I love feeling them there." I wanted to roll my head back and bask in the pleasure his hands were doling out, but there was something so primitively erotic about watching him appraise my body that I couldn't look away.

He stepped closer to me, his erection pushing into my pelvis deliciously.

"I thought you were playing hard to get?" I asked him.

His eyes shot to mine, their burning intensity rocketing warmth through my entire body. "I'm not hard to get. *You've* always had *me*."

For a few minutes after he spoke, we did nothing. We didn't speak. We didn't kiss. And truth be told, I couldn't be sure if we even breathed. As always, I instantly got so lost in him, in us, that the thought of doing anything other than just being with him hadn't even crossed my mind. I savored this time spent with him and silently cursed myself for almost ruining the chance to experience it.

Eventually, he moved his mouth purposefully toward mine, and my lips met his with the same intensity. As much as I adored our ability to simply be, I loved these moments too.

When a kiss began slowly, our tongues licking, pulling, and sucking until our hearts began to race faster and our breaths quickened.

I moaned against his mouth, massaging my hands down the length of his spine and back up again, feeling the pull of his skin beneath my fingers. He lowered me onto the bed and his hand immediately found my thigh, draping it over his hip so we could grind softly against one another. I felt myself get even wetter as his cock teased me until I was ready to beg to have him inside me.

He danced his fingers tantalizingly down my legs and settled between my thighs. Reflexively, I thrust my hips against his hand, gaining the friction I craved. "So smooth," he groaned out as he slid a finger inside me, expertly stroking the most sensitive part of me.

He increased the speed of his fingers, causing more of the slickness to slide into his palm as he swirled and stroked me toward orgasm. When I reached down to grip his shaft, he moved it away slowly. "Mmm-mmm," he groaned teasingly. "You'll feel me when I'm inside you. Not until then."

I whined playfully, but the truth was I liked it. The idea that I couldn't please him right away only turned me on more. He took his time licking his way down every inch of my body, across my arms and down my stomach to my toes and back up my legs, until his warm mouth finally ceased its torturously long journey and came to a stop at just the right spot.

Slowly at first, and then with increasing speed, he made love to me with his tongue—licking, thrusting, flicking, and sucking wildly until my need to have him inside me was excruciating. My subtle sounds grew steadily louder until I was sure the whole street knew what we were up to.

I bit my bottom lip to keep from screaming as his tongue and fingers worked inside me perfectly. "Please," I finally begged, knowing that I couldn't hold out much longer. But he didn't let up. He teased me, bringing me just to the brink of orgasm before slowly tapering off his movements. *God, he knows me better than I know myself.*

Slowly, he brought his mouth back up to mine, kissing every speck of skin on the path up to my lips. I writhed beneath him, waiting impatiently for him to fill the emptiness in me that only he could ever fill. Then he pulled away for a moment, his gaze finding mine before speaking. "What is it you want?" he asked, a slight smile peeking out from the corners of his mouth.

I stilled my body before speaking, my eyes returning his intimate stare. "What I always want," I said simply, knowing he loved to hear it. "You."

And that's exactly what he gave. What he'd always given. And as he thrust solidly into me, causing my body to climb even closer toward release, I was so incredibly thankful for getting this chance that I really hadn't deserved. And as he pounded into me and brought me to the brink of shattering, love swelled even more in my chest because I knew that he'd be there to pick up the pieces after. In his arms, I'd always be whole.

"Let go, doll. I wanna see you fall apart beneath me."

I met his thrusts, wildly working my hands over his body, until finally my body seized and my orgasm rocked through me.

He continued to pump inside of me, causing my body to continue to shake as my muscles contracted, making me even tighter for him.

He groaned his release, emptying inside of me. "God, I'm

so glad we stopped using condoms. The feel of you around me with nothing between us is incredible." He lowered himself onto his side so that half of his body draped over me.

I laughed. "You are a true romantic, you know that?"

"Just speaking the truth," he replied as he buried his face in the crook of my neck.

"So did I show you?" I asked.

"Show me what?"

I turned so that we were facing each other. "How much I love you," I whispered.

His sexy smirk primed my body for him again. "You did. But maybe you should show me again. Just to be sure."

"Whatever it takes," I replied sincerely.

And as we began to get lost in each other again, I knew, beyond a shadow of a doubt, that I loved this man. He was my one, my only, my Max.

epilogue

m a x

Nearly five years later . . .

"In five, four, three, two . . ." Scott pointed at me.

"We're here with Anton Gavrikov," I began, "who scored the tying goal in the Flyers come-from-behind victory. Gav, at the start of the third period, you were down by three goals. What was the secret to today's win?"

Gav brushed his sweaty hair from his eyes with his fingers as he leaned toward the mic I was holding and spoke with a thick accent that reminded me of Arnold Schwarzenegger's. "We were never out of it, you know. All the guys worked together." He looked toward his teammates, who were filing excitedly toward the locker room. "We just kept up our speed and never stopped attacking. And I guess it paid off 'cause we won in the end."

It was no secret that I loved when the Flyers won. How could I not love my home team, especially when I was one of the on-ice broadcasters? But what I loved more than just watching the Flyers win was watching them win when they were the underdogs. Just when you thought they were down and out, they'd pull off nothing short of a miracle at the end. "You know, these are the kinda games fans love to watch, Gav. New York's favored, they're up by three in the third. It looks like they're gonna win, and then you take a risky shot that could quite possibly result in New York recovering the puck and holding it 'til the buzzer. If you'd missed, fans might've said you should've been more patient, waited 'til the right time to strike, gotten a little closer to the net. What made you take the shot when you did?"

"Well, there wasn't much thought that went into it. More reflex than anything else. I saw an opportunity and I took it. Didn't really think about *not* taking it. Just brought my stick back and focused my eyes on the goal."

I chuckled at Gav's confidence. I knew what it was like to fight for something you wanted—something you *needed*. To know that sometimes you just had to go for it and fuck what anyone else thought. Because while you might miss nine out of ten times, it was the one time that you made it that everyone would remember. That one time—that was the game changer.

"Then that gave us the opportunity we had in overtime. It's almost like a new game when that happens. A fresh start. Plus you're pumped up 'cause you've just come back from behind. There's already a feeling that you've won."

"And you think that attitude is what helped you finish the game?"

"Yeah, they gave us a second chance. We weren't gonna screw it up again."

"Well, it paid off. People were pulling for you, and you found a way to win. The only thing that matters is the score at the end." I shook his hand, signaling that our brief interview was coming to a close. "Well, I'll let you go celebrate with the guys. Great win today."

❤

Thankfully, the drive home didn't take long. Saturday afternoon games were my favorite. I'd be home in time for dinner and to put Maddie to bed. Those were the moments I cherished most now. As much as I loved the fast-paced atmosphere that broadcasting provided, nothing beat reading a bedtime story to my daughter. Except maybe holding her mother in my arms as we lay in bed together after a hectic day.

The smell of homemade Italian food and Maddie's eager embrace greeted me the second I entered the door. "Daddy!" she screeched with her little arms stretched around my legs. "We made you dinner." I knelt down to scoop her into my arms and squeeze her against my chest.

"What'd you make together?" I asked, overemphasizing my excitement. "It smells great."

"Chicken . . ." She held her finger to her lips like she was deep in thought. "With cheese," she added. "And sauce . . ."

I carried Maddie into the kitchen, and Lily turned around to face me, leaning against the counter. "Chicken parm," she mouthed with a coy grin. "Shh," she warned, not wanting to spoil our three-year-old daughter's fun at remembering the dinner she helped cook.

As I watched Maddie try to remember the menu, I smiled widely. I'd recognize that face anywhere: the way the left corner of her mouth raised slightly more than her right when she smiled, how her hazel eyes shimmered with specks of bronze when the light hit them just right. Maddie's dark hair hung to her shoulders and her brow was furrowed, deep in thought. "You know," I said, tapping her on the nose playfully, "you look just like Mommy when you do that." I held up my finger to my lips to imitate her expression, and she giggled at me.

My eyes raised to Lily, who pushed off the counter and walked slowly, gracefully across the kitchen toward me. "She does, does she?"

"Yup, dead ringer," I said, pulling her into me so I could hold them both close. "I think we're in trouble. Is it wrong to keep her locked in the house for the next thirty years?"

Lily's expression told me I'd probably have a tough time doing that. "How was your day?" she asked.

"Great. Flyers won," I said, giving Maddie a kiss on the forehead before lowering her to the ground. "Even better now that I get to see you," I said, placing a soft kiss on Lily's warm lips. Even after all this time, it was still nearly impossible for me to kiss her without wanting to take things further. I brought my fingers up to the locket I had given her a few months after we met and untwisted the chain. I was always happy to see her wearing it, knowing she was keeping a piece of me close to her.

"Why don't you go wash your hands for dinner, honey?" Lily said, and Maddie turned to scamper down the hall toward the bathroom.

"You know how beautiful you are?" I asked, cradling Lily's chin with my hand as I looked into her eyes.

"Oh, stop, Max," she replied with a shy smile. "Even like this?" She ran a hand over her growing belly, and I placed mine over hers, hoping to get a feel of my son moving around.

I gazed into her warm eyes before answering her question. "*Especially* like this."

❤

Forty-five minutes later, Lily had Maddie in the bath, and I was finishing up with the dishes before putting Maddie to bed. When she was finished, Maddie came bounding down the stairs at rapid speed. *She may have gotten her looks from her mother, but she definitely got her recklessness from me.* The thought made me grin. She was a perfect combination of the two of us.

"What are you doing down here?" I asked her. "I thought I was gonna come up and tuck you in?"

"You are. Come on." She tugged lightly on my shirt, and I scooped her up in my arms.

Once we reached the second floor, I lowered Maddie to the ground. "Why don't you go into your room and pick out a bedtime story? I'll be there in a minute." As Maddie disappeared to pick out a book, Lily came out of the bathroom. "You know how I like a good wet T-shirt contest," I said, gesturing to her dampened shirt. "And you didn't even invite me?"

"Your daughter," she laughed. "She's wild."

"Yeah, I've been thinking about that. And I'm pretty sure she gets that trait from me."

"Oh, ya think?" she joked.

"Hey, speaking of wild, how'd the writing go today?"

"Eh, could be better." She shrugged. "Got a little done. Writer's block, I guess."

"Hmm," I said with a hint of subtle seduction that I knew she'd pick up on. I swept her hair away from her neck and leaned down, allowing my breath to tickle her ear as I spoke. "I bet I can alleviate that writer's block you were talking about.

You know I can be very inspirational."

Just then I heard the pitter-patter of Maddie's little feet as she ran toward us excitedly. "Daddy, what about this one?"

"Let's see. What do we have here?" I asked, turning away from Lily and taking the book from Maddie's hand to give her my attention. "*Sleeping Beauty.* Excellent choice." Then I leaned in to give Lily's earlobe another teasing nibble. "I can't wait to sleep with *this* beauty later," I whispered. *That'll get her.*

"Stop it," she scolded with a playful swat to my chest.

"I was just talking about the book," I said innocently, feigning shock as best I could and pointing to the cover.

Her look told me she knew better than to believe that.

"What?" I replied, plastering on the boyish grin I knew she couldn't resist. "Girl meets guy . . . they fall in love, but they can't be together. A bunch of other crap happens, and neither one of them realizes they were destined to spend the rest of their lives with each other until the dashingly handsome prince kisses her to wake her up from her hellish nightmare."

She couldn't help but smile at my plot summary. Even I was impressed by how quickly I'd come up with it. "Hmm . . . I dunno. I always sort of had you pegged as more of a knight."

I laughed softly through my nose as I planted a kiss on her forehead. "Whatever works for you as long as the ending's still the same. They get married, have babies, and have tons of great sex," I added quickly under my breath to be sure Maddie couldn't hear.

She shook her head at my last addition. *Works every time.* "Only you can make a fairy tale sound dirty." She laughed, wrapping her arms around my neck and pulling me in close.

I took a moment to gaze into those eyes that would always

remind me that it was always her. She was my piece of perfect. And she always would be. "Aw, come on, doll," I said with a seductive smirk. "You know how I love happy endings."

Her expression fell somewhere between playful scolding and heated desire. But her voice held sincerity when she spoke. "Me too, Max." She smiled. "Me too."

also in the

love lessons series

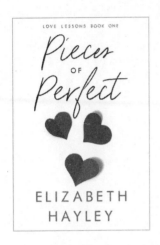

LOVE LESSONS BOOK ONE

Pieces
OF
Perfect

ELIZABETH
HAYLEY

LOVE LESSONS BOOK THREE

Perfectly
EVER
After

ELIZABETH
HAYLEY

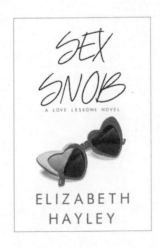

SEX
SNOB
A LOVE LESSONS NOVEL

ELIZABETH
HAYLEY

also by
elizabeth hayley

Love Lessons:
Pieces of Perfect
Picking Up the Pieces
Perfectly Ever After

❤

Sex Snob
(A Love Lessons Novel)

Misadventures:
Misadventures with My Roommate
Misadventures with a Country Boy
Misadventures in a Threesome
Misadventures with a Twin
Misadventures with a Sexpert

acknowledgments

Our Husbands: Different book, same story. We're not sure how you both put up with us, but you somehow manage to. And we love you immensely for it.

Bloggers: So many of you have been instrumental in getting our names out there that there are simply too many to name. But we love each of you beyond words. Thanks for all your pimping, for putting up with us and our ridiculous requests, and for just being 100% awesome 100% of the time.

Alison Bliss: What can we say? If it weren't for you, people would be throwing their kindles at the wall right now because our ending would have been a disaster. Thank you for always pulling us out of the hole we continuously dig ourselves, for giving us phenomenal suggestions, and for always believing that we are great writers (even when we're not). Love you!

Amanda: New York, baby! You've been part of our journey from the beginning, and it means so much to us that you're always in our corner. You're our first fan and also one of our greatest friends. Love you, Petal.

Lauren Bearzatto: Words can't express the gratitude we have for your editing skills. How an Australian can write American English better than we can will remain a mystery. But it's absolutely true! Without you, our manuscript would have looked like we texted it to each other.

Beta Readers: We can't thank you enough for reading so quickly and for providing such honest feedback. You helped us see flaws in our writing we wouldn't have otherwise seen. We'd like to especially thank Stephanie, Allison, Becky, Sim, and Lauren for going above and beyond the call for us. It means everything.

Friends we've made on social media: Holy Cow, where do we start with you loons? You are always there to brighten our day, participate in our nonsense, and remind us that this dream is worth pursuing. Thank you doesn't even begin to cover the appreciation we have for you.

We thought we'd do something a little different this time. In typical self-praising Elizabeth Hayley fashion, we'd like to bash each other while complimenting ourselves.

To Hayley (from Hayley): I'd like to thank myself for constantly reminding Elizabeth that she needs to write our smut instead of just reading other people's. Hayley, thanks for making sure that every orgasm is described in vivid detail. (I sort of have a pet peeve about that.) Thank you for cheering Elizabeth up because she's always down. If it weren't for my witty and unmatched sense of humor, Elizabeth would never smile. And thank you for fixing all of her elementary grammar mistakes—commas, homonyms, spelling, etc. Hayley, if it weren't for you, it would have looked like a third grader wrote half the book.

Oh, fine. I guess I should also thank Elizabeth. You are my soul mate (the one I *don't* sleep with) and my partner in crime. Thank you for making me feel like less of a sexual deviant because you're just as bad as I am. Thanks for talking me down off a ledge time after time after time when I was stressed about not getting the book finished. We are in this together, and I love you for standing beside me every step of the way. SYATEC!

To Elizabeth (from Elizabeth): I thank myself for not strangling Hayley over her incessant issues with plot continuity and character logistics. I also thank myself for constantly fixing her missing quotation mark issue, usually without even telling her because, well, what's the point? I can't fix stupid. If I weren't there to correct all of her mistakes and write flawless prose myself, it wouldn't seem like a third grader wrote it, because nothing would be written at all. Or at least nothing with any attention paid to time and space.

Okay, seriously, I need to thank Hayley for understanding me on a level few people ever have. You're the yin to my yang, and together we achieve a balance so oddly perfect, I can only attribute our meeting to fate. We were destined for this. Destined to be business partners, friends, sisters. Always remember: shoes are for suckers. Love you and SYATEC (probably sooner rather than later).

about

elizabeth hayley

Elizabeth Hayley is actually "Elizabeth" and "Hayley," two friends who love reading romance novels to obsessive levels. This mutual love prompted them to put their English degrees to good use by penning their own. The product is *Pieces of Perfect*, their debut novel. They learned a ton about one another through the process, like how they clearly share a brain and have a persistent need to text each other constantly (much to their husbands' chagrin).

They live with their husbands and kids in a Philadelphia suburb. Thankfully, their children are still too young to read their books.

Visit them at AuthorElizabethHayley.com